# PRAISE FOR ALTAHA

"With the release of *Altaha*, Jefferson Glass has once again scratched my itch for another outstanding Conor Armenta mystery thriller...one could say, 'Glass has become a master in his own class!'"

— W. MICHAEL GEAR, *NEW YORK TIMES* BESTSELLING AUTHOR

"Jefferson Glass spins a gripping tale where the past haunts every page. *Altaha* weaves deceit and danger into a narrative as crisp and clear as the Nevada air. Sheriff Conor Armenta—a character destined to become iconic—provides the heart of an intriguing story."

— PRESTON LEWIS, SPUR AWARD-WINNING AUTHOR

"As always, Glass masterfully intertwines history, cultures, and complex characters with nuanced pasts to create an action-packed adventure that will leave readers craving more."

— JENNIFER KOCHER, AWARD-WINNING AUTHOR AND JOURNALIST

# ALTAHA

# ALSO BY JEFFERSON GLASS

**Conor Armenta Mystery Series**

*The First Light of Dawn*

*Shifting Sand*

*Sons of the Texas Star*

# ALTAHA

## A CONOR ARMENTA MYSTERY
### BOOK FOUR

## JEFFERSON GLASS

**WOLFPACK PUBLISHING**
— EST 2013 —

**Altaha**
Paperback Edition
Copyright © 2024 by Jefferson Glass

Wolfpack Publishing
1707 E. Diana Street
Tampa, FL 33610

www.wolfpackpublishing.com

Paperback ISBN 978-1-63977-549-1
Ebook ISBN 978-1-63977-548-4
LCCN 2024950065

*Dedicated to my wife Debbie,*
*the inspiration for so many of the pages in this novel.*

# ALTAHA

# 1

Sheriff Conor Armenta and his prisoner, Dutch Wagner, boarded the train bound for Salt Lake City with connection to Carson City, Nevada at four-fifteen in the morning. He carried an old-fashioned carpetbag containing his razor, suit jacket, and a change of clothes. Two days there, execution on Thursday, then two days back home. A lone passenger car attached to the rear of the express car trailed behind more than a dozen freight cars on this working-man's train. A half-dozen boxcars and a fading red caboose followed. Conor guided Dutch to a seat on the right near the front and directed him to the window. He unlatched Wagner's left handcuff and connected it to the framework of the seat in front of him. The smug expression on Dutch's face in the dimly lit car caught the sheriff's attention.

"The less you have to say, Dutch," he told him, "the better we'll get along."

One other passenger occupied the car: a man dressed in miner's gear with dirty overalls and slouch hat. He sat near the rear on the lefthand side. Con sat down across the aisle, one row back from Dutch. As he watched the brakeman hurriedly checking the undercarriage of the train, the conductor entered the rear of the car.

"Got your ticket there?" he asked the miner, who handed it to him.

"You're on the wrong train, mister," he told the man as he returned the ticket to him. "Your train won't leave for another couple of hours."

"Oh! Sorry," the man said as he jumped to his feet and scampered toward the rear door.

"Better hurry," the conductor told him just as the car lurched and began to move.

Conor watched the man bail off the rear of the car, dash across the platform, and out of sight into the darkness. The conductor ambled his way up the aisle toward them. Con handed two tickets to him.

"One round-trip ticket to Carson City," he noted as he punched holes in it. "And one...one way." He glanced knowingly at Dutch, cuffed to the seat in front of him. "Enjoy your trip, Sheriff," the conductor added as he handed the tickets back to him.

The chug of the steam engine could barely be heard above the creaks and groans of the car as they gradually accelerated. A slight surge of anxiety had brewed a restless night for Armenta. The sensation lingered as the lilting roll of the car tried to relax him and the train ambled northward. He glanced across at Wagner in the dim light, still wearing the same slight smirk of a grin when Conor had cuffed him to the seat.

"Whatever it is that you're hatching in that pea brain of yours, Dutch," he told him, "don't set your hopes too high."

Wagner snorted through his nostrils in reply and slumped further down in his seat as he turned his face to the darkness through the window beside him.

Nearly an hour had passed since their departure when dawn began to break across the desert.

"Know where we are, Dutch?" Con spoke to the back of his prisoner's head.

"Not particularly."

"This is where we found the first pieces of Jimmy Garza's body," Conor informed him just as their car crossed the trestle at Crystal.

"I found his head right here," he added a moment later, "then most of the upper half of him about here." The train slugged along up the track. He watched Wagner as he shared the gruesome details without response.

"Right here was the last of him. A quarter mile from the start. Looked like a pair of Levis laying there until you could see the bottom half of him was still inside of them." Armenta started to continue, but Wagner's shoulders jerked forward as he struggled to control the bile boiling up inside his throat. It took all the sheriff could muster to control his rage. He desperately wanted to make this man suffer for the murders he had committed, the pain he inflicted on the families of his victims. He wanted to push the issue harder but had no desire to smell Dutch Wagner's stinking vomit all the way to Salt Lake City in a hot railcar.

At Moapa, the brakes complained profusely as they slowed to a stop with the engine precisely beneath the downspout of the water tower. The sun cleared the eastern horizon as Conor's eyes scanned the area surrounding the train station. Long shadows streaked across the dusty streets. His recital as they passed Crystal had dissolved the subtle grin on Dutch's face, but not whatever mayhem the grin may have foretold of what lay in wait ahead. Wagner may have been unaware of the details of the plot. His demeanor nevertheless, belied the impending doom of a man enroute to his extinction.

Dutch received no visitors or mail since his sentencing. He certainly appeared confident though, that something would happen to reverse his circumstance before they arrived at their destination. Time passed slowly while they took on water. Con felt like a tin duck in the BB-gun gallery at a carnival. Anticipating a shot from any direction that could take him out, he continued, relentlessly scrutinizing every place that might harbor an assailant. Nothing moved. Not even a stray cat.

After a seeming eternity, brakes released with a loud hiss and the car began to move with a jolt when the locomotive eliminated the slack from every coupling between them and the front of the train. His eyes continued to probe the shadows as the train slowly gained momentum and the last buildings of Moapa fell in the distance behind them.

The engine labored to gain speed on the gradual three-mile incline to Acton. The fireman caught his breath as the grade leveled off to Guelph then wiped his brow and flung the door of the firebox wide as he redoubled his efforts to fill it to capacity with coal for the steeper climb to Rox and keep it stoked all the way to Caliente.

Armenta glanced toward Dutch Wagner as they passed the home of Jimmy Garza's mother at Acton. The morning sun flooded the interior of the car and his prisoner appeared to be dozing. Conor adjusted his Stetson and noted the tension in his neck and shoulders seemed to be lessening slightly. He felt more at ease in the mostly open country...and in full daylight. He almost allowed himself to doze as they crossed into Lincoln County just south of Rox. Meadow Valley began to narrow while the train crept up the grade. The eastern slopes gained in height and cast shadows intermittently across the car.

\* \* \*

Tinkling glass and a sharp thud at the seatback in front of him jolted Conor into action. Adrenaline surged through his body, transitioning the world around him into slow motion. Con turned in his seat and rushed down the aisle toward the emergency brake cable at the rear of the car. Glancing at Dutch bent forward over the seat in front of him, the left half of his skull was missing. Rising from a crouching run just two steps away, the cable dangled from the roof. As he grabbed hold of it, the momentum carried his body crashing full speed into the rear wall, but he held his grip long enough to activate the brake before tumbling onto the last seat of the row.

Showers of sparks sprayed from iron against steel, screaming in agony as every wheel of the train slid on the rails to a halt. The abruptness slammed Conner into the seat in front of him, then to the floor. When he rose to peer out the window, the glass shattered before him as something tugged at his Stetson, tossing it across the car. He carefully raised his bare head to peek again over the sill of the window. The sun barely cleared the bluff to the east. A momentary glint of reflection below the glare caught Con's attention. His face ground into the seat when he ducked back down, out of sight. Another shot never came. On his third glimpse out the window, a man carrying what he suspected to be a rifle rounded a rock outcropping shaped like a loaf of bread high up the ridge in retreat. Looking directly into the sun, he couldn't be certain.

When he stood, dots of blood spotted where he had pressed his face into the seat. He picked up his hat from across the aisle. A bullet had clipped the brim, cut a furrow through the left front of it and down the side, missing his head by less than three inches. He slipped it back on his head and pulled it down tight as he raced out the door of the car.

"What's going on?" the conductor hollered, maneuvering toward him beside the cars across the rough ballast of the railbed.

"Look in there," Conor replied, pointing with his thumb toward the car behind him. Clambering across the bar ditch, he shouted back, "Don't touch anything!"

\* \* \*

As Conor worked his way up the steep incline, he kept the rock formation in his view where he had seen the man from the railroad car. He followed an irregular game trail up the incline.

Thankfully, as Meadow Valley narrowed into the canyon, his climb was on the shaded side of the chasm. Both due to the increase in elevation and the time of year, the morning air remained comfortably cool. He continued on. Pausing further along to catch his breath, Con assessed his surroundings. Behind and below him, the train crew stood beside the passenger car, each watching his ascent with hands shading their brows. At least four hundred yards, he thought. Maybe closer to five. He turned around examining the slope above. The stone protrusion he had been heading toward remained another hundred yards ahead. He needed to focus on likely positions for the shooter's stand and take care not to disturb any evidence. He proceeded ahead.

Half the distance to his targeted precipice, Sheriff Armenta spotted what he'd been looking for. A nearly flat oblong indention about two feet by three feet interrupted the center of the trail he was on. A bed used by a rather large animal. Possibly a mule deer or perhaps, considering the terrain, a desert big horn sheep. Regardless of its identity, the regular denizen of the bed had pawed out a miniature terrace in the mountainside cleared of stones. A comfortable place to rest with a wide range of view from which to spot predators...hopefully in time to escape before the enemy detected them.

The most recent occupant of the spot, however, was a mammal of a different ilk. A two-legged predator. He chose the spot for the same reason as his predecessor, the expansive view. From there, he could watch his prey approach from a great distance and shoot from near anonymity. If his victim might try to spot him on the vast hillside...a blinding sun arose at his back.

Conor found four rifle casings within a couple of feet, .30-06 Springfield. There were several butts from hand-rolled cigarettes, smoked down to stubs and the remnants of matches that had lit them. And there were tracks. Moccasin tracks. The right foot smaller than the left and oddly misshapen. These few clues were left by the assailant. Without better options, he put the casings and cigarette butts into his shirt pocket and began following the tracks of the man who ran up the trail ahead of him. It was an odd gait he thought. The damaged foot must cause a severe limp. Judging by the stride and depth of tracks on the trail, the sheriff estimated a man of short stature and fairly lightweight. Even when carrying a heavy rifle, he doubted over 130 pounds.

Immediately beyond where Conor had seen him round the outcropping, the man mounted a small unshod horse. Judging the animal stride and depth of tracks, he guessed the horse to be lean and less than fourteen hands. The shooter had trotted away on a similar trail to the one Con had arrived on. It headed a northeasterly direction. There was no visible movement on the landscape, but the feeling of being watched stood the hairs on the back of Conor's neck at attention as he gazed into the distance.

\* \* \*

"I need to get ahold of Sheriff Reynolds in Pioche," Conor told the conductor when he returned to the train.

"Well," he contemplated, scratching his chin. "The nearest telephone is back at Rox. Six miles. There's a siding there. We can back up and drop this car off on the siding...along with what's left of your prisoner inside there. Otherwise, it's all the way to Caliente."

"Okay," Con acknowledged. "Let's go to Rox."

While the engineer and fireman made their way back to the locomotive, Conor took a red bandana from his pocket and tied it to a branch of sagebrush beside the track. The conductor and brakemen waited by the steps at the rear of the passenger car.

As Con joined them, the conductor motioned toward the caboose. "We'll be back here."

He nodded in understanding and entered the door of the car. Studying the window where the bullet pierced the glass before striking his hat, he lined up the approximate trajectory and found where it entered the far side of the car. With little to slow it down, the bullet most likely continued through the thin wall and beyond.

When the car started rolling, Con moved forward to his former seat and continued the inspection. Rigor mortis had begun to set in on Dutch Wagner. The movement of the car had little effect on the stillness of his body. A mist of blood from the exit wound began at Dutch's shoulder, across the back of the seat beside him and dissipated on the seatback in front of the sheriff. Fragments of bone, flesh and hair accompanied it proportionately. Recalling the chain of events; a thud at the seat in front of him seemed nearly simultaneous to the sound of glass breaking. The frump sound of the bullet hitting flesh had been overwhelmed by the thud of it hitting the seat. He hadn't realized Wagner had been hit until seeing him when he turned to access the emergency brake.

Looking over to the front of the seatback ahead of him revealed the final point of impact. An angled furrow into the back of the seat terminating without an exit. As he contemplated the evidence, his transport began to slow. He glanced at his pocket watch. Just shy of a half hour. They were at Rox.

"We're here, Sheriff," came the voice of the conductor from the door. "I'll get you to the telephone while they jockey this car onto the siding."

Con turned and followed the conductor down the steps and across a sterile breadth of several yards to a six-by-six-foot corrugated tin shed. The conductor removed a massive padlock and opened the door. An oak telephone hung from the wall. Caliente and Moapa were penciled on the wall at opposite ends of the double throw electrical switch mounted between them. It was set to Caliente.

"You turn that crank; it should ring you through to the station at Caliente," the conductor instructed. "They should be able to patch you through to public telephone service in Pioche. Throw that switch the other way and the folks in Moapa can hook you up to Las Vegas. If you can't get through on one, try the other."

He stepped outside and leaned against the shady side of the shed.

Con stepped up to the telephone and cranked it while holding the handpiece to his ear.

"Hallo, this is Tom. Whadaya need?"

"This is Clark County Sheriff Conor Armenta. I need to talk to Sheriff Bill Reynolds in Pioche. It's an emergency."

"Yessir, Sheriff. I ain't real good at workin' this machine, but hang tight, I'll getcha through. I Promise!"

Con could hear Tom's muffled voice in the background, then silence and a couple more sporadic conversations. Then he came back on the line.

"Ya still there, sir?"

"I sure am."

"When yuh hear a loud bunch of clicks, you'll be hooked up to them. If I lose yuh, crank me back again."

After a series of clicks, a female voice came on the line. "Hello?"

"Hello. This is Sheriff Armenta—"

"Yes, Sheriff," the voice interrupted. "Bill…Sheriff Reynolds will be right with you."

"Con! What the hell are you doin' in Rox?"

"I was transporting a prisoner to Carson City until someone killed him about six miles north of here a couple of hours ago. Shot from ambush. I think I was the actual target, but they missed."

"That the pimp that murdered his own mother?"

"That's the one."

"Are you sure it wasn't some upstanding citizen that killed the S.O.B.? Maybe wanting to make sure that no one screwed up in Carson City or pardoned him at the last minute?"

"Maybe. It'd be more convincing if the second shot hadn't missed my head by less than three inches. I tracked him about a quarter mile. He's on horseback now and pointed north of the Mormon Mountains."

"Well, I can see your concern and that's some rough country. What would you like me to do?"

"I would like your permission to handle the case outside of my own jurisdiction and pursue the shooter."

"You've got my blessing. My nearest deputy right now is five or six hours away from you and I'm too old to go chasin' some fool around in the pucker brush for miles. What's your plan?"

"I'll get my coroner up here, then commandeer a horse and go after him."

"Well, I'll do my best to get some help to you if you'd like."

"I don't give up too easy. If I get in a bind, I'll send up smoke signals."

Bill Reynolds chuckled. "Good luck to you, Conor. Be careful."

* * *

Hazel answered the telephone when Con was patched through to Las Vegas. "Where are you?"

"Rox. It's a spot on the railroad north of Moapa. Just across the Lincoln County line."

"What are you doing there?"

"Dutch has been killed. Shot from ambush. I'm getting ready to go after the shooter. Get Hal up here. Have Ben come with him and bring my pickup."

"But you're in Lincoln County."

"Yep, I've already talked to Sheriff Reynolds in Pioche. He approved my plan."

"I'll call Dr. Martin and have Ben accompany him up there. What else would you like me to do?"

His thoughts quickly turned to his fiancée. "I need you to call June."

"No, you should call her."

"I'm on a railroad telephone line. It's quite an ordeal to make a call. Tell her what happened, that I'm okay, and that I love her."

"Oh, please. She'll be worried," Hazel pleaded. "I really don't want to."

"It'll be okay. Ben, Hal, get them up here as quickly as you can. I've got to go."

"She won't be happy."

"Well, neither am I right now. She'll understand."

"Okay," Hazel grumbled.

He heard the stiffness in her voice as he hung up the telephone. When he walked around the shack to the conductor, the passenger car sat on the siding while the brakeman recoupled the caboose behind the boxcars.

"Can you get that car down to Las Vegas after we're done here?"

He looked at his watch. "Southbound freight will come through here about six o'clock this evening. Is that enough time?"

"Yep. Tell them to call the Clark County Sheriff's Department when they get to Las Vegas with it."

"It'll be in the middle of the night, Sheriff."

"That's okay. They'll answer."

* * *

Two hours had passed since the train left Sheriff Conor Armenta and the passenger car at the switch station called Rox. An hour ago, he parked himself in the shade on the bottom step of the car. He tried to doze intermittently between continually rolling over the events of the past nine hours in his head. Unsure of whether he first heard the footsteps or saw the movement through the slits between his eyelids, a woman approached from a dozen yards away. He sat up straighter.

"Howdy," he greeted as she continued closer.

His elder by perhaps a decade, she wore an aging cotton dress hemmed at her calves and men's work boots laced up to the same height. "Howdy," she returned, changing hands with the flour sack she carried.

"You're a bit far from town," Conor commented.

"So are you. Difference is...I live here," she replied as she snatched a tress of hair that escaped her ponytail and corralled it behind her ear.

He glanced away, almost guiltily. Uncomfortable conversing with strangers that happened to be women, he chose silence for the moment.

"You a marshal?" she asked, noting his badge.

"Sheriff." He turned back to look her in the eye.

"I thought Bill Reynolds was still the sheriff."

"He is," Con clarified as he stood and offered his hand. "Clark County Sheriff, Conor Armenta."

She kept the flour sack in her right hand and didn't accept his. "You're a couple of miles out of your jurisdiction, Sheriff."

"Yes, I am. Sheriff Reynolds knows I'm here."

"Why?"

The response startled him. "What do you mean?"

"What are you doing here?"

"Waiting for the coroner and one of my deputies to arrive from Las Vegas."

"Coroner?"

Con motioned to the car behind him. "There's a dead man inside."

She looked at the shattered windows. "He'll be stinkin' to high heaven before sundown in this heat."

"They should be here in a couple of hours," Conor said as he examined his pocket watch.

The woman held the flour sack out to him. "Biscuits left from breakfast and water."

"Well thanks. That's kind of you. Where do you live?"

"Up the wash." She motioned behind her. "We've got a shack and a little mine up there."

"Gold?"

"Dirt mostly." She smiled. Her even white teeth brought life to her plain face.

He smiled back. "You seen anybody ride by here recently?"

"Before sunup. Off to the east. A dark horse. A long way off. There's a kind of mesa up past this first bunch of hills." She pointed. "Past our place."

"Headed which way?"

"North."

"Thanks."

"Sure," she said and turned to walk away, then looked back. "Leave the sack by the shed. They're hard to come by."

"I will. Thanks again."

Conor watched her gangly stride as she traversed the main track and made her way across the barren expanse past the lonely tin shed that sat in the midst of it. When she reached the far side, her back disappeared into the jungle of mesquite that choked the mouth of the smaller wash that joined Meadow Valley Wash where it crossed the tracks.

Opening the flour sack revealed a quart mason jar filled with tepid water that was nearly clear and a clean red bandanna containing three large biscuits and a modest slab of ivory colored cheese. When he began to eat, he realized he was hungry. He looked at his watch: one thirty. He and Dutch had eaten a slice of pie and drank coffee at the station in Las Vegas. That was more than nine hours ago. He washed down mouthfuls of dry biscuit with the warm water. Both tasted delicious, though his opinion may have been tainted by his appetite. He saved the cheese until last. It was good, obviously from cow's milk, but still he preferred the Irish cheddar cheese his mother made from ewe's milk. Con rationed out the second half of his water to last until Hal and Ben would arrive. Having nothing to drink for several hours, he knew he needed to drink it all, though sparingly.

# 2

The distant roar of a car's motor roused Sheriff Armenta as he dozed on the steps of the railcar. The sound became quieter as he looked south along the dirt road that paralleled the railroad track. A thick coating of gray dust did little to disguise the coroner's sedan delivery as it topped a low hill less than a quarter mile away. The road behind lay hidden in the powdery cloud left by the vehicle. As it neared the driver slowed, his pudgy elbow protruding from the open window. Conor stood and checked his watch while the car eased to a stop adjacent to the main rail line between them.

The driver cut the engine. Dr. Harold Martin swung the door open and crawled from behind the wheel. Gaining his feet, the aging coroner removed his sweat-stained straw fedora and proceeded to beat the dust from his clothing with it. Stuffing the hat back onto his bulbous head he turned toward the sheriff. Propping his hands on his hips and puffing out his chest, he stared at Con through spectacles so consumed in dust that his eyes could barely be seen through them. The pose was nearly laughable, but the sheriff kept a straight face.

"Conor!" he blurted out. "You come up with some of the damnedest places for me to examine a corpse."

The sheriff was about to respond when a second engine's rumble distracted him. Watching the road, his official sheriff's pickup truck soon came into view. Barely recognizable, Deputy Bennett Neilly rolled to a stop behind Hal's sedan. With his Stetson pulled down low, bandana up over his nose and no less than a quarter inch of dust covering his entirety, he resembled a cowboy riding drag on a cattle drive much more than a deputy sheriff.

Conor returned his attention to the coroner. "What took so long?" he inquired earnestly.

"Those track workers may consider this a road, but most of those dry washes we had to cross took some serious maneuvering."

"That," Ben added, "and your fiancée insisted we bring some supplies she thought you'd want to have along with you."

With Ben's comment, Conor's face flushed, and Hal struggled to suppress his grin. Ben finished beating as much of the dust off himself as he could with his hat. When he pulled the bandana off his face, the band of encrusted, sweat-soaked dust between his bare forehead and cheeks looked like a racoon's mask. Hal and Con both chuckled.

"What?" Ben asked, unaware of the joke.

"El Zorro?" Hal snickered.

Conor stifled a snort trying to contain himself. "Wipe the dirt off around your eyes, Ben."

Ben shook as much dust as possible from his bandana and complied. "Better?"

"Better." He paused for a moment with a puzzled expression, then crossed the mainline tracks to his pickup. "What would June think that I would want to take along?"

"She might know you better than you think, Sheriff," Ben

noted as he pulled back a small canvas tarp protecting the provisions from sun and dust in the pickup bed. "She had me meet her at your house."

The first thing Con noticed was his Model '94 Winchester in its scabbard. "Where did she find this?"

"That was the very first thing. She knew right where to look. It was under the seat of your car."

Conor was abashed. As more and more strangers arrived in Clark County, so had the crime rate risen. Becoming wary of the increasing dangers surrounding his position as sheriff, he seldom ventured anywhere without having a firearm within close proximity, especially if June was along. Knowing it bothered her to constantly have guns around when off duty, he'd begun hiding the rifle and his 1911 Colt automatic under the seat of his car any time they were together. Concealing the practice from his fiancé had evidently been unsuccessful.

As he studied the assortment of articles, Con was impressed with June's foresight. He picked up two boxes of .30-30 cartridges and two of .45.

"Mrs. Sommers found those in your top dresser drawer," Ben noted. "She said she thought you would understand her going through your personal things, but she didn't want to miss anything."

"Of course." He blushed. "I don't think I would have the courage to do the same, if our circumstances were reversed though."

Ben blushed in response to the thought. "Me neither."

He glanced at a shoebox, then picked it up. There were a few stains near the bottom where something of its contents were bleeding through.

"Fried chicken," Ben explained. "Left over from last night, she said. She made me promise not to eat any of it myself before giving it to you."

"June makes great fried chicken," Conor responded through a broad grin and moved to the corrugated cardboard box beside it.

"That's stuff from your folks' café," Ben offered.

Con's parents owned and operated the Mesquite Café on Fremont Street, a block and a half from the sheriff's office. The box contained an ample supply of lamb jerky, his father's frybread, and of course a wedge of his mother's Irish cheddar cheese. All staples traditional to living in a sheep camp, such as the sheriff had through much of his growing up.

In addition, there were his bedroll, flashlight, a well-worn and blood-stained leather vest, and a full canteen, and desert waterbag. She had thought of everything he would have packed up himself. She was very smart…and intuitive, two of the many reasons that he loved her.

"She wanted to send your field glasses too," Ben commented, "but she couldn't find them."

Conor pointed to the cab of the truck. "They should be in the glove box."

"Well, let's get to work," Con quickly changes the subject. "Grab your camera, Hal. We've got a couple hours, then a southbound will pick up this car and take it to Las Vegas. There, you can finish up anything we don't have time or equipment to do here."

"Me?" Hal balked. "What about you?"

"I'll be out here hunting a killer."

Ben and Hal followed when Conor mounted the steps into the railcar. He explained where he sat when the first shot hit Dutch and how he had scrambled to the emergency brake cable. Then he described when the second shot took off his hat.

Hal noted the furrow gouged through the brim of Con's nearly new Boss of the Plains Stetson. "Close," he commented dryly.

Remembering an earlier encounter that had penetrated the crown of the sheriff's previous headwear and left a singed crease through the hair on his scalp he added, "You're beginning to make a habit of this."

"Not intentionally," Conor responded.

He reached into his shirt pocket and produced four .30-06 casings and a handful of cigarette butts. He handed them to Hal, who placed the butts in an envelope and shifted to the casings. With experienced eye, he examined the base of one of the casings.

"Military," he proclaimed.

"Yep," the sheriff agreed.

"Where'd you find them?"

"Six miles north of here, you'll find my red bandana tied to a sagebrush. On the east side of the tracks. Six hundred yards up that east side, there's a rock outcropping. It looks sorta like a loaf of bread standing on end. Just below that rock. That's where the bushwhacker shot from...and where I found those." Con nodded to the casings.

"And you want me to turn into a Billy goat and shuffle my fat old ass up a mountainside to take a picture?"

"No. Just take pictures from the tracks and bring back my bandana."

"And where are you gonna be?"

"I'm heading to Acton."

"Acton?"

"Gotta see a man about a horse."

* * *

At five o'clock the Clark County sheriff's pickup pulled up in front of the home of Rayno and Tomanie Pete in the area known as Acton, Nevada. They were the mother and stepfather of Jimmy Garza, the final victim of Dutch Wagner's series of murders and members of the Moapa band of the Paiute tribe. They were sheep-herders like Sheriff Connor Armenta's family had been, and his younger brother continued to be. Conor shut off the engine and started toward the door. Tomanie stepped out onto the porch before he reached it.

"Mrs. Pete," he greeted as he removed his hat.

"Is something wrong, Sheriff?" she asked.

"No, and yes. I need to borrow a horse," he began, "or rent one, I should say. The county will pay. I don't really have time to go all the way to Las Vegas and bring my own horse all the way back up here."

"Oh. You will need to talk to Rayno about that." She paused momentarily then continued almost as if in another conversation. "We heard that evil man is going to die in the electric chair. Did he escape?"

"No, but this *is* about him." He paused not wishing to tell the whole story twice. "Is Rayno home? I'd like to explain this to both of you."

"He's out in the barn. I will ring the bell and he will think it is time to eat."

She disappeared into the small house. A moment later a loud bell began to ring from the back. By the tone he suspected it to be a large wrought-iron triangle being struck by an iron bar. Tomanie soon reappeared.

"He is coming. I waited until I saw him."

Moments later Rayno Pete appeared in the doorway behind her. He halted at Conor's presence.

"Mr. Pete," he acknowledged.

"What's wrong, Sheriff?" he asked.

"It's about the evil man," Tomanie interrupted.

"What has happened?" Rayno clarified.

"I left Las Vegas this morning on the train," Con began, "escorting Dutch Wagner to Carson City and his execution. Just after sunup, a bushwhacker killed him. We were about six miles past Rox."

Rayno and Tomanie both solemnly nodded in understanding.

"The second shot barely missed me." He stuck his finger through the hole in the brim of his hat. Rayno let out a slow whistle.

"I think both shots were intended for me." Con continued, "I caught a glimpse of the shooter's escape and went after him. I found casings where he had been and tracked him until he climbed aboard an unshod horse and headed toward the north end of the Mormon Mountains. I need a horse. I don't have time to get my own up here from Las Vegas. It'll be dark in an hour. The county will pay."

"I know that country well. I've grazed sheep all over this side of those mountains. It is very rugged. A wilderness."

"I have heard that it is."

"It is because of that mountain that I no longer own horses. Only mules. They are tougher and more dependable," Rayno explained. "There is another problem too."

"And what is that?" Con asked.

"Darkness. There will be no moon to guide us tonight and only a sliver for the next few nights."

"Hold on there. I just need a horse...or mule it seems. I can track an animal or man. I don't expect you to take me there." He paused a moment. "Mr. Pete, I can understand you wanting to avenge Jimmy's murder, but the man who killed Jimmy is already dead as it turns out. I'm going after the man who's trying to kill me. I can't be getting you hurt in the process."

"We don't believe in revenge. We believe in honor. You have shown honor to the one who has left us and to our family. You are our friend. My friend. My name is Rayno, Sheriff. I would like to be called by that. I will go with you. We will find this man who wants to kill you."

Conor did not know if the *we* that did not believe in revenge were he and Tomanie, his family, his band, or his tribe. And he understood honor. It definitely was an honorable thing that Rayno Pete offered. It was however, beyond Con's scope of understanding. He and June had engaged in this conversation a few months ago. Conor had no friends. He had never had a friend. Now this man that he barely knew called him his friend and seemed for some unknown reason to be willing to confront whatever perils might be instore in the name of honor and friendship.

"No. I can't let you do this. I will rent the mule from you. Or I will buy the mule, saddle, tack, everything."

"They are my mules, Sheriff. I will go with you or my mules will not. We are in this together and if we don't start soon, we'll be loading up in the dark."

Con agreed without saying it that Rayno was right...in one aspect anyway. A black moonless night was soon to fall upon them. They needed to hurry. There was no time to argue.

"Okay, Rayno. We're in this together. Let's get packed up."

"Bring your truck around to the barn, Conor...may I call you Conor, as Luis does?"

\* \* \*

An hour later, Rayno Pete and Con rode north on the road that followed the railroad tracks. Conor had eaten June's fried chicken while driving down from Rox, but felt obliged to gorge himself on the lamb stew that Tomanie offered. He had over indulged and hoped the ride would encourage the digestive process and ease the discomfort. Rayno had eaten three times as much as he had and seemed to be suffering no ill effects. Con smiled into the darkness recalling an old Army scout's musing about Indians that he had told Conor when just a boy.

"Let me tell you something," the old man had said. "An Indian can ride for six or seven days without a single bite of food nor any sort of rest, then squat himself down by the fire and eat a half a buffalo without taking a breath."

Rayno led them...barely visible in the darkness on his black mule though only a dozen feet ahead of him. Con ran a single wrap of the lead rope for the third mule that carried their supplies around his saddle horn. They rode in silence for the first hour. A tawny, tannish-gray dog accompanied them somewhere out there in the night. An unusual looking breed that Conor suspected to be a cross between some sort of collie and a coyote. It bore a striking resemblance to a dog that Rayno had given to Luis many years ago. With nothing to see in the blackness, his mind wandered. They must be near Guelph he thought. The stars did little to illuminate any clues.

Far ahead in the distance, perhaps two or three miles away, the single light of a southbound train appeared. A few minutes later, Rayno turned his mule to face east and stopped in the middle of the road. Conor did the same, stopping beside him. He stared into the night, uncertain what he was looking for.

"Close your eyes and wait until the train passes," Rayno said. "Then your eyes won't have to readjust to the darkness."

After a few minutes, Con broke the silence. "There's something I haven't told you."

"Oh?" Rayno questioned.

"The man we're looking for is probably Indian."

"Why do you think so?"

"He wore moccasins."

"Many people wear moccasins...but it's something to consider."

The night returned to silence until the chugging sound of the locomotive broke through the invisible mire. The faint clack of iron wheels striking the joints between the steel rails soon followed. The harmonies of the orchestra gradually grew, reaching a crescendo in passing as the train shook the ground a couple of dozen yards behind them. When the sounds of the train dissipated in the distance, a creak of saddle leather and soft snort of mule indicated that Rayno was resuming the trek.

"What was it like where the man shot at you from?"

"A rock formation that looked like a loaf of bread standing on end."

"I know this place," Rayno confirmed. "About three more hours."

As they plodded through the moonless night, an occasional beam of light began coming into view ahead.

"There is a car coming," Rayno announced.

"That will be the coroner and one of my deputies," Conor replied.

Rayno stopped. "Let me have the lead rope. When they get close, I'll move off the road and wait. Try to keep one eye closed, so you can still see with the other when they leave."

"Okay. I don't think I will be able to see the road well enough to go on afterward."

"When I come back to the road, if you let him, your mule will follow me until you can see better."

They rode on until the headlights no longer disappeared intermittently. Rayno led the pack mule off the road and stopped with his back to him. Conor closed his right eye while he stopped and waited for Hal to pull up.

"Odd looking horses you're riding there, Con," he stated flatly.

"Long-eared horses. More agile in the mountains."

"Who's the other fellow."

"Rayno Pete. He says we're in this together and not letting me go it alone."

Hal handed Con's bandana out the window. "I'll bet he's good one to ride the trail with, Conor."

"I believe he is. I'll see you when I get back."

Hal tipped his hat and bade Con an adios. Ben gave a single finger salute to the brim of his Stetson from the passenger seat, barely visible in the lights from the dashboard as the car pulled away. The mule Conor rode was a lanky dun named Abe. With a slight lift of the reins, he ambled forward and fell in behind when Rayno reentered the road. A mile further along, the road crossed the tracks and climbed a hundred feet up the west side of the valley while the tracks and the wash cut through a narrow gap for another mile before the valley opened back up again. There Rayno turned down from the road to the wash and they dismounted for the first time since leaving his house.

"Lower Cone Springs," he said as he led the two mules to the water. "Better water than what the rains leave in the puddles of the wash."

Con dismounted and stumbled behind in the dark. After the mules drank their fill, the duo climbed back into their saddles then returned to the road and continued on. Con resumed leading the pack mule while following behind Rayno. The road soon recrossed the tracks following the wash around a sweeping horseshoe bend while the tracks cut across it. When they topped the hill beyond the bend, Rox lay directly ahead of them. Even on this moonless night the tin shed that housed the telephone was fairly visible in the center of the empty work yard.

As they progressed, the hills to the east gradually rose. An hour and a half later, a four-hundred-foot bluff hid a quarter of the stars from the sky. Hugging the base of the cliff, the tracks eventually crowded the road between them until it was forced to return to the west side of them. As they passed around the precipice, Rayno gradually slowed to a stop.

"This should be the place...or very near it," he said as he moved into a flat clear space near the road and dismounted. "We'll sleep here."

Conor would not normally be so compliant, but the savvy Indian had not missed on a single account all evening. In the time it took him to fumble in the darkness to unsaddle his mule, Rayno had unsaddled his own mount, unpacked the pack mule, and located halters and lead ropes for both of their mounts.

"If you could take care of the mules," he asked, "I will get a fire started. Toohoo is edgy. There is no water nearby, but they should be fine until morning. Once we have a little light, I can cook some coffee."

"Do you think your mule's smelled a puma that's making him nervous?"

"No, he's just not used to me riding him. He belongs to the one who has left us, but he'll settle down tomorrow."

Conor regretted reminding Rayno of his deceased stepson. He accepted the gear, unbridled each of the mules they had ridden, and haltered them. None of the trio protested or attempted escape. They knew the routine and patiently awaited the outcome. Leading them into the brush near the wash he tied them securely to smaller branches of the vegetation so that in the event of an attack by predators, a sudden pull against the tether could set them free. He then pulled dried grass and gave each a quick rubdown.

When he turned, his partner had a small blaze started. A blackened enamel coffee pot sat across two adjacent rocks over the edge of the fire as the sticks beneath it burned down into coals. The pot had already begun to emit a whiff of steam and Rayno knelt beside it, slicing bacon from a slab in the light cast by the flames.

\* \* \*

There was little conversation as the duo shared a meal of Rayno's bacon, Con's frybread and partially brewed coffee. The campfire burned down to the dimmest of coals and Conor rolled out his bed with his borrowed saddle for a pillow and his feet toward the fire. He unbuckled his belt and hung it from the saddle horn with his .45 automatic close at hand, should the need for its use arise. Pulling off his boots, he laid atop the blankets and stared up at the immensity of stars against the Prussian blue sky. He was not cold, but the warmth radiating from the embers soothed his stockinged feet in the coolness of the autumn night.

Rayno Pete had assumed a similar position across the fire from him. It approached midnight and Con had nearly fallen asleep when the man spoke. "How is Luis?"

The question almost startled him. Luis Garza was Con's father's lifelong best friend. Luis had been a mentor and surrogate uncle to Conor in his adolescence. He suddenly became aware of the Winchester in the scabbard beneath his shoulders. Perhaps Con's most prized possession, it had been a gift from Luis when Conor was a teenager.

"He's still mourning," Conor finally replied as he lay lost in contemplation as thoughts of the complicated events surrounding Luis' relationship with the man across the fire raced through his head. A relationship that had been kept secret over twenty years until just a few months ago. Luis had been married to Tomanie Pahgoroo. He was much older than Tomanie, but they were very much in love. They lived at Luis's sheep camp near Moapa. And they had a son together...Jimmy.

In the beginning, Tomah Pahgoroo, Tomanie's father had approved of the marriage. When Jimmy was born, Luis built a house on the homestead he had southeast of Las Vegas. When he returned to Moapa to bring his family to their new home, Tomah was outraged that Luis would take his daughter and grandson away. He drove Luis away, trying to kill him in the process. He nearly succeeded. Tomah was a leader among the Moapa Paiute band and arranged Tomanie's marriage to Rayno. Jimmy Garza, who was raised as Jimmy Pete, was murdered by Dutch Wagner. The tragedy suddenly brought the old secret to the surface, the past overflowing into the present.

"So is Tomanie." The words broke the silence and Conor's reverie.

"You know that he still loves her."

"Yes, and she loves him...and me...but in a different way."

"Luis would never do anything to come between you."

"I know. And Tomanie will never leave me for him." Rayno Pete drifted into contemplation for several minutes before resuming the conversation. "You told me once that it was sad Luis and I could not be friends; those unfortunate circumstances had forever divided us."

"It is true," Conor offered. "The two of you are very much alike in many ways."

"And so are you too. You may have learned it from him. Honor. It is honor that sets you apart from others. Honor...and understanding. Do you remember the day that Simon and I came to the morgue? The day that I saw the remnants of the one who has left us?"

"Yes. I remember the day."

"What overcame me was not honorable. When I saw him, I was crushed. I wanted to share the pain he had suffered. It over-whelmed me...and shamed me."

"It's difficult to see such a thing. A loved one in such condition."

"You were not a courageous sheriff that day, Conor. You were a kind and understanding friend. You consoled me and shared in my suffering. I knew then that I should be your friend. I also knew then who you were, the boy I had met who came with Luis to the Moapa Trading Post so many years ago. The boy I had hoped would become Luis's substitute son and help heal the wounds Tomah Pahgoroo had inflicted upon him. I hoped that someday you might act as an older brother to the one who has left us. You have already been my friend. This is why I want to become your friend."

Rayno held nothing back. He bared his soul and it penetrated Conor as deeply. Stunned, he let the feeling steadily soak through him in the stillness of the dark night while he gathered his thoughts.

"Toohoo?" Conor questioned.

"Yes."

"What does it mean?"

"Black." Rayno stifled a quiet chuckle. "The one who has left us wasn't very imaginative when choosing names."

"Well. It suits him," Conor admitted. The two men shared in a subdued momentary laugh as Conor caught a glimpse into the young victim's personality and Rayno reminisced over a cheerful memory of the son he so tragically lost.

They soon retreated, each into their own thoughts until Conor again broke the silence. "You are my friend, Rayno Pete. I will try to be a good friend to you. We *are* in this together."

* * *

WEDNESDAY, OCTOBER 22, 1930

Conor woke to Rayno's dog licking residual bacon grease from his fingers left there the previous night. He reached up to scratch around his neck, but the dog quickly jumped back releasing a cautious low growl in the process.

"Where did you disappear to last night, partner?" he asked rhetorically, as the dog stood watching him in a half-crouched stance a few feet away.

Rayno had rekindled the fire and the coffeepot already steamed beside it. The sun had yet to clear the bluff to the east even though it was well past dawn. It surprised him that he had slept so late. That was not a normal habit. He had gotten up at two o'clock yesterday morning in order to get Dutch to the train on time, then was well onto midnight by the time he went to sleep.

"Foraging," Rayno answered for the dog. "He feeds himself when we're away from home."

"What's his name?"

"Nukwi Sari-chi." Rayno answered. "He doesn't understand English."

"What does it mean?"

"Running Dog."

"Sounds appropriate."

Rayno let out a deep belly laugh. "You will see today." He looked up the steep hillside. "Are we close?"

"Right over there." Conor pointed northeast of their position. "We're close." He shook out his boots and stepped into them.

"I've got bacon skewered on sticks ready to cook over the fire. Do you have any more bread?"

"I have more frybread, lamb jerky, and ewe's milk Irish cheddar cheese."

"Great! We'll have some of your bread with the bacon. We can chew on jerky while we ride and eat some of the cheese tonight," Rayno planned. "I have canned beans and peaches too. We will feast like kings."

"I'll saddle the mules if you cook the bacon," Con offered. "I'll ask your help with the packs when we finish eating, but we can skedaddle out of here pretty darned quick."

"It's a deal," Rayno agreed.

Conor went to work with the mules and had them saddled with bedrolls tied down by the time Rayno had the bacon roasted. Drips of fat hissed blue flame as they struck coals when he lifted the skewers from the fire. They ate standing and tossed the dregs of their coffee over the dying embers as they broke camp. Rayno, a veteran packer, had the packs tied down in seconds while Con held them in place.

"You lead, Conor. You know where we're going. Don't baby old Abe. He'll go anywhere a big-horned sheep can. I'll follow with the pack mule."

Con crossed the tracks then followed them north a short distance to where the train had stopped. The sun was just cresting the outcropping where the shooter had been. Looking into the sun, his view was about the same as yesterday. He pointed Abe up the game trail he followed the day before. The mule scrambled over even the steepest places with little effort. Where the trail leveled out a little bit near the rifleman's stand, he slowed to let Rayno and the pack mule catch up, but when he looked back, Toohoo was right behind him.

A few yards from the game bed where he found the cartridges, Conor stopped and dismounted. Abe had yet to break a sweat and was barely breathing hard. He tied the reins to the dead stump of a scrubby bush and advanced. He had not been careful to preserve the moccasin tracks when he pursued the man yesterday, but remarkedly most were still intact. Rayno stepped up beside him when he stopped.

Con pointed to the tracks. "This is where he shot from. There were four .30-06 casings and a half-dozen cigarette butts. I figure he must have been waiting a while for the train to get here."

As if on cue, the rumble of an approaching locomotive came up the valley. "Must be about the same time as yesterday," Rayno commented. He pointed a foot or so below the game bed at a small round indention in the slope. "Did you see that?"

"No, I hadn't," Con admitted. "What is it?"

"Fifty years ago, or more, buffalo hunters out on the prairie would use a forked stick to prop up those big heavy Sharps rifles they used while they were shooting. Though he wears moccasins, this man may be a White man. Buffalo Bill often wore moccasins. So have many others, before and since." He looked down the slope at the passing train. "What do you figure the distance is from here?"

"Five hundred yards or more."

"I would need something to steady my rifle at that distance, even if it wasn't a heavy old Sharps," Rayno commented. "Would you?"

"Yep."

"And it's downhill too. I think this man took a lesson from the old buffalo hunters."

"I already figured the extra two shots were to test his range," Con told him with a little bravado. "I never heard of this forked stick thing before though."

Rayno looked around. "I don't see anything around here he might have used. He probably carries one with him."

Con looked around for a clear print of the right moccasin, then pointed it out to Rayno. "What do you make of that right footprint?"

Rayno looked, then dropped to one knee for closer examination. His face had lost all expression. He moved up the trail to find another example, then a third. Kneeling down for a closer look at each of them.

"Well?" Con asked.

Rayno came to his feet but had not yet turned to face him. He removed his flat-brimmed palm-leaf hat. It was not yet hot, but he took out his bandana and wiped the sweat from his brow and face. He put his hat back on and turned to face the sheriff. The person Con saw before him now was not the same man he rode here with. The relaxed expression had disappeared from his face. "I think I know who this man is."

"Who?"

"Altaha."

"What does that mean? Is it an Indian name? Who is he?"

"He is a hunter."

"Like a buffalo hunter, right?"

"A hunter of men. He hunts men for money."

"Like a bounty hunter then?" Con began to regain a little composure, but Rayno's expression had not improved.

"He kills men for money. If you want somebody killed, you give him money, and it's done. Who wants to kill you, Conor?"

"Dutch Wagner. But he's already dead."

"And who would want wanted *him* dead?"

"Beside you and me?"

Rayno nodded while contemplating, then answered, "Yes, besides you and me, Tomanie, and Luis."

"Leonora Campbell, her son and daughter, Dutch's sister Katie, Al Drago...maybe a dozen others...the list of suspects would be long."

"Maybe Altaha did his job."

"Why would someone hire a hitman to kill Dutch Wagner? He was going to be executed tomorrow anyway."

"I don't know, but it sounds like he had a lot more enemies than you."

"Well, I don't know who this Altaha guy is, or even if that's who we're after, but the man we're hunting is small. His stride is short and tracks are shallow," Con shared with Rayno. "He's probably less than five-foot-two or three inches tall. Weighs about one-ten. I doubt over one-twenty. He probably hobbles when he walks. His stride coming off that bum foot is shorter than the other. I tracked the horse for a little bit. He's small too. Unshod, small feet, short stride…six or seven hundred pounds probably."

"Mexican pony," Rayno muttered more to himself than in conversation.

"What?" Con asked.

"Probably a Mexican pony," Rayno replied. "You don't see them up here very much, but there's a lot of them down in Mexico, just like the wild mustangs up here, but smaller. They're quick and agile, but their backs are a little week for a fat man like me." He smiled for the first time since seeing the moccasin tracks. "I've heard the conquistadores, your ancestors, brought them from Spain and they got loose and thrived on their own. Apache's like them."

"Is Altaha Apache?"

Rayno Pete did not answer. He walked past Abe and mounted his mule on the narrow trail. Con watched as he grabbed the lead rope of the pack mule and settled himself into the saddle. "We should get going," he said. "He's a whole day ahead of us."

Con grabbed Abe's saddle horn and swung himself up onto the animal's back. He rode up the trail at a trot. When he rounded the rock outcropping, Con slowed Abe to a walk and turned in the saddle to address Rayno.

"This is where he had his horse," Con told him and continued up the trail. It crested a finger-like ridge that culminated at the outcropping and continued a more gradual ascent to the top of the main bluff. The horse's tracks were easy to see and stayed on the main trail up to the top. They followed them at a trot.

# 3

Southwest of Casper, Wyoming

Seventeen-year-old Roscoe Taylor found his Texas-bred buckskin cowpony lying dead and frozen in the corral near the line shack at the mouth of Tietz Draw. The thermometer hanging by the door read minus thirty-six. This was not the way he planned to start his morning. He considered his circumstances. Marty Tietz, the owner of the outfit, provided a lanky, broom-tailed, blue roan for a second horse that Ross had chosen not to ride for a few days. Consequently, he left the animal out to graze among the cattle up the draw. He wished now he had tossed a loop over the roan's head and brought him in when he finished his round of the herd yesterday.

Unable to come up with an alternative, he returned inside and untied the riata from his saddle. The young cowboy wore a wool shirt and pants over his long johns beneath a moth-eaten sweater, the warmest clothing he owned. He had a long slicker and angora chaps, but both were too cumbersome for serious walking. After stuffing a handful of elk jerky into the pocket of his sweater, he tied a large bandanna over his bare face and ears. Before retrieving his rabbit fur mittens that hung above the little iron stove, he pulled his felt hat down snug on his head to hold it all in place. When passing the corral Roscoe took a last glance at the mound of frozen horseflesh that had been his beloved cowpony. Then he set out up the draw. The tiny flakes of snow falling in the bitter cold had already provided a thin white blanket of powder over the buckskin's coat. Within a few hours the remains would be completely hidden.

Temperatures had remained in the single digits for several days. They fluctuated across the line marking zero between them depending on whether it be daytime or night. The vicious cold brought with it a continual light snowfall accumulating three or four inches each day, now totaling a foot and a half. Though the fluffy blanket did little to impede his stride, it camouflaged a multitude of obstacles hidden beneath it to stumble over. Furthermore, the overcast skies veiled any semblance of shadow in the sea of white thus robbing Ross of his sense of depth perception. Combined with the cold sucking every ounce of energy from his body, he was exhausted by midday.

When he reached the cowherd, he easily spotted the roan among them, but barely had the vigor to continue. As he tried to approach, the horse was wary of the lone man on foot and kept thirty or forty yards between them. After an hour of softly coaxing his target and slow cautious movements, Roscoe never came close enough to consider tossing his riata. He abandoned the pursuit.

It was difficult to be certain in the grayness, but he thought dusk would soon overtake him. There was no point in stumbling in the dark all the way back to the line shack. He knew of an overhanging rock above a shallow cave in a nearby bank. Ross had once used it for shelter from a hailstorm. Presently, it offered his best refuge from the weather. The cave had been large enough to protect him and his horse from the quarter-size hail stones that were pelting them when he found it. Last fall he cached a pile of dry sticks and branches there for just such an emergency as this. The shelter was in a dry wash on the southwest side of Tietz Draw. Everything looked different in the snow, but he was pretty sure it was in one of the two washes presently in view. He found it on his second attempt just as the sky began to darken.

The cave, barely more than an indention in the bank, offered enough cover that it had remained dry. No part of him was warm, but his fingers still functioned within his fur mittens. He removed them and began breaking the smallest of twigs, splintering them as best he could. Securing a match from his shirt pocket, he struck it on a rock and cupped it in his hands. The instant warmth from the flame was tempting to just hold it there, but he placed it beneath the little pile and coaxed it into a small blaze. Roscoe removed his bandana. Condensation from his breath in addition to falling snow encrusted it with ice in a reversed impression of his face. He hovered over the little fire, gradually adding larger sticks and blowing on it periodically to help it grow. The legs of his wool pants formed two frozen stovepipes from his thighs down. They dug into the backs of his legs as he knelt by the fire.

The little campfire began generating enough heat for Ross to move back a little bit from it and he unbuttoned his sweater to allow the heat to radiate against his chest. His feet were numb and had been for several hours. He didn't know much about frostbite, but the thought of losing toes scared him. He continued to add larger sticks and branches until he had a moderate bonfire going. Heat began to bounce back from the wall behind him and he sat back against it, holding his feet near the fire.

As the snow and ice slowly melted from his boots and pants, he began trying to wiggle his toes. As soon as he could see some movement, he slowly and carefully removed his boots. Feeling his stockinged feet, they were cold to the touch, but wet, not frozen. He was afraid to look at them, so left his socks on and resumed his former position with his feet near the fire.

He continued to wiggle his toes as best he could and watched the steam roll up from them into the night as they began drying. His pants began to steam too. Pretty soon his toes began to tingle as the circulation started to return. It was not long before the tingle turned to burning. He sat up and desperately massaged his toes through the nearly dry socks attempting to relieve the pain. The burn turned to ache, but he could feel his hands on his toes and it encouraged him to continue.

As more and more feeling returned to his toes, the ice on his pants melted, and the water started soaking his long johns. He took his pants off and laid them over a nearby boulder with his bandana. He stoked more wood on the fire and resumed his spot against the back wall, wiggling his toes and occasionally massaging them. Finally working up the nerve, he removed his socks.

His feet and toes were red, not black as he had heard they would be with frostbite. "Maybe from rubbing them," he thought aloud. "They're all right," he convinced himself.

Gazing into the soothing fire, Roscoe chewed on morsels of jerky and reveled in the warming glow before him. Amid the rest and warmth, he dozed, still leaning against the clay bank in his long underwear, shirt, and sweater.

* * *

Cold reawakened him in total darkness except for the slight red glow from the embers of his fire. Scurrying on his hands and knees, he found the firewood and worked the end of a branch down into the coals. The dry wood ignited quickly and began to glow, providing enough light to restoke the fire. Soon regaining a substantial blaze, he donned his now-dried pants and bandana before returning to his semi-reclined position between the fire and the wall. Unable to judge the time, he chewed on another scrap of jerky before drifting back to sleep.

* * *

THURSDAY, JANUARY 9, 1913

When Roscoe Taylor next awoke, darkness still surrounded him. Again, he roused the flames back to life and fortified them with about half of the remaining branches. His boots were now mostly dry, so he stomped his feet into the shrunken leather then paced around the fire working mobility back into his tired, sore body. When he got a few steps away, it seemed the ambient temperature had risen. Probably back to single digits, he guessed.

Returning to his previous seat, he felt uninclined to sleep. He occasionally thought he heard movement in the darkness, but every time he tried to focus his ear on the sound, a spark popped in the fire and all returned to silence. Not inclined to spook easily, the random noise began to wear on his nerves. A sudden, loud snort within a dozen yards jerked him to his feet. He stared wide-eyed into the obscurity but watching his campfire had limited his ability so see anything in the darkness. He walked to the outer side of the light attempting to adjust his eyes. A second snort stood every hair of his body on end. It sounded very close. Maybe less than twenty feet. Probably following the scent of his tracks in the snow. It must be a bear.

He had an old, worn-out Colt peacemaker back at the line shack. He'd deemed it too cold and heavy to carry when he left there yesterday. First, he failed to catch the roan when he could have and because of it, he was afoot. Now the pistol. It would have been smarter to carry it. Disappointed in himself and his poor judgment, thoughts began to pick up momentum as they passed through his head. The pistol would be nearly useless against a bear anyway. And bears should be hibernating now. But a groggy bear would be looking for an easy meal and...

The thought had yet to conclude when he heard a footstep. It moved but remained invisible in the night. It seemed large. Heavy.

"Oh, God," escaped his lips in a whimper. "It's a griz."

Another brainwave blasted into his head. Fire! Wild animals are afraid of fire!

He nearly dove at the woodpile and piled every branch onto the campfire. All but one. A large one. About three feet long and as many inches in diameter. He slung it over his shoulder like a caveman with a club.

"C'mon, you bastard!" he yelled. "I ain't goin' down without no fight!"

He was no longer cold. Blood surged through his veins as he paced around the perimeter of light. But the glow failed to penetrate the murky abyss surrounding him. The flames dwindled as the hours passed and though he was not cold, Ross began to regret his third poor judgment, burning all of his firewood.

"Bad luck comes in threes," he muttered aloud. "If'n I get et' by a bear, it's my own damned fault."

When the faint red glow of the embers scarcely shown through the ashes, Roscoe burrowed his club into them. The action instantly produced a glowing flame. He commenced his vigil from his seat behind the fire. As the blaze consumed half of the club, he repositioned the unburned portion to the center of the fire. Watching it as the last flames evaporated into glowing red embers, the adrenaline was gone. Weariness overtook him and again he slept.

\* \* \*

Something nuzzled at his hat and breathed on the right side of his face. Startled awake but conscious of the need to pretend being dead, he managed to suppress his movement. The breath smelled horrific. He supposed that was normal for a bear who had just slept for a couple of months. He slowly opened his left eye. It was daylight. He scanned to the right expecting perhaps to glimpse a black furry paw with long claws on the ground from across the bridge of his nose.

What he saw instead was the black and gray stripes of the right front hoof of a tall blue roan with a little hint of appaloosa in his blood from some ancient ancestor. The horse was wise to cowboys and wore a few rope-burned scars on his neck and ankles to prove it. Ross had not known him long enough to learn whether the horse had a mean streak that earned him those scars or if some ignorant wrangler or farrier had handed them over to him out of spite. The array of brands that adorned his hips and shoulders suggested it might be the former. Roscoe was not in a situation that allowed for any more misjudgments.

Opening his right eye, the horse's nuzzle was only inches away from it. The cowboy slowly rose his right hand to gently rub the horse's jaw and simultaneously crab-walked the fingers of his left hand toward the last known vicinity of his riata. Unaware of any other name and for lack of better imagination, Ross had been calling him Blue.

"Good morning, Blue," he whispered a moment before he touched him. "I bet yer lookin' fer that handful of oats yuh get when I ride yuh."

Blue pushed Roscoe's hat up and sniffed at his hair.

"Well, sir," Ross continued. "Y'ul haf'ta earn them oats."

Just short of a miracle in Roscoe's mind, the riata was where he thought it would be. Without looking toward it, he followed the coil around until his fingers reached the hondo, then played the coil out to what he hoped was about a two-foot loop. Still rubbing and petting Blue's jaw, he worked his way to rubbing his neck, talking softly all the time as his hand roamed. Without free use of either hand, Ross slid his feet up as close as he could to his haunches and carefully pushed himself erect, sliding his back up the bank. Through all this he somehow managed to keep from spooking Blue away. On the other hand, Blue had one eye fastened on Roscoe and the other on the riata.

"It's okay, boy," Ross spoke calmly, "Yuh know I won't hurt'cha."

Keeping in mind the old adage, "If you control the horse's head, you control the horse," Roscoe cautiously worked his right hand up Blue's neck and rubbed behind his ears. Preparing to grab around his neck in a bear-hug if necessary to attempt preventing an escape, he let all but the loop of his riata fall to the ground. At the motion, Blue pulled back a bit, but stood fast.

"Now take it easy, fella. Everthin's okay."

The big roan raised his head and eyed the riata suspiciously but allowed Ross to slip it over his head.

"See. I told yuh," Roscoe continued talking as he went back to rubbing behind Blue's ears.

Ross then pulled the riata loosely up around Blue's throat and made a half hitch around his nose fashioning a makeshift cross between a bosal and a halter. Looping the end of the riata across the withers and back to the bosal he had reins. He coiled the rest of the riata to carry in one hand as he rode. The young cowboy knew from experience that Blue sometimes liked to crow-hop when first mounted in the morning and he dreaded that possibility riding bareback. Grabbing a handful of mane, he took a one-step run and jumped as high as he could to get a leg on the tall horse.

Much to Roscoe's satisfaction, Blue took a couple of steps sideways to center himself beneath his rider and walked off as if he had been doing this his whole life.

The mound of snow in the corral at the line shack reminded Ross of his initial task. He tied Blue to a post and ducked inside to gather his saddle and bridle. The roan seemed unaffected by the nearby snowy heap. Roscoe saddled the roan and removed the riata from his head, then slipped the bridle on in its place. Removing the riata from Blue's neck, he looped the noose around the hind feet of the cowpony. Ross stepped into the saddle and took three dallies with the riata around the horn. Taking up the slack, he walked the horse toward the gate. Feeling the rawhide pulling tight against his hip, Blue paused. Roscoe nudged him ahead and after some effort, the hump of snow cracked and the carcass pulled free from the frozen ground beneath it. The roan only outweighed the cowpony by a couple hundred pounds, but once started, the load slid fairly well on the snow as they dragged him across the draw and into the sagebrush away from the shack.

After unsaddling Blue, he rubbed him down with the saddle blanket and turned him loose in the corral. He carried his rig into the shack and returned with a block of hay and handful of oats from the lean-to attached to the side.

Not yet recuperated from the recent ordeal, Ross headed to the line shack. The thermometer by the door read eight degrees. Maybe it was warming up.

* * *

*SATURDAY, JANUARY 11, 1913*

Roscoe Taylor spent the previous day making his rounds, checking the mixed herd of mostly yearling steers wintering in Tietz Draw. The thermometer read a miserable minus twelve when he returned. Minus nineteen that morning with a biting breeze.

He spent all of yesterday debating with himself before deciding. It was time to pull his picket pin and move on. This morning, he rolled the Colt Peacemaker and spare shirt into his bedroll. The gun would shoot and he had cartridges, but he felt uncomfortable carrying it. He then caught the roan in the corral and led him out to the lean-to shed where he fed hay and oats as he saddled him up.

"Too damned cold for this cowboy," he muttered to the horse as he pulled the rawhide strings tight around his bedroll behind the cantle.

Back inside, he pulled his angora shotgun chaps on over his wool pants, then shrugged into his oilskin slicker over the three layers of clothing already covering his upper body. The slicker added little insulation, but it broke the wind. After threading the latchstring through the hole in the door, he pulled it closed for the last time, slipped on his rabbit fur mittens, and swung his leg over the saddle...then headed for the home ranch to collect his final pay.

Roscoe turned from the road toward the Tietz Ranch headquarters three hours later. As he approached Dobbin Spring Reservoir, he spotted two people gliding around on the twenty-acre sheet of ice. When he got closer, Ross recognized the larger of the two as Eddy Tietz, the boss's eldest son. He reined Blue to a stop and pulled the bandana down from his face to watch them. Eddy was only a year younger than Ross and the two had ridden together the previous summer until Eddy moved to the family's big brick house in town last fall to go to school. He enjoyed Eddy's company but knew his own place as a hired hand. Eddy's companion was obviously his younger sister. Even her layers of heavy clothing could not disguise the gangly fourteen-year-old's stature. She had an odd German name, but everybody just called her Sis.

"Hey, Ross!" Eddy exclaimed as he slid to a stop nearby.

"Howdy, Eddy," he replied quizzically. "What the hell're yuh doin' out here in this cold?"

"Skating!" the young man replied, holding up a foot to show off a strange, gleaming metal apparatus strapped to his boot. "Dad says everybody does it back east. It's fun!"

"Yer out here in this stinkin' cold fer fun?" he asked incredulously.

"Well...yeah...it's not so cold once you get skating around."

Roscoe just shook his head in disbelief.

"What are you doing down here?" Eddy asked him.

"I come ta' fetch my pay an' ketch me a train back ta' Texas if I can pay fer a ticket."

"What about your horse?"

"He died a few nights ago. Too da—" Ross caught himself

mid-cuss word as Sis sashayed up behind Eddy. It might not go well if the boss heard that he was swearing in front of his daughter before he collected his pay. "It was too derned cold fer him an' fer me too," he corrected. "It's time ta' be movin' on."

"Hi, Roscoe." Sis beamed from behind the knit scarf covering her face.

"Howdy, Sis." He knew Sis had sort of a crush on him and didn't want to hurt her feelings, but he really wasn't in the mood for it today. Besides, it wasn't likely she'd ever see him again anyhow.

"What's going on?"

"Ross is going back to Texas," Eddy interrupted.

"Well, who am I going to marry when I get old enough if you go back to Texas?" she asked coyly.

"Some bloke that likes this God-fer-sakin' place a hel…a heck of a lot better'n me," Roscoe snapped back at her and put the spurs to Blue.

"Good luck, Ross," Eddy hollered to his back.

Ross waved a mittened hand in thanks and acceptance.

* * *

Marty Tietz sat at the kitchen table sipping a strong cup of coffee. He gazed out the window as the biting wind whipped the leaf-bare branches of the cottonwood trees surrounding the small ranch house. He recognized the horse before his rider when he rode up to the gate. Dismounting, the young man tied the reins to the hitching ring mounted in the stone gatepost by the yard. The light-gray horse blended well into the mottled landscape behind him where the wind blew the blanket of snow into heaps behind each sagebrush leaving barren spaces of frozen dirt between. Wisps of steam exiting the nostrils of both horse and rider then disappeared instantly in the squall.

The possible circumstances causing his range rider's arrival troubled Tietz. He opened the door just as the hand pulled off a mitten to knock on it.

"C'mon in," Tietz ordered. "Get by the stove and thaw yourself out."

"Obliged, sir," Ross muttered as he staggered on numb feet toward the big iron cookstove. He could feel the heat radiating from it from across the cool room. It almost seemed the inanimate device came alive to battle the tempest raging outside.

Tietz filled a heavy blue and white ceramic mug with coffee from a blue-gray enameled tin pot that simmered atop the cookstove.

As he presented it to Ross he asked, "Can you hold on to it?"

Roscoe nodded taking the cup in both hands allowing the heat to slowly penetrate his frozen fingers.

Tietz returned to his place at the table sipping his coffee. After allowing a suitable time for the rider to somewhat recover, he finally asked, "Where's that little cowpony of yours?"

"Dead."

"What happened?"

"Froze ta' death I s'pect. Found him in the corral a few days ago. Froze hard as a anvil."

"Well, that's too bad, Roscoe. He seemed to be a good little horse and I know you've had him for quite a while." Tietz thought for a minute. "I can't pay what he probably was worth to you, but you can have your pick of any of my horses up on the school section. I'll give you a bill of sale. The horse will be yours free and clear."

"That's mighty decent of ya, Mr. Tietz, but ya might wanna hold that offer fer a little bit."

"And why might that be? Something wrong up the draw that I should know about?"

"No, nothin' like that, sir. I drug my pony off inta' the sagebrush across the draw. I made my round last evening and the herd's in good shape. Water's all froze up, but their eatin' snow fer drink, an' seem to be doin' fine."

"So, why would I change my mind?"

"It's the cold, sir. I can't take no more of it. I got on every stitch o' clothes I own an' can't keep my teeth from rattlin'. I had my fill. I come ta' fetch my wages an' light out. I figger I got a month an' a half comin'. I hope that's enough to buy a train ticket back ta' Texas. If it ain't, it'll git me a to somewhere a hell of lot warmer'n here."

"Well," Tietz assessed. "You've been a good hand, Ross. I figure it's closer to three months you've got coming. I'll have to write you a check, but any business in town will cash it for you."

"I'm obliged. I'll need to be goin' ta' git inta Casper by dark."

"You'll need to get warmed up before you get back out in that." He nodded toward the window. "Pull your slicker off and have a seat," Tietz ordered, then retrieved a heavy ceramic bowl from a cupboard. It was the same delft blue on white as the mug. He lifted the cast-iron lid from the Dutch oven on the stove and ladled up a substantial serving of mutton stew from the pot. "That'll help warm you up on the inside," he told Roscoe when he sat the steaming bowl in front of him.

"Obliged," the cowhand replied. He didn't care much for mutton, but when the aroma from the hot bowl of stew hit him, the growl from his stomach convinced him otherwise.

Marty Tietz left the room and returned with a liquor bottle. He poured the now empty coffee mug half full of the clear liquid. Roscoe looked suspiciously at the German writing on the label.

"Kirschwasser," the boss replied to the unasked question. "Cherry water in English. Try it."

Roscoe sniffed the mug. It was clearly alcohol, but not so harsh as to burn his nostrils. He took a sip. It was sweet and warm as it flowed down his throat. He drew a quick deep breath to keep from coughing and set the mug back on the table, thankful for the three or four mouthfuls of stew that cushioned the impact of the Kirschwasser hitting the bottom of his belly.

"Cherry brandy," Tietz clarified. "That'll finish warming up whatever the stew misses."

Roscoe continued eating the stew alternating with sips of the sweet cherry brandy. When he had nearly finished the meal, Tietz again left the room and returned this time with an official-looking book, pen and ink, and a well-worn sheepskin coat. Roscoe was about the same stature as Tietz, who handed him the coat.

"That'll help keep out some of the cold until you get to warmer country. I've been planning to buy a new one for some time now anyway." He sat down in his chair and opened the book full of checks in front of him.

Roscoe stood and shrugged into the heavy coat. It was warmer than anything he had ever worn before. As Tietz dipped the pen into the ink, Roscoe stammered, "I'll be ridin' the roan inta town. I'll leave him at Duhling's Livery to fetch back whenever it suits ya."

Tietz paused. "If that's the case," he began to write, "I'll throw in another thirty dollars to offset the loss of your little horse." He waited without response then turned to the young cowboy. "If that's agreeable," he added.

"Yessir, Mr. Tietz. That'd be jus' fine."

Marty Tietz finished filling out the check and signed it. He pulled it from the book and softly blew the ink dry as he came to his feet. "An honest day's work for an honest day's pay. That's what I ask of the people who work for me and that's what you gave me."

"I ride fer the brand, sir."

Tietz extended the check in his left hand and reached for Roscoe's with his right. "Good luck to you in Texas, Mr. Taylor," he said as they grasped each other's hands.

"Thank you, sir," he replied as he stuffed the check into his shirt without looking at it. Throwing his slicker over his shoulder, he walked out the door.

# 4

Sheriff Conor Armenta and Rayno Pete kept on the trail of the gunman at a rapid pace for two hours. The Mormon Mountains rose steadily to the east at four to five hundred feet per mile. The powdery soil bore a thin crust leaving a clear trail northeast in nearly a straight line. Rayno's Running Dog took the outrider position, occasionally hesitating to sniff after some unknown rodent in the distance. Here the rate of incline doubled and with it came rockier slopes of large boulders and outcroppings creating a multitude of cover for a would-be attacker. The shooter could be miles away...or watching their every move. They continued on warily.

The trail turned due east, pointing directly at Mormon Peak looming thirty-five hundred feet above and four miles away. The foothills rose a thousand feet and a mile apart on either side to the north and south. The ground between the rocks turned gravelly and the patches of soil among them became less frequent. Vegetation nearly disappeared completely as the sidehills closed in around them. Tracks were more difficult to perceive slowing

Conor to a sluggish walk as the duo edged forward through the maze of hideouts. A half mile farther, the trail vanished completely.

Con turned in his saddle and spoke for the first time since they left the spot where their quarry had mounted his horse yesterday. "What do you make of it?"

"You know what it's like when someone is watching you? The hair stands up on the back of your neck?"

"Yep. I know that feeling."

"I don't feel it."

Conor thought about it momentarily. "Me neither."

"I think Altaha knew there was no easy way to disguise his tracks out in the open so he just rode straight here." Rayno scanned their surroundings. "Up here he doesn't have to hide his tracks, just watch where his horse steps."

"Good point."

"And he knows we have to be more cautious up here with all the places to hide."

Conor gazed ahead. The little valley continued to narrow in the distance.

"Another mile," Rayno continued, "and this turns into a box canyon. Our mules could climb out of it, but his Mexican pony can't."

"But does he know that?"

"Yes, I think so. I think he has every step of his escape planned."

Rayno turned his attention to the slope to the north. Con's eyes followed.

"There's a saddle across the ridge up there. I think he went that way."

"And if you're wrong?"

"We follow the top of the crest toward the peak."

"I'll take the pack mule," Conor replied. "You lead."

Rayno nudged Toohoo ahead and handed the lead rope to Conor when he passed and turned north. As they worked their way up the sidehill Con noticed the occasional track of a small unshod horse on their route. A half mile farther and a thousand feet higher, Rayno paused at the windblown crest of the saddle. The ridge ended abruptly a thousand feet higher yet in a promontory another half mile to the northwest. Faint remnants of their adversary's tracks crossed the dozen yards of baren soil as the wind continued to mitigate them. Conor rode up and stopped beside him.

"He headed to the bottom," Rayno stated flatly as he nodded his head in the general direction. "I think he crossed over there." He pointed to the saddle on another ridge two miles away to the northwest.

"Why that way?"

"There's a cave. Our ancestors have used it for many generations."

"How would he know about this cave?"

"I don't know," Rayno contemplated, "but he knows this mountain. We'll traverse the slope just beneath the rimrock on the mules. His little horse wouldn't make it."

They followed an intermittent trail beneath the rimrock on their right. A half mile farther, a trickle of water fell from the cliff above and quickly disappeared beneath the surface of the steep wash leading down the hill. Rayno paused to let his mule drink from the tiny pool at the base of the rivulet. Then he crossed the wash and waited a short distance up the trail for Conor to do the same.

The trail widened just enough for Conor to ride up beside Rayno where he stopped. Turning in his seat, Con reached into the saddlebag for a handful of lamb jerky that he shared with his comrade.

"This is the best place to take a break for a while," Rayno commented as he stood in his stirrups and stretched his back. "Do you need to get down?"

"Nope, I'm fine," Conor answered after tearing off a bite of jerky between his teeth. "How far to this cave?"

"Four or five miles. Double that for our horseman...and twice the time."

Con glanced up at the sun, then pulled the watch from his pocket, ten thirty. "How's the trail?"

"Rough. Up around this next bend we've got a quarter mile of scree to cross. The next water is beyond that if it's not dried up this late in the year."

"Scree?"

"Loose rock on a steep slope. If you lose your footing, you wake up at the bottom...or you don't wake up. A horse can't cross it."

"And these guys can?" Conor asked skeptically.

"Mules take little steps and their hind feet step right where the front one just was. If it's a soft or loose footing, they know it before the back foot gets there," Rayno explained. "Their eyes are farther apart than a horse too. They can look at all four of their feet while they walk. A horse can only see their two front feet."

"So, besides being a narrower foot than a horse, if you're tracking a mule, they only leave two tracks instead of four."

"Well, sort of. It's kind of a track on top of a track so you can usually see a ghost of the front track beneath the rear."

"Hmm." Con nodded. "Interesting."

The duo continued on. As they crossed the scree field, Conor watched the hind feet of Rayno's mule ahead of him. The loose rocks barely moved when he put his weight down on them. "Interesting," he repeated aloud to himself.

A quarter mile past the scree, they came to another dribbling stream. The mules knew from experience to drink their fill when given an opportunity as their next chance may be distant. Rayno let his mule drink and continued a short distance ahead to wait. When Con rode up with the packhorse they stopped single file behind him.

"I used to graze my sheep in this valley and the next one across the ridge," he told Conor. "They usually have good grass in the spring."

"That's how you learned the area so well? Grazing sheep here?"

"Like my father before me and his before him," Rayno replied. "Many, many years. Many ancestors," he added, then nudged his mule ahead.

A single set of tracks made by a small horse preceded them across the saddle of the unnamed ridge when they reached it.

The tracks were more pronounced than on the previous ridge. "We're gaining on him," Rayno observed as he squatted near the tracks. "Moreso than just the shortcut we took," he added behind the puzzled expression on his face. "It was nearly dark when he crossed here."

"Maybe he was expecting me to follow him," Conor contemplated. Standing beside his partner, he scanned the countryside with an observing eye. "He might have been waiting to drygulch me."

"Or looking for food," Rayno considered. "If he thought you were following him, he wouldn't chance shooting his rifle and giving away his location. He may have been trying to catch a rabbit among the brush in the valley."

As if on cue, Running Dog appeared alongside them with tufts of rabbit fur adorning his muzzle from a recent meal. Neither Rayno nor Conor felt the need to comment. They remounted their mules and Rayno led off contouring the slope to their right and continued on a northeasterly course.

After a half mile, the two men rounded a point on their right where the valley narrowed and proceeded due east up the mountain. After crossing the dry wash in the center, Rayno turned northeast again and began the rather steep five hundred foot ascent on a rarely used game trail up the far ridge. At the top, he paused for Conor's arrival.

"The cave is in the far wall of the gorge behind the point on that next little ridge. We'll follow this wash northward to the foot then turn up the ravine to the cave."

He urged his mule ahead and they began the descent on a

slightly milder grade than their route up the other side. When they reached the sandy bottom, they rode side by side up the canyon.

"We just cut another four miles off our horseman's trail," Rayno noted. "It must have been dark by the time he got here. Considering how black it was out in the open last night, I'll bet it was really dark down here."

It was difficult to discern the source of the tracks in the sand, but clearly, a large animal had recently passed this way. A few minutes later, they arrived at the cave. Conor's attention was immediately drawn to the array of petroglyphs adorning the walls. Some were of people seemingly wearing some sort of masks and costumes. Others were symbols, but most were animals. Easily distinguished were tortoises, lizards, and snakes as well as large animals like deer, elk, and bighorn sheep.

He nearly tripped over an empty canvas waterbag before looking down at the evidence left by the mysterious rifleman. He had built a fire and roasted a rabbit. The stick that it had been skewered on had apparently become firewood, but wildlife had not yet carted off the picked-clean bones. A clear imprint of the butt of his rifle positioned beside the wall was accompanied by the indentation of the small man who had slept near it.

Moccasin tracks were everywhere. Conor was particularly intrigued by those near the walls facing the petroglyphs. Judging by the man's perceived height, it seemed he had wandered the gallery, reaching up and touching the images...almost mystical... or reverent. Perhaps he had performed some sort of ritual honoring the ancient artisans.

"See anything interesting?" Rayno interrupted his trance.

"It's almost eerie, isn't it?"

"I can feel the spirit of my ancestors every time I come to one of these places."

"I understand. I can feel it too. But perhaps my feeling is more of an intruder. Like I've entered a forbidden—no...a holy place."

Rayno nodded, "Sacred."

"Have I broken some sort of taboo by being in here?"

"I don't think so. You might want to ask Tomanie's brother, Simon when we get back though. He will know. Might need a ceremony."

"Sure," Con affirmed as he tried to turn his thoughts toward evidence left by the shooter. He picked up the desert waterbag. "Still damp. He must have given the last of it to his horse this morning."

"And it tells us there's no water in the canyon."

"Why would he leave the waterbag?" Conor asked himself aloud. "He must have his escape route planned from one water-hole to the next. If this canyon is dry, where's the nearest water?"

"Horse Spring."

"How far?"

"Seven, eight miles maybe," Rayno replied. "Davies Spring is closer, but it's on the other side of Mormon Peak."

Conor puzzled over the possibilities. "But which way did our shooter go? That's the question."

"His pony is watered up. Our mules aren't, but they can go a lot farther without it," Rayno considered. "My guess is Horse Spring, but we'll know soon enough. Those tracks in the sand are his and they're headed up the canyon. This sandy bottom don't run far and we're back into dirt. He'll be easier to follow then."

Conor's confidence in Rayno's tracking and knowledge of the terrain had grown through the day. "You know where we're going, I'll trail along."

A half mile up the narrow canyon it made an abrupt right turn to the southeast. As Rayno had predicted, the sandy floor became soft dirt with a thin crust from the most recent rain. He picked up the pace to a fast trot and continued their gradual ascent. Abe followed with a remarkably smooth gait that might have been bone-jarring astride many horses. Before long the chasm began a series of turns. Unexpectedly, Rayno took a trail into a steep trib-utary up the south wall of the canyon. Con glanced around for the pony's tracks but failed to spot them at the speed they rode.

In a mile they had gained five hundred feet in elevation. Rayno slowed Toohoo to a walk. Still not seeing tracks of the pony, Conor rode up alongside his escort.

"I'm not seeing any tracks. Have we lost him?"

"He stayed on the main wash. This is a shortcut to Horse Spring. We're halfway to the top. It gets steeper up ahead. These guys"—Rayno patted Toohoo's neck—"they'll have caught their breath before we start the climb."

"So, where's Altaha?"

"If he's headed to Horse Spring, we'll beat him there. If he follows the South Fork of Toquop Wash when he drops off the ridge, we'll still gain another five miles on him."

"If he's going to this Horse Spring, why wouldn't he come this way?"

They were beginning to climb. Rayno stopped before they were forced to ride single file. He looked toward the jagged ridgeline ahead. "It's twice as steep down the other side and there's only one trail down it. It's hard to find and only a few people know about it."

Rayno nudged Toohoo ahead and Abe fell in behind him. Conor caught a momentarily glance of Running Dog paralleling them three hundred yards to their right before the image evaporated into the rugged landscape. An hour later they topped the ridge.

"Stay here while I find the trail," Rayno told him then proceeded along the rimrock on the eastern edge. "Over here!" he hollered back to Conor, then vanished over the edge.

When he reached the place, a meager thirty yards away, Rayno was nowhere in sight below him. He gazed at the nearly sheer drop-off ahead in disbelief. Almost deciding he was at the wrong spot, the fresh scrape mark of a steel mule shoe sliding on smooth rock caught his eye. A moment later, the sound of loose scree clattering down the mountainside drew his attention to the base of a cliff fifty feet below and to his left just in time to see the rocks sliding down the mountain. A moment later, the back of

Rayno's right arm waving his hat appeared from around the corner of the cliff.

"This way, Conor," Rayno yelled at the same instant and the hat disappeared.

Con gauged the descent ahead of him. The first step was no less than three feet down for Abe. He slackened the lead rope for the pack mule nearly to its end and made three wraps around his saddle horn. Standing in the stirrups and leaned back as far into the cantle as possible, Conor gave Abe his head. The wily old mule walked down off the ledge with all the grace of a ballet dancer.

Rayno was beyond Con's view more often than not. Abe needed no guidance. He sensed what his owner described as a trail more than saw it and followed Toohoo down it without faltering. The pack mule marched along behind in perfect step, never letting the lead rope touch the ground nor pull taut. The eastern descent lay in afternoon shadow making it difficult to perceive irregularities in the rocky topography.

A half mile down the slope, Rayno stopped on the only ground level enough to do so. When Conor arrived, he had already dismounted and was checking Toohoo's feet and ankles for injury before proceeding.

"Are you sure that this is a trail?" Conor asked sarcastically as he stepped down.

"It's the only place that you can get off the rim and not fall off a cliff in the process," he grinned. "I've never tried to go up it."

After they ensured the animals had survived the worst of the descent unscathed, Con handed Rayno two pieces of lamb jerky from his vest pocket.

"It's another half mile to the bottom and we'll be in another wash and a gradual downslope to the east."

They mounted up and continued down the mountain on a less severe grade. At the bottom, Rayno turned left and prodded Toohoo into a trot. The entire valley fell under the late afternoon shadow of Mormon Peak. Abe's longer stride made the jaunt effortless. A half mile down the wash, it intersected with a much larger tributary and Rayno slowed the pace to a walk as he hunted for tracks of the adversary. Conor joined in the search.

Within a few minutes Rayno spoke up. "This is the South Fork of Toquop Wash. If our man is headed to Horse Spring, we're ahead of him."

"You know this country. What're your thoughts?"

"It's late in the year and water is scarce. When he left the waterbag in the cave, he figured he wouldn't need it. He either has another one with him or he knows where to find water within a day." Rayno motioned up the wash to their right. "Two miles to Horse Spring." Then nodded his head down the wash before them. "Nine miles to the next spring. There's a good place to camp a mile down this way and we've got enough water to hold the mules for tonight. Our man is below us. If he's headed our way, we should be two or three hours ahead of him. If he's staying eastbound, he'll be an hour or two ahead of us. Either way, we've gained a few hours on him. It'll be dark soon. He won't be able to see any better than us. Even so, if it is Altaha..." He paused in contemplation. "I don't want to meet up with him in the dark."

"What about this place to camp?"

"An old ruin."

"A ruin?"

"Like the 'Lost City' over by St. Thomas. It's three hundred yards off the trail. If you don't know where it is, you won't see it."

Conor evaluated the options. "I vote for the ruin."

As if an omen, Running Dog trotted down the trail from the right and continued past them without pausing toward the east. Rayno clucked his tongue to Toohoo and they were underway.

In the last glimmer of twilight, Rayno rode Toohoo through what had been the doorway and into a round room twenty feet across. The crumbling walls varied from three to five feet in height and nothing of the roof remained. He dismounted and awaited Conor and the pack mule to enter. In near darkness, he quickly unloaded the pack mule and blockaded the doorway, thus corralling the animals within.

Con unsaddled Abe and Toohoo then removed their bridles. Both immediately began browsing on the scattered bunches of grass in the enclosure. He filled both canteens from the waterbag and removed his hat, the Stetson he'd purchased only a few months ago that now sported a new diagonal bullet hole across the brim. Regretfully, he filled it a third full and offered it to the first mule that quickly emptied it. Repeating the process, the waterbag ran dry as he filled his hat the third time. All three got a meager drink, but after filling up earlier today, it was enough to sustain them.

"I've got cans of beans and peaches," Rayno grumbled, "but I can't find them in the dark."

"I might be able to help," Conor offered and began feeling his way around in his saddlebags. In a moment, the rummaging produced his flashlight. He turned it on and handed it to Rayno. "As long as we keep it pointed downward, I don't think our nemesis will see it outside these walls."

"Aha! A rare luxury out here."

With the marginal light they rolled out beds and situated saddles for the night. Rayno located two cans of beans and spoons. After opening them he handed one to Con along with the flashlight. He seated himself on his blanket, reclined against his saddle and began devouring his paltry supper. After returning the flashlight, Conor hung his gun belt from his saddle horn, removed his boots and did the same.

Before long, the sound of spoons scraping the insides of empty cans subsided to be drowned out by nearby munching mules.

"I doubt there's much chance we'll be detected before we start moving in the morning," Con finally commented. "There's something puzzling me though."

"What's that?"

"How did he know where I was sitting on the train? He had to know. He could see someone in a seat, but not who from that distance."

"Somebody seen you at Moapa maybe."

"He was near Rox before dawn. The sun was up when the train pulled into Moapa. How would they of got word to him in time?"

"I don't know. How'd you know he was at Rox?"

"A woman who lives near there told me."

"Mary?"

"She didn't share her name. Said her and her husband have some sort of mine near there."

"That'd be Mary Davis. She's pretty quiet. Don't say much. When did you talk to her?"

"She brought me biscuits and water yesterday. I was waiting with the railcar at the siding for my troops to arrive from Las Vegas. She saw a man on a dark horse riding north on the mesa east of their place before sunup."

Conor contemplated the possibilities. Someone had to have seen where he sat on the train long before they arrived at Moapa. Then they had to call the rider somewhere within a couple of hours ride to the site of the ambush.

"Is there a telephone at Guelph?"

"Howling Moon has a telephone. He lives right by there."

"Who's this Howling Moon?"

"A crazy White man. He goes off into the night when there's a full moon and howls like a coyote or a lobo. Some of the Indians think he talks to the spirits. Like he's magic."

"How long has he lived there?"

"A few years. Four or five, I think."

"Would this Altaha know him?"

"I guess he could. I don't know where Howling Moon came from. He's old enough to have been in the war, I think. Maybe they knew each other then."

* * *

*THURSDAY, OCTOBER 23, 1930*

Conor woke as the sky began to brighten over an unnamed peak
two miles to the east. He rose cautiously and peered over the
northern arc of the stone wall. His view was dim, but a rider on a
dark horse would be visible against the lighter background of the
valley floor. Running Dog, curled on the ground at Rayno's feet,
raised his head to study him. Conor had no idea when the canine
joined them during the night. Still in stocking feet, he fished a small
piece of jerky from his vest pocket. Biting off half of it, he tossed the
remainder within a few inches of the dog's face. Conor slowly
chewed his snack and watched the dog's fluctuating nostrils as
they warily tested the scent in the air but made no move to take his
eyes off the stranger nor retrieve the morsel in front of him.

Taking a seat on his blankets, Con removed his socks and
shook the dirt from them before sliding them and his boot onto
his feet. Before standing, he bit off another half piece of jerky. This
time he leaned over with the second half between his fingers and
gradually moved it closer to Running Dog until he held it less
than a foot from the dog's actively flaring nostrils. Hoping to gain
acceptance from Rayno's companion instead brought a soft
rumbling growl from deep within his chest. Though barely audi-
ble, the sound also instantly drew Rayno's attention as one eye
popped open and darted around the ruin searching for danger
without the slightest movement from any other portion of the
Indian's body.

"You all right?" he asked, barely over a whisper when Conor
came into his view.

"Mm-hmm," Conor hummed through his own nostrils, "but
I'm trying not to move too quickly, thus avoiding him taking off
my hand instead of the jerky."

Rayno spoke in Paiute and Running Dog grabbed the jerky

from between Con's fingers without touching them. Swallowing it whole, he then recovered the first serving from the ground and wolfed it down also. The entire process took less time than a quickdraw artist's pistol would need to clear its leather holster.

"That's why I was being careful."

Rayno let out a soft chuckle. "He don't trust strangers much."

"I see that."

Conor donned his hat, then stood, stomped feet firmly into his boots and strapped on his gun belt.

"I'm gonna take a look around," he told Rayno. He slipped his field glasses around his neck and slid the Winchester from its scabbard. Running Dog watched as he removed the packsaddle from the doorway then followed him out.

"Oh, so now we're buddies?" he questioned rhetorically. He wasn't sure but thought for a moment he saw a quick single wag of Running Dog's tail in response.

Working his way across the valley, Conor scanned the distant surroundings intermingled with watching the ground below him for tracks. Running Dog patrolled the perimeter. Con took extra care in scouting for tracks where he crossed the trail that he and Rayno had followed down the valley. The sun kissed the peaks of the Mormon Mountains to the west and though remaining in shadow, dawn washed the lower elevations in light. As he continued his way north, Running Dog paralleled his route twenty feet to the east.

Con nearly evacuated his skin as a resounding thud accompanied a spray of dirt at his feet. Almost simultaneously, Running Dog let out a yelp and bit at his tail when Con glanced that way as he hit the ground. Excitement overcame him and it seemed a long time before the report from the rifle arrived.

They were in knee-deep scattered sagebrush and out of the shooter's view where they lay. Conor's rifle lay a few feet away where he dropped it in the melee. The bullet had cut Running Dog's tail in two before landing at Con's feet. The amputation occurred about midway of the tail's length and the severed portion dangled from a scrap of skin and hair. *Another victim of a bullet intended for me.* Con surmised guiltily as the dog half sat, half laid and gnawed intently at his wound. *At least this one wasn't fatal.*

Conor crawled to his rifle and examined it. The barrel was clear and it appeared unhurt other than a little dust. He had a clear view between the brush of the ruin. The ears of all three mules clearly marked the origin of the shot as they listened and stared toward the source. A whiff of smoke rose from behind the crumbling wall. Rayno had started a fire most likely intending to make coffee and roast bacon. He was nowhere in sight.

Conor removed his hat and raised up to peer through the upper branches of the tallest sagebrush nearby. In the distance lay a low mound of dirt and rocks in the middle of the valley. A dark-colored horse stood watching toward him from the far side of it. Con studied it through his field glasses. *At least seven hundred yards,* he thought to himself. *Far beyond the range of a .30-30 Winchester.*

# 5

*Casper, Wyoming*

Roscoe Taylor rode the lanky roan down snow-covered Center Street under electric lights. A Model-T Ford sat beneath the wintery blanket outside the Stock Exchange Saloon in hopes of a chinook wind that might raise the temperature enough for it to start. Roscoe stepped down beside it and tied Blue to the hitching rail. Inside, four cowboys sat sullenly playing cards around a table they had moved close to the large pot-bellied stove in the center of the room. The bartender sat in a chair facing the stove along with two other cowboys. A hostess bundled inside an over-sized wool coat filled a chair between them.

"Pull up a stump," the bartender offered Taylor as he came to his feet. "What'll you have?"

"Whiskey. Too damn cold fer anything else," he replied as he pulled his mittens off and stuffed them into the pocket of his newly acquired coat. He crossed the room to the stove and warmed his hands over it.

"You from around here?" the bartender asked as he filled a glass at the bar.

"Been working for Mr. Tietz southwest of here."

"What brings you to town?"

"My horse froze ta death four nights ago an' I'm ketchin' a train outa' this God fersakin' place in the mornin'."

The bartender handed Roscoe his drink. "Well young man, you won't be catching that train tomorrow. A steampipe froze an' broke on the engine about the same time your horse died. It's been sitting in front of the station ever since. The engineer and a blacksmith have been trying to figure out how to fix it."

Roscoe accepted the drink staring at the bartender in disbelief. "Yer pullin' my leg."

"I wish I was, son, but that's the honest to God's truth."

He found a nearby chair and plopped himself into it with his feet up to the stove. Sipping his whiskey in silence, he gazed at the orange light flickering through the broken eisenglass window of the door on the stove. As he neared the bottom of his glass, he looked over at the bartender who had resumed his seat.

"If that don't beat all," he muttered and downed the remainder of his whiskey. He held up the empty glass peering through it at the light hanging from the ceiling. "I guess I better have another while I think on this."

After emptying the second glass he held it up again. "Another."

"Look, you're a nice kid and I understand your dilemma, but you need to get some food in your belly, and I need to see some greenbacks."

Roscoe pulled Tietz's check from his shirt pocket and handed it to the bartender who recognized the signature.

"That'll do. I've got peanuts, pickles, crackers, pickled eggs, bread, and roast beef. What'll it be?"

"Roast beef an' bread…an' peanuts too."

"You want coffee with that?" seeing a blank response, he added, "it's free."

"Okay, sure."

Three of the card players had left along with the other two cowboys. The fourth player, a man twice Roscoe's age, sat at the table idly shuffling the deck of cards. The bartender sat a plate with two slices of bread and a slab of roast beef across the table from the card player. Setting his empty glass beside it, Roscoe took the chair where the meal awaited him. The card player picked up the bottle of whiskey beside him and filled Roscoe's glass. As Taylor took a large bite from his sandwich, the bartender returned with a basket of peanuts and a steaming cup of coffee.

Roscoe devoured the sandwich and gulped down the coffee. When he started shelling peanuts, the card player resumed shuffling the deck of cards. "Care to play a game?"

"I don't play cards for money with folks I don't know," Roscoe replied.

The bartender nearly snorted a mouthful of his own coffee out of his nose. "He's got you pegged, Yates." He laughed.

The scowl on his face that appeared at Roscoe's response turned to a grin. "Maybe not as green as he'd make some folks think," Yates commented as he shuffled the deck again.

An hour later, the hostess had given up for the night and the bartender had gone into an adjoining storeroom.

"Where you been working for old Marty at?" Yates asked as he refilled Roscoe's glass.

"Out Tietz Draw. It's about five miles past the main ranch."

"I know that place. Stayin' in the line shack?"

"Yep."

"I'll bet that was colder 'n Hell."

"It has been lately."

The bartender returned from the storeroom with a large pasteboard box that he sat on the end of the bar. Yates scanned the room.

"You know. We should be gettin' out'ta here."

"Yeah, I need ta get a room somewheres 'fore it gets too late."

"I got a place down on the sandbar. A couch to sleep on and a shed out back for your horse. Better'n the livery and cheaper too. Be easier to figger your options tomorrow in the daylight anyhow."

"'Prish'ate yer offer. I'll take yuh up on it. Let me git settled up here an' I'll be ready ta' go."

Taylor crossed the room and spoke to the bartender. "I'd like ta' cash out now."

The bartender examined Marty Tietz's check. "What's your name, son?"

"Roscoe Taylor," he said while the bartender confirmed the payee's name.

"Just put your mark on the back there," he said as he placed the check face down on the bar and laid a pencil beside it.

Roscoe picked up the pencil and scrawled his name on the back. Somewhat surprised that the young man could write, the bartender put it in his cash drawer and brought out four silver dollars and a handful of bills. He counted out one-hundred-fifteen dollars and laid the stack on the bar beside the coins.

"That ain't right," Taylor said.

The bartender snorted at the tipsy youngster, retrieved the check from the drawer and verified the amount before slapping it down on the bar.

"Six bits for your drinks, two bits for your food, and a hundred-nineteen dollars. That makes one-twenty, Mr. Taylor." He held the check up to Roscoe's face. "You got a problem with that?" the bartender growled.

"Uh...uh, no sir. I didn't figger the check was fer that much," he stammered, scooping the money up and putting it into his coat pocket.

Yates looked on, also surprised at the amount.

* * *

*SUNDAY, JANUARY 12, 1913*

Roscoe Taylor opened one eye to investigate his surroundings. The man called Yates stood over a small woodburning cookstove poking a fork into an iron skillet. Steam billowed from the spout of the coffee pot beside it. A Hoosier cabinet stood against the wall near the stove. The aroma of coffee and bacon filled the room, accompanied by subdued light entering through the only window. It was frosted over, but Roscoe suspected it was still cloudy and perhaps snowing outside. A small white table with two chairs sat beneath the window. Faded wallpaper adorned the walls. His coat and hat hung from a peg near the door. A tarnished twin-size brass bed nested in the corner nearest his feet and the couch he laid on pushed against the remaining wall to complete the furnishings crowded into the one-room house. Everything looked neat and clean. Yates was watching him when his eye wandered back toward the stove.

"Mornin', Roscoe Taylor. We weren't properly introduced last night, but my name is Yates. Frank Yates, but everybody just calls me Yates. How's your head?"

Roscoe's mouth felt like it was stuffed with cotton. He ran his tongue around the inside to see if it still worked before answering.

"I think I left it over yonder." He pointed randomly across the room.

"Pick your poison." Yates chuckled as held up a bottle of Castor oil and a pint of whiskey. "Either one might cure or kill you."

"Coffee," Roscoe answered as he worked himself into a sitting position on the couch he'd slept on.

"First, you need to crawl your ass over to this table or you might never make it off that couch today."

Roscoe stood and obeyed his host.

Yates forked bacon from the skillet onto a plate and sat it with a cup of coffee in front of him, then did the same for himself and sat down in the other chair. He chewed off a bite from a slab of bacon and chewed it slowly as he sized up the young cowboy in front of him.

"You strike me as a pretty tough kid for your age, but you look like Hell right now, boy."

"Whadaya mean?'"

"You can barely stand up an' your eyes look like a couple of piss-holes in a snowbank. That's what I mean. An' shit boy, you just slept for nine hours straight besides. Next time around you better lay off that hootch a little earlier in the evening."

"I'll be all right," he said as he washed down a mouthful of bacon with scalding coffee.

"I've been thinking while you've been snoring," Yates began. "How many head you been riding herd on over in the draw?"

"A hundred thirty-nine. Why?"

"Cows with calves?"

"Mostly. Forty-three are yearlin's," Roscoe replied while trying to comprehend in his muddled brain where this conversation was heading. "Why you askin'?"

"Well, you're wanting to light out'a here and the train's not running. I've been thinking the same thing. So, why not pick up a little scratch on our way out'a town?"

"Scratch?"

"Money."

Roscoe chewed on a mouthful of bacon. "How?"

"Those yearlings are worth fifty bucks a head in Rock Springs."

"You wanna rustle old man Tietz's yearlin's?" Roscoe had never stolen more than a stick of hard candy in his entire life. Even thinking about it stood the hair up on the back of his neck.

"We could cut them out, then push them up over Red Creek onto Lone Tree and re-brand them. It'll take the old man a couple of days to get a new man out there. They might not even notice them missing at first. With a little luck, snow'll prob'ly cover our tracks before they figure it out."

"Tietz's got a dozen sheepherders scattered all over that Lone Tree country."

"Brought three thousand head of sheep down from there and put 'em out onto the flats ten miles north of town two months ago. Some of them sheep camps out on Lone Tree have cabins. We can spend a couple of nights in one of them and keep outta the weather while we brand. When we're done? Drive them up over the rim and south across Shirley Basin."

"How do we get them to Rock Springs without gettin' caught? Herdin' cattle in January'll look pretty fishy."

"There's trails that nobody pays much mind to. Past Medicine Bow and over to Baggs. Then down the Little Snake River and out to Brown's Park. By then the brands'll be healed up. We run them up to Rock Springs, sell them and light out for Utah before they butcher the first one and see that bar-T brand on the underside of the hide beneath ours."

"What about supplies?"

"We can get a few things here, but not enough to draw attention. Then do the same at Bessemer. That should hold us until we get to Medicine Bow. They're used to folks passing through down there and don't pay much attention. Same at Baggs."

"Sounds to me like you done this b'fore," Roscoe surmised as the food and coffee began to heal his hangover.

Yates chuckled. "Only a time er two."

\* \* \*

*TUESDAY, MARCH 18, 1913*

As the sun rose in the east, Roscoe Taylor watched the herd two miles south of town. Frank Yates rode into Rock Springs and arranged to sell their stolen cattle. The yearlings anxiously grazed on newly sprouting green grass. The ground was muddy as sunny days rapidly melted most of the snow. Its remnants huddled precariously amid the shadows beneath the scattered sagebrush. Roscoe sat half-dozing in the saddle as he let the midmorning sun soak its warmth through him. Yates came into view returning from town.

"Good news partner, railroad man will give us seven dollars a hundred cash money today. Needs the beef for a track crew building new line out east of here. We just need to run them into the stockyard right here in town."

"Seven dollars a hundred. What's that mean?"

"He'll give us seven dollars for every hundred pounds of beef on the hoof. That's top dollar. I'll bet most these fellas'll go over eight hundred," he added, gazing over the herd. "They got a scale right there at the Union Pacific stockyard."

An hour later they drove the cattle into a big corral alongside the tracks at the edge of town. A cowboy on foot with a long stick closed the gate behind them.

"I'll start running them through the scale," he said. "We should be able to get eight or ten at a time."

The cowboy waded through the herd to a building at the far end of the corral that looked like a miniature covered bridge with a gate on each end. He opened the gate, then stood aside and waved Roscoe and Yates to move them ahead. A moment later he poked the last couple of animals into the building with the stick and closed the gate. Soon he was prodding them out the back gate into another corral and reopening the gate on the front. They repeated the process until all forty-three steers and heifers had crossed the scale. When they were finished, he gave Yates a handful of scale tickets.

"Take them to Mr. Johnston and he'll pay you."

The two men rode to the train station near the center of town and went in.

Roscoe stood aside while Mr. Johnston took a stack of money from a safe and counted out twenty-four one-hundred-dollar bills and two tens onto his desk. He then reached into his pants pocket and added four copper pennies beside the pile of bills.

"Thirty-four-thousand, five hundred-seventy-two pounds at seven dollars a hundred makes twenty-four-hundred-twenty dollars and four cents, Mr. Davis," he told Yates as he slid a paper forward beside the money. "If you'll sign right here, you can take it and be on your way."

"It's been a pleasure doing business with you, Mr. Johnston," Yates replied as he signed *Frank Davis* on the paper and slid it back before reaching for Johnston's hand.

"Likewise," Johnston replied as Yates crammed the wad of bills into his jeans.

"Davis?" Roscoe questioned as the two men stepped out onto the stone walk in front of the station.

"You didn't think I was going to give them my real name, did you?"

"S'pose not."

A rather large man wearing clean, new-looking clothes and a light-gray cowboy hat stood near their horses. Yates untied his sorrel and stepped into the saddle. As Roscoe untied Blue, the man spoke up.

"That your horse?" he asked.

"Yessir."

"Peculiar combination of hieroglyphics he's wearing."

"Hydro-what?"

"Brands," the man clarified.

"Yeah." Roscoe grinned. "I think he's been traded around some."

"I stood next to Marty Tietz about this time last year in Laramie. Big horse sale going on. He bought this horse and a couple dozen others there."

"Is that right?"

"Yep. That bar-T on the right shoulder is Marty's brand."

Roscoe didn't reply.

"How did you come by him?"

"I bought him from a fella up in Casper a couple of months ago."

"You didn't happen to get a bill of sale?"

"No sir. I did not. Neither of us knowed how to write so's we didn't see much point."

The big man chuckled. "No, I suppose not. What was that fellow's name?"

"Taylor, I think."

"And a first name?"

"I don't recall. Might not of heard it." He turned to Yates. "Do you recall hearing that fella's name, Mr. Davis?"

"Can't say that I do," Yates replied, miffed that Roscoe identified him as being in Casper right before the herd of cattle disappeared.

The big man turned to Yates. "So, you witnessed this transaction?"

"Yessir, I did."

"What did this Taylor fellow look like?"

"Young kid. Sixteen or so. Falling down drunk. Said he was going to Texas, I think. Gonna ride the train. Didn't need the horse no more."

"Where did all of this happen?"

"Outside o' the Stock Exchange. That's a saloon. Late at night an' colder'n Hell as I recall it."

"Well, thanks for your help, Mr. Davis." The big man turned and walked up the street.

Roscoe swung a leg over the saddle on Blue, and the duo rode to the Stock Growers' Mercantile. Yates set out a bag of ground coffee and a sack of dried beans. When he added a handful of cigars, Roscoe added a similar amount of horehound candy sticks. Yates snorted and paid the bill. He had yet to offer Roscoe his half of the revenue from the stolen cattle.

Outside Yates handed Roscoe his candy and the sack of beans.

"Tie that on with your bedroll," he ordered while he did the same with the coffee.

Yates mounted his sorrel just as Roscoe tightened the rawhide strings around the sack of beans.

"Roscoe Taylor," a voice boomed from the corner of the mercantile building.

Roscoe's head snapped toward the voice. A tall man peered from under the wide brim of his hat. The sun was at the man's back. Little of the man was recognizable beyond a dark silhouette. Blue stood between him and the man.

"You're under arrest for horse stealin', Taylor," the voice boomed again.

At that instant, Yates drew his pistol and fired twice while turning his horse and burying spurs into his sides. Roscoe turned toward Yates at the sound of gunfire. He could not tell if he heard it or felt it when the bullet from the lawman's pistol whizzed past his ear striking Yates in the right shoulder as he fled.

Roscoe grabbed a handful of mane and saddle horn. Swinging his right leg up to knee Blue in the flank, he held on for dear life as the tall roan bolted in the opposite direction of Yates's retreat thus keeping between Roscoe and the lawman. A block away, Roscoe finally managed to get aboard the four-legged rocket that flew down the streets of Rock Springs. He laid low clinging to Blue's neck as the saddle horn burrowed itself into his belly. He had no idea where the reins were nor stirrups as they raced through the town. The world flashed past in slow motion as the blood surged through Roscoe's veins.

A mile or maybe two east of the hamlet, the strands of blue's mane that had been whipping his face became wet from sweat and began to sting. Roscoe sat up enough to allow his feet to find stirrups. With his left hand gripping the saddle horn, he worked his way far enough down the horse's right side to reach a rein flapping in the breeze. Gently easing back on the single rein, the terrified horse began to slow. Roscoe leaned forward and rubbed Blue's neck with his left hand. Eventually calming him down, he slowed to a trot, and then a walk. Blue's left rein had been broken in the scramble, but

Roscoe wanted to let him cool down slowly so let him amble along at an easy pace.

The bluffs to the south began to fall back opening into a wide basin. He knew he needed to circle the town and work his way west. Remembering a spring that Yates had earlier pointed out south of town, Roscoe left the road and pointed Blue in that general direction.

As his racing pulse subsided, Roscoe's thoughts drifted back to the chaos in front of the mercantile. Somewhere in the earliest seconds of his escape, he glanced back toward Yates. He had dropped the pistol when the bullet struck his shoulder and within a few more strides, fallen from his horse. If he survived the ordeal, he was captured and in jail. Roscoe's share of the money Yates got for the cattle they stole was gone.

\* \* \*

*THURSDAY, JUNE 28, 1917*

*Elko, Nevada*

Even at nine o'clock in the morning, the courtroom in the Elko County Courthouse was hot and stuffy. Roscoe Taylor sat awaiting sentencing after being found guilty of stealing fifteen horses.

"All rise! The Circuit Court of Elko County, Nevada is now convened, Judge Horatio Adams presiding." the bailiff bellowed.

A rather short rotund gentleman in his sixties entered the room wearing a long black robe. He lumbered up three steps behind the bench and took a seat there looking down over the population of his courtroom from the lofty position.

"This court is now in session," he announced gruffly and

struck the sound block with his gavel with a resonating result. "You may be seated."

Judge Adams looked through several papers on the bench. Peering over the top of his spectacles, he eyed Roscoe. "Mr. Roscoe Taylor, it seems you have existed in Elko County for the past few years. During which time, it appears that you have been seeking some sort of notoriety. There have been numerous occasions that you have partaken in similar crimes as the one you are here before me for today. You have not yet been arrested for any of these offenses in Elko County nor any other county in the state that I can find. It hasn't been because you weren't involved that you haven't been arrested for these crimes; it's because our only evidence has been eyewitness accounts of your horse being at the scene of these crimes. Both I and the district attorney have found no legislation that would allow us to arrest your horse for any offense other than being coerced into performing these acts.

"This particular horse has numerous brands from several previous owners throughout much of the western United States and Mexico. It takes no expert to identify him. Any toddler who has ever seen a horse before would remember this one. I recently discovered that the horse in question does not actually even belong to you. It in fact belongs to your former employer"—he glanced at one of the papers before him—"a Mr. Marty Tietz of Casper, Wyoming. It says here that Mr. Tietz offered to give you the horse in payment for a horse belonging to you that died while you were in his employ. Yet you chose cash instead and then took the horse anyway. For this offense there is a warrant for your arrest issued in the state of Wyoming, but that is not the issue here at the moment.

"I suspect, Mr. Taylor, that you have at times profited from these illegal excursions of yours. It baffles me why you have never taken some of your ill-gotten gains and bought a less conspicuous animal to ride on these forays. I don't want an answer, I'm just blowing off steam.

"There are two reasons that you were caught and convicted

this time. First, you stole these horses from Mr. Amos Boles. Mr. Boles happens to be the brother-in-law of Sheriff Tom Tilson. The second reason is that in the chase, your comrades abandoned you, leaving you like a set of bedraggled drawers hanging out to dry in the wind. The bottom line, Mr. Taylor is that you have outlived any reason for clemency for your actions. Thirty years ago, a judge may have looked the other way at some of this tomfoolery, but that day has long since passed.

"The penalty in the State of Nevada for this crime is ten to twenty years at hard labor in the Nevada State Prison. Independence Day is next week, and our country is at war in Europe. For that reason and the fact that you appear to be a healthy young man, I'm feeling patriotic. I am offering you something that I have never offered a convicted criminal before. You can choose prison or join the Army and fight for your country. You can enlist in the US Army for a period of not less than three years, or the end of the war, whichever comes later. What'll it be?"

"I ain't never kilt nobody. Ain't never shot nobody neither. Hell, I don't even carry a gun 'cept an old six-shooter rolled up in the bedroll on my horse."

* * *

*TUESDAY, MARCH 12, 1918*

*US Army Sniper Training, British Army Sniper School, Somewhere in France*

"Private Roscoe Taylor, good morning. You have been selected to become a sniper for the United States Army because of a particular group of skills you acquired as a civilian; primarily your ability to sneak around without getting caught. You will receive special training here to add to those skills by British experts in this type of warfare."

A young Native American entered the room.

"Private Taylor, this is Private George Altaha. He also has been selected for the program. George is a Chiricahua Apache. His father was with Geronimo when he was captured in '86. He doesn't speak English, but he does speak a little Spanish. You also speak some Spanish. The same Mexican dialect as George, so it seems. From this day forward, until one or both of you leave this service, you will be partners. Your very lives will depend on this partnership. You will become close friends, brothers so to speak, or you will not survive."

# 6

Running Dog lay a few feet from Conor Armenta making an odd sound, something between a moan and a growl, as he gnawed at the remnant of skin attaching his severed tail. Con crawled to him and carefully reached out to his neck. The dog stopped in silence at his touch then slowly turn to look at the man who had accompanied his master the past two days. Conor rubbed his fingers through the thick fur surrounding the dog's neck and spoke calmly to him as he reached for his jackknife with his free hand.

"Don't worry, boy. I know it stings, but you'll feel some better in a minute."

Conor kept his knife razor sharp. He had learned a valuable lesson from having an unsharpened knife once as an adolescent. Opening it, he swiftly and as painlessly as possible completed the amputation. Running Dog immediately began licking the stub of his tail and soon came to his feet. Seemingly pleased that the weight of the dangling remnant of his tail no longer tugged at the wound, he watched his make-do surgeon intently.

Conor returned his attention to the assailant. Peering with his field glasses through the sagebrush to the mound where the horse stood, he could see a small dark hump at its summit. It might be a rock or sagebrush, but the sheriff suspected it was Altaha. The sniper would have his .30-06 trained on the spot where Con last appeared. He would now be certain of the range and would compensate accordingly. The hump did not move. He remained glued to the bald mound offering the smallest of targets should Conor attempt a shot.

The horse suddenly noticed the mules and raised its head that direction, searching for their scent...then whinnied to them. The hump jerked and Altaha's head shot up searching for an adversary in the direction of his horse's gaze.

Con jumped to his feet and dashed toward the bed of the wash. The sound of the horse's whinny reached his ears just as Running Dog sped past him in slow motion. Conor's smooth-soled boots dug for traction in the soft soil as he pushed with all of his might at every stride. He thought he saw a puff of dust a few feet in front of him, but was uncertain. Feeling the breeze through the sweat that trickled down his face, he ran. The view seen of the sea of sagebrush before him belied his efforts as it slowly slid past in an adrenaline induced fog.

The sagebrush grew thicker and grabbed at Conor's legs as he sprinted through them. The thought rushed through his mind that he should have reached the wash by now. At the sharp sound from Altaha's rifle reaching him, he dove into the sagebrush. Running Dog had disappeared ahead of him and Con tried to keep his rifle from striking the ground when he landed. The sagebrush tugged at his rifle and scraped his hands and face as he fell. Suspended in their grasp the branches slowed his pace as he fell through them over the bank and somersaulted down into the wash.

At this point the South Fork of Toquop Wash was dry, about six feet deep and two to three times that in width. Running Dog stood nearby panting as Conor took in his surroundings. As he sat in the dirt catching his breath the adrenaline rush began to subside. A swallow of water would have tasted good right then, but a scrap of lamb jerky from his vest pocket would have to suffice. He shared it with Running Dog who accepted his portion gratefully.

"Oh, so now that I'm about to get killed I'm okay, huh?" Conor asked him rhetorically.

Blowing dust from his Winchester, Con checked the action then the condition of his field glasses. Pushing himself to his feet, he brushed some of the dust from his clothing and concluded that thus far, he was uninjured. He headed down the wash. Using the high bank for cover, Conor planned to approach Altaha from a flanking position. A few minutes later he judged the mound should be nearby. Removing his hat, he peeked over the edge of the bank of the wash. The patch of sagebrush upstream had dissipated. An intermittent scattering of grassy stubble was all that covered the parched earth. The mound, fifty yards away was bare. The horse and Altaha were gone.

Conor scanned the surrounding terrain for his opponent. Gradually raising himself from concealment, he took in more and more of the landscape. Eventually he stood erect atop the bank of the wash looking over the countryside through his field glasses. As his view took in the descending wash to the east, he caught movement. He focused in on the object. Nearly a mile away, a lone horseman rode eastward at a trot. As Conor watched him, Altaha rounded the base of a ridge on the south side of the wash and disappeared.

When Con brought down his field glasses, Running Dog sat at his feet. He picked up his rifle and walked toward the stone ruin. The mules watched as they neared and he noticed fresh smoke rising from the campfire. Rayno evidently watched Altaha leave and resumed his morning routine. The rising sun soothed his back as he ambled along. The deadly scene of less than an hour ago took on an almost pastoral serenity. His thoughts turned to his fiancée, June Sommers, as he walked a rather leisurely pace to the ruin. What would she think of the situation? He quickly concluded that she would love the scenery but hate the circumstances. He seldom willingly allowed the distraction of her to interrupt his concentration on the job. He surmised his own thoughts were about the same. Returning to business, Conor reminded himself that complacency was an unaffordable luxury that could quickly become fatal. He tried to erase her from his thoughts for the time being.

"Are you ready for some coffee?" Rayno asked casually. Not waiting for an answer, he lifted the pot from the fire and filled the tin cup resting atop a nearby rock. Conor noticed a well-worn revolver tucked into Rayno's waistband when handing him the cup.

"You wait out the foray in here?" Con asked as he glanced around the crumbling stone walls.

Rayno grinned motioning with his head in the general direction. "When the shooting started, I jumped the back wall and scampered like a scared jackrabbit into the rocks up the bottom of that ridge."

"Smart thinking." Con glanced at the pistol. "I haven't seen that before."

"It's been in my saddlebags. I wanted Altaha to think I was your guide and not your deputy."

"That's smart too."

"I changed my mind. I'm sure he's been watching us from a distance. Probably has a telescope on his rifle."

"I'd bet money you're right on both counts. Did you see him?"

"I could see him from where I hid in the rocks. At first, I could only see his horse. Then the horse smelled our mules and whinnied. Altaha moved. Then I could see him. I was watching when he fired the second shot."

Conor sat down on his blankets. Leaning against his saddle he watched bacon strips sizzle over the fire as he sipped the scalding coffee. Drops of melting fat from the bacon popped as they landed in the fire. Running Dog curled up beside him and began licking his tail.

"Two shots. How close were they to you?"

"The first one took half of Running Dog's tail off. Well, mostly anyway."

Rayno looked shocked as he diverted his attention to the dog. "He looks okay now."

"It was left dangling by a strip of skin. That really bothered him until I cut it off with my jackknife."

"He just let you do that?"

"I think he knew I was helping him. We were both running for the wash when Altaha fired the second time. It hit the ground right in front of me and I lunged to the ground...well, into the sagebrush, and fell into the wash."

"I didn't see that. I was watching him."

"When did he leave?"

"Right after that. He was far away and I couldn't see him very good. I think he was looking for you maybe. Then he snuck off the back of the mound and sat up. I looked around for you and never saw you. When I looked back, Altaha was getting on his horse. Pretty soon he was down where the trail crosses the wash, but he stayed on this side. Then the point of that first ridge blocked my view."

"As soon as I caught my breath, I headed down the wash to get close enough to shoot back. By the time I got there he was gone."

"I stayed hid. I thought he might be cutting around to get up above us and shoot the mules. When I saw you stand up real close to where he was before, I though you musta knew where he went, and I felt safer. Then you headed this way, I came back and got the fire going again."

"When I stood up, he was already rounding the next ridge east. Must be a mile away or better."

Knowing the terrain, Rayno nodded in agreement as he handed Conor a bacon shish kabob.

"We interrupted his plan." Con blew on the bacon to cool it. "How far to the next water?"

"Seven, eight miles."

"Unless he had another waterbag, his horse has been dry for quite a while. He was moving at a trot when I saw him. Gotta slow down pretty soon, I think...or hope."

Rayno poured himself coffee and refilled Con's cup in silence. Then he sat down on an adjacent rock and chewed bacon from another stick.

When Conor finished his bacon, he saved the last morsel for Running Dog. He gently accepted it from between Con's fingertips...licking them in the process. He gulped down his last swallow of coffee then stood and began saddling the mules.

The dry sticks Rayno had used for the fire burned quickly and were nearly gone when he splashed the last dregs from the coffeepot over them. Conor already had the packsaddle on the mule when Rayno rearranged their gear and slung it over the crossbucks. Working well together the two men were soon loaded up and ready to go. In a matter of minutes Conor ducked his head under the arched remnants of the doorway as Abe followed Toohoo out of the ruin.

* * *

Where the trail crossed to the north side of the South Fork of Toquop Wash, Rayno followed Altaha's tracks on the south side. When he rounded the first point a few yards ahead, he stopped and waited for Conor to ride alongside.

Indicating another point, a mile to the east of them he asked, "Is that where you saw him last?"

"Yep."

"He could circle around and come up the backside of this ridge about three-quarters of the way between here and there. The other side is a little steeper than this, but I think his little horse could make it. If he did that we'll be in his line of fire in a half-a-mile. If I was outa water, I wouldn't wanna put my horse through that. But I ain't him."

"What's our choice?"

"About a quarter mile up here, we can go up this side and ride down the other. If he's in the best spot for an ambush, he won't be able to see us until we're a half mile down this wash. If he's up there and we go over the top first, we'll ride right past behind him. Right now, we're most of an hour behind him. If he ain't up there, he'll be more'n two hours ahead of us when we get down off the back side of this ridge."

"What do you think, Rayno?"

"I think you're the sheriff and me and my mules are just here to help you out. Them little Mexican ponies are usually tougher than nails, but he's getting' thirsty. These mules are tough too. Probably tougher than that pony, but they're thirsty too. Thirstier than that pony."

Conor only thought about it for a moment and grinned. "Let's ride into a trap."

Rayno smiled and tapped the butt of his revolver as he motioned Con past him. "If need be, I can put you out of your misery if he don't kill you with his first shot."

Conor shook his head and handed off the lead rope for the pack mule to him. "Thanks for your vote of confidence."

"No thanks needed, but you're welcome anyhow."

A half mile ahead Con approached another point jutting out from the ridge. *This is the point of no return*, he told himself. *No looking back now.* His heels nudged Abe ahead into a slightly faster walk. The sun struck his face as he rounded the point, knowing he was an open target for Altaha's rifle if he lay in wait for them. *Don't outthink yourself, Conor. First instinct is usually the best instinct*, but the ridge to the south dominated his attention. The trail crossed back to the south side of the wash. He had to force himself to glance down intermittently to verify that the single set of horse tracks followed it between the base of the ridge and the wash. He heard Toohoo and the pack mule walking behind, but never looked back to see them. The ridge ended abruptly after their quarter mile of exposure. It took less than five minutes to get there, but seemed an eternity.

The trail turned southeast at the end of the ridge and the mountainous terrain opened out into a broad desert plain that gradually sloped off toward the east. The trail pointed straight into the rising sun for at least a couple of miles, maybe more. Conor stopped and raised his field glasses to no avail. The glare was too intense for the optics.

Studying the trail, the only tracks belonged to the Mexican pony. The little horse was making good time at a fast trot. Conor urged Abe to do the same. The longer stride of the mules should easily outpace the smaller horse while expending the same amount of effort. The trail drifted away from the wash by about a quarter mile making it less likely their adversary would be able to use it for an ambush. Conor only slowed enough periodically to verify he stayed on Altaha's trail. Running Dog kept pace effortlessly. Two miles down the trail Con paused and lifted his field glasses. The sun had risen enough not to interfere with his view as he scanned the expanse before them.

Rayno stopped beside him. "What do you see?"

"Nothing moving as far as I can see. It's farther to those mountains than I thought though. I figured we'd of got to them by now."

"The East Mormon Mountains. They're about another mile away yet. A single string of them runs north and south. This wash cuts them in two and the trail splits there. We go south about a mile past there. The spring is up in the foothills on the eastern side there if you know where to look."

"Well, our man is still ahead of us. I guess we'll find out if he knows where he's going when we get there." He reached forward and patted Abe's neck. "Another couple of miles and we'll get you a drink, Pard."

Just before the gap in the mountains, the wash grew shallow and the trail crossed back to the north side of it. This time Altaha had stayed on the trail. Conor slowed Abe to a walk and followed. As he entered the gap, he pulled his Winchester from the scabbard. With reins in his left hand, he rested the rifle across the pommel in his right. Rayno fell back allowing several yards between them. Unsure how Abe might respond to someone shooting from his saddle, Con proceeded warily.

Crossing through the gap was tense, but uneventful. It was nearly noon and the sun rode high in the sky. Temperatures this late in the season were moderate, but the sweat trickling down between Con's shoulder blades contradicted the fact. On the east side, the trail forked as Rayno told him it would. Altaha had taken the left fork that turned northeast. It brought Conor to an abrupt halt. He balanced the rifle across his thighs and studied the landscape through his field glasses. He lowered them when Rayno joined him.

"What do you make of that?" he asked, pointing to the tracks on the trail.

"Tule Spring. Five or six miles away. It's at the foot of those hills in the distance. They're named for it."

"Where would he go from there?"

"Take your pick; trails run north, south, or east…or back here."

"Where do they go?"

"North cuts through the hills and into the Tule Desert. Ten miles wide and fifteen miles long."

"How about east?"

"Goes around the south end of the Tule Springs Hills then over into Arizona. Comes out at the Virgin River down below the mouth of the canyon."

"And south?"

"Bunkerville."

Conor considered the options for less than a minute. "First, we need water. This spring is about a mile down this other trail?"

"Yes."

"That'll give us time to think on it. Should be safe. You lead, I'll follow."

Rayno passed the lead rope to Con and ambled at a somewhat leisurely pace down the trail to the right. Fifteen minutes later he turned off the trail into what looked like a bone-dry cut into the flank of the mountain. As it grew steeper, he seemed to follow a dim game trail. Suddenly a trickle of water showed itself tumbling down a steep, rocky bank from above. With barely room enough for one mule at a time, it fell into a tiny pool no larger than a bowler hat then disappeared into the rocks below.

Conor waited a few yards below as Rayno remained mounted and let Toohoo drink his fill. When he lifted his head, Running Dog squirmed himself past to take his turn. Access to the water was too tight to turn the mule around. Rayno backed Toohoo down the narrow trail to Conor's position that provided just enough room to occupy all three animals.

"Hand me the lead rope and ride Abe up. I'll walk this girl up when you're done, then we can take a break and eat some jerky and canned beans right here."

When finished watering the mules, Rayno located their canned goods while Con refilled canteens and waterbags. He had commandeered the one abandoned in the cave yesterday and added it to their gear. Returning to the makeshift picnic area, he slung the waterbags over the packsaddle and canteens over their saddle horns. When he turned, Rayno put a can of beans with a spoon protruding from it into his hand.

Rayno sat down on a large boulder nearby to savor the meager meal. After two days in the saddle and more yet to come, Conor chose to remain standing. The mules all stood ground-tied on the little patch of somewhat level ground, while Running Dog napped in a spot of shade beneath them.

Rayno watched Conor as he surveyed the plain to the east from their elevated vantage point. "What are you thinking?"

"I'm pretty sure that when we took the shortcut over the mountain yesterday, Altaha thought he'd lost us. What's the fastest way back to Moapa from that Horse Spring that he was headed to?"

"Straight south. There's a saddle across the mountain and down to Wiregrass Spring. It's pretty steep, but that little horse could make it. It's only a mile or two. After that there's a real good trail all the way to the Moapa Valley. It's been used by generations of our ancestors. There's ruins all over that side of the mountain."

"How far to Moapa from there?"

"Twenty-five, thirty miles."

"I think that was his getaway plan. We just got in his way when we cut him off at those ruins. He doesn't know about this place, so now he's riding six miles in the wrong direction for water. By the way, how did *you* ever find this place?"

"My father showed it to me when I was little. His father before him."

Conor tried to force that information into his memory for further discussion later. "If he's really wanting to get away from us, he might try heading north through the desert. My guess is that he's plenty savvy enough to do it, but he never would have left the waterbag, if that was his original plan. If he doesn't know where to find water in that desert, he might kill his horse trying to escape that direction. If he's Apache, he probably lives in southern Arizona or New Mexico—"

"I never said he was Apache," Rayno interrupted.

"You didn't have to," Conor continued. "If he heads east, he'll get to Arizona soon enough and we—*I*—have authority to pursue a suspected felon into Arizona. But going east from here, he'd be crossing hundreds of miles of rivers and canyons to get anywhere near where he'd want to end up. Once again, he could probably do it. Seems he's been living off the land out here for the last three days and it doesn't appear to have slowed him down much. But that's a tough way to travel when you're so close to a train."

Rayno mulled over Conor's assessment without comment.

"How far are we from Bunkerville?"

"Fifteen miles. More maybe?"

"Then another thirty to Moapa?"

"At least."

"Where's the trail at from Tule Spring to Bunkerville?"

"The other side of Toquop Wash. Not the south fork. The main wash that this one runs into. It's six or seven miles east of here. It's deep and steep. I only know one place to cross it. That's a mile or so down from where the south fork meets it."

"How far is that from here?"

"Five or six miles. Add at least an hour to cross the wash."

"And from Tule Spring?"

"About the same, but he don't half to cross the wash here. It's shallow and wide where he'll cross it."

The duo watered their mules again before Conor led off down the narrow game trail to the bottom of the cut where he pointed Abe east. Leaving the trail they rode in on, he continued eastward across the gradually descending desert. The South Fork of Toquop Wash occasionally appeared to the north as they rode cross country toward its confluence with the main wash. Two hours later, Rayno rode up alongside him. Conor stopped as he was handed the lead rope.

"I'll take over here. There is only one place to go down. If we miss it, it could take us hours to cross the main wash."

"How far?"

"A couple more miles yet, but there are deep cuts on this side. We need to be going between the right ones to get there."

An hour later, Rayno dropped off the west rim of Toquop Wash on a steep and narrow trail that contoured its way toward the bottom. Running Dog followed on Toohoo's heels. Conor stood in his stirrups and leaned back over the cantle and his bedroll as Abe stepped off the edge of the rim. The late afternoon sun still hung high over Mormon Peak, but quickly disappeared in the depths of the wash. The mules carefully chose their steps nearly sliding on their haunches in the descent. Rayno paused when they reached the sandy dry bed more than a hundred feet below the rim. He pointed to a highwater line twenty feet up the side of the narrow gorge.

"Not a good place to be when it rains. No clouds here, but who knows what's going on twenty miles from here?"

"Good point," Conor agreed as he eyed the stain on the wall. "Chances of surviving that one would be slim to none."

They each took swallows of water from their canteens. "The trail up is not so steep, but more than twice as far and scree fields to cross in places. The sun might be down before we get to the top."

"Nice and cool down here, but we best get going, then."

Rayno nodded and tapped his heels to Toohoo's flanks. Halfway up, the wall of the wash began tapering back and a mix of brush and cacti began showing up among the nooks and crannies between the rocks. The trail made a sweeping turn eastward and advanced straight up the receding slope. The brush grew in density until very near the top where it ended abruptly and returned into a nearly barren desert. Rayno halted a few yards within the border of vegetation. The riders cast long shadows across the arid landscape before them.

"The trail is a couple hundred yards out," Rayno announced.

Conor dismounted and pulled his Winchester from its scabbard. "Find us a spot for a cold camp back here out of sight." He took a swig of water from his canteen and returned it to his saddle horn. "I'm going to look around."

Taking advantage of the disappearing sunlight, Conor walked to higher ground a few yards beyond the brush at the nondescript edge of the east rim. Running Dog accompanied him a short distance away. With field glasses, he studied the surroundings, paying particular attention toward the north, where he suspected Altaha to be coming from. Discovering no visible movement, he continued in the direction of the trail to Bunkerville. There was no evidence of the trail he and Rayno traveled while crossing the gorge.

Two large heaps of stone lay ahead. They were so conspicuous in the midst of the vast empty plain, it almost appeared they were put there by human hands. A laborious task considering the distance to the nearest source of materials and an apparent lack of purpose. When reaching the first pile of rocks, he realized the second was farther away than he expected. A good fifty yards at least. The trail crossed midway between them. Conor examined the trail closely for tracks. Most recent were those of a vehicle and they were a few weeks old.

A slight whimper from Running Dog drew his attention to the second rockpile just in time to see the dog's head dive among the rocks. The shortened tail wagged profusely from the protruding aft portion of the animal. The rest of him soon came into view as he extracted a wriggling rabbit from its fortress. Fear of losing his prey among the maze, prompted the canine to carry it into the open where he held it with a forepaw and concluded killing his supper.

The sun slid behind Mormon Peak as Conor mounted the second rockpile for a better view. He noticed from this vantage point that the first rockpile aligned perfectly with the point that he and Rayno had exited the wash. The discovery caused a rethinking on the placement of the two rockpiles and their possible connection to the ruins and petroglyphs they had been seeing these past two days. They could be seen for miles from three of the four compass points.

As he gazed toward the foot of the East Mormon Mountains and the spring they drank from earlier today, he mumbled aloud, "Or from every direction."

Taking advantage of his elevated position and the remaining dusky light, he again surveyed the area through his field glasses. The smallest movements of a tiny dark dot to the north caught his attention. He studied it more closely. A horseman. Coming toward him. Altaha.

Realizing he was silhouetted against a darker background, Conor hoped Altaha was too far away to distinguish his presence.

Even so, he very slowly lowered himself to his knees. The dot disappeared below the horizon.

Conor took in the glow of sunset over the Mormon Mountains. Their dominance far overshadowed their much humbler little brothers to their east. Dusk would surrender to dark in about a half hour. Perhaps a little longer with light refraction from the sunset. He guessed Altaha to be about two miles away. The trail would probably be mostly level and smooth. The rifleman should arrive there just before dark. Sooner if he was in a hurry.

Running Dog finished dining and lay beside the rockpile licking his chops. As if on premonition of his approaching nemesis, he moved to licking the stump of his abbreviated tail. Conor seated himself among the rubble on the leeward side of the protective cover and sucked on a sliver of lamb jerky. Evidently satisfied with his meal, Running Dog continued attending his wound and ignored him.

A short time later, Conor slowly rose and peered over the heap of stones. Through the dimming light, the horseman advanced at a fast trot from a quarter mile away. Conor checked his Winchester for the third time, found a comfortable rest for it among the uppermost rocks, and eased the hammer back. When the adversary reached a hundred feet away, the sheriff hollered,

"Altaha! Stop in your tracks!"

With unimaginable speed, flashes of light erupted from Altaha's right hand. In the flurry of bullets ricocheting off the rocks around him, Conor pulled the trigger of his Winchester and levered a second round into the firing chamber. Wishing he had relied on his 1911 Colt automatic instead of the rifle, he fired his second shot just as Altaha sped between him and the first rockpile. At the same instant he saw what he thought was the eighth and final flash from Altaha's own automatic pistol. In a matter of seconds from beginning to end, Altaha was gone. The clatter of racing hoofbeats diminishing in the distance succumbed to the darkness.

# 7

Conor Armenta awoke to the sounds of Rayno Pete rummaging through the packs containing their provisions. After another moonless night, the eastern horizon barely showed a pale yellow line at its meeting with the sky. The motion of the silhouette could have easily been mistaken for that of a bear in the darkness. Rayno grumbled in Paiute as he searched mostly by feel for whatever he was hunting.

"Good morning," Conor interrupted the complaint.

"I got canned peaches somewhere in here."

"It'll be light out soon."

"You think that Chiricahua will be waiting for daylight?"

Conor was thankful that his grin was hidden by the darkness as he swallowed his laugh. "No, I suppose not."

"It's over twenty miles to the Virgin River and there ain't a drop of water to be found until we get there. I gave the water from one of the bags to the mules when we got here last evening. They'll need the other this morning...no fire...can't see nothin'…" The oration continued in muffled Paiute as he returned to the packs.

Conor dug into the saddlebag near his bed and retrieved the flashlight. He turned it on and handed it to him. "You can start a fire now, if you want to."

"Oh," came the only reply.

As Con took turns among the mules sharing water from his hat, Rayno found the peaches. He didn't start a fire. It was nearly light out when the mules were finished. Rayno handed him a can of peaches with a fork in it and his flashlight.

"I forgot you had that. Thanks."

"We can get packed up," Con told him as they ate their peaches, "but I'll need to take another look around out there before we pull out."

They saddled and loaded the mules and Conor led Abe as he walked back to the trail about where he thought Altaha had been when he confronted him. The sun just began to wink over the unnamed mesa in the east. The pattern of horse's tracks changed from trot to gallop. Conor picked up two shiny brass shell casings as the tracks ran between the rocks. They were of a design unknown to him as well as the notations on the base. He knew there would be more but couldn't justify a need to search for them.

He was about to board Abe as the first splash of the sun's rays cut through the sparse vegetation of the plain. A black object a few feet from the trail caught his eye in the bright light. Moments earlier, he might have missed it. He walked over and picked up the angular-framed pistol by its barrel.

"What the hell is that?" Rayno exclaimed as he rode up, leading the pack mule.

"A German Luger pistol. I've seen pictures of them before. He probably stole it from one of his victims in the war."

As the sun hit it from a slightly different angle, he noticed a slight streak of dried blood on the left side of the frame just above the grip.

"There's something else."

"What?"

"Blood. I might have winged him."

Conor pulled the bandana from his pocket and carefully wrapped the pistol in it. It seemed a longshot, but there was still the possibility of fingerprints remaining on the gun that would positively identify its owner. Cautiously, he placed the bundle into a saddlebag in such a way he thought it unlikely to move, thus resulting in an opportunity for the bandana to erase any evidence remaining on the pistol within it.

The mesa atop the east rim of Toquop Wash spanned an area two miles wide and five or six miles in length. They had climbed from the gorge near the uppermost part at its northern end. Conor led off heading south toward Bunkerville on the trail that paralleled the rim. Altaha had fled last night at a gallop. His horse's tracks were easy to follow and other than an occasional minor deviation had stayed on the trail even in the moonless night.

Two miles south, the trail left the wash and turned southeast across the mesa. Before and after the turn, the trail ran almost straight. Conor had no trouble following the fresh galloping tracks at a fast trot. After another three miles the trail led them into the head of another wash. The first two hundred yards were a fairly steep descent, but below that it leveled off again to follow the sandy bottom and continue down its mostly southeasterly course. The valley that lay ahead was a half mile wide and a hundred-fifty feet deep with a multitude of boulders and outcroppings capable of concealing an ambusher. He slowed Abe to a walk then stopped on the last point of the mesa before making the initial descent. The sun made a significant morning climb and began warming the mesa. Running dog stood panting in Abe's shadow. They had been on the trail for most of an hour. Rayno stopped beside them.

"I figure we've made about five miles so far. Fifteen more to the river?"

Rayno nodded. "Pretty close I think."

Conor gazed at a plateau about their same elevation in the distance. "Flat Top Mesa?" he asked as he looked over the terrain through his field glasses.

Rayno nodded, then answered, "Yes," when he realized Conor was looking the other direction.

"Another five miles?"

"Seven or eight, I think. The trail follows the base of it back to Toquop. Then another five miles to the river."

"And a million places for Altaha to hide along the way."

"Yeah, pretty much."

Conor lowered the field glasses. "He was still riding faster than we are now when he came by here. I have no idea how he could see where he rode in the dark as fast as he was moving. The moon was just a sliver and even that disappeared right after sunset. We'll need to be cautious from here on out. We'd be easy targets from anywhere he chooses between here and the river."

"That is so," the Indian replied.

Conor nudged Abe ahead and worked his way down the steep slope. Tracks were sporadic down the slope, but Altaha had not slowed very much. The bottom was sandy and tracks less pronounced, but judging by the stride, the little horse was back into a full run.

A mile and a half down the wash, the tracks slowed to a walk, then turned left off the trail. Conor stepped down from the saddle and pulled his Winchester from the scabbard. The tracks rounded the end of a point three hundred yards to the east that marked the entrance of a smaller wash joining from the north. He took a swig of water from his canteen and handed his reins to Rayno.

"Get outta sight if you can but be ready to make a run for it if need be."

Conor made a crouching half-run-half-trot to the end of the point. There he crept among the rocks working to find a vantage point to survey the other side. He soon discovered where the little horse had been tied to a half-grown mesquite tree. By the amount of manure on the ground, he must have been there overnight. Altaha's unique moccasin tracks were all around. Then Con found a bloody shirtsleeve cut off at the elbow. One of the shots he fired from his Winchester had found its mark striking Altaha's forearm. Probably the second one...when he dropped the pistol.

On further reconnaissance he found where the Apache must have slept. No bed and no indication he even unsaddled his horse. He simply laid down in the dirt only a few feet away and did not move. Nothing at the scene drew Running Dog's attention except the scent of the man where he had slept and the smell of blood on the shirtsleeve.

Other evidence showed he stripped yucca leaves to eat or maybe to bind or medicate his wounded arm. Conor had no knowledge of medicinal properties of the spiny plants, but this must have occurred in the morning light. His own experiences with the serrated, sword-like leaves were never pleasant. Their blades always left him bleeding.

Regardless, Altaha had plainly slept here and left. The tracks departing the rest stop pointed back toward the trail a quarter mile beyond where Rayno and the mules awaited his return. The tracks were about two hours old and the horse departed at a trot. When he came into view, Con waved Rayno to join him on the trail with the mules.

They rode cautiously at a walk for the next three miles where the wash became shallow and the valley widened to over a mile. Here the trail turned due south into the sun. Its surface became an alternating mixture of hardened soil and fine, natural loose gravel. With considerably less chance of an ambush, Conor urged Abe into a quick trot that matched or slightly exceeded the pace of their quarry. As another three miles passed beneath them, they neared the base of Flat Top Mesa looming three hundred feet into the eastern sky.

The trail followed the wash as it made an abrupt turn to the east followed by a sweeping horseshoe bend worn a half mile deep into the foot of the cliffs and just as wide. Altaha's tracks kept to the trail. Conor pointed Abe south cutting across the bend and eliminating two-thirds of the distance. They rejoined the trail just as it plunged into a narrow ravine. Bordered by a hundred-fifty-foot-high bank to the west and Flat Top Mesa to the east, the walls containing the wash closed in around them. Altaha maintained his pace. Leary of being trapped, Conor slowed theirs.

They emerged atop the east bank of Toquop Wash four miles later. Out in the open, Rayno rode up beside him.

"It's five miles from here to the Virgin River," he commented, "but something puzzles me."

"What's that?" Conor asked.

"Why hasn't he tried to slow us down?"

"I've been wondering the same thing. There's been plenty of opportunity to ambush us. Even if he doesn't want to kill us, a couple of well-placed shots could have slowed us down by hours."

"I don't think he's trying to kill you, Conor. I think he shot off the tail of *Nukwi Sari-chi* as a warning." Hearing his Paiute name drew Running Dog's full attention. He stood with eyes and ears focused on Rayno who seemed not to notice. "I think his second shot missed you on purpose."

Conor removed his Stetson and poked his index finger through the bullet hole in its brim. "What about this?"

"Altaha doesn't miss his target. The man who died on the train? *He* was the man who was supposed to die on the train. You told me that he had many enemies. One of them paid Altaha to kill *him*, not to kill you."

"What about last night? He unloaded a Luger automatic shooting at me."

"Did he hit you?"

"No."

"But you shot *him*."

"In self-defense!"

"I don't think he wants to hurt either one of us. He just wants to get away."

"Five miles to the river," Conor remarked and buried his heels into Abe's flanks.

The mule crow-hopped in protest, but galloped off down the trail. Rayno followed at a fast trot. Conor's irritation cooled while the temperature rose in the midday sun. After a quarter mile sprint he brought Abe back to a slow trot. The trail that had been barely passable by a motor vehicle earlier, became more well-traveled at Toqoup Wash. It followed the top of the east rim and had very few obstructions. The tracks from Altaha's horse were still the most recent.

After two miles the gorge of Toquop Wash dissipated into a wide, nearly flat valley. Rayno caught up to Con there. They talked as they rode side by side at a walk.

"I'm not trying to kill anybody, Rayno. Somebody murdered Dutch Wagner as he sat six feet away from me on the train. That same person shot the hat off my head, missing me by mere inches. Yesterday, the same guy shot at me two more times. You said this guy is some kind of hired assassin named Altaha. You might be right. He might just be trying to escape, but whoever he is, he's willing to kill me or you or anybody else who gets in his way doing it."

"If this is Altaha, and I think it is, he's legendary among the Indians," Rayno reported. "I've never heard of him killing another Indian."

"Well now, that's comforting to know," Conor acknowledged sarcastically.

The heat reminded him they were at a significantly lower elevation than the past two days. The valley floor consisted mostly of sandy soil that had washed from the canyon over centuries of flash floods. In some places it was firm enough that Altaha's tracks were clearly identifiable. In others, they were only round dimples lined across the soft sand.

A mile from the river, a homesteader's shack sat backed up against a low bluff a quarter mile to the west. From that direction, a two-track trail much like the ones he and Rayno traveled for the past two days joined the road they now traveled. A single set of tire tracks coming from it covered Altaha's tracks ahead of them.

"It seems we have company," Conor commented. "Looks like that homesteader's headed into town behind Altaha."

"Might have been going the other way."

"Not by the way the rear tires covered the front when it came onto the road."

"You can tell that?"

"Yep."

"You're a better tracker that I am."

"When it comes to tracking automobiles? Maybe."

Altaha's tracks were occasionally visible where the car hadn't quite covered them. A half mile down the road, Altaha rode a few feet off to the side then stopped. The car had stopped beside him then drove on. From there the road was mostly a coating of dust over packed dirt. The tracks were easy to follow as Altaha rode at a trot. Conor did the same.

With the river in sight, the road swept eastward toward Bunkerville. In the midst of the turn, they met a dusty Model-T Ford pickup truck. A thin man in his forties sat behind the wheel and rolled to a stop. He wore a sweat-stained straw hat and faded bibbed overalls with a dirty white t-shirt beneath them.

"Are you Sheriff Armenta?"

"As a matter of fact, I am."

"I seen your picture in the paper once't." The man looked at Rayno, then back to Conor. "You wouldn't be chasin' after a scrawny Indian with a bum wing, would ya?"

Con looked back to Rayno whose hand concealed the butt of the pistol tucked into his waistband, then returned his attention to the man in the truck.

"I might be...you seen one?"

"'Bout four hours ago. On this very road. Up ahead a piece."

"You talk to him?"

"Tried to. Couldn't understand much he said 'cept he pointed at that trussed up arm an' I made out the word, doctor. I told him there weren't no doc in Bunkerville. He kept carryin' on in gibberish. I finally told him the nearest doctor is in St. Thomas. He started ridin' soze I just drove on by him and on into town."

"He never showed up in town?"

"I sure never seen him a'gin."

"Thank you." Conor touched the brim of his hat in a casual salute.

The man in the pickup truck drove on up the road. When Con turned to follow his departure, Rayno rode up beside him.

"He make you nervous?" Con tormented.

"White men talking about Indians always make me nervous. Especially when I'm outnumbered." He smiled wryly then urged Toohoo ahead.

Con prodded Abe back alongside him. "Since Altaha never kills Indians, it might be smart to let you ride ahead. Then again, he'd probably let us both pass by then shoot me in the back... I'd just as soon see what's coming." With a cluck of Con's tongue Abe returned to a trot and Rayno fell in behind leading the pack mule.

A couple dozen yards further, Altaha left the road and angled down to the river. Conor grinned to himself as he looked toward the rickety wooden bridge ahead. *Either Altaha didn't trust the aging bridge or he was very thirsty*, he thought to himself. He followed the tracks.

The Virgin River Valley was even sandier than Toquop Wash. Altaha's tracks led straight into the water at a section of the river that was shallow and wide. Surprising to Conor, both the bank and river bottom seemed firm. He stopped a few feet from the edge of the water. Tracks went in, but none came back out. Looking through his field glasses, he quickly spotted evidence of the exit on the far bank. Dismounting he led Abe the last few steps to the river and let him drink. Rayno and the other two mules soon joined them.

"Where'd he go?"

Conor motioned with his head. "Straight across."

"Why?"

"Isn't the road to the Key West Mine right around here somewhere?"

"Just about straight across," Rayno answered.

"How are our supplies holding out?"

"There's enough food for another day. Two if we're careful."

"How far to the mine?"

"Ten miles or so."

"Terrain?"

"Pretty easy going."

Conor calculated their pursuit. "I'm pretty sure he's heading for St. Thomas. It won't take long once we're across to know for sure. There's plenty of water at the mine and probably better tasting than from the river here. We'll fill up everything here anyway. It's getting late, but if we push it, I'm hoping we can make Key West by dark."

They filled the waterbags and topped off their canteens. Water in the Virgin River ran low this time of year. Melting snow from the mountains dwindled months ago and it was nearly as long since the last significant rain. Water barely covered the mules' ankles when they crossed.

"That was easier than expected," Conor commented when they climbed the low bank on the south side.

"I think they used to ford the river here before they built the bridge."

"It's definitely a good spot to do it."

He traced Altaha's path to remnants of an abandoned road that their suspect followed. It led to the foot of a steep bank below the new gravel highway that was built a few years earlier from Moapa through the Virgin River Canyon then on to St. George, Utah. He had kept in a southeasterly direction along the bottom of the bank until he found a spot to access the new highway. In less than a half mile the road to Key West Mine intersected the highway. Altaha had taken it. Any question of his intended destination was all but eliminated.

Keeping on Altaha's trail, Conor and Rayno rode their mules hard, but failed to significantly gain much time on their opponent. The Mexican pony seemed tireless considering the pace his rider held him to. Cutting straight across country when coming off Bunkerville Ridge shaved an extra half mile from their route and brought them back on the tracks of their adversary when returning to the road. Nickel Creek was dry when they crossed it and followed Altaha directly to North Key West Spring, they arrived there just after sunset. It too was nearly dry and by all appearances, even the wildlife had abandoned the soupy mudpuddle as a source of water. Altaha had barely slowed down as he passed it. His tracks looked no fresher to either man than when fording the Virgin River.

Key West Mine sat among the crags to the east of the road and five hundred feet above it as they passed below. The buildings dangled precariously from the mountainside in the waning light. Arriving at South Key West Spring only moments before dark, Conor clicked on his flashlight to examine Altaha's tracks. The killer again had not dismounted. He rode the little horse into the pool of water and back out again. What mud that was stirred from the bottom in doing so was completely settled back down, leaving the water crystal clear. He was still hours ahead of them.

* * *

*SATURDAY, OCTOBER 25, 1930*

Dawn found the two men in the saddle leaving South Key West Spring at a trot. The mules were filled up on the fresh clear water from the spring as were the waterbags and canteens. The riders were filled with coffee, bacon, and beans. The road was practically straight, a gradual even descent all the way to St. Thomas five hours away. Four if they were lucky.

A small dark-bay horse stood tied to a porch post in front of the railway station in St. Thomas. The reins were stretched to their limit as the pony sought to escape the late morning sun in the last dwindling slice of shade. Conor dismounted at the mercantile a block away and stole to the station. He entered the lobby from the platform at the rear. It was empty apart from the clerk reading a magazine at the desk behind the ticket window.

"What can I do for you?" he asked when he looked up. "Uh, Sheriff?" he added, noticing the badge pinned to Conor's vest.

"Have you seen the man riding that horse out front?"

"Indian fella with his right arm in a sling?"

"That would be him."

"Bought a ticket through to Las Vegas last night. Paid with a brand new double eagle."

"Gold?"

"Yep. I barely had enough change."

"When did he leave?"

"Rolled outta here right on time at nine o'clock sharp."

"This morning?"

"Last night. I never noticed the horse out there until I got here this morning. He looked pretty tired...and thirsty, so I gave him a bucket of water. He drank down almost all of it."

Conor scratched at his four-days growth of beard while absorbing the information. "What time would he get to Las Vegas?"

"Eight thirty this morning if it was on time."

He looked at the clock on the wall. Almost three hours ago. "Did you see what all he carried with him when he got onto the train?"

"Yeah. He had a long buckskin sheath or scabbard with fringe. It looked like it had a rifle in it. Then saddlebags, and a bedroll too. Had some trouble packin' it all. He looked really beat up. Walked with a pretty bad limp. And that arm was bleedin' through the bandages."

"Thanks for all of your help," Con offered as he started to leave, then turned back. "I hear there's a doctor here in town. Where might I find him?"

"Her. Doc Herschler. One block down. Turn east at the mercantile, then three blocks over. Yellow house on the corner. She's got a shingle hangin' on the fence."

"Thanks again."

Running Dog greeted him with one wag of his abbreviated tail, when Conor stepped out onto the porch in front of the station. Altaha's horse had abandoned its quest for shade and stood mournfully in the sun. An empty canteen made out of a gourd with a wooden stopper hung by a rawhide string from the saddle horn. Con untied the reins from the post and led him down the street.

Rayno sat in the shade on a bench in front of the mercantile. The mules were tied to a hitching rail facing him. The vintage rail might have seemed out of place in other small towns of the era, but St. Thomas appeared to still support a significant percentage of equine transportation. Conor added the horse to the mules at the rail.

"Looks like our man has been in Las Vegas for the better part of three hours," he informed Rayno as he unsaddled his captive. "Caught the train out of here last night."

"What about the doctor?"

"She's three blocks down this street."

"She?"

"She," Conor verified as he rested the Mexican saddle atop the rail.

Con was in the saddle and trotting down the dirt side-street almost before Rayno realized it. Scrambling to his feet, he climbed aboard Toohoo and galloped to join the sheriff in the first block.

A yellow ochre house stood on the corner. The sign read, Dr. C.E. Herschler, M.D. It hung from a picket fence that had seen many layers of whitewash in its lifetime and was in need of a fresh coat. Like the store up the street, a hitching rail adorned a short-cropped patch of grass outside the fence. The condition of the grass and an array of road apples of varying age confirmed its frequent use.

A sign on the front door noted, *Come on in.* Conor followed the orders and entered a glassed-in porch. Most of the windows were open allowing an intermittent breeze to cool the space. Several well-worn chairs occupied the area and a bell hung from the casing of the door into the house. The next sign hung beside the bell with more explicit instructions.

> *Ring the bell.*
> *If I don't come running, I'm busy and I'll be out soon.*
> *If you're bleeding on my floor, ring the bell again.*

Conor rang the bell then stood back from the door with his hat in hand. A moment later it opened. A plump elderly woman filled the space. Her long mane of gray hair was drawn back and contained beneath a bandana pulled across her forehead and tied at the nape of her neck. A faded cotton dress with tiny flowers hid behind a clean white bibbed apron. She peered over the top of round spectacles that rode on the tip of her nose. Her gaze began at the sheriff's face, then down to the badge on his chest before returning to look him straight in the eye.

"Sheriff Armenta, you don't look sick nor hurt," she growled. "And you ain't bleedin' on my porch, so what do you want?"

"You have the advantage. I don't recall meeting before."

"We haven't, but I've seen yer picture."

Con smiled and nodded. "Did you work on an Indian man last night? Short, thin build, doesn't speak much English?"

"I figured as much." She shook her head. "You the one who shot him?"

Con nodded again.

"What'd he do?" she asked, antagonism in her voice seeped through her teeth.

"Murdered a man four days ago."

"Could have been self-defense," she accused.

"It could have been, but it wasn't. He'll get his day in court. The victim was handcuffed to the seat of a Union Pacific passenger car."

The expression on her face softened slightly as her eyebrows arched momentarily. "I suppose he was shootin' at you when you shot him."

Conor didn't like being interrogated by the witness, but abided for the moment. "Third time in three days." He poked his finger through the hole in the brim of his hat. "This time I shot back."

The old doctor's demeanor relaxed considerably. "Showed up right after dark. I was right in the middle of my supper when the bell rang. I tried to hurry up and finish, but the bell rang again. He was just getting' ready to ring a third time when I got to the door. He was bleedin' all over hell and gone."

"Then what?"

"I asked him his name. He told me it was George. In Mex though. Hore-hay. You know what I'm sayin'? He talked a little English, but mostly Mex with some Indian throwed in here an' there, Apache, I think. Not that I know any of it, but it sounded like them Apaches down south do. I lived down there on the border for a number of years. I was down there when Villa was on the rampage. I know Mex pretty good. Anyway, I got him inside and under some light. That arm is really tore up."

"How so?"

She sat down in one of the chairs and motioned Conor toward another before continuing. "I've saw plenty of bullet wounds down south, but none worse than this...that lived through it anyhow. The bullet went in on the underside of his hand right where the thumb meets the palm." She used her own hand as a model to show him. "He said he had his pistol in his hand at the time. I don't know how, but it missed the bone and the grip of his pistol or it would'a been way worse.

"From there the bullet come out the back of his hand and went back into his forearm just above the wrist. Then it run all the way up the inside of his forearm and come to a stop wedged between the ulna and the radius at the elbow."

"Between the what?" Con interrupted.

"The two bones in the lower part of your arm." Dr. Herschler held up her forearm showing him which bones. "If it hadn't hit his hand first and slowed down some, I believe it'd a' took his arm off at the elbow and you'd brought him to town draped over his saddle. He'd a bled out fast. Damn near did anyhow.

"Let me tell you, Sheriff, that little Indian's the toughest son-of-a-bitch I ever saw in my life. I had him in a chair with his arm propped up on the table. When I saw how bad it was, I tried to give him ether. He'd have none of it. Pulled out a toad sticker with his left hand and held it up for me to see an' never laid it down. I don't know half of what he was sayin', but I got the gist of it.

"Anyways, I just about fileted that arm an' he barely flinched. I got to the elbow and try as I might, I couldn't get that bullet out. Sweat was pourin' down my face, and he just sat there cool as a cucumber watchin' me work. I looked him in the face an' shook my head. 'Cóselo,' he says. You know, 'Sew it up.' And I done just that. It about quit bleedin' by the time I finished an' I got him bandaged up as best I could.

"I's washin' up an' turned back to him. The blade had disappeared from his left hand to who knows where. He lays a shiny new double eagle on the table. 'Nuff?' he asks. 'Enough,' I tells him, 'But I ain't done yet.' He looks at me kind'a funny. 'Sin terminar,' I said. He got that and nodded.

"I fetched a pint o' whiskey out'a the cabinet and took a pull then offered it to him. He shook his head, so I put it away, then made up a sling for his arm. 'Done,' I tells him. He nodded an' went out the door. When I finished cleanin' up there's a second double eagle on the table atop the first. Damned if I know when he put it there, but I ain't complainin'. Forty dollars for an hour's work? That's double what I make in most any month."

"Which way did he go when he left?"

"Uptown."

Conor opened the outside door, then turned back to face her. "Thank you, Doctor."

"You gonna hunt him down?"

"Yep," he replied confidently.

"Never met him in my life 'fore last night, but try not to kill the little bastard?" she asked with a lump stuck in her throat. "Gotta admire anybody who's got that much sand in their craw."

"I hope I don't have to, ma'am," he replied while putting on his hat. "I need to know where that pocketful of double eagles came from," Con concluded and closed the door behind him.

# 8

*Somewhere in France*

At one o'clock in the morning Roscoe Taylor and George Altaha were both making final checks of their weaponry. They sat on the ground at the edge of their currently assigned US Army encampment on the western fringe of the Argonne Forest. Both carried Enfield P17 bolt-action sniper rifles. Upon their meeting seven months earlier, they spent four weeks together in accelerated training at the British Army Sniper School outside of Paris. There they were introduced to the fine art of assassination. In the six months that followed, they refined their skills, adapting to new sets of circumstances for every mission they embarked on. Roscoe counted the notches he had cut into the fore-stock of his Enfield for each of those missions, thirty-six. He discovered after the first few missions that the notches improved his grip when aiming the rifle. An excuse to continue the morbid ritual.

Both men also wore sidearms. Roscoe carried an Army-issued Colt 1911 automatic. George retired his Colt after appropriating a Luger P08 from a German officer he had just exterminated. Roscoe had not felt so inclined but did admire the much more practical design of the Luger's holster than that of the Colt. At the next opportunity, he confiscated a Luger holster and modified it to accept his Colt.

They had also been issued bayonets for their Enfields, but neither found them practical. The sniper version of the rifles they carried had longer barrels and telescopic sights for improved long range accuracy. The extra size and weight of these improvements made them too cumbersome to be effective in hand-to-hand combat except for a club. Consequently, Roscoe had long since abandoned his. George altered his bayonet into a long, well-balanced dagger that he carried tucked into the top of his left boot. Roscoe knew of him using it to neutralize a target more than once.

As he checked his ammunition, Roscoe contemplated what he and George Altaha had been through together. On the day they met, the commander of the sniper school had told them that they would form a bond like brothers. Their lives would depend on it. He had been accurate in his prophecy.

George's native tongue was Apache. Roscoe's was English. Both men had picked up a little Spanish in their travels, but neither were fluent in it. Since their beginning, George learned some English and Roscoe some Apache. By necessity they concocted a mingled blend of the three languages that very few others would even recognize. They both now spoke and understood this uniquely morphed dialectal language effortlessly.

Roscoe's concentration returned to his inventory. The Enfield carried six rounds in the magazine. In addition, he had six 5-round stripper clips of .30-06 Springfield ammunition for quick reloading. He had a fully loaded 7-round clip in his Colt and two additional clips of .45 ammunition for backup.

Fifty-seven rounds. George would carry about the same. They had two men to kill three miles behind enemy lines. Roscoe hoped that over a hundred rounds of ammunition would be enough to get them back here alive.

\* \* \*

The old mess-sergeant slid three fried eggs from the cast-iron skillet onto each of the two sniper's plates. They joined a pile of chopped mutton, onions and potatoes fried into a facsimile of hash. Roscoe looked up at the grizzled face. In the flickering candlelight of the mess tent, it nearly resembled a face he'd seen on one of the gargoyles of a cathedral in Paris.

"Where'd you get these?" he asked of the eggs.

"One of the soldiers found a partridge nest in a field yesterday. He brought them in so I could cook them up for Captain Schaeffer. You two deserve them more than he does. Who knows how long this breakfast might have to last 'til you find yourselves another meal?"

With that final comment, the cook topped off their cups with scalding coffee and returned to his portable kitchen in preparation for feeding a thousand hungry men before daylight...and commencement of another day's shooting.

While George and Roscoe were in the sniper school, the German offensive known as Operation Michael captured 1,200 square miles of France and advanced their front line 40 miles. Allied intelligence sources indicated the Germans were again on the cusp of launching a similar offensive against them. George and Roscoe were assigned the task of eliminating the German colonel and lieutenant colonel commanding this sector. Their orders, both simple and vague accompanied a crudely sketched map of the commanders' last known encampment. The team was left to its own devices regarding whatever methods were deemed necessary to accomplish the task.

They wolfed down every morsel of the breakfast and cleared the passageway by chugging the last dregs of the blistering coffee. Outside, the perpetual drizzling rain had returned to welcome them. Their issued trench coats, though waterproof, were far too unyielding for subversive activity. Roscoe recalled his education on functional clothing from a Wyoming winter a decade ago. Woolen shirts absorbed the rain but remained insulative even when wet. Each man wore double layers of them. The doughboy tin helmets they were given might deflect an enemy bullet if struck a glancing blow at an acute angle but offered a bright and glistening target when reflecting their wet surface. Both men adopted black French berets instead. Also made from wool, they offered the same properties as their shirts.

Sometime before three a.m., the duo slithered across the top of an earthen dike that marked the eastern edge of their camp. They literally slid down the far side of the muddy barrier like a couple of otters sledding on their bellies down a snowy slope. Roscoe swore that George could see in the dark, but he himself, eventually began acquiring some of George's natural ability and intuition in navigating uncertain terrain with very little illumination. He discovered with practice that when sight was limited, his sense of feel, smell and hearing could become more elevated. He followed a few yards behind George in silence.

They progressed by weaving their way through a maze of fallen trees, stumps, and craters left by many relentless barrages of artillery fire. Roscoe lost all sense of direction in the process, but felt they were getting closer to something of strategic importance since the terrain was becoming significantly more riddled by the ravaging bombardment of mortars. Guided only by an occasional shadow in the darkness, the sound of a foot stepping cautiously placed into a soupy mudhole or an abrupt breath caused by an unexpected exertion, he continued on.

George emitted a sudden gasp. A subdued, "Oaf!" and disappeared completely from any semblance of view.

Roscoe froze...listening intently for the slightest sound that might indicate what had happened. Nothing. He took a careful step forward. Then another. He could see nothing. With each step, he paused to listen, but heard nothing. After a dozen steps, he heard a whisper. It seemed to be coming from right under his feet.

"What?" he whispered back.

"Ten cuidado," he cautioned in Spanish.

Their muffled conversation continued in their oblique dialect.

"Where are you?"

"Down here."

"Are you all right?"

"Yes."

"What happened?"

"I fell into a trench. I think it's abandoned. It's deep. I can't reach the top."

Roscoe got on his knees and groped for the edge. It was only a couple of feet in front of him.

"I'll let my rifle down. See if you can reach it?"

A moment later, Roscoe felt George take hold of the butt of his Enfield.

"I've got it. You can let go."

Roscoe abided, then felt his way up and down the bank in search of anything that might help in lowering himself into the trench. He found an exposed tree root. He had no way of knowing how firmly attached it might be or its length, but it was all there was. Laying on his belly, he reached as far down the root as he could. Getting his best possible grip on it, he slid himself over the edge. His muddy hands slid down the root and soon escaped off its end. He dropped only a foot or two more before sliding in the mud unscathed to the bottom.

"I'm here," he gasped as quietly as he could beneath his

heightened pulse. A moment later George's hand touched his shoulder as he half sat leaning against the bank.

"Here's your rifle," George said as he handed it to him. "The barrel has touched nothing. It is safe to fire...I'm not sure about mine. I lost hold of it when I fell. I cannot trust it until its light enough to check the muzzle."

"So, how do we get out of here?"

"This trench has to be German. It's not on the map and it has to be accessible somewhere from the back."

"You lead, I'll follow."

Before long, George found an exit that led them further eastward and deeper into enemy territory. As the black sky barely began to lighten into a dark gloomy gray, he stopped unexpectedly. Roscoe could hardly make out his shape in the predawn obscurity. He strained to hear what might have caught his comrade's attention to no avail and failed to detect any motion ahead.

A twig snapped somewhere in the distance and George's vague silhouette melted into the mottled terrain. Roscoe sunk to the ground and squirmed on his belly toward the last glimpse he had of his teammate.

"Down here," came the faintest of whispers to his ears. In the darkness, Roscoe could make out a faint depression to his left and moved toward it. Larger than expected, it happened to be a crater left by some previous explosion. George lay dead-still in the bottom. As their surroundings slowly brightened in the murky dawn, he noticed the dagger tucked beneath George's pant leg in his left hand. His right hand was not visible, but Roscoe suspected it held a pistol in similar concealment. Roscoe retrieved the Colt from his holster. Tucking it into his left armpit to muffle the sound, he slowly cocked it. George responded with a slight snort escaping his nostrils.

They lay in silence for several more minutes before Roscoe began hearing the sounds of German troops moving through the ravaged forest around them. It seemed they were undetected until the sound of footsteps came nearer. Roscoe closed his eyes; took slow shallow breaths in hope the motion would go unnoticed and listened. Two pairs of footsteps he thought as they neared. His suspicion was confirmed when one set stopped a moment before the other.

"Franc-Tireurs," a voice announced.

"Sie müssen gestern in das Mörserfeuer geraten sein,"

"Du willst irgendwelche Souveniers?"

"Zu viel Arbeit, um da wieder rauszukommen."

The sound of footsteps resumed and receded into the distance. Their playing possum had thus far succeeded in eluding their foes. Roscoe had little understanding of the German language but thought the men had said something about French guerrillas and souvenirs. In the dim light. the berets had led the two soldiers to confuse their nationality.

A significant amount of time had passed since Roscoe had last heard any movement surrounding them when George sat up and ejected the cartridge from the chamber of his Enfield. He uncoiled a section of stiff wire and ran it through the chamber and out the barrel. When the end reached the magazine, he hooked a fragment of cloth in the end and dragged it out of the barrel. The process cleared enough mud from the muzzle to have caused a serious obstruction had it gone undetected. He coiled the wire back up and it disappeared into its former unobserved location somewhere on his person.

A light drizzle continued intermittently since leaving the American camp a few hours ago. While on the move, the exertion had been sufficient in keeping the cold dampness at bay. After an hour of unprotected stillness, the chill settled in. When George reloaded his rifle and came to his feet, Roscoe welcomed resuming their advance. In another hour, a new day would dawn, if you could call it that. The rain-filled black clouds would lighten to charcoal gray. The rain would continue to fall. Beneath the curtain of mist and featureless sky, the gunmen slipped through the lifeless mire eastward.

* * *

Around ten a.m. George Altaha paused behind the trunk of a large fallen oak tree on the crest of a ridge. Many of the nearby pines still bore needles on their branches. They had been spared by the artillery being so far back from the unmarked lines of the battle. George wiped clean the lenses of the telescope mounted to his rifle. Sliding it over the log, he rose to look through the sight and scan the magnified valley below.

"We're here," he whispered without taking his gaze from the camp.

Roscoe found a similar vantage point a few yards away and replicated George's preparations before taking a peek himself. A dozen tents stood apart in the gray gloom from many more that obviously housed the German soldiers now battling the dough-boys to the west. Sounds of the encounter raging a few miles behind them were subdued by the weather.

Closer, but still five hundred yards away, the rear guard, a sergeant and private warmed their hands over a fire contained in a repurposed oil drum. It sat in an open area near what seemed to be the mess tent. Black smoke escaped the barrel suggesting it was fueled by coal or heating oil. The wet, pointy helmets of the men glistened even on this dark day. Their rifles, complete with bayonets hung from their shoulders.

Another hundred yards beyond the guards, two men stood across a table from each other. The canvas sides of the tent they occupied were rolled up and tied to allow what daylight shown to help illuminate their field office.

Both of the riflemen knew the scenario without speaking. There was no chance of killing both targets without being heard. They would each have their chosen man. They would shoot from ambush, preferably within three hundred yards. Head shots only. Fire simultaneously. No second shots. Immediate escape was absolutely essential. Speed and stealth in retreat would be their only defense.

George clicked his tongue to attract Roscoe's attention then signaled to join up.

"You see that grove of pine trees about two hundred yards this side of the camp?" Roscoe whispered.

George nodded. "About forty feet tall."

Roscoe nodded.

"You take the left," George whispered.

The copse of pines in question nearly concealed their approach completely. The falling rain would cloak nearly any sound they might make as they advanced. They quickly stole their way to the trees. Roscoe picked a tree slightly taller than others nearby. Slinging the rifle over his shoulder, he scaled the tree with expertise. Finding a good spot to shoot from, he glanced toward George who was already checking his aim.

Roscoe did the same. They were higher than their targets, so Roscoe marked his target at the base of his victim's neck. With the angle and distance of trajectory, his bullet should strike eight inches higher, the center of his victim's skull.

He looked back at George who held one finger up. The beginning of the five-second countdown. He raised a second finger, then a third. "Four," Roscoe whispered to himself as the crosshairs landed at the base of his target's neck and he began applying pressure to the trigger of his rifle. "Five."

The heavy rifle barely quivered as the bullet sped from the barrel. George's shot was so accurately synchronized that the report was unheard.

"Bang!"

Where did that come from? Adrenaline surged through Roscoe's veins. The German sergeant rose from one knee where his rifle had rested. Roscoe glanced to his right to see George tumbling from his nest.

Roscoe drove another cartridge into the chamber of his rifle as he raised it to fire. His aim was mechanical. As the crosshairs found the center of the grinning sergeant's chest, the bullet struck the German's throat just below his Adam's apple.

Roscoe did not remember seeing the private even though he stood right beside the sergeant. As Roscoe began his escape from the tree, a bullet from the private's rifle shattered the stock of Roscoe's weapon barely missing his right hand. The broken rifle bounced through the branches to arrive at the base of the tree seconds before Roscoe hit the ground running toward George.

George sat up facing the camp, Luger in his right hand, bayonet-dagger in his left. At a glimpse, George's right boot was missing, and the foot was a bloody mass of raw meat. George's rifle stood nearby, speared, barrel first two feet deep into the mud. Roscoe hurriedly tugged to remove its sling.

"Go," George yelled. "Go!"

But Roscoe ignored him. With the sling from George's rifle, he fashioned a tourniquet around George's right ankle.

"Go!" George yelled as Roscoe grabbed a handful of the front of his shirt and propped him against the tree while jerking him to his feet.

Roscoe crouched in front of George to carry him piggyback. "Climb on," he ordered.

"Go," George yelled. "Get away!"

"Climb on you son-of-a-bitch or I'll club ya and throw you over my shoulder."

Blurting a fusillade of profanities in Apache, George stuffed the bayonet into his left boot and climbed aboard, all the time keeping his Luger ready in his right hand and holding onto Roscoe with his left.

Assessing the demise of his two commanding officers and his sergeant, the German private was not in a terrific hurry to pursue his adversaries. Roscoe, however, could hear him coming as he scrambled with his passenger up the hill. Just as he was about to stop to re-evaluate the situation, the thought was interrupted by four rapid shots from George's Luger and a sharp yelp from down the hill.

\* \* \*

In midafternoon, the sound of fighting was getting very close ahead of them. Roscoe spotted an artillery crater with the roots of a large tree stump hanging over the west side of it. George was still hanging on so Roscoe figured he was either still cognizant or his subconscious muscle memory had taken over. Regardless, he wriggled the two of them into the crater and unloaded George beneath the tree roots.

"Are you tired?" George whispered.

"Nah," Roscoe replied. "Just hungry. I figure I'll leave you here and go on to camp for supper. Then I might come back and drag your carcass over there later."

George muffled a snort. "Better make sure I'm dead before you come back, or I might make sure that you will get that way."

Roscoe grinned and changed the subject. "How's your foot?"

"Numb."

"I better let some blood get to it," Roscoe began to loosen the tourniquet. "I've heard this might hurt like hell," he warned.

George winced but made no sound.

Roscoe was uncertain how to properly maintain the torniquet but let George's foot bleed slowly for several minutes then tightened it back up. After that he removed his outer shirt and used it to bandage the foot as best he could. Sometime during the process, George drifted off to sleep.

* * *

At dark, the shooting ceased. Roscoe woke his partner.

"They've quit shooting," he whispered. "Should be coming back pretty soon."

As suspected the German troops began their retreat a half hour later. It continued for nearly an hour before the last of them had passed.

George finally spoke. "What took 'em so long?"

"Carrying wounded, maybe?"

"Maybe."

After some time, Roscoe spoke again. "Are you warm enough?"

"Why?"

"I think we should stay here until daylight. I don't wanna trip and fall in the dark."

"The Germans will come back here before daylight."

"I'm hoping when they find all the chiefs gone, the Indians will give up the fight."

"Indians never give up the fight." George smirked.

"Just a parable."

"A what?"

"A story."

"What if the doughboys shoot us when they see us, thinking we're Germans?"

"They never have yet."

\* \* \*

*SATURDAY, OCTOBER 5, 1918*

At eight thirty that morning Roscoe carried George into the mess tent. The grizzled old cook who fed them the previous day looked to see if anyone watched, then poured them coffee when they sat down.

"Can't let any of these boys see me showing favoritism," he explained.

Roscoe thanked him.

"I'll have something cooked up in a jiffy."

As Roscoe and George drank their coffee, Captain Schaeffer rushed in to the mess tent.

"We need to get you to the infirmary," he blurted to George.

"I wait," George replied.

"No, you need to go now."

George pulled the Luger from his holster and laid it on the rough wood table. "After I eat," he replied in his best English.

# 9

Conor crossed Dr. Herschler's yard to Rayno Pete, leaning against the picket fence in the shade. "I know now why he hasn't tried to ambush us again."

"Why's that?" Rayno asked.

"Same reason he hasn't unsaddled his horse for two days. He's working with one arm...his left one."

"So, one of your shots *did* strike home two nights ago?"

Con nodded somberly. "Evidently."

"Now what?" Rayno asked.

"I need to make another stop at the station."

The two men rode to the waiting pack mule and Altaha's pony in front of the mercantile.

"Grab those two and meet up with me at the depot," Con told him as he rode ahead up the street. The complaint from unoiled hinges on the door brought the clerk's face up from the desk full of papers when the sheriff entered the waiting area.

"What can I do for you, Sheriff?"

"Can you get me through on your telephone to my office in Las Vegas?"

"Yeah." He grinned. "Probably." He picked up the earpiece from the oak box hanging on the wall and spun the crank on its side a turn and a half. The clerk, probably ten years Armenta's junior reminded him of his deputy, Jesse Slater. Young and perhaps a bit naïve, but savvy for his age, nonetheless.

"Hey Clyde, patch me through to Las Vegas," he told the mouthpiece jutting from the box toward him. His face reddened at an unheard response. "No, I got the sheriff standing here needing to get through to his office. Patch me through."

A moment later the conversation resumed. "Hi," he began. "This is Ned in St. Thomas. I have Sheriff Armenta here and he needs to talk to his office...yes, ma'am."

He waited a moment, then passed the earpiece to Conor, "It's ringing. Would you like me to step outside?"

"That won't be necessary," he replied as a voice came on the line.

"Clark County Sheriff's Office."

"Hello, Hazel. What are you doing there on Saturday?"

"Just enjoying a quiet morning, Sheriff," she replied sarcastically.

"Who's on today?"

"Jesse and Whit."

"Good. We've got a murder suspect in our midst. He should have gotten off the southbound train in Las Vegas about eight thirty this morning. His name is George Altaha. He's a Chiricahua Apache Indian, small build, about five-foot-two or three maybe, walks with a limp. His right arm is bandaged and might be in a sling. He's carrying a rifle in a fringed sheath and a bedroll. He's probably looking for a doctor or a horse. Maybe both. Tell the boys to be real careful around him. He's sly as a fox and slick as a rattler."

"And he's got a big knife stuck in the top of his left moccasin?" she interrupted.

Conor nearly dropped the earpiece. "That would be him."

"Doesn't speak English and meaner than hell. Pardon my French."

"That would be him."

"Jesse and Whit have been looking for him for about two hours. He found Doc Anderson around nine o'clock this morning. Doc couldn't understand him, but recognized some Spanish among what he was saying. He couldn't get ahold of you, so he called your dad at the café. Juan went over to the Doc's house and managed to communicate somewhat with the Indian. Doc's wife, Jenny was helping Doc unbandage his arm. I guess she wasn't looking right at it when Doc got it where he could see it. Juan was standing right there trying to mediate when Jenny saw the gruesome wound and fainted. Doc tried to help her when the Indian poked this big knife in his face and says, 'fix.' Then your dad tried to help Jenny, and he got the up-close view of that knife too, along with something in Spanish that made him change his mind.

"By this time Jenny woke up but pretended not to. Her condition had escalated from sickened to frightened. As Juan and Doc worked on the Indian, she somehow managed to slip out of the room and over to the neighbor's house. When nobody answered the phone here, she called me at home. I saw Whit on my way here and he said he knew where Jesse was and that he'd round up the posse and hot foot it over to Doc's."

"And that was two hours ago?"

"Yes. Somewhere along the line, Whit managed to sneak into the house. When the Indian spotted him, he put the knife up to Doc's throat and yelled something that no one understood. Juan talked in Spanish, and then he told Whit to move slow and go outside, then wait in the street where the Indian could see him. He told Whit not to worry, that he and Doc would take care of things and everyone would be okay.

"After Whit left, I guess the Indian backed off some with the knife and Doc went to work digging a bullet out of his elbow. All this time, the Indian wouldn't take any ether. He just sat there holding the knife ready and watched Doc work. Juan said he couldn't bear watching, but just tried to keep the Indian calm as best he could. When Doc got the man sewed and bandaged up, he stood and backed out of the room waving that big knife at them. When he got out of that dining room where the Doc works, the Indian closed the door behind him. Doc sat down at his desk and told Juan to have a seat. Then he produced a flask and they each took a snort.

"A short time later, Jenny comes in. She never saw the Indian but saw Whit and Jesse chasing after him. They were going out through the brush behind the house with their pistols drawn. After a while, she figured it was safe and came back home."

"What about Jesse and Whit?"

"The last I knew was just what I told you. When the three of them calmed down, Doc called me and told me what I just told you. Doc called back a half hour later and said he didn't know when or how, but when he cleaned up the table where he worked on the Indian, there were three gold double eagles laying there."

"The price for surgery went up."

"What?"

"We're at the train station in St. Thomas. The doctor here worked on Altaha last night. She couldn't get the bullet out. He paid her with two double eagles."

"We? Who's with you?"

"Rayno Pete. We have three of his mules and Altaha's horse. We still have a long ride back to Acton. I'll be home sometime tomorrow."

"And you're on a railroad telephone?"

"Yes."

"So, you want me to call June."

"And call the FBI too. Find out what they know about George Altaha."

"All right, but I'd rather you called your fiancée."

"I know, but she probably likes hearing from you better than me anyway."

"Poo! You know that's not true."

"She worries less."

"Okay, that might be true."

Rayno Pete sat in the shade on the porch in front of the station when Conor came out the door. "Where to now?"

"Dinner."

Rayno's puzzled expression begged further explanation.

"The second-best Irish cooking in Clark County."

"The Shamrock Café in Overton," Rayno surmised. "My niece works there."

"I know. I've talked to her."

Conor let that part of the conversation diminish as he began sharing Altaha's activities in Las Vegas this morning.

"So, he got away?"

"So far," he replied before urging Abe into a brisk trot over the half-dozen miles to Overton. Running Dog fell in at his usual outrider's post loping along fifty yards off to their left.

* * *

Dellis Tido brought two orders of lambchops from the kitchen and sat them in front of Sheriff Armenta and her Uncle Rayno. They were her only customers on a warm Saturday midafternoon.

"What brings you two down here today? I didn't realize that you even knew each other except through Jimmy."

Her statement sharpened Rayno's attention. It irked him that she spoke the name of his deceased son. These young people have no respect for the dead he thought, nor the tribal customs of a hundred generations. This was her cousin. They grew up together. How could she do such a thing, arousing his spirit by mentioning his name?

"The one who is gone brought us together," Rayno replied

through clenched teeth. "Now we help each other as the one who is gone would have helped us both."

"Oh, I see," Dellis backpedaled, realizing she had broken taboo. "What would he have been helping you with?" She glanced out the window to escape her uncle's glare and noticed the trail weary mules and small horse.

"Tracking a murderer."

Thus far the sheriff had not spoken to her other than to place his order and thank her for the Coca-Cola she brought him without asking. The details began congealing together for her; their dusty clothing; the long stubble protruding from the sheriff's unshaven chin; the heavily laden pack mule tied outside, they had been on the trail for days.

"Is he here?" she asked, suddenly aware of the situation. "The killer, in Overton?"

"Not anymore," her uncle replied, stuffing a mouthful of lamb into his mouth to avoid continuing the conversation.

Sheriff Armenta drank from his bottle of Coca-Cola while looking the other direction. The waitress filled her uncle's coffee cup and brought another bottle of Coca-Cola to the sheriff before slipping away into the kitchen. Conor savored the first true meal the men had eaten in four days.

"Fifteen miles to Acton?" he asked between bites.

"Give or take," Rayno replied. "I didn't intend to share our mission with the public. I'm sorry."

"No need to be." Con changed the subject. "The mules are tired. What do you think? Five hours?"

"We'll be close to Muddy River most of the way. They'll get water often. It won't hurt to push them a little."

Dellis had not returned when they finished their meal. Ignoring Rayno's protests, Conor paid for both, leaving the money on the table. Outside, he took the lead rope for the pack mule. The horse was tethered behind.

"You lead, I'll follow," he told Rayno.

* * *

At half past eight, the weary riders stopped beside the sheriff's pickup truck by the barn behind Rayno and Tomanie Pete's little white house at Acton. With a full belly and Abe following Toohoo at a lazy, rolling walk, Conor had dozed intermittently since sunset. He slid from the saddle and nearly collapsed when his feet hit the ground. The jolt shook him awake and he immediately began transferring his gear into the truck.

"You're tired, Conor. Go into the house and go to sleep," Rayno urged him.

"I need to get back to home." Con shirked.

"Then at least drink some coffee. Tomanie will cook it. There is fire in the stove. It won't take long."

"Okay," he conceded and led Abe to the corral. Running Dog followed on Con's heels while Rayno dashed inside. Lights appeared through the window in the door and a moment later they both were unpacking the packsaddle and unsaddling the horse and mules.

"I'll be back in a few days to get the horse. The county will pay for his board."

"He seems very gentle. He might make a great horse for kids," Rayno encouraged.

"Or maybe after that Apache rode him halfway into his grave, the horse is too stinking tired to put up a fight," Conor countered. "Today was probably the easiest day of his entire life."

"Maybe," Rayno surrendered. "It was just a thought."

At that moment, Tomanie rang the dinner bell from the back porch, and the men headed toward the house. Running Dog laid down at the door and waited. A plate stacked with hot, fresh frybread sat in the middle of the kitchen table and a gray enameled coffee pot steamed on the woodburning kitchen stove. Tomanie was fully dressed. Her long hair fell in a thick, single braid down the middle of her back. She looked fresh as she scurried about the kitchen with no semblance of recently being awakened from a sound sleep.

"Would you like sugar?" she asked as she filled the cup before him. "I have no milk or cream."

"No, thanks. Black is just fine."

Rayno took a piece of frybread and passed the plate to Con. Unpacking and taking care of the mules had roused the sheriff from his drowsiness. The coffee and food further invigorated him. As he finished his third cup of coffee and second piece frybread, Tomanie wrapped the three remaining pieces in a dishtowel and placed them on the table in front of him. At the same time Rayno produced a Stanley bottle from a nearby cupboard and filled it with coffee.

He sat it beside the frybread and ordered, "Take them."

"I can't take this," Conor hefted the steel coffee bottle as he stood. "It's brand new."

"It was a gift from the one who is gone. I've used it a few times. Bring it back when you come for the little horse."

Con embraced the man who stood with him. "Thank you for everything. You will be repaid."

"You've already paid me, my friend. Nothing more is needed."

Rayno walked Conor to his truck and Running Dog followed close on their heels. When Con opened the door, Running Dog jumped in and took a place on the far end of the seat.

"You're not going with me," Conor told him as he tried to extricate the animal by the nape of his neck. Running Dog would have none of it and without a collar, Armenta failed to secure an effective grip in the thick mane of fur surrounding his throat.

"Take him with you. He's been yours ever since he got his tail shot off."

"But he's your dog."

"No, he just followed me. Now he follows you...he'll work sheep for you if you ask him to."

"I don't speak the language."

"Remember the dog I gave Luis twenty-five years ago? You two got it worked out with her, didn't you?"

\* \* \*

The brakes of Conor's pickup complained slightly as it rolled to a stop beside the brown Chevrolet coupe parked behind his house. He had rationed the coffee and frybread to last the duration of the trip home. Swallowing the last dregs of the coffee, he then split the remaining half piece of frybread with Running Dog as they drove into town. After gathering up his rifle and all of the gear from the bed of his truck, Conor made one trip through the back door. The Stanley bottle and dishtowel landed on the kitchen table and everything else on the sofa in the living room. He draped his gun belt over the bedpost, hung his hat over it, and pulled off his boots. Con stretched out, fully clothed atop the blankets and heard the first three dings from the clock on the mantel as it struck twelve.

\* \* \*

*SUNDAY, OCTOBER 26, 1930*

A low muffled growl from Running Dog roused Conor awake. After four nights of sleeping on the ground under the stars, it took a moment for him to realize where he was. Through one opened eye, the sun shone brightly through the window illuminating the room around him. A second low growl followed by a short snort heightened Con's senses. He smelled coffee...and bacon. Turning on his side, his eye following the floor to the door and caught a glimpse of tan shoes. Working its way up came slender ankles and the hem of a blue checked dress dappled with yellow daisies.

"What is that?" June Sommers asked so softly she could barely be heard.

Conor's other eye opened and took in the rest of his fiancé, cup of steaming coffee in hand, standing in the doorway. "That is Running Dog. *Nukwi Sari-chi*, to be exact."

"Is he friendly?"

"Not particularly…until he gets to know you…and that can be awkward since he doesn't speak English."

June stifled a snicker which helped her fear subside somewhat. "Where did he come from?"

"He adopted me. Before that, he belonged to Rayno Pete."

"What do you mean, he adopted you?"

"It's a long story. I'll tell you about it later. What are *you* doing here?"

"When I came here to get your rifle and supplies last week, I left things looking like the place had been ransacked. Hazel told me you would be home sometime today, so I came over before church to air the house out and straighten up my mess. You were already here and asleep, so I stayed as quiet as I could, made coffee, cleaned the kitchen, and mopped the floor. At nine o'clock, I decided to skip church and make you breakfast."

"It's nine o'clock?"

"Now it is ten o'clock."

Conor got up and sat on the side of the bed. "I've not been out of these clothes since Monday night. You might not want to get too close to me. I need to shave, brush my teeth, and take a bath before I eat breakfast. I'd love to spend the day with you, but I'll need to get back after a murderer before he's gone. First, I'll need to catch up with Jesse and Whit who are on his trail."

"He got away," June informed him. "I talked to Maggie last night, and Juan had heard from them yesterday afternoon. She said they tracked him south of town a couple of miles. Even caught a glimpse of him twice. Then he just disappeared. No tracks. Nothing…just vanished."

June took a step closer to give him his coffee. When Running Dog reminded her of his presence she stopped abruptly and sat the cup on the corner of the dresser.

"I will let you and your bodyguard enjoy each other's company. Biscuits, bacon, and potatoes are staying warm in the oven. Holler when you are ready and I will start your eggs." At that she backed out of the door and escaped into the living room.

"Ready," he called out twenty minutes later and appeared in the kitchen clean shaven, bathed and shined shortly thereafter. "You look wonderful," he told her as she slid eggs from a skillet onto two plates.

"You look pretty snappy yourself," she teased with a grin as she sat the skillet down and untied the dishtowel from her waist she had used for an apron.

When she turned back to face him, Conor's arm replaced the apron around her waist. He held her close to him and kissed her. She returned the favor.

"I've missed you," he told her when they broke their embrace.

"It has been a long week," June contemplated, "but in a way I think I prefer the way it turned out over how it was supposed to. The alternative may have been more difficult to undergo than you would have been comfortable with...or maybe just for me to know that you had experienced it."

"I wanted him to suffer. To atone for the pain he caused...both physically and emotionally. Instead, he smirked most of the time he was on the train. He showed no remorse whatsoever. It made me wonder if there was a planned escape waiting ahead. In the end...he never felt a thing. He was dead before the sound of breaking glass, just inches away, reached his ear."

"I am sorry. I was so happy that you were here. Now I have slipped back into the same blue mood that I have been in for days. Only now I have brought you along with me."

"It's all right. I've been trying to make sense of this whole thing ever since it began. I thought the hitman killed Dutch by mistake, that I was his intended target. His second shot missed me by mere inches."

June's eyes widened at the realization that those inches may have been all that separated the difference in life and death of the man she loved. Conor had not intended to share that information with her yet and quickly plowed past the comment to continue telling of the multiple encounters with the assassin.

"Rayno believes the hitman killed the man he was supposed to. He thought Dutch was the intended victim from the beginning." Conor paused to collect his thoughts. "The killer has shot at me three times. He shot half of Running Dog's tail off the second time, and I shot him in the arm the third time. I know that it sounds crazy, but I'm starting to think maybe Rayno is right. He could have killed me easily the second time but didn't." He continued his account before June could digest what he just told her. "The third time, I surprised him. I was the one hiding in the rocks when I yelled at him. He started spitting bullets in my direction from the back of a running horse hoping to get away before I could fire back. He couldn't have taken aim if his life depended on it...and it did. But he misjudged me. I shot back. I didn't even know that I hit him until the next morning."

June's face was flushed. Hearing what had happened terrified her, but she did everything in her power to conceal it.

"We need to eat our breakfast before it gets cold," she interjected. Neither one mentioned saying grace, but June closed her eyes momentarily and thanked God for bringing Conor home to her alive.

For the past several minutes, Running Dog warily studied June's movements through the legs of the kitchen table and chairs. Deeming the current situation lacked a need for urgency, he settled on the floor behind Conor's chair and hoped the aroma of bacon foretold the arrival of fortune in the very near future.

Conversation eventually resumed through guarded small talk as they ate. By eleven o'clock, Con collected his gun belt and hat. June noticed the bullet hole in the brim and the generally disheveled condition of his nearly new Stetson from watering mules from it for the past few days. She made no mention of it when she waylaid him at the back door for a prolonged goodbye kiss.

"I love you more than anything in the world, Conor Armenta. Please be careful."

\* \* \*

Deputy Jesse Slater sat behind Hazel's desk filling out a lengthy report when Con entered the office and hung his hat on the peg by the door.

"Boy, am I glad to see you," he said when he looked up from his work.

"I've already got the highlights," the sheriff told him as he poured himself a cup of coffee and sat down at the second desk in the outer office. "Fill me in on the rest."

"I was hiding behind the neighbor's lilac bush near Doc Anderson's back door. Whit had told me what happened inside and waited like your dad told him in the street. It had been close to an hour when the Indian bolted out the back door. He had his bedroll slung over his shoulder with a piece of twine. His right arm was in a sling and he carried that fringed scabbard in his left hand. That rifle looked pretty heavy, but he still moved durned quick on that gimpy foot. It startled me when he came busting out of there like he did. I didn't even get my gun outta the holster 'til he was already into the brush outta sight behind the house.

"I gotta admit we were both pretty scared of this guy. Whit said he had a knife as long as a sword and looked meaner than... well he was real spooky. We gave chase into the brush. This guy wore moccasins and left a real odd track with that bad foot. Just the same, we tried to hurry but half expected to catch a bullet from that rifle before we had a chance to hear the gun go off."

"You were right to be cautious," Conor praised him as he stood and collected his hat from the peg. Poking his index finger through the hole in the brim he held it up for Jesse to see. "This doesn't look near as scary now as it felt when he shot it off my head through the glass of a train car window from five hundred yards away."

Jesse expelled a slow diminishing whistle.

"He's a very good shot with that rifle."

Jesse's face had lost some of its color, but he continued. "We caught a glimpse of him once more about a half mile south of Charleston Boulevard. We took off straight to where we saw him and picked up his trail again pretty quickly. About another mile he turned west toward Bracken. His tracks went right up onto the road to Los Angeles and disappeared. We scoured both sides of the road a mile north and south for tracks...nothing.

"After Hazel called the FBI, they put out an alert. The town marshal in Searchlight called this morning." Jesse handed Conor the note he had written and continued. "Yesterday afternoon, a rancher north of there sold a horse and saddle to a big White man and a little Indian." Jesse handed over much more detailed notes from Hazel's conversation with the FBI.

He continued, "This George Altaha has quite a history. I guess he's a Chiricahua Apache. His grandfather was one of Geronimo's warriors. His father was ten years old when Geronimo was captured. This George is known throughout most of the Indian reservations as some sort of hero of their people. He was a sniper in France in the Great War and must have been very good at what he did. When he got back home, he became a hired assassin. Mostly for gangsters back east, but sometimes south of the border.

"He had a partner in the Army. A guy named Roscoe Taylor. I guess they knocked off some pretty important German officers in the war. The FBI lost track of this Roscoe guy after the war, but before the war he was some kind of outlaw up around Elko. He's a White guy. You don't suppose he might be the guy that bought the horse with him in Searchlight, do you?"

Sheriff Conor Armenta pored over Jesse and Hazel's notes

and sighed. What now seemed like a month ago, he was simply escorting a convicted triple murderer to his execution at the state prison. It seemed an almost mundane task. Why are things never easy anymore?

"I'll be in Searchlight."

# 10

On his way out of town, Conor stopped back by his house. He had chosen not to alarm June during his earlier departure, but now slid his Winchester under the seat of his pickup. Running Dog eyed him curiously when he returned the paraphernalia from his earlier excursion with Rayno Pete into the open truck bed. Con fought with himself whether or not he should call her. Guilt finally won out over fear. He picked up the telephone and dialed 1-4-2.

"Hello, Sommers residence," April answered.

"Good afternoon, Miss April. Is your mama there?"

"Are you scared?" she asked without answering his question.

"What? Uh…why should I be scared?"

"Mama said you are after a really bad man. She said he shot his gun at you."

"Well, yes, your mama's right. I'm going after a really bad guy. And yes, he did shoot at me. But I'm not scared. I am concerned though and I'm being cautious too, because this man has shot other people before. But I'll be really careful and everything will be okay. I'll be safe. You don't have to worry. I'll be okay."

"Okay," she finally said. "I'll get Mama for you."

A moment later, June picked up the telephone. "Hello, sweetheart," she greeted cautiously. "Is everything all right?"

"The man I'm after bought a horse yesterday just north of Searchlight. I'm headed down there now."

"Oh," she replied. "I was hoping you could have dinner with us tonight."

Con was unsure if it was fear or disappointment he heard in her voice. "And I was hoping you would invite me, but I'm afraid that's out of the question for right now." He forced a subdued chuckle. "Unfortunately, once again, my job is interfering with personal lives."

"Oh, Conor. This man scares me."

"I know he does, and I appreciate you being honest with April about it too. I talked to her and assured her that I will be okay. And I will. I promise. It might be a couple of days, but I'll be wanting to collect on that dinner invitation as soon as I get back."

"We would be delighted to have you." His reassurance had struck home and he could hear a bit of relief in her voice. "What can we plan to make for you?"

"Oh, I've liked everything you've ever cooked for me." He laughed. "You pick whatever you want to."

"Okay, pretend you are sitting in the dining room of Sommers's Café de Excelencia studying the menu. You already know every entree. Which one would you pick?"

"Hmmm. I love them all, but it's been a while since I've had your meatloaf. How about meatloaf and April's fresh-baked peach cobbler?"

"I think the market does still have peaches. If not? We'll substitute whatever they do have. It's a deal."

"It's a date. With my two favorite ladies, I might add."

"Yes, a date. I love you, Sheriff Conor Armenta. I know that it is not just your job, it is who you are, and I respect that. Please be careful."

"And I love you too, June Sommers. More than anything. I'll be back sitting at your kitchen table before you'll hardly notice that I left..."

* * *

Realizing it was Sunday and the market was closed, Conor motored his pickup southward on the highway to Searchlight. Running Dog hung his head out the passenger side window, his tongue waving in the twenty-five-mile-per-hour breeze. A short distance past the end of the pavement Con turned his pickup down a side road to the Chavez family's produce farm. Juanita came from the barn wiping her hands on a well-worn apron as she watched the sheriff's pickup roll to a stop in front of her.

"What brings you out here on a Sunday, Conor?" It was at that moment she noticed Running Dog. "And what's that thing in the truck with you?"

"That's Running Dog. He decided to adopt me a few days ago and I can't seem to get rid of him."

"Does he like bones?" she asked and disappeared into the barn without waiting for an answer. She returned a moment later with a massive beef leg bone. "I get these from the butcher shop for our dogs. Keep a few in the cooler."

She handed the bone to Running Dog who, much to Conor's surprise, accepted it and immediately laid down on the seat to gnaw on it. Then before he could stop her, Juanita reached through the window and began scratching his neck and ears without incident.

"Well, so much for his disliking strangers," Con thought aloud to himself as he came around the truck. "Must be getting used to so many new people being around all the time."

Juanita let the dog enjoy his present and turned. "So, what brings you all the way out here on a Sunday, Conor? Last time you were wooing a pretty girl as I recall. Your mama says you're getting married. Must have been the cantaloupes you bought. That'll get 'em every time."

Con blushed. "You're probably right. I know I didn't have much else to offer a woman."

Juanita snorted. "Give yourself some credit, Con. Every girl in Clarke County knows you've been the most eligible bachelor in Las Vegas for years. It just took that pretty city gal to turn your head."

Con continued to blush and found no discourse to ward off the chiding.

"Okay, so what do you need?"

"Groceries. I'm likely going to be on the trail for a few days. Sunday and all. You're my best chance."

"I figured as much when I saw your bedroll and saddlebags in the back. I've got plenty of apples and pears. Just a few peaches left. Corn and taters are all I have that you can roast on a fire. Hot taters are pretty hard to eat off a stick."

"I'll take apples, pears, and corn. Hernando delivering in town tomorrow?"

"Always does on Monday."

"Have him drop off some peaches to four-sixty-nine south third. Just leave them on the porch if no one is there."

"Want your goods in a flour sack?"

"Yeah, that'd be great." He handed her a two-dollar bill.

"Let me get your change."

"Nah, that's all right."

"Bring your pretty fiancée by sometime. She'll get a better choice than what's been picked over at the market in town."

"Thank you, Juanita. I'll do that." He tipped his hat and climbed behind the wheel. Driving down the road he maintained his twenty-five miles per hour as the road permitted. His truck could run a little bit faster, but it struggled to do so. His conversation with Juanita, and June beforehand, left him sullen. June's eleven-year-old daughter had been right. He should be scared going after a professional killer. Con was relatively sure that April did not understand how dangerous this man really was, but June did, and it scared her. She never said it, but she probably was afraid more for April than herself.

The thought struck Conor like a freight train. What if April suddenly became an orphan for the second time before she ever got to call him Daddy. He struggled to suppress the tears that wanted to escape his eyes. He had to keep his wits about him. He made a promise that could not be broken...to both of them...to come home...to what soon would be a home for all of them...a family. This was no time to get distracted from his task at hand.

Jesse's notes said the rancher that sold Altaha the horse was about five or six miles north of town near the cut-off to the Searchlight Ferry. Conor's duties did not bring him this far south in the county very often but he recognized the terrain well enough to know that he was getting close. He slowed down in hopes of spotting a clue that might suggest which ranch to go to. He soon saw it. A three-foot-long board, weathered and bleached by the sun, nailed to a fence post. The message painted crudely in barn-red paint down its length was accompanied by an arrow pointing to the right.

## HORSES 4 SALE

The deeply rutted dirt track indicated by the sign told that at some historic point in time it had rained here. It now billowed a thankless plume of dust high into the breathless blue sky at a modest five miles per hour. A small, wagging dog barked relentlessly as Conor eased to a stop in the ranch yard. Running Dog stared, baring his teeth beneath curled lips, but keeping silent. Con closed the door behind him, indicating to his dog in sign language he hoped, to stay inside.

"Stay," he reinforced the command as he approached the gated picket fence that surrounded the house. A man in his midsixties came out onto the porch and stifled his own dog.

"What can I do for you?"

"I'm Sherriff Conor Armenta. I heard you sold a horse to a short Indian yesterday."

"Well, I sold the horse along with a saddle to a tall White man, but there *was* a short Indian with him."

"I'm only after the Indian for now, but circumstances might change as time passes."

"What did he do?"

"Murdered a man about a hundred miles north of here five days ago."

"Are you sure?"

"I was about six feet away when the bullet hit him. From what the FBI says, there's been many others before."

"This guy looked like he'd been in a train wreck. Arm all bandaged up in a sling and walking with bad limp."

"That's the man. He had the limp beforehand. The bandaged arm was from returned fire when he shot at me a couple of days later."

"I see." The rancher seemed to ponder as he scratched several days of stubble on his neck. "Name's Haygood, Bert Haygood," he offered along with his hand over the white gate between them. "They bought a little blue roan gelding. About fourteen hands. A bit small for most folks around here, but that Indian seemed to like him. Three-year-old and spunky," he added. "I threw in an old McClellan saddle. Paid forty dollars in gold coin for the whole kit and kaboodle."

"Two shiny new double eagles?"

"Yeah. How'd you know?"

"He's been leaving a trail of them everywhere he's been the last few days." Conor scratched at his own freshly shaven chin as he contemplated the circumstances. "So, he rode outta here on a gray horse." It was a statement more than a question.

"No, they loaded him up in that old truck and drove away with him."

Con tried not to look surprised. "What old truck?"

"The one that White fella drove them in here with."

"What kind of truck?"

"An old Model-T Ford."

"What did it look like? Anything unusual about it?"

The rancher chuckled. "Every fender on it was bent up. Had mud caked up and dried by the back wheels like he'd been stuck somewhere. Lord knows where he might have found enough mud to get stuck around here. It had a rickety wood stock rack on the back with a drop-down ramp for a tailgate, but the floor and the ramp looked solid."

Conor grinned. Haygood was more concerned about the condition of the stock rack than anything else. Regardless of what future follies might develop, he didn't want the horse he just sold getting hurt when it left his care. The man failed to notice the sheriff's amusement.

"That old truck sure ran good though. Lit right off on the first crank that cowboy gave her."

The fact he called the man with Altaha a cowboy caught Con's attention. "So, what did the White fella look like?"

"Tall, kinda lanky, but not skinny, if you know what I mean."

Conor nodded.

"Black hair, long, curly, and pulled back in a ponytail. Sun-tanned, damned near as dark as the Indian. He wore a sweat-stained straw hat with an eagle feather stuck in it. Had a vest that looked to be made from a Mexican poncho or an Indian blanket and wore-out blue jeans. Not from riding. The seat of his jeans and inner thighs were in better shape than the front of the legs and his cowboy boots were tall. The tops were tooled and had been fancy once, but they were wore out too. Heels all run over, more from walkin' than ridin'. He'd spent plenty of time in the saddle in his past, though. Had the bowed legs to show it, but not lately."

Conor began to admire this horse rancher's savvy. He knew every trait of an experienced rider and recognized many of them in the cowboy that accompanied Altaha. "How old do you suppose this fella might be?"

"About your age. Midthirties, I'd guess."

"How'd he talk?"

"Southern, I'd say. A bit of a drawl, but not as bad as some. When him and the Indian talked it was a mix of Mexican and something else. A word or two in English sometimes, but I couldn't get much out of it."

"Apache."

"Hmmm."

"Did you see which way they went when they left?"

"Down the road to the river."

"I don't suppose you'd have a good horse and saddle to rent, would you?" Conor asked.

The two men had meandered toward the sheriff's pickup as they talked. "I've been expecting that question ever since I saw your saddlebags and bedroll in the back of your truck. So, I've been thinking about what you'll need. I have a big buckskin mare whose mother was a thoroughbred-morgan cross. Never quite figured out who her daddy was. She stands about sixteen hands and can step out and put some ground between here and yonder at a pretty fair clip...and won't shake your kidneys loose doin' it neither. She's ten or twelve years old and bred to foal in April. She's early enough along and been through it enough times that it won't bother her at all. She's fresh shod and you can have her for five dollars a day. If you bring her back tore up, it'll be double."

"You've got a deal. If she comes back hurt, I'll have the scars to prove I did everything I could to prevent it."

He reached out and offered his hand to seal the deal. Bert Haygood accepted.

"That Indian is a full day ahead of you. I'll guess it'll take you two or three days to run that little roan down depending on where he went once't he crossed the river. I see you got a waterbag and a canteen with you. There were two waterbags hangin' from the stock rack of that Model-T. At the time, I figured the old truck must use some water. I'm not so inclined now.

"I've got a truck behind the barn. I can haul you and the horse to the ferry. That'll save you about two hours to start."

"I'd appreciate that."

"And I have a telephone in the house if you need to call the Mohave County Sheriff and tell him you're coming. I'll grab Belle and saddle her up while you make your call. Just knock on the door. My wife will show you where the telephone is."

* * *

Conor was unsuccessful reaching anyone at the sheriff's office in Kingman. Much like his own office on Sundays, the local telephone operator took most calls and, in an emergency, went down a list of deputies if the sheriff could not be reached. He left a message with the operator for the sheriff that he was in pursuit of a murder suspect and would enter Arizona on the Searchlight Ferry within two hours. In addition, he advised the department to be on the lookout for the man and recommended that the sheriff contact the FBI for further information on George Altaha.

As Con stepped off the porch, the rancher came from the barn leading a beautiful buckskin mare with a rafter-H brand on her right shoulder. Belle stood nearly his own height at her withers.

"Ain't she a beauty?" Haygood asked beaming with pride.

"Yessir, she certainly is that. Trouble is, while I'm tracking this Indian, I'm not sure I can read sign from that high up." Con laughed, and the rancher joined him.

"Speaking of that, there's something you should know. That roan is freshly shod too. He wears a size 0 on every foot except his right front. On that foot, he wears a size 1. That may not mean much to most folks and it doesn't affect the way he walks or runs. What it does mean is that the right front shoe is a quarter inch wider and three-eighths of an inch longer than the rest. If you're a good tracker, you could sort that out if there weren't too many sets of tracks to pick from. Never know, might be useful some-where along the line."

"Much obliged," Conor replied as he began loading his gear on the horse. Bert watched as he sandwiched his flour sack of apples, pears and corn between his saddlebags and bedroll.

"Traveling pretty light on groceries, aren't you?"

"I got in late last night after five days on the trail. No place open this morning. I picked this stuff up from a farmer I know on my way here."

"Let me see what I can rustle up to go with that," he offered, and dashed off to the house.

Con finished loading his gear and was adjusting the stirrups on the saddle when Bert returned with a generous portion from a ham and a bagful of biscuits.

"That might stick to your ribs a little better," the rancher offered as he handed them to him. "I've got a few pounds of oats set out to take along for her too. I wouldn't normally bother, but you'll be ridin' her pretty hard and with that foal in her belly, a little boost in her feed might do her good."

Conor opened the door of his pickup and Running Dog followed. As he led Belle toward the barn, Bert fired up his truck and brought it around. The nearly new Chevrolet had a similar stock rack to what he described Altaha and his partner were using, but there was nothing dilapidated about this setup. Conor loosened the cinch on Belle's saddle and led her up the ramp. Running Dog seemed satisfied to ride with the horse in the confined space and they were underway in short order.

An hour later, Bert Haygood slowed the truck to a stop at the approach to the Searchlight Ferry. Running Dog bailed out of the back of the truck wagging his half-tail as soon as the ramp was lowered. Belle backed down the ramp as if she had done it a thousand times before. Conor tightened the cinch and reached out to shake Bert's hand.

"I'll be seeing you in a few days," Haygood told him before he released his grip.

"Yessir," Con replied as he climbed into the saddle of the tall horse, then rode down to the dock at the river's edge and onto the ferry. Running Dog paused momentarily as if waiting for the ferry to sink under the weight of the horse, then dashed across the ramp behind them.

"That'll be a half dollar for you and the horse," the ferry operator told him as Conor stepped down. "The dog is free."

"Have an Indian with a banged-up arm cross yesterday?" he asked as he paid the man.

The ferryman eyed the badge on his chest and pocketed the money. "Yep, just about this time of day. They unloaded his horse right where you fellas did. The guy with him walked down and paid the toll. Said the Injun didn't speak no English. He never got off his horse, but they talked a bit before the other fella went back up to the truck. I couldn't understand what they said."

Con scanned the hills to the east. It appeared to be a gradual incline for the first mile or so, then across a low ridge. Five or six miles beyond that spanned a higher mountain range. The road contoured southward between the river and the first low ridge disappearing in the distance before turning east over the Black Mountains.

"Did you notice if he followed the road after he crossed?"

"For about a half mile then he cut back to the north. Never saw him after that."

Conor continued to study the terrain ahead as the ferry motored across the Colorado River. He slipped his badge into his vest pocket as they neared the east bank. Turning to the west, the sun hung low in the sky. In an hour it would disappear completely. A quarter moon had been showing since noon. He would have its limited illumination for a few hours after dusk.

Riding Belle to the riverbank for a drink before they departed was sufficient reason for Running Dog to follow suit. As soon as they were on the road, Belle fell into a smooth-gaited trot. With her long stride, they made good progress, but Con failed to maneuver her into a lope for more than a few strides before she would break into a gallop. He would need to work on her with that.

True to the ferry operator's word, a set of hoofprints departed the left side of the road turning east toward the low ridge. Thankful for the remaining sunlight, Conor dismounted and examined them closely. The soil was hard and dry leaving clear impressions. In just a few strides, the larger right front shoe became apparent. Under the right conditions, this might become a very useful tool.

Altaha's trail steered in a sweeping turn to follow the ridge northward over a mile from the river. It seemed he was using the summit of a small mountain three or four miles ahead as a landmark. Conor did the same. Unknown to him, local prospectors called the lone pinnacle Mount Davis, rising six miles west of the Black Mountains. When a mile and a half away from the little peak, he realized that it actually rose over a thousand feet above him and a smaller crag of half its height actually stood between them. A wide sandy wash lay before the first point. Altaha's tracks vanished into the deep sand. Conor stayed his course.

When he and Belle reached the far side of the wash, Altaha's tracks were nowhere to be seen. With some searching, Con recovered the trail a quarter mile to the west skirting the smaller point. On the far side, the trail again disappeared into a second wide sandy wash that ran east to west between the two peaks ending a couple of miles away at the river. This time it was nearly a mile up the wash to the east before the unique set of tracks emerged from the sand to climb over a low saddle on the southeast corner of Mount Davis.

The sun had set, and Conor raced against the growing shadows to stay on Altaha's trail. Another mile northeast, they fell into a shallow ravine that continued to climb the foothills of the Black Mountains to the east. Two miles farther, the ravine opened into a valley nearly a half mile wide. In the last glimmer of dusky light, a spot of white in the trail drew Con's attention.

He dismounted to find it a crumpled piece of paper. There as something folded up in it.

He scrambled to find his flashlight to see what he had found. He carefully unfolded it under the light. Pills. Some sort of pain pills most likely. There was something written on the paper.

*Beware —*
*This man is very dangerous.*
*Dr. Joe Anderson*
*Las Vegas*

Doc Anderson had given Altaha what were probably pain pills. In the event that someone came across him either unconscious or asleep, he tried to warn them. Con folded the pills back into the paper and placed them in his pocket then glanced around the area with his flashlight. It would have been late. Probably as dark as now when Altaha got to this place last night.

Then he saw it. An indention in the dirt where Altaha had lain. He may have been groggy from the pills and fallen from his horse, thus losing them in the darkness. He might have dismounted intentionally to sleep. By all indications he never let go of the reins. He could have tied them to his foot when he stopped to sleep or perhaps, around his good wrist understanding the possibility of passing out and losing his seat.

While retrieving an apple from his provisions, he returned the flashlight to his saddlebag. Conor sat down in the middle of the trail to eat his apple while his eyes readjusted to the lack of light. Running Dog materialized out of the obscurity and sniffed at the apple before finding a spot beside him to curl up. Con ate the fruit down to the meagerest scrap of core that he then gave to Belle before returning to the saddle. He glanced at the slender quarter moon that would remain for another hour or two then gave Belle a soft click of his tongue to proceed.

Staring at the dim outlines of hoofprints in the darkness, Conor continued his pursuit.

# 11

C onor rode on into the night. Altaha seemed to be following a trail of sorts. Perhaps left by game animals migrating to and from closer proximity to the Colorado River depending on the season or perhaps by prospectors...or both. It was difficult to discern in the dim starlit sky, but clearly from the hoofprints left by Altaha's horse, they were the only recent passersby. They must be heading nearly due east by the vague shadow he and Belle cast before them.

A couple of miles up the wide valley, the mountains closed in, forming a narrow gap between them. The hoofprints stayed on the trail whose gradual ascent became steeper. Belle began breathing a little harder as the grade increased, but she did not balk as they progressed. After another mile, the mountains again fell away beyond Conor's scope of vision. The trail maintained the same approximate grade without deviating its course for a half mile then made an abrupt turn south, dropping into a slender wash. In the last waning light of the moon, he realized he had lost the hoofprints of Altaha's horse in the darkness. He would wait until daylight to scout the trail of his crafty adversary.

As the crescent moon sliced a hole through the darkness, Conor shook out his bedroll before stowing his rifle, saddlebags, and canteen nearby. He offered Belle a handful of oats from the sack that Bert sent along and she ate it carefully, barely touching his hand. For lack of anything visible to tether to, he tied her to the pommel of the saddle with a short rope. Lacking a brush, he gave the big mare a quick rubdown with gloved hands before adjusting his bed and repositioning the saddle for his pillow.

"We have to share," he told the slightly lighter than dark form of the buckskin horse, "so, be a lady."

With a slight snort, she obliged.

"Just like my little sister," he mumbled to himself. "Always has to get the last word in."

He pulled off his boots and stretched out on his bed. In the darkness, Con carved a slab from the cured ham Bert had provided and added a pear from his flour sack for supper. Leaning against the saddle, he ate his meager meal and washed it down with lukewarm water from the canteen. The stars glittered like broken glass in the sun as he gazed up at them. He wished he knew the constellations better. Thinking it must be past nine o'clock, those that he did know seemed to be in about the right places.

\* \* \*

*MONDAY, OCTOBER 27, 1930*

Conor woke to the flat gray of predawn light. Belle dozed on her feet. The short rope had a relaxing sag between her and the saddle. Running Dog might have been mistaken as dormant had it not been for the slit of a half-opened eye staring toward him. He thought the dog frowned at him, possibly in contempt for not sharing the ham that still lingered on his lips. Con rose on one elbow and took a swig of water, rinsing his mouth before swallowing it in an attempt to slow the aftereffect of last night's salty meal.

Sitting up, he pulled off his socks and shook the dust from them before slipping them onto his feet. He did the same with his boots before planting his feet back into them. As Conor viewed the Black Mountains two miles to the east, they appeared an insurmountable wall fifteen hundred feet above him. He strapped on his gun belt, then walked over the trail he had followed Altaha on for the past several miles. Over three miles back, Altaha had laid down. That was probably Saturday night. Conor had pushed past that point into the night attempting to narrow the interval between him and his prey. It had taken him three or four hours in darkness to cover what would have been less than an hour's ride in daylight. The only set of tracks on the trail were Belle's.

He hurriedly saddled her up and packed up his camp. Stepping into the saddle, he carefully retraced his path searching for the blue roan's unique hoofprints. A quarter mile back he found them. They veered north into a wash that continued east past the turn in the trail he had followed in the dark. The rays of sunlight just broke over the mountain range to the east. He had spent nearly an hour backtracking to find his quarry's path. All he gained by riding late into the night was lost.

On the fresh trail he put Belle into her fast trot. A half mile up the wash, Altaha rode up the north bank of the wash and turned north across a vast open area that gradually sloped off to the west. Conor tried to push Belle into a lope that he was certain would suit her stride perfectly if only she understood what he was asking of her. Twice more he tried and both times she loped for a few strides then broke into a gallop. When he eased back on the reins the second time, she turned her head far enough to look at him out the corner of her eye as if to say, "Make up your mind, fast or slow."

Con was discouraged with his own misjudgment and last

night's wasted time, along with Belle's misunderstanding what he was asking her to do. It forced him to accept the situation as it was and continue on with the job at hand, regardless of impending circumstances.

The open area soon ended at another wash. This one quickly narrowed and climbed northeasterly up the foot of the mountain. Mount Perkins, the highest peak in the chain stood nearly straight ahead of them. In spite of the five or six hundred feet they had already gained in altitude this morning, it still loomed another fifteen hundred feet above them. The incline up the wash was not terribly steep and Belle tore up it as if it were nothing.

When they had gained half the elevation to the summit, Altaha again left the wash to turn due north. Here he contoured the sidehill to the east only climbing slightly as he went. At a point about a mile from the wash, he crossed a steep scree field. Unlike the one Con and Rayno had traversed on the mules a few days ago. There was no trail to follow across this one. Altaha's course was clearly marked by displaced stones at each step of his horse along the way. At one point the roan had slid down the slope several feet, scrambling to find a more secure footing.

While Conor contemplated the best route in order to avoid Altaha's mishap, Running Dog scampered ahead with only a few stones barely moving as he ran. Trying to map Running Dog's undisturbed path in his mind Con urged Belle ahead. She proceeded quite solidly. At one point her feet sliding on the slippery rock spooked her and she lunged ahead briefly before regaining her confidence to complete the crossing safely.

A mile ahead, Altaha took a more aggressive angle to the contour and soon broke out onto a saddle between the main ridge and a rock outcropping to the west. Instead of crossing the saddle, he turned straight up the hillside to the crest of the Black Mountain range. Rather than crossing it, he turned back south as if to follow it to the summit of Mount Perkins. Instead, he began contouring down the much more gradual eastern slope. When nearly straight below the peak, he turned down a rather steep wash that ran again to the northeast for a few hundred yards. A small copse of stunted cottonwood trees indicated a source of water amid the barren landscape and the sound of it trickling down the gully soon confirmed it.

The water was cool and clear. Conor drank his fill. After Running Dog and Belle did the same, he refilled both his canteen and the water bag. He ate another apple and one of Mrs. Haygood's biscuits, feeding the core to Belle before continuing on Altaha's trail. As he rode, he tried to evaluate the man he hunted. Doc Anderson warned on his note to beware. Conor himself probably had more reason to fear him than most, but, as he had told the little girl that soon would become his daughter, he was not afraid. Maybe he should be. As much as he wanted to catch this outlaw and bring him to justice, he found himself respecting him.

"The little warrior is unbelievably tough," he muttered aloud, causing Belle to turn an ear his direction. "He must be in a great deal of pain from being shot in the arm, not to mention two surgeries in as many days without anesthesia. Yet he's making a ride that most riders in perfect health would have difficulty keeping up with." Conor continued his one-sided conversation, which by now Belle chose to ignore. "And on top of all that, without question, he is the best shot with a rifle I've ever seen."

He proceeded down the slope, steep enough to cause Belle to squat on her haunches. The water from the spring vanished beneath the ground nearly as quickly as it had appeared. Con followed Altaha down the wash below. A second spring soon rose to the surface in the bottom of the same wash.

"Probably the same spring, just returning to the surface," he continued his introspective monologue. "And then there are other things...like this." His gaze swept over the surroundings. "According to the FBI, he's spent most of his life several hundred miles southeast of here, yet he knows where the water is and how to reach it. Rayno Pete spent his entire life herding sheep in the Mormon Mountains and only knows of a few more watering holes than Altaha does." Conor's thoughts became more pensive. "It's no wonder so many tribesmen revere him."

He nearly bit his lip to silence the thought before it escaped his lips, "And now he's leading me right into the middle of several of them. Any one of these people I should encounter, might be willing to kill me in order to protect *him*."

Conor struggled to push the thought from his mind. He could not allow himself to become distracted. At the second spring, the narrow wash turned north for a quarter mile before widening out and sloping more gradually east again. After two miles, it dumped out into a prehistoric alluvial fan. It began in a vast plane of soft sand that had blown into a series of small dunes resembling waves in a landlocked sea of sand.

It looked like Altaha had cut across the southern border of the obstacle to continue eastward. The hoofprints left behind had long since evaporated into the sea of desert. Conor held his course across the apex of the perimeter, but when he emerged on hard ground the unique prints of Altaha's horse were nowhere to be seen. Taking in the topography in every direction he decided the Apache must have turned south, the closest escape from the sand. He turned Belle back west following the southern border of the sand. After a quarter mile, he was back to the point where he entered the sand, and Altaha before him.

Aggravated by yet another setback, he turned Belle around to retrace their most recent steps. The slightly longer distance on much firmer ground would be faster and easier on his pregnant conveyance than renegotiating the sand. They covered most of the distance at a quick trot. Con felt no need to frustrate his trans-port with another lesson in loping for the meantime considering the short distance. They slowed to a walk when arriving back at their earlier exit from the sand and followed the outskirts while scouting for tracks. Throughout the ordeal Running Dog seemed not to notice any difference in negotiating the array of terrain. He did however give Conor a look as if he had lost some of his faculties when they returned to the exact same spot, they had just been only a short time ago.

The further Con rode around the circle of sand without any sign of Altaha's passing, the more he began to agree with his canine partner. Consequently, Running Dog closed in his outrider position in a conspicuous attempt to avoid being too far afield when his human companion might choose to suddenly turn around and go back the other way. Again.

"You're probably right, *Nukwi Sari-chi.*" Running Dog jerked to a stop, eyes and ears alert, giving Conor every ounce of his attention upon hearing his Paiute name. "You're right," he repeated. "I've probably lost my marbles."

With a cluck of his tongue Belle moved ahead while Con continued his search for Altaha's exit from the sand. When he had gone three-quarters of the way around the circle of sand and nearly a mile in the process, Altaha's tracks emerged heading north along the eastern foot of the Black Mountains. He had lost another hour.

After a mile Altaha stopped and dismounted. It seemed he had checked the left rear foot of his mount, though Conor had noticed no peculiarity in the prints he had left to indicate any lameness. From there, his adversary turned east at a fast trot. The sun hung high in the sky and the tracks were twenty-four hours old. He desperately needed to make up for lost time and somehow overtake his quarry.

"It's now or never, old girl," he commented to Belle as he touched his heels to her flanks and turned her east. Within a hundred yards, he urged her into a lope that in a dozen strides she accelerated into a gallop. When he pulled back ever so lightly on the reins, she reverted to her fast trot. After a quarter mile, he tried again. She stayed in the lope and with her long stride easily doubled Altaha's pace across the Detrital Valley a tad north of due east. In addition, Altaha had stopped twice more to check the left hind hoof of his horse.

They crossed the road from El Dorado Ferry to Kingman reaching the far side of the valley in less than an hour. Altaha picked up a well-traveled trail northward into the southern end of the White Hills. Two miles into the hills, the Indian camped at a spring. He had roasted a jackrabbit over the campfire on a stick and pried the shoes from his horse there. Most likely with the big knife Conor heard he carried tucked in the top of his moccasin.

Running Dog sniffed the remnants of bandages among the ashes. "The arm must be getting better," Con muttered to himself as he stepped back into the saddle. He glanced up at the sun beginning its descent to the west. "Four more hours of daylight."

The barefoot horse was still easy enough for the sheriff to track. The one larger hoof could still be identified with only slightly more effort than before. The left rear shoe must have been coming loose, possibly triggered by the slip crossing the scree, instigating Altaha's frequent stops.

An hour later Conor crossed a saddle at the western foot of a flat-topped mesa several hundred feet below its rim. Belle had adapted to her loping gait and made the gradual ascent from the spring only slowing to a trot for short distances while negotiating less hospitable terrain. For the most part Con had let her have her head as both horse and rider were becoming more accustomed to each other.

Another mile to the northeast, Altaha's trail again turned east around the north end of the mesa. A half hour later, the small valley they were following spilled out into the Hualapai Valley, twenty miles across with Hualapai Indian Reservation in the mountains on its eastern flank.

Conor eased Belle to a halt staring at Garnet Mountain and the Grand Wash Cliffs in the distance. Altaha was leading him into a trap among his Hualapai allies in those mountains. He would have little chance if confronted by a dozen men willing to fight to protect the man they believed represented the last of their ancestral warriors.

He retrieved the field glasses from his saddlebag. Even on this moderately cool day, heatwaves waltzed across the vast plane before him obscuring his view and rendering the magnification useless. Con returned the field glasses to his saddlebag and drank a swallow of warm water from his canteen, hoping to wash down the lump in his throat.

*"Are you scared? Mama said you are after a really bad man. She said he shot his gun at you."*

The words shot through his pounding heart like a bullet. When was that? Last week? When sweet, innocent, April voiced her own fears for his life? He had reassured her. Told her he would be careful. That everything would be okay. Then why was sweat trickling from his temples and down his neck when it was only seventy degrees out, with a light breeze to boot. When was that, again? Yesterday. Barely older than the tracks on the ground in front of him. Twenty miles of open ground. The best marksman in the southwest, maybe the entire country lay in wait for him.

With a cluck of his tongue, Belle moved ahead. Her trot grew into the now familiar lope and Running Dog raced from behind to pass them both down Altaha's trail. A mile ahead lay the tip of the tail of what resembled a sleeping dragon named the Cerbat Mountains. The snout lay forty miles south at Kingman. Just before reaching the tail, Altaha's trail made an abrupt turn south. The sudden change in direction caught Conor so off guard he dismounted to carefully inspect the tracks and ensure he was still on the right trail. After a fastidious examination of every detail, he concluded that the right front foot was in fact slightly larger than the other three. Returning to his saddle, he turned south along the west side of the tail.

A mile and a half south, Altaha ventured toward the mouth of a gap in the dragon's tail but returned to follow the west slope of the mountain. The same distance down the face, he repeated the action, but again returned to continue down the west slope. Relieved to be moving away from the Hualapai Reservation, Conor was puzzled by Altaha's actions. He seemed to be looking for a landmark of sorts. The string of mountains bent westward and widened as it did. Three miles further, Altaha again ventured into the foothills. This time he did not return. Con followed.

The trail climbed five hundred feet in a mile then dropped over a narrow saddle and down a steep and rocky ravine. In another mile they were in the foothills of the east slope and three hundred feet lower than they started on the west. Upon exiting the rocks, Altaha's horse had a quarter-sized divot missing from the two o'clock position of his oversized right front foot. He appeared to be walking without pain so evidently the damage was superficial. For Conor, it made tracking him much simpler.

Altaha did not descend completely from the mountain. Turning south, he followed a contour four to five hundred feet up in the foothills picking saddles across the various points extending into the valley below. Three miles south, he turned up a wash that led to a spring a mile above. On the shady side of the mountain the sun had already set and soon it would fall into darkness. There was firewood nearby, grass for Belle to graze on and fresh cold water from the spring. The locale was perfect, and Conor chose to make camp.

He unsaddled Belle not surprised to find her back barely damp with sweat beneath the blanket. He rubbed her down with handfuls of dry grass and she found a flat spot to roll. Conor grinned, suspecting the foal in her belly may be causing a little discomfort. When she stood back up, she shook intensely until everything returned to its proper place.

"You feel better now?" he asked rhetorically. She blew a short snort and stared at him, which he accepted for *yes* as he picketed her in knee-high grass where she could also reach the spring. After giving her a handful of oats, he went about preparing his own supper.

Rustling up dry sticks and branches, he started a fire. While allowing it to burn down to coals, Conor rolled out his bed. He rummaged through his food supplies and brought out the ham, an apple, and two ears of corn. Con stabbed one of the ears on a green stick and propped it over the fire to roast. He reclined on his bed, leaning against the saddle and munched on a hefty serving of cold ham while his corn hissed over the fire. Chewing the meat from the rind, he tossed the scrap to Running Dog who had lunched on a ground squirrel earlier in the day.

Donning his leather gloves, he swapped his roasted ear of corn for the fresh one and commenced to peel back the browned husk and silk to munch on the sweet, hot, and juicy treat from the fire. When finished, he tossed the now-cooled cob within Belle's reach and repeated the entire process with the second ear.

In his camp, the mountain already blocked the slice of moon from view rendering the night black as molasses. The campfire, burned down to ashy coals providing a dim glow on his immediate surroundings as he pulled off his boots and laid back on his bed. Eating his apple, Conor stared up at a Prussian blue sky. The stars poked through pinholes of the darkness.

"June would love this."

* * *

*TUESDAY, OCTOBER 28, 1930*

The approaching sunrise lit up the sky overlooking the wash between the foothills to the east. The terrain was rocky, but Altaha's mount chose his footsteps between them mostly, still providing a comfortable trail for Con to follow. The morning air on the east side of the mountain range was cooler than he suspected it would be. His adversary's trail crossed the narrow valley and he could see Belle's breath as she climbed toward a notch between the foothills to the south. Altaha kept his distance from the open Hualapai Valley to the east. He contoured the upper foothills mostly maintaining about five hundred feet above the open plain below.

For the first five miles, their path ran pretty much southeast before a band of hills broke off to the east forming a valley about a mile and a half wide that ran south between them and the main range. Altaha held his same contour above the valley. Five miles further south, the Cerbat Mountains bulged eastward about the same distance. The Indian stayed his course, turning up a canyon that ran a little bit west of south and straight into the center of the mountain range.

Two hours later they broke out onto the backbone of the sleeping dragon, three thousand feet above their start. They were in timber for the last two miles. A forest of juniper and pinyon trees. Even the wily Indian had dismounted and scrambled through the rocks leading his horse up the last mile of the climb. Here was a well-traveled trail that followed the crest of the mountain range. The trail was a maze of mule tracks migrating both directions. None were newer than the hoofprints left yesterday by Altaha's horse. He rode south and Conor followed.

Numerous smaller trails entered and exited the one he was on. Three miles down the trail he met a packer riding a mule and leading six more with heavy packs.

"Rufus Jones," the heavily whiskered gent introduced himself and held out his hand. "You lookin' fer somebody?"

"What makes you ask that?" Conor queried as he accepted the handshake.

"Where should I start?" Rufus mused, scratching at a cheek buried somewhere beneath his massive gray beard. "How about that automatic pistol yer packin'? Or the Winchester in yer scabbard? Could even be that desert waterbag hangin' from yer saddle horn clear up here on a mountaintop where there's a half-dozen freshwater springs every couple of miles?"

"I can see how that might pique some curiosity," Con replied as he dug his badge from his vest pocket. "Sheriff Conor Armenta, Clark County, Nevada."

The thick whiskers moved into the shape of a wide grin from somewhere behind the tangle of facial growth. "Pleasure, Sheriff," he acknowledged with a tug on the short brim of his tattered fedora. "Might have also noted that I seen ya stop twice in the last half mile lookin' at tracks tryin' ta pick out those of the first horse I seen up here in over two years. Anyone on a horse up here ain't plannin' on bein' here long."

"And when might you have seen this other fella?"

"Yesterday afternoon. Down on the lower trail."

"Let me guess. Indian fella, don't speak English. A little over five feet tall, right arm in a sling. On a blue roan horse about fourteen hands. Old McClellan saddle. That about right?"

"You forgot to mention the rifle in the fringed buckskin sheath and two desert waterbags tied together and draped across the pommel of the McClellen. I never saw no sling."

"Arm must be healing up."

"What happened to it?"

"I shot him a week ago."

"Oh."

"How do I find this lower trail?"

"Stay on this one here. About two miles you'll be sneakin' up on Cherum Peak. Just beneath it, the trail falls off the east side of the ridge. Little over a mile from there, it splits. Stay left. It drops pretty quick. A mile past the fork, the trail turns sharp to the north. Bail off the west side right there. There's a bit of a trail. Try to stay on it where you can. Either way, go straight to the bottom. It's steep. Six, eight hundred feet down in a half mile. At the bottom, you'll be right in the middle of the lower trail. Turn left. It'll take you right out to Hualapai Valley. Turn right, you'll be in a box canyon."

"Thanks for your help. I'm obliged to you."

"Always try to stay on the right side of the law, Sheriff. I need to get movin' now. If you sit tight fer just a minute, I'll be outta yer way and you can be on yers in a jiffy. I got three stops to make yet today and two more tomorrow."

The packer, Rufus Jones was moving before he finished talking. The string of pack mules followed him like a brood of ducklings follow their mama. The whole bunch were gone past him in less than a minute. Running Dog waited patiently as the mules passed then trotted ahead down the trail. When they reached the sharp turn in the trail back north, Conor peered down the steep hillside Rufus had told him about. When he was about to call the old packer a liar, he spotted the trail twenty yards away that the old man had brought his string of mules up.

"Well, old girl," he told Belle. "If heavy loaded mules came up it, surely we can go down."

And they did. Belle slid on her haunches, skidded, trotted, stomped, and snorted herself all the way to the bottom...in a matter of minutes. When they reached the lower trail, she turned her head far enough to look at him with her left eye. Conor was uncertain what her exact thoughts might be. He was sure of one thing, it most likely included profanity.

The lower trail followed a narrow, semi-forested valley eastward. Two miles down the valley, the trail split around a range of foothills two miles across. Altaha's path turned right through a slender gap between the hills for a mile. He left the trail on the other end of the gap skirting a rocky point to the right, then southwest straight across another open valley and into a cleft gouged out of the mountain and climbing five hundred feet back up its side. It flattened out on top crossing the road from Mineral Park that traversed the mountain and ran southwest halfway across the Hualapai Valley to meet the Santa Fe Railroad northeast of Kingman at Berry.

It was past midday. There was a spring near the road. Since daybreak they had been from the bottom of the mountain to the top. Slid most of the way back down and now were nearly back to the top again. Conor picketed Belle in a grassy patch with a little shade and within reach of the spring. Then he pulled her saddle off. She gave him the same look Running Dog had given him yesterday. As if she had just checked her watch to make sure it was actually as early in the day as she thought it was. The "have you lost your marbles" look.

Con did not reply. He rubbed the sweat from her back with handfuls of dry grass. Then gave her a portion of oats. After finding an apple in his grub bag, he quartered it and doled the entire apple out to her before taking another for himself and the last two of Mrs. Haygood's biscuits. Running Dog laid nearby looking wishfully at the biscuits as Conor ate his lunch.

"Don't give me that look. You didn't have half as tough of a morning as she did."

After his first biscuit and some water to wash it down with, he ate the apple. When finished, he tossed the core to Running Dog who caught it midair and gulped it down as if it were a steak. Halfway through washing down the second biscuit, Con came to a realization. It might be that he was less hungry than he thought or perhaps, the biscuit, halfway through the third day of its cold, dry, stale life, just was not quite as palatable as it had been on day one. He tossed the remainder to Running Dog who disagreed; it was scrumptious.

Belle seemed disappointed when Conor saddled her back up, but tolerated the situation, nonetheless. The hoofprints of Altaha's horse led down the road toward Berry, but there had been a considerable amount of traffic over the road since his passing a day ago. Initially, he rode down the right shoulder of the road. Most of the tracks were visible though heavily dusted by the passing motor vehicles.

When the road crossed to the west bank of the creek it shared the valley with, Altaha moved over to the outside bank of the barrow ditch. Conor now could pick up his pace and within a quarter mile things got much better when Altaha abandoned the road altogether and turned south between two of the foothills. On the other side, it opened into a valley about a half mile wide that ran west to east. The Indian turned west and the hoofprints broke into a gallop for a mile up the valley and continued at that pace up a ravine between the tallest two of the nearby foothills.

Four hundred feet above the valley floor, the ravine suddenly ended in a large flat shelf a half mile across in every direction. The peak to the northwest rose over a thousand feet above it. An extended arm of the mountain formed a ridge bordering the north side three hundred feet above the shelf. Two-thirds of the way up the arm, a gaping hole fortified with timbers looked out over the flatland below it. A sizable pile of rubble excavated from the mine covered the mountainside below it. Conor halted Belle abruptly. Even with his naked eye from over a quarter mile away, he could see the light-gray horse standing at the entrance to the mine.

# 12

Conor turned Belle around and slipped out of view below the lip of the shelf. He rode back to the northeast for nearly a half mile where the eastern end of the ridge descended toward the valley below. It was midafternoon but remained moderately cool at their elevation. Here he caught the crest of the arm and stayed just beyond the skyline on the partially shaded north face as they climbed westward above the entrance to the mineshaft. He tied Belle to the crumpled remains of a juniper tree on the otherwise nearly barren slope.

Running Dog watched in anticipation as Con checked his Colt automatic and the Model '94 Winchester he had carried since he was fourteen. He took a swig of water from his canteen and started to leave, then turned back and slipped his flashlight into the left hip pocket of his blue jeans. Peering over the crest, he was a hundred yards east and twenty feet above the mine. Running Dog scampered over the hill and immediately caught the horse's attention. Had there been any doubt, the rafter-H brand on his right shoulder confirmed the blue roan's identity. The horse nickered, cutting through the silence of the afternoon sun. The alarm was sounded to every napping creature within earshot.

Con ducked behind a boulder and held his rifle ready. He waited for any sign from the gelding watching him that Altaha was coming from the mine. After twenty minutes, the horse's eyes and ears never left him. Conor transferred the Winchester to his left hand and pulled his Colt from its holster, pulling back the hammer as he did so. He rose slowly from behind the boulder and worked his way toward the level top of the tailings pile, never taking his eyes off the roan in the process. As he approached, he noticed the rifle and bedroll still tied to the saddle and the full waterbags draped over the pommel. It made him no less wary of the rider.

Running Dog must have sensed the danger. He stayed close at Conor's side as they came nearer the horse and the tunnel bored into the mountainside. When just a few feet away, the horse took two steps toward them, as near as the reins tied to a mine timber allowed. When he did, two wide boards nailed crisscross over the opening came into view. The words painted in red across them clearly spelled out their warning; "DANGER" and "KEEP OUT." Their message had made no more sense to the Apache than if they were written in Egyptian hieroglyphics.

A clear pair of moccasin tracks in the dust marked where the wearer ducked beneath the boards and entered the shaft. The twisted print of Altaha's crippled right foot allowed no mistake as to who left them. The vertical timber to the right of the entrance blocked Conor's silhouette from view of anyone more than a few feet inside. He removed his hat and prudently peeked around the timber. With eyes unaccustomed to the darkness within, no shape or feature could be distinguished.

Con leaned his rifle against the timber, slid the flashlight from his pocket and shined it inside. The walls of the mine were so dark, the light barely penetrated the passage. The only perceivable features were the gray timbers and dusty floor. Altaha's footprints quickly disappeared into the darkness. Though the

Indian's rifle remained outside on his horse, he might have acquired another pistol since leaving St. Thomas. Even without a pistol, the two accounts he heard both indicated his deft ability when handling his sword-like knife. Leaving his rifle behind and his pistol drawn, Conor ducked beneath the warning and dashed inside. He plastered himself to the wall behind what cover the third set of timbers could offer him.

After a few minutes of listening to Running Dog's panting in the silence, he ventured to shine his light further into the abyss. Altaha's footprints continue another dozen yards and around a curve where the shaft angled to the right. Conor moved cautiously ahead, pausing every few steps to listen to the growing silence. After turning, the mineshaft began a slight descent. Suddenly, something moved in the darkness ahead of him. He tried unsuccessfully to catch it in the light, but Running Dog saw it and barked. The sound was deafening in the confined space as Running Dog blasted ahead. Conor repeatedly tried to identify whatever the squealing and hissing animal was that the dog was attempting to corner. A moment later it escaped Running Dog's pursuit and ran straight toward Con. He finally identified the sizable packrat as it rocketed past him with Running Dog hot on its tail.

Conor struggled to force himself into taking long deep breaths as he attempted to rein in the blood pulsing through his veins and slow his racing heartbeat.

"So much for stealth," he gasped in irony.

When his nerves finally recovered to the best of his ability, Con moved past the scene of Running Dog's melee and resumed following Altaha deeper into the mine. More than fifty yards from the entrance, the batteries in his flashlight began to fade. Because of it, the footprints were becoming more difficult to see. The print from the left foot was clear, but the next step from the right was smeared and drug forward. As Conor looked for the step of the left to follow, he nearly stepped off a ledge.

Shining his light around, he discovered a large hole, just

inches narrower than the width of the tunnel, thus about six feet across. The shaft ended less than a dozen feet past it. Shining the light toward the ceiling revealed a large wooden pulley hanging from the timbers. It looked to be long out of use and covered in heavy dust. From all appearances, Altaha had stepped off into the pit. He could hardly imagine him finding his way this deep into the mine without any light, but it looked as though he had carried nothing with him. He took a step with his left foot that had fallen on nothing solid and his right foot drug in the dirt as he tumbled into the pit. Conor could see nothing in its depths. He wondered how far down it went. Picking up a stone a few inches across, he tossed it in expecting to hear it hit bottom, to ring if hitting stone or thud if Altaha's body. It seemed an eternity had passed when he heard the splash.

He repeated the process. This time he tried to count the seconds it took for the stone to hit the water. About two, he thought, maybe a little less. He was unsure how many feet that might be, maybe a hundred.

Conor did not know George Altaha. He was a criminal. Yet he felt sorry that the tough little sharp-shooter should come to his end in such a ghastly way. He was nauseated as he found his way back toward sunlight. When he reached the mouth of the tunnel, Running Dog sat just inside the shade at the opening licking his chops. It drew his attention momentarily away from his recent discovery of the tragedy.

"You look pleased with yourself," Conor mused. "Good rat?"

He looked over the blue roan. At his best guess, the horse had probably been standing here since last evening. The waterbags were full so he probably had nothing to drink since around noon yesterday. By chance, an old washtub laid nearby. The bottom was rusted through on one side, but the opposite one looked pretty solid. He propped it at an angle and poured one waterbag into it. The horse sucked it down in a hurry.

"Okay, that'll hold you until I get back."

He picked up his rifle and headed up the hill to get Belle.

When he returned, the two horses exchanged pleasantries in their own native lingo. He gave the roan the other bag of water before leading him behind Belle down the hill. There was a road from the mine off the west side of the tailings pile and Conor followed it. The sun had nearly set and he hoped they weren't far from Kingman. He passed five other mines before he left the flat. Two of them were active, and he proceeded past two more soon after starting down from the mountain. Three miles below, the road he was on joined a more well-traveled thoroughfare headed south. It was nearly dark when he hit the hamlet of Berry, and the Atchison, Topeka, and Santa Fe Railroad. Berry consisted primarily of a couple of dozen houses secondary to a thriving shipping and supply point supporting the mining districts to the north. An electric light hung over the door of a large barn as he approached the community. Mules and Livery in two-foot-tall letters adorned the rough-cut board and batten siding illuminated by the dim light. The sliding door stood open below it with more brilliant light from within washing the street in front of the building.

A man appeared in the doorway as Conor brought Belle to a stop.

"You got room for two more?"

"Yessir, two bits each for water and hay. That includes unsaddled and brushed down. Ten cents more for grain."

"That'll do," Conor accepted as he climbed down. "I've got some oats for them myself," he added as he slipped the sack from under his bedroll. "Just a handful each," he told the man as he handed it to him. "Is there a hotel in town?"

"Mrs. Appleton's boarding house. Three doors down on the left," he glanced at his watch. "If you hurry, you can make it in time for supper. She's a good cook, too too."

Conor pulled the two rifles from their scabbards as Running Dog waited in anticipation.

"Mrs. Appleton won't allow your mutt inside."

Running Dog looked indignantly at the stable keeper as if understanding the derogatory moniker.

"He'll stay outside," Con replied as he gave the man a half dollar and walked down the street.

The well-lit two-story clapboard house stood a short distance back from the street. A small sign, barely visible in the dark, hung on the fence by the gate. ROOMS, it read. Conor climbed the steps to a well-furnished front porch with several chairs and a swing. Running Dog sat down beside him beneath the porch light while he spun the knob to ring the bell in the center of the door. It opened a few moments later to a thin stern-faced woman ten years his senior. Her gaze landed on the two rifles under his arm then moved to the dog at his feet. When it finally reached his unshaven face the expression on hers had not improved.

"Sheriff Conor Armenta, Clark County, Nevada," he introduced himself as he pulled the badge from his vest pocket. "I'm hoping you have a room available tonight."

The corners of her mouth lifted slightly. "Come on in, Sheriff." Running Dog came to his feet. "The dog stays outside."

"Nukwi Sari-chi," Conor spoke in a commanding voice.

Running Dog immediately sat back down into a posture akin to a soldier standing at attention.

"What was it that you said to him?" Mrs. Appleton asked.

"His name. It's the only two words I know in Paiute."

"What does it mean?"

"Running Dog."

She raised an eyebrow as she nodded. "Supper's on the table," Mrs. Appleton told him. "You can stand your rifles in the corner and wash up at the kitchen sink." She pointed the way.

When he returned to the dining room, Mrs. Appleton ladled a generous portion of beef stew into a bowl from the large tureen in the center of the table and handed it to him. Two thick slices of buttered bread already occupied a plate where she had seated him. As he began to eat, she introduced him around the table to her regular boarders; a woman about his own age and her teenage daughter, and a heavily mustachioed gentleman in his late sixties who wore a business suit.

The stew was delicious and after three days of meager meals, he ate it more quickly than good-manners would recommend. When Mrs. Appleton offered to refill his bowl, Conor did not refuse. It embarrassed him that the others sat awaiting dessert while he completed his second serving of the stew. When he was finished, the hostess brought custard pie for all and coffee for him and Mr. Mustache. Conor was the last to finish eating and Mrs. Appleton began clearing the table.

"Would your dog like the last of this stew?"

"I'm sure that he would, but it really isn't necessary."

"It's not a problem. I have an old pie tin I use to feed my chickens for a dish," she offered. "Besides, I made this from yesterday's leftover pot roast. I don't intend for my guests to eat the same thing three evenings in a row."

"Okay, but I'll take it out to him. He sometimes gets aggressive when around food and strangers at the same time."

She smiled as she left the room. Soon returning with a dented pie tin, Mrs. Appleton emptied the tureen into it. Running Dog's portion easily equaled the two bowls full of stew Conor had eaten. When he sat it down on the porch the dog quickly began devouring it. Mr. Mustache was standing at the far end of the porch enjoying a cigar. They entered into casual conversation. When Running Dog had concluded herding the tin around the porch trying to lick his way through its metallic surface, Con spoke again to the man.

"I'd like to take a bath and shave," he began. "I wonder if I could borrow a razor."

"Why, certainly, Sheriff. You'll find my shaving mug with soap and my safety razor in the medicine cabinet. There's a fresh pack of blades there, also. Help yourself."

**\* \* \***

WEDNESDAY, OCTOBER 29, 1930

Conor awoke to a glint of sunshine through the window curtain. The bed and room of the boarding house were clean and comfortable. After over a week in the saddle between his two excursions, the long, hot bath had soothed his aches and relaxed him. He felt clean, rested, and refreshed. From his upstairs window he could see the train station. A column of smoke slowly drifted away from a locomotive down the tracks as a crew wheeled carts of cargo from a boxcar across a ramp and into a warehouse parallel to them.

The aroma of sausage and biscuits filled the air when Con opened the door of his room.

"My, are you the same trail weary sheriff who rang my doorbell last evening?" Mrs. Appleton greeted from the bottom of the stairs.

"I certainly feel much better than I did then," Conor replied.

"Well, I have sausage and biscuits keeping warm in the oven and hot coffee on the stove," she offered as he descended the stairwell. "Would you like me to fry you some eggs to go with them?"

"What about your other guests?"

"They've already gone about their business for the day," she told him.

Conor was stunned. "What time is it?" he asked as he dug in his pocket for his watch.

"A few minutes past seven."

"Well then, yes. I suppose that I do have time for another good meal before I start my own day."

"Have a seat at the table and I'll bring your coffee."

After breakfast, Conor walked to the livery, saddled both horses, and slid the rifles back into their scabbards. He refilled his canteen and all three waterbags before climbing aboard Belle and leading the roan down the road. The sign said six miles to Kingman as he rode to the Mohave County Sheriff's Office. After tying the two horses to a tree in the park, he crossed the street and mounted the steps to the office. Running Dog laid down outside when Conor entered the door.

A woman in her early twenties sat behind a desk where he entered the office. "What can I do for you, sir?"

"Is Sheriff Blaine in?"

"May I ask who's calling?"

"Sheriff Conor Armenta, Clark County, Nevada," he told her as he pulled the badge from his vest pocket.

"You're the one chasing the murderer who's wanted by the FBI?"

"Yes, ma'am."

She crossed the room to a solid wooden door marked Private and knocked. Then she cracked it open and talked to someone inside.

"Sheriff?" she said as she turned. "Right this way."

A gray-haired man appeared in the doorway. He was tall, over six feet, and big, two-forty...maybe more. His grin was welcoming.

"How are you, Con?"

"Al," he acknowledged.

"C'mon in." He motioned with his hand. "Bring us some coffee, El."

He ushered Conor into the office and seated him in front of his desk. "You were a green recruit deputy the last time I saw you. You should stop in when you're down this a way."

"That was the one and only time I've been here until now," Con replied. "I don't have the opportunity to get outside of Clark County very often."

"I saw in the *Gazette* where you were appointed interim sheriff when Baker had his stroke. That must of worked out okay, huh?"

"Special election a few months later. I won."

"Good for you."

Elaine came in with two cups of coffee. She handed the first to Con. When Sheriff Albert Blaine accepted his, he moved behind the desk and took a seat. "Thank you, sweetheart," he told the young lady. "Close the door on your way out, would you?"

Con grinned as the old man flirted with the young girl.

"I see the look in your eye and the grin, Armenta. I know what you're thinking."

"Okay, what am I thinking?"

"You're thinking that she's awful young for an old buffalo like me. Right?"

"Well, pretty close."

"And you're right. She's way too young for me, but she should be. After all, she *is* my granddaughter."

Conor turned beet red. "Well, you got me, Al. Suckered me right in and I took the bait. You haven't lost your touch."

The old sheriff nearly blew coffee out his nose containing himself when Conor realized he had been hoodwinked. He took another sip of coffee. "Okay, I've had my fun at your expense. So, what's going on with this killer you're looking for? You must of got a tip of some kind or you wouldn't be sitting here."

"I did get a tip. Sunday morning. He bought a horse in Searchlight Saturday afternoon."

"And it took you 'til Wednesday to get here? You deserve the shellacking I just gave you."

"I've been on his trail since Sunday afternoon. His horse is standing in the shade across the street." Conor took a sip of his coffee while he let the information sink in and watched the older man's face as he processed it.

"So, where's the Indian? Dead?"

"Most likely. He walked off into a pit inside of an abandoned mine about ten or twelve miles from here. Probably Monday evening is my guess."

"The mine sits up on a steep sidehill facing south?"

"That's it."

"Heart of the Dragon," Blaine muttered as he stared blankly in Con's general direction.

"What?"

"The Dragon's Heart," he muttered before drifting back into the present. "Or the Heart of the Dragon, depending on who's telling the story. There must be over a thousand abandoned mines on that mountain. I know the names of a dozen or so, but I know more than just the name of that one."

"Okay, so what's to know?"

"Back in the late eighties this fellow from Pennsylvania showed up out here looking for gold. I was just a kid. Seventeen or eighteen. I don't remember, but this fellow had some history behind him. About thirty years old or so I guess, when he showed up. His name was Joseph Wren. Like the bird. He was a White man, but he said he was raised by a tribe of Indians out east." Blaine sipped his coffee. "Anyway, he'd left the tribe ten years before and tried to fit in with White folks. Along comes this pretty little White girl. A lot younger than him as I recall and her family was pretty rich. So anyway, he falls ass over tea-kettle in love with her and she with him, or so he told everybody. He wants to marry her, but she won't hear of it because he's as poor as dirt. She tells him that he needs to make something of himself before she'll marry him.

"As the story goes, he lights out to make his fortune out west, then he'll go back to Pennsylvania and marry this goddess. At first, he had a few dollars in his poke and tried to make it grow on a Mississippi riverboat. He lost all that he had. So, Wren hears about how somebody struck it rich in a gold mine out here. He hobos his way out here without so much as two nickels to rub together in his pocket. He works in mines for a few others around here until he makes enough money to strike out on his own."

"Did he get rich?" Conor asked.

"Well, he did so to speak, but then, like so many others of these damned miners, they either drink it all up or go insane trying to get richer. Old Joe, he did a little of both. In the early nineties, he hit a vein of gold-filled quartz the likes of what every sourdough this side of anywhere dreams of. He chased it back down into that shaft where it starts downhill in there and followed it all the way back in there to where the pit is. Then the vein turned straight down into the belly of that damned dragon. He dug and dug. Joe got down so far underground that he run out of air. He came to town and cashed in twenty thousand in dust and nuggets to buy this big steam powered bellows to pump air down into the shaft. That's a pretty hefty sack of dirt in anybody's book.

"Folks say he had a lot more than that at the time. Hid all over the mountain, or so the story goes. Wren stayed in town waiting for that air pump to show up. He had it built back east somewhere and shipped it out here on the rail. I guess he knew what he needed from working in coal mines back there in Pennsylvania. The whole time he waited he spent most of it in the saloons. I remember seeing him around town then. Always falling down drunk. I heard there were lots of times he'd spend a hundred dollars a night on whiskey and whores. When he finally got that air pump and got it going, he went right back to digging.

"He bought all kinds of special equipment for that mine. No one was ever inside it except him, but it had some sort of elevator that went up and down in that pit. He had a winch that would pull his ore cart from the top of the pit up to level ground in the horizontal part. Then he could push it on out to this tailing pile."

"But there's water in that pit somewhere down around a hundred feet," Conor interjected.

"Yep. That was the beginning of the end. Around ninety-six or seven Joe Wren was digging in the bottom of the pit. He told folks here and abouts that everything was fine. Then he swung his pick to break loose a big hunk of quartz and it shot water out. Not just a little water. Not hundreds of gallons or even thousands. He struck into some sort of underground river that shot millions of gallons of water into the mine. Like a giant cold water geyser. He somehow managed to stay on top of it as it puked him out, all the way up the shaft and out onto the tailings pile. The flow slowed down some, but ran a stream of water down the mountainside for the better part of an hour before it quit flowing.

"It was no secret. Everybody in the territory was talking about it. I'm surprised you didn't hear about it up in Las Vegas?" Blaine questioned in astonishment.

"I was only two at the time," Conor replied. "If I did hear about it, I wouldn't remember. Besides, my family was there, but Las Vegas didn't even exist until 1905."

"Oh." Al blushed. "Yeah, I forgot. Anyway, Wren bought a huge steam-powered water pump. Like the air pump, it was custom built back east somewheres. When it got here, it cost him three thousand dollars just to get it hauled up to the mine. The freighter had to have a custom wagon built that could haul it and thirty-eight mules to pull it. The teams closest to the wagon were six abreast. There's a picture of the freighter's rig over at the train station. When Wren got it up and running, he ran that pump for twenty-four hours straight, adding more sections of four-inch hose every time he got the water sucked down a bit. At the end of that time, he said the water was back to the lip of the pit. He and the man he had hired stoking the steam engine took a break. An hour later it was filled back up to the bend in the horizontal shaft.

"There wasn't enough firewood in the county to keep that pump running, so he bought coal from the railroad and had it hauled up to the mine. That single pump never got the water below about ten foot down into the pit. He had a second pump built. With both pumps running nonstop, they got the water down to about fifty feet below where it's at now. Joe Wren spent the next six years and every cent he had trying to get back down into that pit and digging for gold. After he run out of money, he still hung around here 'til 1906 trying to recruit investors. When that failed, he finally loaded up a pack mule with all of his worldly goods, saddled another, and rode out of here. Said he was heading down to some mountains he knew about in the southeast part of the territory. Down by Tombstone, I suspect. Nobody ever heard from him again. If he's still alive, he must be past eighty."

"So, what's happened since? There's no steam engines or pumps laying around up there."

"After he left, a few miners poked around up there for a while. An engineer surveyed the tailings pile and estimated from the volume and the size of the shaft that the pit must be at least five hundred feet deep. Maybe less if there's a room dug out down there before that.

"As far as the equipment goes, a fella went in there during the war and hauled it all out piece by piece to the railroad and sold it for scrap iron. He took ore carts and tracks, pumps, boilers, everything he could get his hands on that would come apart into small enough pieces to haul away.

"That was about the end of it until '24. Three teenage boys went up there. They got horsing around in there and one of them fell into the pit. It took us four days to get down in there and another four before the body ballooned out and came to the surface. Then two more to drag his corpse out. He was all bloated up and unrecognizable by then. If they're still there, I nailed some boards across the entrance after that. I painted, 'Danger – Keep Out,' on them."

"They're still there."

"So why do you suppose this renegade Indian went in there?" Sheriff Blaine queried as he scratched his chin.

"Well, first, he couldn't speak English, so I doubt he could have read your warning. But I don't think it would have stopped him even if he could have read it. Ever since he first got into this country it seemed like he was looking for landmarks. Especially after he got to the north end of these mountains. Then the last couple of miles, he broke that horse into a full gallop. Charged up that ravine to the east of there on a dead run. George Altaha knew exactly where he was going before he ever got to that mine. He even left his rifle, water, everything on his horse, outside."

"The only person that could have told him about that mine would have been Joseph Wren."

"Well, get this," Conor added to the puzzle. "This Altaha is a

Chiricahua Apache. He's Descended from Geronimo or some such thing, but most importantly, he grew up in the mountains of southeast Arizona, southwest New Mexico, and northern old Mexico."

"Right where Joe Wren was headed when he left here," Blaine reconfirmed to himself. "How old is this guy?"

"I think the FBI said around thirty."

"Just the right age for some eight-year-old kid to hang on every word around the campfire of some old prospector's yarns."

"Some eight-year-old kid who doesn't know a word of English?"

"Are you telling me that Joseph Wren's an Apache?"

"I'm not telling you anything about Joseph Wren," Conor countered. "I never heard of the man in my entire life...not until an hour ago."

# 13

SUNDAY, OCTOBER 13, 1918

Le Cateau, France

At two o'clock in the morning, Private Roscoe Taylor worked his way through the backstreets of Le Cateau toward the shelled-out skeleton of a cathedral near the center of town. The stone bell tower of the structure had by some quirk of fate survived multiple bombardments. According to his orders, a field head-quarters for the Kaiser's troops lay five to seven hundred yards beyond it. The tower's height and proximity made it the perfect position from which to stage his ambush. It also made it the most likely candidate for an enemy observation post.

When he peered around the corner of an empty building, the moonlit silhouette of the bell tower loomed ahead, the epicenter in a surrounding maze of ruins and rubble. Less than a dozen yards away from him, the idle barrel of a tripod mounted machinegun pointed toward the stars. It sat amid the chaotic landscape behind a low wall of sandbags. Closer observation revealed similar fortifications a hundred yards apart in either direction. The perimeter of their operation.

Leaning against the wall, he was close enough for the occasional whiff of a burning cigarette to penetrate the cool night air. Sporadic wisps of smoke appearing over the sandbags of the nearest installation indicated the source while intermittent voices quietly uttered unknown words in German. They were not minding their post very well.

Roscoe studied the terrain, mapping in his mind a route around his would-be assailants and stalked past them. After eluding the machine gunners, he had no further encounters with the enemy en route to the cathedral. Sliding into what had been the nave of the building, he looked toward the remnants of the sanctuary and altar. Splintered fragments of the roof lay heaped atop crushed remains of pews. Partial walls reached half the distance they once had toward the open sky above.

"God's house," he whispered to himself.

The words sent a shiver up his spine. His first experience in such a place. It left him feeling uneasy. Especially when his thoughts returned to what he came here to do. His gaze turned to the tower, in clear view through what once was the roof. He made his way to the doorway at its base. It was dark inside. Only scant slivers of light from the half-moon outside penetrated through narrow slits of window openings halfway to the top. A very narrow stairway with no railing clung to the outer walls as it climbed steeply to the windows then disappeared into darkness above.

Roscoe hung the heavy rifle over his left shoulder by the sling, then unholstered his pistol. The click from the Colt automatic nearly echoed within the confined walls of the belltower when he pulled back the hammer. Carefully placing his foot on the first wooden step, he gradually increased his bodyweight onto it, finally lifting the lower foot to repeat the process. Alternating each step over and over eighty times, he finally reached the slits that once held windows. There, the stairs ended and a ladder began. Dropping the pistol back into its holster, he continued his climb on up. What began with minimal visibility became completely blackness near the top.

Anticipating one or more soldiers above, he proceeded warily in total darkness. Eventually, when he reached for the next rung, his hand touched the bottom of a floor. More correctly, the bottom of a trapdoor. If no one was on top of it, he thought it should open fairly easily. Not unlike the stairs below, he slowly increased pressure against it until it moved. As he raised it a few inches, a dim light appeared through the crack. He could see a German soldier wrapped in his long gray wool coat, propped against the outer wall...apparently alone...and asleep, his long Mauser rifle leaning against the wall beside him.

Hoping not to wake him, Roscoe again drew his pistol as he slowly opened the door with his left hand. To his surprise, the hinges did not squeal, and he quietly rested the hatch against the wall. Easing his way closer, the soldier woke just as Taylor's hand reached the Mauser. He could see the soldier's mouth open in slow motion as instinct rushed to take control over his mind and body. The man drew a long breath, about to scream...when the steel butt-plate of the Mauser crashed against his left cheekbone. Had it not been for the intensity of the moment, Roscoe would have become ill at the sound of the cheekbone breaking...but he didn't. He grabbed the unconscious man by the front of his coat and threw him headfirst through the open trapdoor. There was a loud crash from within the tower when the body took out a section of the stairway somewhere near the end of the ninety-foot drop.

Not knowing how he might be able to retreat past the damaged stairway, Roscoe was more concerned that the crash might have been heard outside of the belltower. He knelt behind the lower half of the belfry wall catching his breath while attempting to calm his shaking hands and racing pulse.

The belfry itself was eight or ten feet square. Each of the four walls had large Moorish openings that had previously been enclosed with louvers. The bells and mechanisms were also gone. He discovered his pistol in the middle of the floor. He must have dropped it in the melee but could not recall it. The Mauser lay not far from it. He decided to drop the rifle through the trapdoor and close it. If someone were coming to relieve the soldier and found his body and rifle at the bottom of the tower with the door closed above, he might think the soldier fell while exiting the tower earlier for some unknown reason. If the stairway was as heavily damaged as suspected, he doubted anyone would attempt scaling it without strong reason.

As dawn began to break, Roscoe scanned the area surrounding all four sides of the cathedral. He discovered no movement. Turning his attention to the east where the field office should be, he studied the area through the telescopic sight on his rifle. At the far edge of the rubble field stood a row of less-damaged structures. Early morning activity began showing around one particular building in the predawn light. It may have been a bank or some sort of government building in an earlier life. Now several men in German uniforms scurried up and down the wide stone steps in front of the building. Thus far he had seen only one of them in an officer's uniform.

As usual for this type of operation, his orders were vague. Ten or more commissioned officers should occupy the field office. Neutralize as many officers as possible. If time allows, continue with enlisted personnel. When completed, retreat by the most expedient method available.

The morning sky began to brighten over the horizon beyond the field office. In a matter of minutes, he would be staring directly into the blazing fireball of sunrise. He glanced into the sky above him. The eastern stars had faded into the grayness of dawn. A bank of black clouds slowly approached from the west but would not arrive in time to assist in his mission. He checked to ensure there was a round in the chamber of his .45 automatic, then eased the hammer forward and returned the pistol to its holster. He felt his right front shirt pocket; two extra clips of ammunition for emergencies.

Checking his Enfield, it carried six rounds in the magazine and one in the chamber. Each of his coat pockets held three five-round stripper clips of .30-06 Springfield cartridges for the rifle. He took two of them from the left pocket and placed them by his right knee for quick access. The bottom of the window opening before him was about four feet above the floor. Just right for the lanky cowboy to kneel comfortably behind while using it to support the heavy rifle atop it to steady his aim.

In firing position, he again scanned the area in front of the field office before raising his head and calculating the range with his naked eye. He estimated the distance at seven hundred yards and a hundred feet below his own position in the tower. Unscrewing the cap from the elevation setting on the optics of the scope, he turned it to his mark for five hundred yards. Knowing that the downward angle of trajectory would make the bullet strike higher than if shooting at a target level with his own elevation, he compensated for the change. He doubted his estimate would be exact, but with no opportunity to test it, it should be close. He could adjust his aim accordingly after firing his first shot. As he screwed the cap back over the mechanism, a long sedan stopped at the foot of the steps. He may not have long to wait.

When the car stopped, an officer stepped out of the front passenger seat and opened the rear door. He could not recognize the second man's rank at the distance, but it was clearly superior to that of the first man. Roscoe clicked his rifle off the *safe* position and touched the trigger guard with his index finger. He felt the rush welling up again in his chest and warming his face. Two more officers exited the other side of the car and it pulled away. The junior officer stepped behind his superior who stood a head shorter than the younger man. The foursome all remained at the curb. Steam from their mouths in the cool air suggested they were discussing something.

He positioned the back of the senior officer's head in the crosshairs of the rifle. Roscoe's finger moved inside the trigger guard. He took a deep breath and let it halfway out, then gently squeezed the trigger. The junior officer's hat jumped into the air along with the top half of his head.

"One. Still too high," Taylor scolded himself.

The senior officer jerked before the sound of the first shot reached him. As he started to take a step forward, Roscoe realigned his crosshairs on the point directly between the man's shoulder blades. The round exited the comandante's nose.

"Two." He had established his range.

Just as the report from the first shot reached them, the two other officers moved to assist their comrades. The nearest received a bullet just behind his right armpit that exited near his left nipple.

"Three."

The fourth man turned to locate the source of the ambush just in time to catch his end in the center of his chest.

"Four."

Roscoe detected movement in the right upper quadrant of the scope. An officer looked out an upstairs window trying to comprehend the chaos on the steps outside. The bullet that struck him carried remnants with it of the Maltese cross that had adorned his throat as it split the tissue between his collarbones.

"Five."

The first enlisted man's foot landed on the fourth step down as the second man dashed out the door to receive a bullet in his right upper chest.

"Six."

The first enlisted man caught a bullet in his right shoulder blade as he rolled the senior officer onto his back.

"Seven," Roscoe counted as he slid the cartridges on the first stripper clip into the magazine.

Gliding the bolt forward to chamber the next round, he resumed his firing position. With nothing visible at the front of the field office, he scrutinized the rubble field between him and the building. A half-dozen men were clambering among the debris toward him less than three hundred yards away. Among them, an officer wielding a Luger pistol in his hand.

"And what do you 'spect to do with that pea-shooter at this distance?" he asked rhetorically.

Guessing where to take aim at the much closer and moving targets, he again took a deep breath and let it halfway out...then squeezed the trigger. The bullet hit the officer's right bicep, shattering the humerus, and nearly amputating the arm.

"You may live through it, but you're *neutralized* for sure. One."

The squad of infantry dissipated into the rubble. One rose and began a dash for better positioning. He never made it.

"Two."

Roscoe was so far from reestablishing range he simply resorted to aiming at the belt buckle and hoping to hit somewhere in the upper torso. To further complicate his situation, the rising sun now blazed into the optics of his telescopic sight. He missed his third shot completely and his fourth struck a man he wasn't aiming at. He reset the elevation on his scope for one hundred yards and again missed his fifth shot completely.

"Time to get the hell outta Dodge, Roscoe," he muttered to himself. "You done wore out your welcome here."

When he crossed to the far side of the belfry and stood to load the second stripper clip into his rifle, a barrage of machinegun fire ripped through the air. One or more of the guns he had slipped past in the wee hours of morning had come back to haunt him.

"Three hundred yards and a half-dozen machineguns aimed at me, George," he spoke to the spirit of his wounded former partner. "Damned good time to get yourself shot up and leave me out here to figger this shit out on my own. What the hell would you do?"

Roscoe wondered if God had trapped him here...punishing him for desecrating his house. He thought George Altaha must have spoken to him through some weird Apache vision. He suddenly had an idea. The Germans had him trapped between east and west. There were more Germans to the north too. He would head south.

After reloading his rifle, he tried to make himself invisible as he studied the western perimeter. He needed to buy some time and to do that, he had to spook those boys manning the machine-guns. Their sandbag fortifications mostly protected those guns from the west. The east side of several of them were wide open. As he moved his sights from one to the next, at about the center of the line, one of the guns was aimed directly at him and appeared ready to shoot. Forgetting he had lost all track of range; Roscoe took aim and moved his index finger inside the trigger guard. He took a deep breath and let it halfway out, then squeezed the trigger. The soldier wilted over the gun in front of him.

"One."

Two positions to the left of his first target, he spotted a similar situation and took aim.

"Two," he counted as the gunner's assistant moved to take over the gun.

"Three."

A shot suddenly rang out from below him and ricocheted off the stone tower. Looking nearly straight down through the missing roof of the cathedral, two soldiers had entered the nave. He never aimed, just pointed. A soldier fell. He fired at the second man and missed as he ducked back out of the cathedral.

Digging a third stripper clip from his pocket, he slid the cartridges into his rifle's magazine. The world moved in slow motion around him as his mind raced through his exit strategy. Most urgently, he had to escape the tower before more soldiers arrived in the nave and blocked his only exit. Slinging the rifle over his shoulder, Roscoe drew his pistol, took a deep breath, and flung open the trapdoor in the floor. Sunlight through the open doorway below shined on the corpse of the soldier who had manned the belfry just a short time ago. Nothing moved. Returning the .45 to its holster, he climbed down the first few rungs of the ladder where he paused just long enough to pull the hatch closed behind him. It completely darkened the inside of the tower above the windows forty feet below. Now he would not be seen from below until he reached the windows.

Holding on to the iron rails of the ladder, he mostly slid down it to the small landing at the top of the stairway. Alighting with a jolt, he began his descent down the steep stairway. The wooden treads of the steps were barely over six inches deep and only allowed room for about two-thirds of the length of his boots. He slipped several times as he jostled his way down them, thankful for the iron handrail embedded in the stone wall to hold onto. Twenty feet from the bottom, a sizable section of the stairway was missing where the falling soldier had struck it. It resumed again ten feet below.

At that instant, two German soldiers burst through the open doorway. Seeing their dead comrade on the floor startled them for an instant. Just long enough for Roscoe to draw his pistol and unload five shots from the automatic into them. Quickly surveying the situation, he opted to jump down the ten feet to the lower section of stairway rather than the twenty feet to the heap of dead bodies on the floor. Re-holstering the Colt, he took the Enfield from his shoulder. Gripping it firmly in both hands, he made the leap.

He landed where he planned to, but failed to catch his balance on the short narrow treads. Losing the grip on his rifle, he tumbled to the bottom of the stairs. The rifle landed nearby. Regaining his feet, he made a brief assessment of its condition. The barrel was clear and the action seemed sound. He had no idea how accurate the scope might be. Stuffing his beret into his jacket pocket, he commandeered a helmet and long, wool coat from his victims. He shrugged into the bulky coat over his own. It was heavy and cumbersome, but he didn't plan on using it for very long. The helmet also felt heavy and odd on his head, but hopefully the outfit would be sufficient to disguise his identity from a few yards away.

Moving to the side of the door, he glanced around the interior of the cathedral. He saw no one. A section of the exterior wall had been blown out thirty feet from the doorway. The breach was conveniently located in the south wall, the direction of his planned escape. Carrying his rifle in a ready posture, he dashed toward the opening and plastered himself against the wall a few feet from the gap. Inching ahead, he looked around the edge of it studying possible routes through the network of rubble. He made his way in short sprints in a general southerly direction.

Once he was away from the cathedral and the majority of the rubble, the effects of adrenaline began to subside. The German troops were in turmoil following his attack. They trotted hither and yon in squads of six or eight as superiors barked orders at them. Roscoe only understood a few words of German and had no idea what they were yelling. He hoped to be gaining enough distance from the center of activity to appear less conspicuous and began moving less urgently. He made his way south carrying the rifle slung on his shoulder down streets that were mostly cleared of debris.

He occasionally made detours to evade squads of soldiers when they came within a block or so, but otherwise maintained a fairly direct course. In a half hour, he reached the outskirts of town and hadn't encountered any soldiers in more than the last half mile. As he walked past a white barn alongside the road, the door slid open and a German officer with a riding crop in his hand suddenly emerged. Roscoe could not help looking at him, then quickly turned away.

"Hören Sie dort auf, privat!" he commanded.

Roscoe only recognized the word "private," and slipped his right hand through the slot by the coat pocket to access inside. He slid his pistol from its holster and continued walking past. He had lost track of how many shots he fired at the two soldiers in the tower. He didn't have time to figure it out.

"Anhalten!"

He understood the "halt" in the middle of that word. He stopped but did not turn toward the man. Right then, a soldier led a beautifully muscled light-gray horse by its halter from the barn. If this officer had been out here riding his horse, he was obviously unaware of what had gone on earlier at his head-quarters.

"Was ist das für ein Gewehr? Wo hast du es her?"

Roscoe turned to look at the angry officer. He had no idea what he had said, but the insignia on his shoulder boards were that of a colonel. When he reached for Roscoe's rifle, Taylor fired through the coat hitting him squarely in the groin. The colonel's eyes widened, and he dropped the crop, then looked down and reached with both hands to grab his wound. As his eyes glazed over, he dropped to his knees and fell over onto his side. His eyes stared at nothing and he did not move.

The magnificent horse shied at the sound of the gunshot and jerked free from the soldier's grasp, bolting back into the barn. Roscoe wriggled the pistol through the access hole in the coat. The slide was closed, indicating there was another fresh round in the chamber.

"Was hast du getan?" the young man yelled in disbelief.

Roscoe raised the Colt and shot him dead-center in the chest. The slide locked open.

Entering the barn, he found the horse standing in the back of an open stall. He took the rifle from his shoulder and leaned it against the railing, then shed the coat and helmet. Ejecting the clip from his pistol, he replaced it with a fresh one from his shirt pocket and released the slide to shove a new cartridge into the chamber. He dropped it back into the holster. As he tugged his beret back onto his head, the sound of an approaching vehicle came from the town. He slung the rifle diagonally across his chest and entered the stall. He had stolen many horses in his earlier career, but never in as dire conditions as stood before him now.

He spoke softly as he approached the wide-eyed animal. "We ain't got time for no messin' around, pardner. I wish it was easier."

He grabbed a fistful of mane and slung his leg over the horse's bare back. Before the animal could realize what was happening, Roscoe buried both heels into his flanks. He had a death-grip with both hands on the horse's mane and was stretched out across his neck as they bolted through the open doorway of the barn. They were passing between the two bodies outside the door when Roscoe heard the first shot.

By the time they jumped the fence on the far side of the road it sounded like a shooting gallery behind them. He laid low across the horse's neck Indian style as they raced across the open hayfield. He thought to himself that George would be proud to see him riding like the wind without bit or saddle. He wished for a moment he had spurs to urge the animal on, then realized he was atop the fastest piece of horseflesh he ever had the opportunity to ride. The shooting had ceased behind them. He rose slightly to look back. They were a half mile away from the barn.

"Yeeee Haw!" he yelled at the top of his lungs.

* * *

TUESDAY, OCTOBER 8, 1930

Roscoe "Howling Moon" Taylor unloaded two fat steers from the back of his truck into a small corral. He'd constructed it from brush woven and wired together in the wash behind his shack east of Guelph.

The steers were stolen from a ranch he once worked for south of Fredonia, Arizona. After the war, he spent a few years roaming between several ranches in northwest Arizona, southern Utah, and Nevada. He worked for a few months at a time, then loafed and drank until the money ran out and forced him back into finding employment again. In the process, he always stayed long enough to learn how they operated and where cattle were apt to be found without being watched too closely.

Guelph was an unassuming community north of the Moapa Indian Reservation. When he discovered it, he squatted in the abandoned shack that became his home. When no one ran him out, he decided to stay. He put the brush corral together for his horse and replaced the leathers in the pump over the water well. He let the black hair he inherited from his half-Mexican mother grow long and braided it into a ponytail that trailed down his back. When money from his last job had nearly run out, he traded his horse and twenty dollars for an old truck. It looked worn out but ran remarkably well.

With lumber salvaged from a tumbling shed and henhouse he constructed stock racks and a ramp-tailgate on the back of the truck. The evening of the first full moon afterward, he drove the truck with one headlight to a ranch along the Virgin River between Bunkerville and St. Thomas where he once worked. There was a holding pen in the corner of a pasture that was far away from the ranch yard. As he hoped, he could see in the moonlight several plump steers were bedded down near the pen. He opened the gate to the pen, then roused the nearest from his sleep and herded him on foot into it. Backing the truck up to the opening, he set the gate at an angle against it, forming a chute, then herded the steer up the ramp and into the truck. In less than an hour, he was driving down the road toward Moapa.

Roscoe could hardly believe his good fortune. He sold the meat at very low prices or traded it to families on the reservation. Soon he was repeating the process at a variety of his former employers' ranches nearly every full moon. He traded cowhides with the local Paiute women in exchange for simple homemade clothing like their husbands wore. Within a short time, he blended quite well into the neighborhood. Rumors began growing that his midnight absences were a ritual where he went to sacred locations and howled at the full moon in some sort of mystical ritual. Many believed he was an Indian belonging to some unnamed tribe in Texas. No one seemed to know his name, but everyone was calling him Howling Moon.

Within a year, his clientele grew to a point requiring installation of a telephone to receive orders from customers in more distant towns.

On a visit to Meriwether's trading post he overheard two White women who were looking at moccasins. They were discussing how some Indian in moccasins was steeling cattle by herding them on foot into the back of a truck. The conversation scared the wits from him and he quickly departed there.

The enlightenment troubled Roscoe for several days. He seriously considered quitting his beef business and leaving the country. As he sipped a glass of whiskey one evening, his thoughts drifted to his first foray into the cattle rustling business. That too, began with a glass of whiskey...several glasses of whiskey actually, a subzero night in Wyoming and a card shark named Yates. His mind wandered to the fourteen-year-old girl everyone called Sis who had a crush on him there and her older brother, Eddy. They had been ice-skating earlier that day...for fun. At forty degrees below zero. He thought they were crazy. They had those skates that they strapped onto the bottoms of their shoes.

Those skates prompted him to make his "cow-shoes." He cut the hooves from one of his victims and mounted them to the bottom of boards that he could strap to the bottoms of his boots. It took him awhile to learn how to walk with them in a way to leave tracks that realistically mimic those of a steer, but he mastered it. He also improved his methods and locations for loading his booty. Now he loaded one or two steers at a time at greater distances from the rest of the herd. Over time he perfected the operation and now, in his estimation, left no trace of human evidence behind him. He considered himself the only true *master* of cattle rustling alive.

He never cut up the cattle he stole, but he would slaughter, skin and quarter these latest two steers on Thursday and deliver them to his client's butcher shop in Beaver, Utah that night. With that in mind, he closed up the ramp-tailgate on his truck and drove it up the trail to his shack. When he crested the rim of the wash, a horse stood in the shade, tied to the rickety porch of his house. As he came closer, it was a small bay horse with a Mexican saddle. There was a rifle in a fringed buckskin sheath strapped to it. A gourd water-jug hung from the horn and two desert waterbags hung across behind the cantle like a pair if saddlebags. No one was in sight.

When he rolled to a stop, Roscoe took the worn, Army-issued Colt automatic from the glove box of the truck before he shut it off. The hammer made its distinctive click when he pulled it back. He held the pistol partially concealed behind his right thigh as he walked cautiously around the corner of the shack.

George Altaha sat on a broken-down chair on what was left of an equally bedraggled porch. He held a German Luger in his right hand that rested on the arm of the chair. Roscoe looked at the pistol, then at George's face.

"I wasn't sure it would be you," Altaha commented in the weird concoction of three languages the two men shared.

"The legendary Altaha," Roscoe replied in the same jargon. "You are known among the Paiutes. I wasn't sure the myth was you either, but now…"

"You have a telephone. I need to receive a call here in two weeks. Can I ask this favor of you?"

"Of course. It's been twelve years since that morning in France when you were shot. What has happened since then?"

"The doctor in France wanted to cut off my foot. I told him if he did, I would cut off his head. They sent me to England instead."

"And your foot?"

"They fixed it."

"Since then?"

"It's kind of like the orders we got in the Army. There is more that happens than what the orders say. The less you know, the better."

He stood and shook Roscoe's hand. He didn't let go. "I'll be back in two weeks."

When George's grip freed him, there were two shiny, new gold double eagles in his palm.

"You don't owe me anything," Roscoe told him.

"I owe you more than that. I owe you my life."

# 14

*WEDNESDAY, OCTOBER 29, 1930*

"Do you want the body?"

The question caught Armenta off guard. "What?"

"You want this Altaha fella's body?" Sheriff Blaine clarified, "We'll hafta charge Clark County for the recovery if you do. We spent a couple of grand dragging that kid outta there in '24. Of course, in that case, we were trying to respect the dead and get the corpse outa the shaft in one piece."

"I don't know. I mean...I don't know if anyone will need it. I'll have to let the powers that be in Las Vegas decide that."

Al Blaine stood and lifted the receiver from his modern style telephone. Laying it on his desk, he motioned for Conor to take his chair. "This might take you a while...and more than one call. Make yourself at home. If I'm not outside when you're finished, Elaine will know where to find me."

Conor began his inquiry with District Court Judge William Tucker, who directed him to Clark County District Attorney Donald D. Davis followed by the FBI office in Los Angeles. He held lengthy conversations with each of the three describing the abandoned Heart of the Dragon Mine and explaining how he believed George Altaha had drowned inside. All concluded that they were in no need of Altaha's body. The FBI agent he spoke to seemed the most interested in the information. He thus determined that he could now move George Altaha's file from active status to inactive.

After over an hour on the telephone, he needed to give his ear a rest. When he emerged to the outer office with cup in hand, Elaine pointed him toward the coffeepot.

"Right over there." She grinned.

Following a sip of the steaming coffee, he asked, "Would it be okay to make a couple more calls? I've been out of touch for several days and really need to check in."

"Gra—" She caught herself. "Sheriff Blaine said you were to have free run of the place." She winked and whispered even though they were the only two people in the office. "That means it's okay to call your fiancée." When Conor looked surprised, she added, "He told me when I asked him if you were single."

"Thank you." Con blushed.

"Don't take too long though, he's planning on buying you lunch at the Santa Fe."

"Santa Fe?"

"It's a diner across the street from the depot."

Conor nodded and closed the office door behind him. Elaine wondered how someone so shy around women ever had the courage to ask someone to marry him.

"Maybe *she* asked him," she questioned herself aloud while stifling a chuckle.

* * *

"Good morning, Hazel," Con replied when she answered the telephone.

"Where in the world are you?"

"Kingman."

"Kingman? I thought you were in Searchlight!"

"That seems like a lifetime ago," he answered as a vision of the past few days raced through his head. "I chased Altaha across two mountain ranges and finally ended up here."

"Where is he?"

"He's dead."

"You killed him?"

"Not exactly. He drowned in the bottom of a mineshaft north of here. I'll give you the complete report when I get home. How are things going there?"

"Oh my gosh. It's hectic. There must be a thousand strangers in town. Rumor has it they're getting ready to start work on the dam and these men started rolling into town looking for work. Most of them with families are camping in tents out east of town."

"I was just there Sunday," he commented incredulously. "They all showed up since then?"

"Well, there were a few last week, but yes. Most of them seem to have come to town since Monday."

"Well, we'll get a handle on all of this when I get back. I should be home by Friday."

"Don't you dare tell me to call, June," she scolded, remembering the two previous conversations she had with her boss. "I'll quit."

"No, no. I'll call her. How's Jesse doing?"

"Pretty well under the circumstances, I think. Neither him nor Whit had any idea how dangerous this Indian was when they were chasing him out through the brush."

"They did their jobs and did them well. It's what counted then and what counts now. No loose cannons."

"You should tell them that."

"I will." Conor thought about Hazel's sound advice and added, "As a matter of fact, have them both meet me in my office first thing Monday. Have Ben come in too. I'll see you then, if not before."

A moment later he was calling Bert Haygood. His wife answered the telephone.

"Is Bert there?"

"Yes, he is, but we're about to sit down for dinner. Is it important?"

"Yes, it is. This is Conor Armenta. It shouldn't take long."

"What is it, Sheriff?" Bert asked.

"I'm wondering if you could pick me and your horses up at the ferry tomorrow? We should be there around noon."

"You and the Indian?"

"No. Just me and the horses."

"I'll be there," he answered and hung up.

Conor sat the receiver down and rubbed his ear. One more call to make. He called the law office of Robert Westcott. June answered the telephone.

"Is this the prettiest girl in all of Las Vegas?" he asked when she answered the telephone.

"I have heard that before, but you know how those lawmen can lie. I was once told that one of those federal boys even called me a *dish*."

"I remember hearing the same thing, but I don't think he was lying…and I know that I'm not."

"Well, I have not heard from you for days now, so you must be very lonely or wanting something."

"As it happens, I am and I do. I want a date with that beautiful young girl who lives with you and if she would like to have a chaperone, her mother can come along too."

"When and where might this tryst be taking place?"

"Friday evening? In the restaurant at the Hotel Nevada? We've dined there before and as I recall, she seemed to enjoy the atmosphere. Shall I pick her up at six?"

"If she is timid, I believe I can convince her to accept. Now however, I want to know something."

"What might that be?"

"Where in heaven's name are you?"

"Kingman, Arizona."

"I have heard of it. I even have an idea of where to find it on a map, but isn't that a little bit out of your jurisdiction? Furthermore, the question *should* be, what are *you* doing there?"

"At the moment I'm at the sheriff's office."

"Were you arrested? How did you end up there?"

Conor gave June an abbreviated version of what had happened since he last spoke to her. "I'll fill in the details later, but for now I wanted to tell you that I'll be home tomorrow night, but I don't want that to be public knowledge quite yet."

"I can keep a secret, but I doubt I will be able to hide how excited I am in anticipation of seeing you."

"You can tell everyone that I should be back Friday, but I'd like to see you by ourselves first. What time will April be in bed?"

"On a school night? Eight o'clock."

"I'll be there at eight thirty."

"I'll be waiting. I love you."

"I've fought to keep you off my mind throughout this ordeal, but I've missed you, and I love you too."

"Tomorrow night then," June replied.

"Tomorrow night," he confirmed.

Conor rode Belle, leading the blue roan to Front Street. Not surprised to see a hitching rail in front of the Santa Fe Diner, he tied the horses there. Running Dog looked disappointed when he laid down in the shadow cast by the two of them. Upon entering, Con hung his hat on a peg at the front door. The inside smelled much like the Mesquite Café in Las Vegas, owned and operated by his parents for some twenty years. His younger sister went to work there as a teenager, she had been their only employee ever since. He looked around the room. Ham steak with corn and mashed potatoes was the lunch special scribbled on a chalkboard behind the counter. Sheriff Al Blaine sat in a booth near the back sipping coffee. He held up his cup in a mock toast when Conor looked his way.

"Everything on the menu is good," he said as Con sat down. "My treat."

A waitress set a cup of coffee and menu in front of him, almost before he took his seat.

"They're used to serving passengers from the trains," Blaine commented. "Always in a hurry."

"So, I see."

"How'd it go back home?"

"No one cares about the corpse. Not there or at the FBI in Los Angeles. The county commissioners are complaining that I've been wasting too much of their money gallivanting around the country. They're questioning why I'm trying so hard to catch the murderer, when the victim was a convicted murderer himself?"

"I didn't know that part. You hafta admit, it seems rather pointless."

"I was escorting the man to his execution at the time." Conor rose and retrieved his hat from its peg by the door. "It didn't feel pointless to me," he added as he returned across the room. He poked his finger through the bullet hole in the brim and continued, "This was his second shot."

"Ooh, yeah, that would make a difference." Blaine nodded. He had been somewhat condescending toward his younger peer since his arrival, but this latest evidence drew a new level of respect from the old veteran. They both ordered the special and conversation fell to small talk. After Conor finished his third cup of coffee, he rose and donned the disheveled Stetson.

"Thanks for lunch, Al, but I gotta get goin'."

"In a hurry?"

"I need to be at the Searchlight Ferry by noon tomorrow."

"That's fifty miles from here."

"Yeah, I know."

"Just west of here is McConnico," Blaine began. "That's where the rail spur to Chloride splits from the mainline. There's a dirt road runs northwest from there to the ferry. It's less traveled and a little rough for a car, but shorter and faster for you. There's a store and gas station where it intersects the road from Chloride over Union Pass to Fort Mohave. About five miles past the store, you'll come on Cottonwood Spring then Willow Spring about a half mile apart. That's just shy of halfway to the ferry. I can't think of any water past there until you reach the river," he concluded and reached for Conor's hand. "You're a good lawman, Con. I'm sorry for ever thinking any less."

"Thank you, Sheriff. That means a lot to me coming from you. Whenever you get up my way, I'll buy *your* lunch at a place we have there. It's every bit as good as this one."

* * *

At four-thirty that afternoon, Conor reached the store that Al Blaine told him about. Finding a bucket, he watered his dog and horses. His food supplies had completely dwindled, so he restocked himself with a can of beans and one of peaches. To complete his purchase, he added a bag of peanuts, a handful of beef jerky, and a Coca-Cola from the cooler outside. Sitting on a bench in the shade, he shared a piece of jerky with Running Dog. He followed up by shelling and eating peanuts, occasionally tossing one to the dog as he ate. When he emptied the bag and finished the Coca-Cola they resumed their journey.

The sun set shortly before they reached Cottonwood Spring. Conor unsaddled the horses and picketed them near the water, then rubbed them both down with dry grass in the last minutes of daylight. A three-quarter moon had risen early and sat a third of the way up in the sky as he rolled out his bed and readied himself for the evening. Sitting on his bedroll and leaning against Belle's saddle, he sat down to eat his can of beans. After cutting the can open with his jackknife, he realized he had no spoon. He peeled back the top. Tipping the can, he poured its contents over the jagged edge and into his mouth, one mouthful at a time. The process was messy but worked. When finished, he went to the spring to wash his face and refilled his canteen with its cool, fresh water.

Returning to his bed, he pulled off his boots and reclined against the saddle. The moon reached its apex as he stared up at the stars. By this time tomorrow evening he would be joining the love of his life, June Sommers, on her front porch swing. It seemed an eternity had passed, he mused, since the last time they had done so. Sleep overcame him.

\* \* \*

*THURSDAY, OCTOBER 30, 1930*

The first hints of morning light outlined the eastern horizon. In an hour the sun would begin showing itself over the Cerbat Mountains fifteen miles away. Conor ate his peaches, skewered on the tip of his jackknife in the darkness, and began packing up immediately afterward. At the break of dawn, he was already in the saddle and moving his entourage northward through the eastern foothills of the Black Mountains. Three hours later, their road angled slightly more westerly and soon joined with the road from Chloride to Searchlight.

The climb had been almost unnoticeable from the store through the foothills, but now they reached the summit and began the steep descent winding down from the rim of the Black Mountains. In another mile, Con could see Cottonwood Island and the Colorado River ten miles to the west and two thousand feet below them. Tatum's Riverside Ranch overlooked the river there. That was where the old ferry crossing had been, but now the road turns and continues north for a few miles to the new Searchlight Ferry.

The sun approached its peak when he rode up to the east landing for the ferry. On the far side of the river, Bert Haygood sat on the running board of his truck under the shade of a cottonwood tree. Conor looked at his pocket watch, a quarter past eleven. A half hour later, he and Bert closed the tailgate on the truck and drove down the road toward Searchlight.

In midafternoon, Conor stowed his gear and George Altaha's belongings into the back of his pickup truck. He brushed down both horses while Bert carried Belle's saddle to the tack-room in the barn and tossed hay into the manger for them.

"What do you want me to do with this guy?" Bert asked, rubbing the roan's neck while Con brushed him.

"I'll pick him up in a few days or send someone for him. He's community property right now. The county will most likely auction him off in a few weeks. Let me know what's owed for renting Belle, both trips to the ferry and boarding...what's his name anyway?"

"Smokey. He was mostly black with just a touch of gray on his rump and shoulders when he was born. Looked like new blue steel. He didn't really roan out 'til he was two."

"He's a little thin but seems to be a pretty good horse."

"Belle's his dam, so he should fill out pretty good. He's been a little slow to mature, and I just gelded him last year," Bert mused. "He might grow another inch or two yet."

"If you want to buy him back, I'll let you know when the auction comes up."

"Nah. I can pick up colts around here as I need 'em, He's the age for sellin', not buyin'."

"Okay. As I started to say before, put together a bill for what's owed and I'll get you paid. The county's usually pretty quick about it."

Bert nodded his satisfaction with the terms.

Con tossed the brush into the wooden box in the corner where he found it. He patted Belle on her rump as he came around her, both as a sign of his appreciation and to let her know he was there.

"And she did her job, well. I worked her into a smooth-gaited lope on the second day and she became comfortable with it. With her stride, Smokey here had to break into a gallop to keep up yesterday."

"Well, I'll be," Bert commented in surprise.

"Who says you can't teach an old dog new tricks?" Conor beamed. "Pick up the reins, stand up a little in your stirrups, and lean forward a bit. She'll go right into it from either a walk or trot."

He had shared with Bert the key points of the last five days during their drive from the ferry. Now he paused for a moment looking out the large doorway over the sunbaked ranch yard from the darkness of the barn. Bert strolled up to join him.

"I want to thank you, Bert. These last few days have been a bit of a journey...and a successful one in the end. They might not have been, if not for your help. Thank you." He reached out and shook Bert's hand.

"It's been my privilege and you're welcome," Bert accepted with an almost uncomfortable grip. "I'm glad I was able to help you out."

After the two-hour drive to Las Vegas, Conor rolled into the county's maintenance yard. All of the regular personnel had gone home for the day. He pulled up to the gas pump and filled his sheriff's pickup. He needed to take a bath and shave before meeting June at eight thirty, which still left him a couple of hours to spare. Firing up the truck he rolled out of town heading west just as the sun dropped behind the red sandstone bluffs.

He came to a stop in the yard of the sheep ranch he grew up on just as dusk was turning to dark. His younger brother, Patrick, resumed the family ranching operation here shortly after graduating high school. The dim light of a kerosene lamp appeared from behind him when he opened the front door.

At that moment his two sheepdogs and Running Dog discovered each other. The two host dogs were warily sniffing the visitor until he took the opportunity to emit a low and menacing growl. That sparked a flurry of barking and growling from all three.

"*Nukwi Sari-chi,*" Conor yelled.

Running Dog froze and looked at his master. Con pointed to the open door of his pickup. He read the sign language and jumped inside.

"What was that and what did you say to him?"

"That was Running Dog, my new deputy. And *Nukwi Sari-chi*? That's his Paiute name."

"Which means?"

"Running Dog."

"So, what's the sheriff doing sneaking around out here in the middle of the night?" he asked sarcastically as he stepped out onto the porch.

"Looking for moonshiners who have electric lights but burn candles and kerosene instead."

"I'm no moonshiner, but electric lights are too bright. I only use them to read. Electricity is better for other things. The refrigerator…radio."

"How are you, Paddy?"

"I'm good. Where is June?" He mocked, "She's nicer than you."

"She's at home. I'll see her later tonight. But since you asked, I'm good too," Conor countered to his brother's cynicism.

Paddy chuckled. "Okay, I got it. But I don't think that's why you drove all the way out here."

"You're right. I want to borrow your truck Saturday."

"What day is it now?"

"Thursday."

"Okay…if you bring June with you."

"That's a great idea. I'll ask her."

"It needs gas."

Now Conor chuckled. "Okay, I got that too. Is there enough gas in it to get to town?"

"I think so. What do you need my truck for anyway?"

"I have to pick up a horse in Searchlight."

"And bring it here?"

"Yes. You'll be boarding him here until the county decides to sell him."

"So, I'm running a stable now?"

"If you don't want a few extra sawbucks coming your way, I can find someone else."

"Oh, no," Paddy backpedaled. "I'm always ready to help out our county however I can."

"Well, that's good because I need to bring another horse down from Acton too. Maybe next Saturday. The county will pay for the use of your truck to get both of them here and board until they are sold."

"Boy." Paddy shook his head teasingly. "I'm sure glad you just stopped by to visit. I was beginning to think you might be needing a favor or something." He grinned. "Is there anything else I could do for my big brother while you're here?"

"Is that lamb stew I'm smelling? I haven't had anything to eat but a can of peaches and two slabs of beef jerky since daylight this morning."

"And the wolf-beast?"

"I shared the second piece of jerky with him and he ate a jackrabbit over in the Black Mountains this morning. He's fine."

"You're kidding, right?" He looked at his brother in the moonlight. "You're not. C'mon in." He disappeared through the open door. Conor followed.

* * *

At seven thirty, Conor pulled into the yard behind his house. He left the old McClellan saddle in Paddy's barn and brought everything from the back of his truck into the house. He shaved and took a hot bath. Wishing to soak longer in the tub soon lost out to seeing June. With a splash of shaving lotion, a fresh shirt, and clean blue jeans he headed for the door. Leaving his decrepit Stetson hanging on the back of a kitchen chair, he rolled his gun belt around the holstered Colt 1911 and stuffed it under the seat of his Chevrolet coupe. When he opened the door, Running Dog jumped in without invitation.

"I don't have time to start tonight," he told the dog, "but we're going to be teaching you a few new rules and some manners."

June sat in the swing on her darkened front porch. When Conor turned off the headlights and engine, she moved to the top of the steps and waited. The dim radiance from lights in the living room showed through the sheer curtains on the windows. She wore a light-colored dress and a crocheted shawl over her shoulders to ward off the chill of the evening air. She doubted she would need it much longer. She already felt a warm glow slowly rising up her chest, then to her neck on its way to her face and ears.

Conor climbed the steps and took her in his arms without speaking a word. She raised her lips to his and he accepted them hungrily. Her nostrils flared as her lungs surged to fill with air and her heart felt as if it would burst hammering in her chest against his. They both sucked in the cool air when their lips parted.

"I've missed you," Conor managed to utter through reasonably controlled breathing.

"Me too," June gasped between lungsful of carefully metered air.

Minutes ticked past as they stood there holding each other in silence. Time restored their breathing. June eventually leaned back slightly to look at Conor's face in the dim light.

She finally broke the silence. "I could stand here in your arms forever, Conor. Having you here would be enough to sustain me." She stifled a giggle, but not before it began to slip out.

"What's funny?"

"You have been chasing an outlaw nearly continuously for two weeks nourishing yourself with whatever meager food you carried with you. April and I had fried chicken with corn and potatoes for supper tonight. I am telling you that I could live on your love alone after eating a full meal while you have been doing without. It seems a little selfish to me."

"Okay, I'll let you feel guilty momentarily, but I've eaten pretty well mostly. For instance, I went out to Paddy's before coming here tonight and ate a delicious bowl of lamb stew."

June looked at him skeptically. "And before that?"

"A can of peaches and two pieces of jerky."

"When?"

"Early this morning," he replied sheepishly, thankful the darkness disguised his inability to look her in the eye.

June was sure that beyond a few intermittent meals, the can of peaches was probably one of the tastier indulgences since his departure. She had no intention of chastising him at their first opportunity to share quality time together in many days, so ignored the thought.

"Speaking of peaches," she continued, "someone anonymously left a bagful of fresh peaches on my porch while I was at work Monday." She stared at his face but failed to read his expression in the darkness. "April made them into her special peach cobbler. Would you care for some desert?"

"I would love some."

"Wait right here," she told him as she released from the embrace. It was only then that she noticed Running Dog sitting on the porch beside them. Without comment, she vanished inside only to halt abruptly to catch the screen door before it slammed noisily against the frame.

Conor eased himself onto the porch swing and unconsciously began to slowly rock it forward and back. Running Dog laid down by the steps. The slightest hint of a squeak drifted down the chains that suspended the swing as they pivoted from the eyebolts attaching it to the ceiling above. He stared blankly into the darkness with thoughts of the wonderful woman dishing cobbler into a bowl inside filling every crevice of his mind. The sound of her footsteps returning to the porch tore him from the trance. She tossed a drumstick of cold fried chicken to the dog and held a brimming bowl out before Con.

"You're not having any?"

"Oh, no. I have already partaken substantially earlier." June did not share that she had held back this serving for him when she and April had eaten their shares earlier.

Conor ate slowly savoring each bite. "It's delicious. Just the way I remember it from a few months ago."

"You will need to pass the compliment on to the cook when you see her tomorrow."

"I will."

June sat quietly beside him as he ate. She studied his profile, this man of few words who held his thoughts and feelings inside mostly, but occasionally released them in profound depths of character. She recalled as she watched him eat the last time they had peach cobbler. It was only a few days after she and Conor had one of *those* conversations. A deep and personal conversation. She had wanted to know his feelings about intercourse before marriage.

The discussion arose following a dinner with another couple. The woman made it clear to her in private that they were sharing that intimate experience. On the drive home, June approached the subject. Conor tried to avoid the question, but she had forced him to confront it…as she would now.

"Do you remember the last time we had peach cobbler?" she asked cautiously.

"I do. April called me at home. She was terribly excited that she had made fresh peach cobbler and invited me to have some. It was very good. Just like this."

"Yes, it was," she replied with what Conor called the smile in her voice. The smile disappeared quickly and her voice quivered as she continued. "Do you remember the conversation we had on our way home from the Campbells a few nights earlier?"

There was a long pause. The silence was nearly unbearable. She heard the brakes squeak from a car several blocks away. The sound of Conor setting the spoon down in the bottom of the empty bowl after his last bite of cobbler. She could hear his soft breathing, but then the sound of her own heartbeat rose above all else. Again…she was forcing him into that same intimate conversation that he did not want to have.

"Yes, I remember," he finally replied so softly she barely heard it.

"Do you…do you remember what I offered to you that night and what you answered?"

"Yes."

"The offer is still there, Conor…if you want it?" Her whisper was nearly inaudible except for the crackle in her voice as she spoke.

"My answer is still the same," he replied in nearly a normal tone.

"Oh, Conor. At times like tonight…when you got here. My emotions nearly consume me. I love you so much. I want to please you. How will I be able to control this until the wedding?"

"You have the advantage, June. You have experienced the joy, the elation that I have only heard about." He paused to choose his words carefully. "I, too, want to please you…with a marriage that is pure between us. I love you more than anything else on earth. I can wait."

"If you can wait, so can I, but I will need your help to control it."

# 15

Expecting the Mesquite Café to be nearly empty at that hour, instead he met a throng of men appearing to be on their way to farm or perhaps construction work. At six-thirty in the morning, Conor Armenta hung his Stetson on a hook by the door. A wave from Judge William Tucker seated at Con's usual corner table drew his attention.

"Coffee, big brother?" Olivia asked in passing while he took the vacant chair across the table from the judge.

"Sure."

"Good morning, Con." Tucker met him with an open hand. "When I heard you were back in town, I hoped to catch you before you get wrapped up in all the hoorah going on around here."

"Good morning, Your Honor." Conor tried to camouflage what he was certain was a dumb look on his face. "How did you hear I was in town?"

"Oh, I have my sources. And call me Bill outside of the court-room." When the puzzled look on Armenta's face remained,

Tucker clarified, "My wife saw you gassing up your pickup truck when she drove past the county shop last evening."

Con nodded as Olivia sat a steaming cup of coffee in front of him and refilled the judge's cup. "Ham and eggs on special with biscuits and gravy."

"Suits me."

"Make that two," Tucker added as he handed her his menu.

"So, what's 'all the hoorah' you're talking about?" Conor asked as he took a sip of scalding coffee.

"Look around," he told him, motioning with a swing of his arm across the room.

Surveying the room, there was scarcely an empty seat in the crowded café. "Where'd they all come from?"

"Everywhere. Like somebody opened a gate and two thousand lost sheep flooded into town."

"Hazel told me something about it Wednesday on the telephone."

"I talked to her not long after you did. The commissioners authorized hiring four additional deputies. I hope you don't mind, but I got it in Wednesday's edition of the *Evening Review.* They got over a hundred applicants yesterday."

"From where?"

Tucker again motioned to the packed café without answering.

"When will I have time to go through a hundred applications?" Conor asked rhetorically.

"I don't mean to be stepping on your toes, Sheriff, but I took the liberty to have my wife join Hazel and your night dispatcher, Dottie, is it? They narrowed it down to ten last evening. That's where my wife was coming from when she saw you at the shop. When I heard how many applications they were getting, I didn't know quite what to think. But all of these men came here hoping for work and there aren't enough jobs going out at the dam yet to hire a tenth of them."

Conor took a sip of coffee. "This isn't quite what I was expecting to come home to. I've had five murders to deal with in the last six months. I've been in the saddle for most of the past two weeks and I have a dead murderer in the bottom of a mineshaft who twice came within inches of killing me…and no one cares less about any of it."

"Oh, they care," Judge Tucker reassured him. "They're just concerned about priorities. With this sudden influx of folks, mostly men in desperation, it's got the majority of our citizenry a little bit nervous."

"Me included."

"Marge says you've got some really good candidates for additional deputies."

"Marge?"

"My wife. She said they had a really tough time narrowing it down to just ten."

"I'm sure Hazel will fill me in with details."

"She's good at her job," Tucker commented as Olivia brought their breakfast. "So's the night girl. You've got a good crew over there, Con. Your department's about to double in size. Build it around that core and you should be fine. You're authorized to promote one of them to undersheriff, a sergeant, your second in command. I assume you'll select Jesse Slater. There'll be an increase in pay along with the title."

Conor swallowed a mouthful of food and washed it down with coffee. "He's my first choice."

"Talk to him about it before you send the paperwork through. The job comes with a lot of responsibility. He'll help you oversee no less than six other deputies and he'll be receiving a monthly salary, just like you. No more hourly wages, no more overtime and as you know, probably a lot more work. He may not be interested in that much of a commitment."

As they ate, their conversation continued with the upcoming construction of Hoover Dam. It mostly centered around the influx of workers affiliated with the project…and the criminal element that would inevitably accompany them. At a quarter to eight,

Conor rose and dug into his pocket to pay the bill. The discussion had left him much to consider.

"My treat," Judge Tucker insisted, extracting a money-clip from his pocket while Olivia cleared the table.

"It's on the house," she interrupted. "Papa's orders."

"Well, you be sure to thank him for us, dear." He slid a two-dollar bill from the clip and laid it as a tip on the table. "For you." He winked.

\* \* \*

Hazel Corbin looked up from her desk in surprise when Conor entered the door. "I didn't expect to see you here," she told him. "At least not this early." She studied Running Dog as he followed her boss into the office.

"I got in last night," he told her as he poured himself a cup of coffee. "I ran into Judge Tucker at breakfast. It sounds like you've been pretty busy since I talked to you."

She picked up a hefty stack of applications. "The good ones," she replied as she took a second group in her other hand. "The best ones. But I'll keep these others handy," she added, indicating the larger group, "just in case." She handed him the selected group again glancing at the dog without comment.

"You know how to get a hold of these fellas?"

"Yes. Most of them are camped out east of town."

"Family men?"

"All but one. It's all in their applications."

He nodded, "This comes first." He indicated the applications. "But I'll have my report on Altaha and the death of Dutch Wagner to you by Monday."

"The boys will all be here for your meeting first thing Monday morning."

"Good. Who's on today?"

"Jesse and Ben. Whit has the weekend."

Conor nodded and went into his office. He left the door open and sat down at his desk to study the applications. Running Dog followed. Selecting a spot beneath the desk near his master's feet, he laid down for a nap. He had just finished reading the fifth application and placed it facedown atop two others that formed the second of two piles on his otherwise fairly clear desk. Hearing the front door closing, he looked up to see Stanley Olsen, the reporter from the *Evening Review* approaching Hazel's desk. He whispered something inaudible causing her to turn and face Conor.

"Sheriff? Do you have time to talk to Stan?"

The young man stood in front of her desk, anxiously awaiting his reply. Conor looked at the clock on the wall behind him. Ten past nine.

"C'mon in, Stan," the sheriff answered. "Have a seat. I can spare about twenty minutes."

Running Dog emitted his low almost imperceptible growl when Stanley sat down.

"*Nukwi Sari-chi.*" Conor nudged him with the toe of his boot. "You might want to slide that chair back a little bit, Stan."

He followed the sheriff's advice and scooted back three or four feet. "What kind of dog is that?"

"I'm not sure. Paiute, I guess."

"He looks kind of like a coyote."

"Probably some of that too."

"What about this Apache guy?"

"Just a minute," Conor said, while raising his right index finger. "Hazel, could you come in here please?"

She came to his office door. "What is it?"

"I'm about to tell Stanley everything that's happened since last Tuesday. If you can write it into a report, I'll sign it. That'll save me spending most of my Sunday writing it out."

She smiled. "And it will save Dottie many long hours of deciphering your handwriting while she's typing out the copy that goes on file for the record."

Stanley tried to hide his reddened face behind the hand

covering his mouth in order to keep himself from laughing aloud. Olsen admired Sheriff Armenta in many ways. The sheriff's exploits, finesse and wile had helped Stan gain a reputation as an honest and trustworthy reporter, not to mention occasional bonuses and an increased salary that resulted from some of the articles he had written about the lawman. Giving credit where credit was due, Sheriff Conor Armenta was Stanley Olsen's hero and rightfully so. There is no way he would ever divulge that the most stalwart man he had ever met suffered from poor penmanship.

Conor either failed to notice Olsen's lapse in composure or chose to ignore it as he began sharing the details of his dogged nine-day pursuit of the Apache assassin, George Altaha. Showing them the bullet hole in the brim of his Stetson and Running Dog's shortened tail, he began detailing the events that escalated to the shootout after sundown atop the mesa east of Toquop Wash on the third night of the quest.

He told how Rayno Pete had helped him with his knowledge of the terrain and the legend among the natives surrounding Altaha, their quarry. He expressed the respect the Apache had earned from him. The man he was after was quite a warrior; displaying amazing skill at long range with a rifle, refusing anesthesia during two major surgeries on his arm to extract the bullet from Conor's rifle, cunningness in the wilderness and his unbelievable stamina. But beneath it all, he was still a killer. According to the FBI, his career began as a sniper for the US Army where he became a professionally trained murderer. The aptitude with which he demonstrated his prowess at this art might suggest previous experience in the profession. Regardless, he continually honed these skills by practicing his deadly craft. When Conor finished, the clock showed eleven o'clock. Twenty minutes became nearly two hours.

"So, there's your story, Stan. Tell it like it happened. Under a separate heading let folks know that by the authority of the Clark County Commissioners I have been ordered to hire four additional deputies immediately. I am reviewing the applications from numerous qualified candidates to fill these positions directly."

"Yessir, Sheriff." Stan nearly fainted when Conor stood and offered his hand. He quickly wiped his own sweaty palm on his pants and accepted the handshake. "Thank you, sir."

Conor had always liked the young reporter. His esteem for the man grew again in the firmness of his grip, even though the soft hand had probably never seen a single day of physical labor. As Stanley left the office, he returned to the applications. By noon he had chosen four that stood out to him. Their backgrounds were diverse and the reasons they attracted him varied. He showed the four contenders to Hazel. She eyed them curiously but made no comment. She, Dottie, and Mable Tucker had spent a considerable amount of time narrowing the field down to the final candidates. She could nearly recite their qualifications by rote.

"I requested background checks for all ten of the finalists. I received the results back a few minutes ago; two had felonies and two had misdemeanors on their records. These men," indicating Conor's four top picks and two others all had clean slates."

"Pull those other four out of the mix. We'll keep the remaining two as backups if any of these don't pan out. Three of these say Tent City, as their address. That's what they are calling the camp out east of town?"

"Uh-huh."

"I saw it when I drove in yesterday. Sounds appropriate." He looked at the fourth. "Arden?"

"His wife's brother-in-law works for the railroad there. They're staying with them."

"When Jesse checks in, tell him to meet me here at four o'clock. I'll be out at Tent City until then and down to Arden Sunday afternoon."

As Conor drove to the encampment, he wished he had more time to make his selection. He had hoped to have some respite when he returned from his ordeal with Altaha, but now it seemed his county was in greater upheaval than ever before. The huge influx of people had not blown the lid off things yet, but he knew it would not take long for them to figure out that his meager staff of deputies were no match for the masses should they become unruly. He had to hire good, sound men…and he needed to do it quickly.

The ramshackle appearance of Tent City, on closer look appeared to have some sense of order. The rows of tents and lean-tos were not necessarily in straight lines, but had meandering narrow lanes between them that sometimes split and turned. This allowed passage for automobiles bicycles, and pedestrians between the makeshift dwellings and occasional wider sections became gathering places for both children and adults, probably similar to the neighborhoods the inhabitants had not long ago called home.

Most, if not all of the residents suffered from some level of desperation that they struggled to shield their families from. A man in rumpled clothing sat near a cookfire drinking coffee from a cup made of fine China. He looked up when the sheriff's pickup stopped.

"I'm looking for Romeo Benelli. Have you seen him?"

"I don't know anyone by that name."

"He's not in any kind of trouble. It's about a job."

"Where the road splits down there." The man pointed ahead. "Turn right. Just past that. A Model-T runabout missing a front fender. New York tags."

"Thanks."

Conor eased his way ahead attempting to raise as little dust as possible. He soon spotted the car described by the man with the China cup and eased to a stop behind it. A woman about Conor's age stirred the pot hanging over her cookfire. She looked up and smiled as he approached.

"Can I help you?"

"Mrs. Benelli?"

"Yes."

"Is your husband here?"

"He's helping a friend with his tent." She turned toward her own. "Tony!" she hollered. "Run and get your father. Hurry."

A young teenage boy emerged lazily from the tent fumbling with the newsboy-styled cap in his hands. When he saw the sheriff, he quickly tugged the cap onto his head and dashed off through the maze of tents.

"If your husband is Romeo Benelli, you must be Juliette?" Conor broke the ice.

"Oh, wouldn't that be wonderful?" she asked dreamily. "No, I'm sorry to spoil the illusion, but I am just Alice, and I'm not, unfortunately, from Wonderland either." She grinned as she offered her hand.

"Sheriff Conor Armenta," he introduced himself as he accepted the handshake. "Pleased to meet you, Alice."

He noted that the dress beneath her apron was only lightly soiled and in pretty good condition. Her hair was pinned up and looked clean. Their tent was in good condition also and the tires on the car had plenty of tread. Aside from the fender, they might be any modestly successful family occupying a house in town.

"Can I get you anything, Sheriff? Perhaps a glass of water?"

"No. I'm fine but thank you for offering."

At that moment a rather robust man about six feet tall negotiated his way around tent ropes and appeared from between his family's tent and a neighbor's lean-to.

"Romeo Benneli? I'm Sheriff Conor Armenta." He offered his hand and almost regretted it. Romeo had a vise-like grip and perhaps because of his enthusiasm in anticipation of becoming a deputy, was a little over-exuberant with his handshake. "I've read your application. Harvard University, PhD in archeology; what brings you to Las Vegas?"

"Long version or short?"

"Let's start with short version and we can expand if we need to."

"Last year, I was working a dig in New York City. A contractor building a skyscraper dug up a grave when excavating for the foundation. Turned out to be a pre-revolutionary cemetery. Things were going great, nice apartment, new car. Along comes the crash. Construction got canceled and so did any funding for the dig. After a year of washing dishes, busing tables and anything else either of us could find to survive..." He looked at his wife and choked back the lump in his throat without finishing the sentence.

"Anyway, a colleague of mine got a hold of me a few weeks ago. He's working this dig out north of here. The Lost City, they call it. Lots of work. They need to completely excavate a large area before this new lake submerges it. I know that it might sound silly since they haven't even started to build the dam yet, but we're talking a twenty-year dig that's being crammed into less than half of that. We sold all we had left in New York, loaded up what little we had left in this little trailer, two kids in the rumble seat of the car, and we head for Nevada. We got here last week planning on camping at the dig until we had enough money to rent a house. No job. They already have more people than they need. We sold our sedan a year ago. Our savings was gone six months ago. We sold what was left of our furniture to buy the trailer and pay for gas on our way out here. So, here we are."

On second look, Conor noticed the belt Benelli wore had several extra inches protruding past the buckle and the waist of his trousers were bunched up around his waist. This man had lost a lot of weight since they had fit properly. Another glance at Alice revealed the dress she wore was also bunched around her slender waist beneath the apron. This couple was starving to feed their children.

"Your application says you also have a daughter. Where is she now?"

Alice answered before Romeo had the opportunity. "After we hit the deer in the middle of the night coming across Kansas, she chose to stay with my cousin in Denver for a couple of months until we could get enough money to rent a house."

No further explanation was needed.

Conor turned back to Romeo. "This isn't on the application and it's the most important question. Why do you think you'd be a good deputy?"

"I told on the application that I worked as a bouncer in night-clubs back in Cambridge. To do that job, you have to be firm in getting the troublemakers out of the club, but not hurt them in the process. It not only takes strength; you have to know how to do it correctly. I put myself through college doing it correctly."

Sheriff Armenta worked his fingers of his right hand and smiled. "You've still got your grip."

Romeo blushed. "The joke among my peers in the field is that an archeologist is just a high-paid ditch digger." He held his arms up and flexed them, then released a hearty laugh.

"Can you shoot?"

"I used to duck hunt. I'm pretty good with a shotgun. I've never shot a pistol nor a rifle."

"We can work with that. I only have one more question. Are you prepared to risk your life in the line of duty?"

Romeo grinned. "How dangerous can it be?"

Conor removed his tattered Stetson and poked his finger through the bullet hole in the brim. "While you were arriving at Lost City, I was onboard a train bound for the state penitentiary. A sniper murdered the prisoner I was escorting. This was his second shot. He was so far away, I couldn't even see him. This job can be dangerous. You have to be willing. And you have to keep your wits about you."

Alice Benelli looked wide-eyed at the hole in the hat, then at her husband. Romeo had lost his smile and become very serious.

"I understand...and I am willing."

"Be in my office at seven o'clock Monday morning. Expect a ten-or-twelve-hour day."

The next candidate was a thirty-year-old carpenter and a

bachelor from Louisiana, Francois Boudreaux. The tarp he had draped as a lean-to from his well-worn Model-T sedan was two rows over from the Benelli family. Conor walked across the camp to it. After initial introductions, he began his interview. Boudreaux clarified the pronunciation of his given name and added that most folks "out here" just called him Frank. He was a couple of inches shorter and several pounds lighter than Con, but appeared very fit in his sleeveless undershirt. His forearms in particular seemed quite muscular, a trait Con attributed to many hours of swinging a hammer.

"Your application says you've been a carpenter for the last four years. Before that, you were a Parish deputy."

Frank Boudreaux nodded.

"Why did you leave the department?"

"My uncle was the sheriff. He shot the governor's son, who he caught raping a young girl. He lost the next election."

"He killed the man?"

"Uh-huh. Three shots."

"Folks thought that was excessive?"

"Some did."

"And you?"

"Families in the bayou country tend to be kind of feudal. The girl was my cousin...his daughter. Had it been me? I might have done the same thing. He was acquitted of all charges, but his career was over and so was mine."

Conor only thought about it for a few seconds. If he caught a man raping June's daughter, April, or his niece, Donna, he doubted the perpetrator would survive either. This young man knew and understood the dangers and duties of the job. There was no need to clarify it. He concluded with the same directions he gave Romeo Benelli.

"Be in my office at seven o'clock Monday morning. Expect a long day."

"Do you furnish the pistol?" Frank asked.

"Yes."

"Can I use my own?"

"May I see it?"

He rummaged around in the back of the car for a minute and produced a Smith & Wesson Model M&P revolver in a black leather gun belt. He handed it to the sheriff. Conor removed the pistol from its holster and swung the cylinder open. .38 Special. The gun was well-used, had a four-inch barrel, and was immaculately clean. There were five cartridges in the cylinder. He closed the cylinder and rolled it over to rest the hammer on the empty chamber. Returning the revolver to its holster, he handed it back to Boudreaux.

"We'll furnish your ammunition," he responded, confirming his approval.

Boudreaux accepted. "I'll see you Monday morning."

The next half hour was spent trying with no avail to locate his third candidate. After inquiring among multiple inhabitants of Tent City, he had yet to locate anyone who had seen him in the past thirty-six hours, at which point Conor returned to town. At two thirty, he rolled down Fremont Street. The sign in the window of the Mesquite Café said closed, but he could see people still eating. He walked in and hung his hat on a hook by the door.

"We closed a half hour ago." Olivia pointed at the clock. "If you haven't ordered before two o'clock, no service," she added haughtily.

"Shush!" their mother chided as she sat a Coca-Cola on the counter for her son. "We were so busy this morning, I never could get over to your table to even say, hi," she told him.

Maggie Armenta was Irish through and through. At fifty-five, her flaming red hair pulled back in a ponytail had a streak of gray springing from atop her forehead and more of the same sprinkled through the rest of the crop. There was never a lack of work to be done in their profession but she and Juan had raised and fed three children to adulthood by feeding others on this counter, six days a week for over twenty years. The lines carved into their faces and arthritic fingers marked their lifetime of labor, but all was experienced with love and joy in their family.

"What'll you have?"

"Just a snack to hold me over until supper. I'm taking June and April out to the Hotel Nevada tonight."

The clamor of Juan cleaning the kitchen quieted momentarily. He had heard the conversation and stuck his head through the window. "We had a three-enchilada dinner on special. I have one enchilada left; no rice or beans. You want it?"

"That'd be perfect."

An instant later, the steaming plate appeared in the window. "It's not as good as the Hotel Nevada," Juan quipped from behind the wall, "but the atmosphere here is much better." He followed up with a brazen cackle.

Maggie poured herself a glass of iced tea and sat beside her eldest child as he ate. The conversation was not notable, but sharing a few minutes together was. He dug in his pocket to pay for the meal while Maggie cleared the counter. She waved him off and kissed his cheek.

"See you Sunday? Father O'Malley's seen June, but has been looking for you," she hinted.

"I sure hope to be there," Con replied.

As he took his Stetson from the hook, he looked at its condition with disdain and walked out the door. He had purchased it barely six months ago to replace a predecessor that suffered a similar fate. He glanced down the street to Beckley's Haberdashery on the corner and proceeded in that direction.

"What can I help you with?" the clerk asked as Con came through the door. He was almost certain it was the same man who sold him the hat he was currently wearing.

"I'm looking for a new hat," Con told him. "I purchased this one here a few months ago," he told him as he handed the man his Stetson. "It hasn't lasted as long as I had hoped."

"Well, sir," the clerk began as he studied the hole in the brim. "It won't have the hole in it, but we...just a minute. I remember you." He looked at Conor's gun and badge. "I didn't recognize you then, but didn't your last hat have a hole in it too?"

"Yes, it did. Up in the top of the crown."

"These are quality hats." He studied the hole closer. "You should try to figure out what's causing this and avoid doing it."

"Bullets," Con commented soberly.

"Say what? What did you say?"

"Bullets. Twice. People shooting at me."

The clerk's face paled. "Well, thank God they missed."

"Yessir," Con agreed. "Thank God they missed *me*."

Rolling the sweatband down, the clerk checked the size tag, then looked to the back of the store and the hat boxes stacked to the ceiling. He climbed a ladder behind the rear counter and began checking sizes. Before long, he was bringing boxes down the ladder. On his third trip, he called out.

"I have three hats in your size, Sheriff. If you can come back to this counter, it will be the best place to show them to you."

By the time Con worked his way down narrow aisles, the clerk had all three boxes opened on the counter. He took the hat from the first box and held it out right side up. It was a very pale gray with a rounded crown and narrow brim. He liked the style in general but had seen other men wearing hats this color and feared it would soon be sweat-stained.

The second one was nearly identical to his present one with a rolled brim. It was a deep gray. "This one is the same model as your last one, just the different color. J. B. Stetson."

"What about the other one?"

The clerk pulled it out. "This is the old traditional style. Stetson calls it 'the Boss of the Plains.' Rounded crown and a flat brim."

It was black and Conor looked it over carefully.

"Would you like to try it out?" he asked.

"Perfect fit," he said when he put it on. Looking in the nearby mirror, he took it off immediately. "I look like an Indian wearing it. Let me try that last one." Placing it on his head, it felt comfortable. "I'll take it," he added after a quick glance in the mirror.

"Is there anything else you need today."

"I could use another shirt."

"What color?"

"Something different, maybe green."

The clerk shuffled around a stack of folded shirts wrapped in tissue paper and pulled one out. "How about this one?" The shirt was light green with dark green pinstripes. Every other stripe had small diamonds of the same color three or four inches apart.

Conor quickly calculated how June might like it and replied, "I think that will do," then paid for the purchase. He donned the new hat and carried the rest to his sheriff's pickup still parked in front of the Mesquite Café.

At the Sheriff's Department, Mark McCoy sat waiting in a chair across the room from Hazel. His twin brother, Matt, had been murdered on the set of a movie being shot on the outskirts of town a few weeks ago. Matt McCoy was in the starring role, and Mark was making his acting debut in *Sons of the Texas Star*. The two local boys had been making a big splash in the little pond of Las Vegas when the dam broke.

"What brings you in here today, Mark?" Con asked as he came to his feet.

"Wednesday's newspaper, Sheriff." He held it up in his left hand. "Dad showed it to me this morning."

"I've been out of town for a few days. What's so interesting in there?"

Mark handed him Wednesday's *Evening Review*. A short column a quarter of the way down the front page was circled in pencil. The heading read, "Sheriff's Department Seeks 4 Additional Deputies!"

"I hadn't seen it." Conor grinned in surprise. "When Judge Tucker told me he got it in Wednesday's paper I didn't realize it was on the front page."

"I'd like to apply. If I'm not too late."

Con glanced at Hazel, who held Mark's application in her hand. "Do you need to see it?"

"I doubt it," he replied as he turned back to Mark. "What about the movies?"

"I don't wanna be famous. I saw what it got my brother. We finished *Sons of the Texas Star* last week. Judge Tucker let Mr. Fredericks and Molly go out to the Campbell place to finish the shootout scene and the ending. Mr. Fredericks directed. I wore Matt's costume and they kept my face off the cameras for the final scene with Molly. My movie career ended a week ago today.

"Whit Ellis brought Molly and Mr. Fredericks out there and guarded them each day. I talked to him some. I kind of decided I might wanna try becoming a deputy. When Dad showed me the paper this morning, it was like…it was like maybe God sent Whit out there to talk to me."

Conor had gotten to know Mark McCoy somewhat during the investigation into his brother's murder. Prior to that, he knew that Mark grew up working on his family's cattle ranch not far from the Armenta family's sheep ranch. Though a decade younger, he thought Mark probably shared some of his own traits and experiences…and hopefully ethics.

"Be here Monday morning at seven and prepared for a long day."

"Thank you, Sheriff," Mark acknowledged as he accepted Con's hand.

At that moment, Deputy Jesse Slater came in the door. He poured himself a cup of coffee as McCoy was leaving.

"Everything okay?" he asked curiously watching the departure.

"New deputy," Conor replied while filling a cup for himself. "C'mon in my office."

Con half leaned and half sat on the edge of his desk.

"Have a seat, Jess," he indicated the chair a few feet in front of the desk. "When Sheriff Baker hired me, you were already a deputy here. How long have you been with the department?"

"Five years in March."

"Almost two years before me. Did it bother you when I was appointed interim sheriff instead of you when Sheriff Baker had to retire?"

"It did at first, but not for long. I kind of had a chip on my shoulder for a couple of weeks when there was that brawl at the Oasis. I was in the middle of it, getting the tar pounded out of me when you walked in. The fracas came to an abrupt halt when you showed up. If you remember it, I'd lost my gun in the melee and might have been dead if you didn't show up when you did. You found my gun on the floor over by the bar, and I ended up with a shiner. I knew then that I was the wrong man for the job."

"How about now?"

"I'd do better now, but only because of what I've learned from you. Sheriff Baker was old. He wasn't ever there by your side to learn from him like you've been."

"What've you learned from me?"

"Mostly how to handle myself around others and how to handle those other people. The biggest part, has been learning how to keep a cool head."

"What's it like when I'm not here and you're in charge?"

"Nothin' much has happened. I've got seniority over Ben and Whit, but we're all about the same age. So far, they've always done what I asked them to."

"Last Saturday?"

"Well, that was different. Mrs. Anderson was scared out of her wits when she called Hazel. Hazel found Whit, who found me, and we figured out a plan. Neither one of us wanted to go in there and that part turned out kind of lucky. I wasn't really the boss during the whole thing. We figured out between us what to do and we just did it."

"But you had the final say so."

Jesse thought for a few seconds. "Yeah, I guess I never thought much about it at the time, but yeah. Whit waited for my approval and we went ahead with our plan."

"I know you've heard that the commissioners authorized us to hire four more deputies. There'll be twice as many deputies and at least twice as much to do."

"I figured as much."

"Will you be able to handle it?"

"Are you leavin'?" Jesse asked in shock.

"No, I'll still be right here, but under Judge Tucker's recommendation the commissioners authorized another change. There will be a new position in the department. It's called an undersheriff. Second in command of this new posse, so to speak."

"Who're you hiring for that?"

"I'm following Judge Tucker's recommendation on that too. I'm hiring you."

# 16

At five forty-five, Conor's freshly washed brown Chevrolet coupe pulled to a stop in front of 469 South 3$^{rd}$ Street. Running Dog sat perched in the rumble seat looking around the righthand side of the passenger compartment. He was eyeing the little blonde-haired girl on the porch and preparing to bail out over the rear fender to introduce himself.

*Nukwi Sari-chi,* in a calm but commanding tone from Con was all that was needed to bring him to attention and seated.

April stood at the top of the steps awaiting Conor's approach and leapt into his arms when he reached the bottom step.

"I've sure missed you, Con,"

"I missed you too, sweet pea," he replied as he hugged her.

April's attention immediately shifted to Running Dog. "Mama said you got a dog. Can I pet him?"

"He's not too friendly to strangers sometimes, but he's getting better about it. Let's see how he does."

"What's his name?"

"Running Dog."

She did not question it. Standing her on the step that kept her at his eye level, he turned his attention to the dog. Snapping his fingers, then patting his thigh brought Running Dog out of his seat and at Conor's feet in three bounds. His tail wagged frantically while sniffing the air surrounding the miniature person in front of him.

"Okay, April. Slowly, and with your palm up, hold out hand your and let him smell it."

Running Dog sniffed her hand then licked her fingers causing April to giggle. So did Conor.

"Now rub under his chin, then slowly work your way back to scratch his neck. Then you can start your way up to scratch around his ears and finally to pet him on his head."

Conor watched her, adoring the excitement mixed with caution in her eyes that accompanied the glowing smile on her face.

"This is how you should always approach an animal who doesn't know you. Whether dog or horse or pretty much anything else, if you start out at their head and especially if your palm is facing down, they might think you want to hurt them. With dogs in particular their natural instinct in that situation is to either run or attack. And you don't want either of those things to happen. After they get to know you and feel safe with you, they won't be as skittish and you can move more easily around them."

Running Dog was eating up the attention he was receiving and licked at April's hands and wrists every chance he could.

"I think he likes me," she commented as she continued to rub and pet him with both hands.

"I think so too, but you still need to be cautious so he builds confidence in you. You're starting off right, but he might not be as quick to become friends as you are so try to let him decide for a while."

As June came out of the house, April and Conor were sitting on the steps with Running Dog. "Well, what's going on out here?" she asked cheerfully.

"I'm learning how to make friends with Running Dog."

"You must be pretty good at it. It sure seems to be working."

"I've got a good teacher," April replied, causing Conor to blush.

"And he is wearing a new shirt...and a new hat too," June observed. "He must think you are pretty special."

"Well, I think you're both pretty special," Con interjected as he scrambled to his feet. "You are beautiful, June," he added as he put his hand around her waist and kissed her. "And you smell wonderful too," he added when their lips parted.

"You look pretty spiffy yourself, cowboy," she replied with a grin. "And I am almost certain that I caught a hint of Donna's foo-foo juice on your cheek too."

"I'm guilty. It's the only shaving lotion I have." He leaned closer and inhaled her scent again before gently kissing her neck.

The kiss sent a shiver up her spine and drew a slight gasp from her lips in the process. She pulled him nearer to her.

"What's that perfume you're wearing?" he asked.

"Honeysuckle."

"You're making me hungry," he replied as he kissed her neck again.

"And that is not all," she added, taking a deep breath as she broke the embrace. "We should be going."

As they headed toward the car, Running Dog soared into the rumble seat with feet barely touching the rubber pad on the fender as he passed.

"Do you want to ride in the back with Running Dog, or up front between Mama and me?" he asked April.

"In the back." She gleamed in anticipation.

Conor gave her a steadying hand as she climbed from the step on the bumper to the fender and in. He then held the door for June before scampering around and climbing in behind the wheel smiling. The drive to the Hotel Nevada took only a few minutes. His right hand rested on the shift knob between them, and June's left hand laid atop his. Her blue pearl and diamond engagement ring glistened on her finger.

"I'm sorry that I was gone so long," he began. "I thought I would only be away for five days."

"When I answered the telephone and heard Hazel's voice, I suspected the worst. I nearly fainted awaiting some form of tragic news that never came. As soon as I realized the reason for her call, all I could think of was gathering everything you would want on your expedition."

"And your choices were amazing. I had everything that I needed."

"I told Hazel to make sure whoever she was sending would meet me at your house before they left. I burst into Mr. Westcott's office, told him you had an emergency and that I would be back as soon as I could. He was with a client and I never even asked. I am still embarrassed even talking about it now."

"What did he say?"

"Take my car!" She shook her head, still in disbelief. "Can you imagine that?"

"Actually?" he replied as he thought for a moment. "No."

That brought a chuckle from them both.

"Right. But he handed me the keys and I ran out the door. I drove straight home to pack you some food, but I only had the fried chicken left over from our supper the night before. I called Maggie at the café and asked her to pack up some groceries for you, then drove to your house. You really should consider locking the door when you go away for a few days," she added. "Ben got there in your pickup truck just as I did and we loaded up everything that we could think of. I was nervous looking through your dresser for the bullets."

"He told me, and while we're on that subject, how did you know where to find my rifle?"

"I saw you sneaking your gun belt out there one time and watched where you put it. When the rifle was not in the house, I guessed. A woman's intuition, maybe."

"And you were right."

"When we left the café, Ben got into your truck and started it up. He asked me if there was anything else that I wanted to send to you. I told him a kiss, but that I was afraid you would never get it. He turned fourteen shades of red." June giggled. "Then he shook his head and drove away,"

"He never told me that part." Conor grinned at they pulled in to the Hotel Nevada. "I'll have to ask him about it."

Only the second time they dined there together, Susie, their waitress recognized June and April immediately as she led the trio to their table. As Con held June's chair for her, Susie mentioned June's necklace.

"I will never be able to keep my eyes off that," she commented in reference to the uniquely shaped blue pearl pendant. Conor had given it to June for her birthday on their previous visit to the restaurant. "It's just so stunning. Forgive me for staring."

June and the young waitress had quickly struck up a tearful kinship in the lady's powder room on their first meeting. June was overjoyed to immediately feel the bond returning on their second encounter.

"It does make me a little bit self-conscious, but I am so proud of it..."

"Oh, my God!" Susie interrupted upon noticing June's engagement ring. "I heard...I mean, after all, this is a small town. I knew you were engaged, but wow. How do you top that? The pearls are the exact same blue color."

June almost shyly held up her hand to allow Susie a closer look. The ring was actually quite simple. It had a modestly sized pale-blue pearl in the center. Less than a quarter inch in diameter, the pearl was guarded by small oval diamonds on either side of it. What drew your attention was the way the diamonds reflected the pale blue of the pearl. The combination nearly glowed of its own accord.

"Please, tell me," she asked. "How does it feel to wear the two most beautiful pieces of jewelry I've ever seen in my life? I just can't comprehend it."

"Loved," June answered as she looked to Conor. "It makes me feel loved beyond measure."

When ordering their supper, June and Conor chose steak. April picked a hot dog as was expected, but only after she confirmed with Con that she could have ice cream afterward if she ate all of her supper. Conor's thoughts wandered in and out of the casual conversation while waiting for the meal to arrive. In recent years, he had felt that his life was incomplete. While enjoying the family that soon would be his own, he felt whole again for the first time in a long time. June noticed the intermittent disconnect.

"Is everything all right?"

"Absolutely. I've just been thinking."

"About what?"

"I think that I'm happier now than I can ever remember."

The statement jolted her and nearly brought a tear to her eye. She desperately wanted to avoid a repeat of the emotional roller coaster she had ridden on her birthday...in this very same restaurant. She leaned over in her chair and put her arm around his neck. She pulled him closer until just inches before their lips met and glanced at April whose face beamed in delight before turning back to him.

"I think that makes three of us," she whispered before kissing him passionately.

When they broke their embrace, Susie was two steps away from serving their supper.

"I hope I'm not interrupting anything," she mentioned as she began placing plates before them.

"They were just smooching," April explained, which brought a chuckle from all three adults.

"I saw that," Susie agreed as she sat April's plate in front of her. "Is there anything else anyone needs?" she asked.

"Mustard and relish, please," April requested.

"Coming right up."

"What happened to the bad man you were chasing?" April asked Con as he took the first bite of his steak.

"He died."

"Did you shoot him?" she asked before he had a chance to clarify the statement.

He did not want to omit any detail that might later be misconstrued as a lie so he sat his knife and fork down and very calmly told a very condensed version of a portion of the story.

"I did shoot him in the arm a few days earlier, but that isn't what he died from. He fell into a mineshaft in Arizona. A long way from here. There was water in the mineshaft and the badman drowned. There were lots of things that happened while I was gone and much of it isn't suitable for conversation while eating. It's a very long story and I will tell you all about it sometime later. Okay?"

"Okay. Where did Running Dog come from?"

"That's part of the story," he replied as June reached over and squeezed his hand in reassurance. "Can I tell you about it later?"

"Sure," April answered cheerfully and resumed eating her hot dog which she had since adorned with generous amounts of mustard and relish.

After they had stuffed themselves with their supper June and Con sipped coffee while contemplating ice cream.

"Have you seen today's *Evening Review*?" she asked him.

"No, I haven't. When I got home I had just enough time to get cleaned up and come to pick you up."

"You should read it; I think you will find it interesting."

"How so?"

At that moment, Susie began clearing their plates. "Ice cream?"

Everyone accepted the offer and June added, "Do you have a copy of the *Evening Review*?"

"Mm-hmm."

"Could you bring it before our ice cream? April needs a minute to finish her hot dog anyway."

A moment later, Susie returned with the newspaper and handed it to June, who passed it over to Conor.

"Quite a story, Sheriff," the waitress added as she collected April's now empty plate. "I'll be back with three ice creams."

Conor opened the newspaper and looked at the headline.

*Killer Meets His End in the Mountains of Arizona After Nine-day Manhunt*

"Stanley always has been a little melodramatic," he commented.

"It gets better," June added.

He moved down to the heading on the actual article.

*The Bizarre Murder of Dutch Wagner (part 1 of 3)*

"Part one of three? Really Stan? He's gonna milk this thing for all it's worth."

"Sells more newspapers. Makes the boss happy. Gets the reporter a bonus, maybe?"

"And makes the public wait for three days to read the rest of the story."

"What? No mystery? No suspense?" June jokingly scolded him. "You, Sheriff Armenta, love that. If not for solving the puzzle behind these cases, I think you would find the daily routine of your job to be quite boring."

Conor flushed when faced with the reality of it. June had him pegged and he knew it. "You might be right," he admitted.

"You are very good at your job, Conor. Read between the lines. You are Stan Olsen's hero. I doubt he would ever discredit you in a story. Just revel in your fifteen minutes of fame. You know in your heart you deserve it."

Susie returned with ice cream providing the opportunity to change the subject of conversation which April sprung upon.

"Have we waited long enough to find out how you got Running Dog?"

"I guess we have," Conor forfeited. "Running Dog belonged to an Indian friend of mine named Rayno Pete. He was helping me track the badman. We were riding Rayno's mules and Running Dog came with us. Running Dog didn't like me very much to begin with. He didn't trust me. I probably smelled differently than the people he was accustomed to being around. Did you know that people smell differently because of what they eat?"

"No," April answered suspiciously.

June thought Conor was teasing her and preferred to remain silent.

"It's true. A dog's sense of smell is a hundred times better than a person's. Maybe more."

April sat wide-eyed in amazement.

"You or me might not be able to tell the difference, but a dog can. If you eat hot dogs and ice cream all of the time, you smell different than someone who never does. I probably smell like Coca-Cola to Running Dog."

April and June both giggled.

"On the second morning, I tried to make friends with him by offering a share of the lamb jerky I was eating. Since Rayno is a sheep rancher like my brother, I thought the smell would be familiar to him, but he wouldn't take it. I could tell he wanted to by the way his nostrils were busy, but he stayed a couple of feet away and growled real low at me. Not really mean but warning me to keep my distance."

"Like he did with me on Sunday morning at your house," June commented more than questioned.

"Yes, exactly like that," Con confirmed. "He was trying to gauge the impact of things under foreign circumstances. He's starting to get better about it now. Anyway, it was just a little piece that I held between my fingers but he wouldn't take it until Rayno spoke to him in Paiute. I don't know what he said, but Running Dog darted forward, grabbed that tiny piece of jerky, and swallowed it whole without ever touching my fingers.

"We took a shortcut the night before, so a little bit later, while Rayno was fixing breakfast, I took my rifle and went looking for the badman's tracks. To my surprise, Running Dog went with me. A few minutes later, Running Dog yelped and jumped, then started biting at his tail. I thought a snake bit his tail until I heard the report from a distant rifle a few seconds later. The badman had shot off part of his tail. I dove for cover in the sagebrush with Running Dog. His tail was only partially severed and he was chewing at it trying to make it quit hurting. While we laid there in the sagebrush, I finished the job with my jackknife and it quit hurting him. Kind of like the fable about the thorn in the lion's paw. But he's been following me around ever since."

"What did you say to him at our house?" April asked.

"Nukwi Sari-chi?"

"What does that mean?"

"It means Running Dog in Paiute,"

"You can talk in Indian?"

"Only his name. Rayno taught it to me. Running Dog doesn't understand English right now, but he will learn more in time."

When they reached the car, April passed a bite of hotdog she had hidden to Running Dog. When Conor looked to June, she had failed to notice the act. He chose to ignore it. When she started to climb her way to the rumble seat, he stopped her.

"It's getting pretty cool out this evening," he began. "I think you should ride up front with us."

"I'm not cold," she reasoned before countering, "If it's too cold out, what about Running Dog?"

"He has a fur coat."

"Ooh-kay," she grumbled in disappointment while climbing into the front seat ahead of her mother.

April struggled to fight off sleep on the short seven-block ride home. She clung her arms drowsily around Conor's neck as he carried her into the house and sat her down on her bed. Running Dog followed from the car, anxious to get better acquainted with the little girl who brought the hot dog, but stopped short when June closed the screen door in front of him.

"Not in my house," she informed him through the screen. "Not until you learn how to mop floors and I doubt that will be soon."

As June began preparing April for bed, Conor retreated to the front porch swing. A few minutes later, June passed through the dimly lit living room to the kitchen, then returned with two glasses of lemonade.

"Have I told lately you how much I love you?" she asked as she sat down beside him.

"Yep, but I never get tired of hearing it," Conor answered, grinning like a Cheshire cat.

"I cannot begin to express the feelings I have for you. I was... and still am in many ways, in love with April's father. But nothing compares to how I feel about you."

"Not lust?"

"Oh, there is that too," she stammered, thankful the half moonlight disguised to Conor how red her face became. "I will not deny it, but I can distinguish the difference. Those hormones are nothing compared to how I truly feel about you. I know of people who jump into relationships with pie-in-the-sky ideas. Infatuations actually, but that is not me. I waited for twelve years after April's father was killed, never expecting to have any feelings for another man until you came along. When you walked in to talk to Mr. and Mrs. Westcott, that day...I was taken aback the moment you stepped through the door. That was the first twinge. After that, I listened to how calmly you spoke to them even when they became angry. I knew then there was something special about you.

"Just a few days later, you were shot. I barely knew you, but it felt like my heart had been cut out and laid on that table beside you. When Dr. Martin said you were going to survive and that you talked to me…or about me when under anesthesia, I knew it was not just me. Consciously or not, I understood then that the feelings were mutual. I believed in my heart that we were meant to be together. It was shortly afterward, I think that you realized it too. Then later you told me how you felt. Though you were not ready yet to accept that feeling as love, I knew."

"I didn't know what it was," Conor replied. "I just knew I'd never felt like this before."

"I would have never dreamt that I could love someone as deeply as I love you."

June sat her now empty glass down and snuggled up beneath his arm to lay her head against his chest. He moved his arm around her shoulders and gently caressed the back of her head and neck. She shivered when his fingers softly fell behind her ears and downward to her neck below. It was the same area he sometimes kissed her that set her body on fire. She raised her head, then her lips to his and struggled to control her breathing through flared nostrils. Her kiss was returned with the same passion it was given and soon forced her to break from it.

"I am on the brink of being beyond control," June confessed with a deep breath as she moved to sit higher in the seat of the swing. "We have to slow down."

"Yes," Conor agreed, regulating his own breathing as he picked up his half-full glass and downed its contents in an instant.

The temperature hovered in the midfifties but felt thirty degrees warmer when June drank the swallow of ice water melted in the bottom of her glass then sucked on the remnant of a cube that remained. After a pause, Conor broke the silence.

"What are your plans for tomorrow?"

"I have none in particular. Why?"

"I need to drive down to Searchlight and pick up a horse that I left there."

"The one that belonged to the outlaw?"

"Yes. I'll go out to Paddy's in the morning and get his truck. It'll be a bit crowded, but if you and April would like to ride along?"

"April is spending tomorrow night with Donna. Olivia is picking her up when she gets off work at two." She glanced to her neighbor's house. The lights were off. "Joyce can probably watch her until then. She has gone to bed now, but I can call her in the morning. She's usually up early, so I might be available." Her grin gone, undetected in the darkness.

"It's getting pretty late and I really should be going," he announced as he came to his feet. "If it turns out you can come along, wear something comfortable. Paddy's truck is pretty rough compared to my car...or even my county pickup."

"What time should I expect to see you?"

"Seven?" he asked, hoping for an early start.

"Six and I'll fix breakfast."

"Six."

# 17

Conor pulled up in front of June's house a few minutes before six. Running Dog bailed out of the rumble seat and followed him to the porch. April stood inside the front door, peering through the screen when they climbed the steps. The smell of bacon wafting in the air around her from the kitchen definitely caught Running Dog's attention. When she held the screen door open, he nudged Running Dog with his knee to stay on the porch.

"Stay!" he ordered.

Running Dog read the sign language more than understanding the command and obeyed.

"Good morning, Con." April beamed.

"Good morning to you too, sweet pea."

"Mama's in the kitchen. Can I pet Running Dog?"

"Sure," he told her.

After the hot dog incident last night, he was almost certain Running Dog would welcome her attention, but paused long enough to ensure his assumption was correct. She followed his earlier instructions on greeting animals to a tee and Running Dog obliged her with a foray of licks to her hands and fingers.

When he hung his hat by the door, Conor noticed June's white straw hat hanging on an adjacent peg. He found no need to ask her if she was joining him when he saw her. She wore her tan riding skirt with boots and a loose white button-down blouse beneath her apron. Her hair was pulled back into a low ponytail and her smile gave away her excitement for the day to come. She dried her hands on the apron when crossing the room to meet him.

"Good morning, sweetheart," she nearly whispered as she wrapped her arms around his neck and kissed him fervently. "I have been waiting for an hour to do that." She giggled.

"Only an hour?" he asked in mock coyness and returned his lips to hers.

"And my whole life before that," she replied when they broke their embrace. "Breakfast is ready and keeping warm in the oven except for the eggs," she added as she returned to the stove and grabbed the coffeepot. An empty cup and a glass filled with orange juice awaited him positioned in front of what had become *his* chair.

"Have you fed Running Dog?" she asked as she filled his cup.

"Yeah, sort of."

"What?"

"What do you mean?"

"What did you feed him?"

"Well, a piece of jerky and a biscuit left from the breakfast you made last Sunday."

"Poo. I have never lived on a sheep ranch, but if you keep a dog in town, you need to feed them, or they will be rummaging through the neighborhood garbage cans looking for whatever they can find."

Conor was about to try to defend himself when she took a can of Vitamont Dog Food from the cupboard and began opening it.

"When did you get that?"

"Yesterday. Ten cents a can at Ward's Cash and Carry." She turned to face the archway leading to the living room. "April! Come in here please."

The front screen door bounced against the frame as June emptied the can into a small mixing bowl.

"What, Mama?"

June handed her the bowl. "This is for Running Dog, and this will be *his* bowl. It has a crack in it and will stay on the porch. I better not find it in my sink with the dishes we eat off of."

"Yes, Mama." She beamed with enthusiasm and ran toward the door.

"Breakfast is ready," June called after her. "Come in and wash your hands as soon as you are finished out there."

She splashed bacon grease into the cast-iron skillet that had been warming on the stove and broke six eggs into it. By the time she turned them April had returned, and June brought the platter with hot biscuits, fried potatoes, and bacon from the oven. Momentarily, the eggs were finished, and she served them from the skillet onto each of the plates on the table; one for April, three for Conor and two for herself.

Most of the talk around the breakfast table was dominated by April and centered on her adoration of Running Dog. Both Conor and June stimulated her discourse on this latest subject in her life, knowing they would have several hours throughout the day for their own private conversations. When they were finished eating, April began clearing the dishes.

"I can get this today, honey," June told her. "You get your things together to bring to Joyce's and then to Donna's. You need to have a dress for church tomorrow. So, fold it nicely, not all wrinkled up."

Conor dried the dishes while June washed and they soon made quick work of it.

Venturing into the living room, June commented, "I need to make sure April has her things in order. I often discover she only hears half of what I say."

Conor looked at Running Dog napping on the mat in front of the screen door. "At least she speaks English."

June caught the correlation and laughed.

By seven o'clock, April was safely in the care of June's neighbor, Joyce Wright, Conor's sister, Olivia McLeod had been notified of the change of venue regarding where to pick up April that afternoon.

June and Conor sped out of town down Charleston Boulevard toward Patrick Armenta's sheep ranch while Running Dog sat in the rumble seat of Conor's coupe joyfully peering around the passenger compartment with his tongue wagging in the breeze.

A half hour later, June waved goodbye to Paddy as they drove out of the yard in his old Model-T truck. June had noticed Conor transferring his pistol from beneath the seat of his car to the truck when they arrived but did not comment. Running Dog poked his head between the slats of the stake-bed to resume his observance ahead when they pulled onto the road.

"You were right," June commented before they were halfway back to town. "It is not nearly as comfortable as your car...or the county's pickup," she added after they struck a chuckhole in the road.

"We should stop back at the house and grab some things for a picnic," June suggested when they stopped at the county shop to fill the truck with gasoline.

"Mrs. Haygood is expecting us for dinner around one or two o'clock," he informed her.

She blushed. "You had this whole thing planned," she accused him.

"Oh, not really. I just called Bert yesterday afternoon to tell him I was coming and that you and April might be joining me. He covered the telephone and spoke to his wife, then asked when I thought we should to be there? When I told him, Bert said Mrs. Haygood would be expecting us for dinner."

"We should at least bring something."

"I figured we'd stop at Chavez's farm."

"You *did* have this whole thing planned."

When Conor made the righthand turn down the road to the Chavez farm, June was reminded of their first outing together.

"We were on our way to Luis Garza's."

"What?" Con asked.

"Oh, nothing," she replied when shaken from her reverie. "I was just thinking out loud."

"What about Luis?"

"The last time we were here. You had just bought your new car." She blushed. "Our first date. Mrs. Chavez told you something in Spanish."

"*Ella es muy amable...y bonita.*" The reminder now caused Conor to blush. "She was right."

"It was something about me. It made you blush then too."

"That you were very kind...and pretty."

*  *  *

Juanita Chavez guarded her eyes from the sun with a raised hand when she came from the barn. The truck's squeaking brakes announced their arrival as it rolled to a stop.

Juanita waved moments before Conor climbed out. "I didn't know the truck, but I recognized your dog."

By the time she ducked back into the barn and returned with a bone, he had opened the passenger door and June stepped out. She gave Running Dog the bone and hurried to wipe her hands on her apron.

"Senorita, it is so nice to see you again." The gleam of bright white teeth dominated her weathered face. "I told Conor to bring you back out here to see us again," she added as she held out her hand. "Did you like your peaches?"

"Yes, we did," June replied, smiling as they shook hands. "My daughter baked a cobbler from them. They were delicious."

"What would you like today?"

"Fruit, I hope?"

"The peaches are gone. I have lots of apples, but only a few pears and cantaloupes left."

June looked to Conor.

"How about four cantaloupes and eight or ten pears?" he suggested.

"Coming right up," Juanita replied and returned to the barn.

June followed. As they perused a table laden with pears, she asked, "Have you known Conor for a long time?"

"Since he was a young boy. Not much when he was real little, but after Juan got hurt, we saw him often."

"What was he like?"

"Always smart…and always a very hard worker. I think with his father crippled; he thought it was his responsibility to support the family. I think he gave everything he earned to his parents for most of his life. Maggie more than Juan, I'm sure."

"What makes you say that?"

"He said something to me one time. When he was a teenager. It was something about how he never wanted his father to think he needed charity. I think Conor was very careful not to hurt Juan's pride, especially when it came to his ability to provide for his family."

"I can see that. Pride," June observed. "In every member of the Armenta family actually. They are a proud group of people… and rightfully so. Not just Conor, either. All of them are hard workers."

"Yes. You are right."

"He spends way too much money on me," June commented in what seemed a total change of the subject to Juanita.

"What do you mean?" Juanita asked.

"He buys me lavish gifts, for example, a very expensive necklace for my birthday. I never made the connection before, but now I wonder if he has been subconsciously trying to show me that he can provide for us financially. Oh, my gosh!" June exclaimed in realization, "I did the very same thing."

"What?"

"I bought him a horse for his birthday. A very nice horse. One that I knew he adored but never would have purchased for himself. I may have injured his own pride in the process."

"You need to talk to him about it," Juanita advised.

"We have never discussed our personal finances before."

"When are you getting married?"

"We've not set a date yet, but soon, I think."

"Are you two having trouble choosing pears or something?" Conor interrupted as he came through the door.

"Make yourself useful," Juanita scolded him as she shoved four cantaloupes into his arms and shooed him out the door.

"You need to have that conversation and others," Juanita encouraged. "Children, female things that men don't have to deal with, likes and dislikes, money, and a million other things that will come up in the future. It's better to muddy the water a little now than try to plug a hole in the dam after you're already married."

She handed June a flour sack full of pears and shuffled her out the door to Paddy's truck. Juanita accepted the two silver dollars Conor gave her as he climbed into the truck, then turned to June seated beside him.

"Lots of things to contemplate, pretty lady," she winked. "And soon too, I think."

June only contemplated for a few minutes how to begin confronting the many issues Jaunita had pointed out that she and Conor should address before marriage.

"When do you think we should get married?" she began as Conor wheeled the truck out onto the highway. "I think pretty soon. Do you agree?"

"Before Christmas?" he asked.

"Oh, that would be wonderful," she exclaimed. "We could spend our first Christmas together as a family. April would be thrilled."

"And you?"

"I would marry you this instant if I could and love you for the rest of my life. I only thought of April because she's never had a family at Christmas, except for my sister that is. Her father was killed in the war before she was born. It has always been just the two of us."

"It must have been hard on you, and for her, not having a father. I can't imagine growing up without Papa."

"She's never known anything different, but she can hardly wait to start calling you, Daddy. Neither can I."

"We shouldn't have our wedding too close to Christmas," Conor began. "Christmas should be very special to April, not about us getting married."

June was unsure which statement surprised her more but tried not to let it show. "Around Thanksgiving then?"

"Yeah," he thought about it for a moment. "The Saturday after Thanksgiving Day, maybe."

The wheels were spinning off their axes in June's head. Four weeks away.

"You probably want a small wedding then?" she asked for clarification.

"Yes." He began making a visual guest list in his head. "Mama and Papa, Paddy, Olivia and Stuart, Luis and whoever you want to be there."

"My sister will probably come up from Riverside. I am sure she will want to be here. Other than that, my friends are mostly your family." June's mind raced as she tried to visualize everything they were discussing. "Where will we have the ceremony?"

"At the church of course."

"But I am not Catholic. April and I can attend, but we cannot even take sacrament there."

"Mama will be disappointed, but you're right." Conor pondered the situation. "And who will marry us if not Father O'Malley?"

"Judge Tucker maybe?"

"That's a good idea. Judge Tucker would be a good choice. I

suppose we could get married at my parent's house. We all manage to fit in there on holidays."

"Or maybe the judge's courtroom."

"That would be better."

After discussing a few more specifics, most of the details were agreed on for their wedding. They were coming to a junction in the road. The sign pointing left said Boulder City – 5; to the right, Searchlight – 38. June glanced at the speedometer on the dashboard, twenty-eight miles per hour. She felt certain that Conor was driving as fast as safely possible in the old truck and the road appeared much less traveled past the junction. Another hour and a half she thought. Maybe more if the road got worse.

"I have never asked you before because I thought it was none of my business, but we are soon-to-be married, and I think we each need to know these things and to make our decisions together. Mr. Westcott pays me very well and I have managed my money carefully. I sold my house in Riverside for more than I paid here, so my mortgage is small. As you know, I have no car so I have no other debts. I went to college and am a certified legal secretary. I make thirty-five dollars a week and my mortgage payment is twenty-four dollars per month. I almost always pay extra and I put money in savings every week so April can go to college when she graduates from high school."

June had not looked at Conor throughout her entire disclosure. She was afraid to see his reaction. She hoped he made more money than she did. She was afraid he might be seriously offended if it turned out otherwise, but she wanted him to know that she and April would not be a financial burden on him.

"You won't have to keep working if you don't want to," he began. "I make enough money to provide for all of us. My house is paid for so there is no mortgage. I owe about three hundred dollars on my car, but I have enough in savings to pay it off whenever I want to. I make forty-three dollars a week. My car payment is twelve dollars a month and like you, I've been paying double. I have a life insurance policy that's two dollars a month and..." He stopped mid-sentence. "You have to promise never to tell this to anyone. Not ever."

June had kept her eyes straight forward just as before but now turned to look at him. What deep, dark secret could he possibly be hiding? "Of course," she said and looked away.

"I give Mama ten dollars every week. I've done it always. Every week since high school. Back then it was more than half what I made. I don't know what she does with it, but I know they've needed it many times over the years. You can't ever tell anybody. Promise."

June choked back tears as she subconsciously crossed her heart with her index finger. "I promise."

Several miles passed beneath them before she spoke again. "I think we should live in my house to begin with."

"To begin with?"

"It will be fine for now, but we will need a bigger house." She looked toward him. The bewildered expression on his face foretold his coming question.

"What for?"

"Children. I want to have more children. Your children. Our children. At least two or three...more I hope...before I am too old. Boys of course. Your sons."

His facial expression had not changed. "How do you know you'll have sons?"

She giggled. "I have no way of knowing any more than you do, but I asked God to let me bear you sons. He did not necessarily answer me, but I have just had this feeling inside me ever since. Now you have to promise me something."

"What?"

"Even if we end up with a whole baseball team of girls..." She waited for a response.

"What? Whatever it is, I promise."

"That you will still love me and every one of them."

He turned down a side road and stopped.

"Are you crazy? What are you doing?" she asked as he sat there staring at her.

He leaned over and kissed her. One of those kisses that took her breath away and left her longing for more. "I promise to never stop loving you and every child you ever bear. I've already started with April."

Four more weeks. She almost said it aloud as she fanned herself with her hat.

Conor put the truck into gear and started on down the side road.

"Where are we going?"

He pointed to the sign on the fence.

*HORSES 4 SALE*

"This is the road to the Haygood's place."

Conor slowed the truck to a crawl to minimize the dust as they neared the house. Bert Haygood had seen them coming and waved from the porch when they pulled up.

"C'mon in," Bert hollered as soon as Conor's feet hit the hard-packed clay of the yard. "Anna will have dinner on the table directly."

June handed Conor, two of the cantaloupes when he opened her door and bundled four pears on her arms. Bert held the back door open as they brought their bounty into the kitchen.

"Oh, let me help you with those, dear," Anna Haygood expressed to June as she bustled to the rescue. "What a lovely treat."

"We stopped at the Chavez farm on the way out of town," June offered. "They have such nice produce there. Juanita is running low on fruit this time of year, but still has a nice selection of vegetables."

"That was so thoughtful of you." She looked around the room.

Conor had left the cantaloupes beside the pears on the counter and followed Bert back onto the porch.

"These men have no sense of manners, I'm Anna Haygood." She smiled at June offering her hand. "That ruffian in the overalls talking to the sheriff is my husband, Bert."

"June Sommers," she replied. "Can I help you with anything?"

"We eat pretty plain around here. I've just cooked a pot roast with potatoes and carrots. All I need to do is dish it up. You could clean and slice one of those cantaloupes you brought if you'd like to though."

She set June up at the counter with a knife and serving bowl, then handed her an apron.

"I hear you're soon-to-be Mrs. Armenta, if the rumor mill in this end of the county is right," she phrased it as a statement, not a question, but awaited June's confirmation, nonetheless.

"Yes." June blushed with her response. "They seem to be correct."

"Not entirely, Miss Sommers. The gossips in Searchlight say that some city gal bamboozled our naïve country boy sheriff and sunk her claws into him. It's mostly just jealousy, I think. A lot of the single ladies around here have considered Sheriff Armenta the ultimate catch for quite some time. Add the fact that nobody down this end of the county has ever seen you before, they've made it out like you're some kind of vixen on a manhunt. I haven't been around you for five minutes missy, but I can clearly tell that you're not that way at all. The opposite, I'd bet. You seem quite the catch yourself, in fact. It wouldn't surprise me if that wind blew the other way altogether."

June's blush grew a little deeper. "I thank you for the compliment, Mrs. Haygood, and I can assure you that our feelings for each other are entirely mutual. I will admit though that the gossips may be partially right. I think I might have gotten the better end of the deal. Conor is a wonderful man."

"We've never leaned one way or another when it comes to

lawmen, but Bert sure is taken by him. We never met him before last week, and I believe Bert would do just about anything Sheriff Armenta asked of him."

At that moment the two men came in the door.

"Better we shut up about it for now," Anna commented to June.

"What were you two talking about?" Bert asked gruffly.

"Horses," Anna replied as she sliced the roast on a platter.

"Horses? You ain't never talked to nobody about a horse in your life."

"Did I say horses? I meant horses' asses. You know the kind. Husbands that sneak off outside, fartin' around in the fresh air while their wives work in a stuffy kitchen to put a nice dinner on the table." Anna turned to face Bert and started to shake her butcher knife at him but thought better of it. "You two get washed up and sit yourselves down at the table," she stared at Bert with clinched teeth until he left the kitchen.

June looked guiltily at Conor biting her lower lip without realizing it until he followed Bert out.

As soon as they were out of earshot, Anna spoke softly to June, "Sometimes you need to cause a little mischief. Keeps them on their toes."

"Does it work?"

"It has so far." She paused to think. "Forty-four years this coming March."

The sound of chairs sliding on the wood floor in the next room announced their return.

"We're on," Anna told June as she removed her apron. "The key is to act like nothing happened." Anna continued as June removed her apron. "You bring the potatoes and cantaloupe. I'll get the roast and carrots."

The men were seated at opposite ends of the table when Anna placed her half of the meal in the center. Conor rose to his feet as June did the same with the other two serving bowls. He held the chair for her when she sat down, then returned to his own seat.

Bert's eyes darted around the table as if expecting a flanking move from the cavalry's next attack as platter and bowls made their way from one seat to the next. When everyone's plates were filled, he made one more scan of the table, sliced a hefty portion of roast beef on his plate and poked it into his mouth. He slowly began chewing. When beyond the point of no return, she sprung it on him.

"Would you like to say grace for our guests, honey?" Anna asked sweetly.

He looked down then closed his eyes and swallowed hard.

"Yeah, sure." He struggled before taking a drink of water. Then bowed his head and clasped his hands. "Lord thank you for bringing Sheriff Armenta and his fiancée...his fiancée..."

"Miss Sommers," Anna whispered.

"His fiancée, Miss Sommers, to share this meal with us. Bless this food we're about to eat. Amen."

Amens followed around the table and eventually the sounds of silverware on plates trailed afterward.

Halfway through the meal, Bert finally broke the silence, "Speaking of horses," he began awkwardly, "Sheriff Arneta and I just loaded up the prettiest little gelding you ever saw."

The statement was obviously directed to June who sat dumbstruck with a forkful of potatoes halfway to her mouth.

"I thought you told me that he's 'a little spunky'?" Conor finally asked.

"Well, he's just a three-year-old, so it's not like he's been ridden thousands of miles yet, but he's finished and ready to go. I'm sure Miss Sommers can handle him. She looks like she would like riding a horse with a little personality."

"I didn't know that Miss Sommers was in the market for a horse," Anna interrupted.

"Well, I just thought since Sheriff Armenta rides, she might want to go along sometimes, since they're gettin' married and all."

"When Conor and I ride together, I ride Chalk, a mare that

belongs to his brother. Chalk and I get along fine," June interjected.

"Doesn't Smokey belong to Clark County now? Why are you trying to sell him?" Anna prodded.

"When he comes up for the sheriff's sale, he'll probably just end up going for dog food. He's a better horse than that."

The conversation quickly dwindled and the four finished their dinner in silence. Afterward, they began the usual, "we really need to be going," conversation, and June and Conor thanked the Haygoods for their hospitality. Con told Bert he should be receiving payment from the county in the next couple of weeks, and they drove away with Smokey's head pointed into the wind looking over the cab of the truck and Running Dog poking his head out the side rails by the horse's knees.

"What was that all about?" Conor asked.

"I have no idea. Anna was a little miffed that Bert dragged you out the door without even having a chance to introduce us, but she was genuinely very nice to me. We talked briefly about the perception of some local women that I came from the big city and stole you away from them, but that was mostly in introduction to how Bert admired you and that the gossipers were mistaken and I was a nice person.

"Then when you guys came back in, out of the blue, she made it sound like we were telling secrets about you guys and tore into Bert. When you went to wash up, she was all sweet again and said women need to cause some mischief now and again to keep their husbands guessing. I asked her how that worked out and she said it had been working for forty-four years with her and Bert."

"Honey, if you need to keep me guessing, could you try to find a nicer way to do it?" he asked sincerely. "I don't want to live like that."

"I promise." She grinned and leaned over to kiss his cheek.

They had discussed most of the things June thought were critical on their way from Las Vegas. Now the conversation took on a more casual tone. They stopped at a corner store and gasoline station at the junction of the road to Nelson and El Dorado. Conor bought them each a Coca-Cola, and June fed Smokey one of their pears. Juice from it spurted from his mouth and all over her when he bit down on it.

"Not quite the same as a carrot or apple." She laughed as she went to the ladies' room to wash her sticky face and hands. The sun was setting and glowed through his mane when she returned. *He really is a pretty horse* she thought to herself as she got back in the truck and they continued up the road.

A dim glow from the kerosene lamps inside Paddy's house barely marked that someone lived there. It suddenly brightened and Paddy appeared in the door with a lantern as he crossed the yard to meet them.

"Full tank of gasoline," Conor told him when they met. "And the truck ran just fine."

The brothers unloaded the blue roan and turned him into the corral. Chalk came over to greet him and to exchange a few mild challenges.

"They have plenty of water for tonight. I'll give them hay in the morning," Paddy noted. "Does he have a name?"

"Smokey."

"I'll take good care of him, Con."

June gathered the pears and cantaloupes, putting them all into the flour sack. Running Dog leapt into the rumble seat as she walked toward Conor's car. She turned back to look at Conor through the darkness. "Don't forget your pistol."

She sat in the passenger seat of the coupe when Conor slipped the pistol under the driver's side.

"How did you know?"

"I looked away for long enough this morning to know you had time to make the transfer...and just to keep you guessing."

"I like your way better than Anna Haygood's."

"So do I."

After Conor shifted the car into high gear, June laid her left hand atop his on the shift knob. It was comforting to be touching. The reassurance. The sensation that as long as she could feel him there, she was safe. Everything would be okay.

"He really is pretty."

Conor understood he was joining into a thought process that had been working in her mind for some time. It only took a moment to guess where this would lead.

"Smokey?"

"Yes. I think he is really a very pretty horse."

"I think so too."

"Will they really make him into dog food?"

"It will depend on who buys him when the time comes."

"But there is nothing wrong with him."

"He has one foot larger than the others."

"What?"

"His right front foot is larger than the other three."

"Does it hurt him?"

"I doubt he even knows it."

"How do *you* know it?"

"I tracked him for three days."

"And you noticed it."

"I might have eventually, but Bert told me. That little tip may have saved me days of tracking Altaha. He was a full day ahead of me to begin with. When Smokey's tracks got mixed in with those of other horses, I could quickly pick his out. When I lost his trail and came across a set of tracks in the vicinity, it was easy to tell if they were his or not."

"None of this really matters though, does it."

"Not really. Buyers for dog food factories tour the country buying mostly old, sick, or crippled horses for really cheap. Depending on how many horses they need, they sometimes by buy healthier ones. The county will eventually want to sell Smokey. When they do, they will run an ad in the newspaper for three days for a sheriff's auction. Those horse-buyers watch for that sort of ad every day. If any of them are in the area when the sale comes up, they will be there hoping to buy him cheap."

"How does the auction work?"

"I hold the auction, usually on the courthouse steps. The highest bidder gets whatever is being sold, the county clerk gets the money and I sign the bill of sale."

"And you would sell him for dog food?"

"I would sell him to whoever the highest bidder is. Lots of horses get sold to make dog food just because no one else wants them. That's how it works."

June got very quiet for the rest of the drive home to her house. She held up the flour sack. "How many of these do you want to take home?"

"A couple of the pears will be fine."

"It's too cold to sit on the porch tonight. Would you like to come in? I can make coffee."

"Sure. It's been a long day. I could use a cup of coffee."

June left two pears on the seat of Conor's car and brought the rest into the kitchen. She poured fresh grounds and water into the percolator and set it on the stove. Conor hung his hat by the door and followed her to the kitchen. When she turned from the stove, he wrapped his arms around her shoulders and held her to his chest. She put her arms around his waist and pulled herself closer. He leaned forward and softly kissed her neck just below her ear.

"I love you, June Sommers."

She lifted her face to his. "And I love you, Conor Armenta," she replied and softly kissed his lips. "Would you like to sit on the sofa?"

"Uh-huh."

June led him into the living room only lit from the kitchen light through the doorway and seated him on the sofa. She took off her riding boots and knelt backward beside and facing him. She leaned forward and kissed him again. Not the soft, tender kiss from the kitchen, but a kiss of heated passion. She gasped for air when their lips separated and buried her face into his shoulder. She sat there breathing heavily, just wrapped in his arms for several minutes. She could hear the percolator in the next room.

"I think our coffee is ready," she muttered as she unwrenched herself from his embrace and went to the kitchen.

Returning moments later, she sat Conor's cup on the end table. Sitting down beside him with her own cup held tightly between her hands, she scrunched her shoulders into the back of the sofa. Snuggled beneath his arm, she leaned sideways against his ribcage and sipped her coffee. After they finished their coffee, June sat her empty cup beside his on the end table. She turned and knelt again beside him with her knees pushed against the back of the sofa. With her arms around his neck, she pulled herself to him and kissed him again as ardently as before.

"Would you like to stay the night?" she asked between gasps for air when their lips parted. "We have the house all to ourselves."

"I've thought about it many times since that night you first offered. I've nearly accepted at other times like this one. Each time has become more difficult. There is nothing keeping me from it, but my own conscience...and your reputation. I need to go home now. I could never face Father O'Malley in the morning if I didn't."

# 18

June and Conor shared coffee and biscuits on her front porch in the fresh morning air. The red-orange leaves of Gambel oak trees in June's yard complimented the bright yellow ones of the cottonwood next door. After coffee, they casually strolled hand in hand the two blocks to the Joan of Arc Roman Catholic Church on Second Street.

Stuart pulled the McLeod family sedan to the curb outside just as they arrived.

"Good morning," Olivia greeted them cheerfully as soon as she exited the car. "Have you two lovebirds set a date yet?"

"As a matter of fact, we have," June replied, beaming. "November twenty-ninth. The Saturday following Thanksgiving Day."

"That gives us four weeks to plan," Olivia responded excitedly, tearing June away from Conor in the process. Juan and Maggie Armenta had just parked alongside the McLeods' vehicle and Olivia immediately recruited her mother into the hen party.

April, as soon as she could extricate herself from the back seat, had her arms wrapped around Conor's waist sharing every detail of her exploits for the past twenty-four hours. As Stuart began herding his own two adolescents toward the church, April ran to catch up to her best friend and soon-to-be cousin, Donna.

Juan came up to join Conor quietly laughing. "They remind me of you three kids when you were that age."

Conor smiled and nodded remembering his childhood before his father's crippling accident. He put his arm around Juan's shoulder and they followed the entourage toward the steps into the church.

At one o'clock, Conor munched on a ham sandwich confiscated from his sister's refrigerator as he drove his county pickup toward Arden. Juan had gone home, Maggie and Olivia were at June's planning their wedding, and April and Donna were playing with dolls at Joyce's. Olivia kept their family car in order to drive her mother home later, so Con drove Stuart and their son, David home after church. He raided the refrigerator in exchange for cab-fare.

When he finished his sandwich, Conor took a swig of luke-warm water from the canteen laying on the seat beside him. A quick calculation brought the realization the water was probably from Cottonwood Spring in Arizona on Thursday morning.

He turned his thoughts to the application folded in his pocket. Carter Simms was a thirty-two-year-old cowboy from Oregon. Only four months on his last job after being a state brand inspector for over a year. That was the job that might help make him a good deputy. Then nothing for almost a year.

Stopping on the outskirts of the community, he reminisced for a moment. He had lived here himself for nearly a decade working for a gypsum mine. He was laid off just short of four years ago and became a deputy. Most of what was left here disappeared this past year after the plaster plant closed. The husband of Simms's wife's sister was unfamiliar to him, but he worked for the railroad so should be easy to find.

As Conor idled his pickup down the street of an area where

most of the railroad workers live, he spotted Amos Browne. The foreman of the Union Pacific track crew sat on his porch in a rocking chair smoking a pipe. Mrs. Browne occupied a similar chair beside him crocheting. Conor eased to a stop and shut off the engine. Amos took a draw on his pipe and exhaled a voluminous cloud of bluish smoke.

"What brings you down here on a Sunday, Sheriff Armenta? We ain't had no trouble out this a way since your deputy hauled Logan and Rae off that Sunday last April."

"There isn't any trouble that I know of right now, Amos. I'm looking for a fella by the name of Carter Simms. He used to be a brand inspector up in Oregon and I heard he's looking for work. Him and his wife are supposed to be staying with a brother-in-law by the name of Johnson who works for the railroad."

"That'd be the cowboy. I know him. Seems to be a good kid and speakin' of kids, they got a houseful. Five or six, I think."

"Where might I find him?"

"Johnson's place is the next block over and down about the third or fourth house. The cowboy has a blue sedan. I don't know the make, but it has Oregon tags."

"Thanks, Amos."

"Anytime, Sheriff."

"Those two hands of yours behaving themselves?"

"They've been like a couple little angels ever since that little vacation in the hoosegow." Amos grinned.

Conor nodded and fired up his pickup. Amos waved, and he returned it with a salute of his index finger on the brim of his Stetson as he pulled out. An old Oldsmobile sedan sat in front of a house the next street over. The license plates were Oregon and it might have been blue beneath the pale coating of dust. The mailbox hanging from the fence read "JOHNSON" on its side. Six children played in the street out front.

"Does Carter Simms live here?" Con asked the mob in general.

The tallest boy quit what he was doing and ran inside without uttering a word.

A moment later a man with sandy-brown hair and about his own build somewhat hesitantly came out the screen door and stood on the porch. The tall boy followed but stayed behind the man.

"Are you Carter Simms?" Conor asked.

"Yessir. I am," he replied questioningly.

"You filled out this application last week?"

"Well, yeah." Simms suddenly relaxed. "I never expected to hear anything about that so soon…or never a-tall for that matter. When the boy said the police were here, I thought there must be something wrong. Brother-in-law's at work and my wife and her sister are over at a church-doings of some sort."

"You want the job?"

"Boy, I sure do, Sheriff." He turned to the boy. "Go on ahead, Bobby. You kids go ahead and play. There's nothing you need to hear about." Bobby descended the steps and passed Con on his return to join the others. "C'mon have a seat, Sheriff." Simms motioned to a couple of weathered chairs on the porch. "Could I get you anything?"

"No. I'm fine, thanks. I'm Sheriff Conor Armenta," Con added and extended his hand when he reached the porch.

"Carter Simms"—when shaking the sheriff's hand nervously —"but I guess you already knew that."

"You don't have anything to be worried about, Carter. I just want to get to know you a little bit."

Both men sat down. Con glanced over the application.

"It says here you graduated high school in Lakeview, Oregon."

"Yessir, 1916."

"But you're not a veteran. Not that there's anything wrong with that, neither am I. It's just not that common."

"My mom was sick. Dad got killed when I was sixteen. They didn't draft me."

"Your mom got better?"

"Some. For a little while. She died in twenty-one. Brights Disease."

"I'm sorry." Conor regretted asking the question. "My story's not a lot different in some ways. Papa got hurt, crippled when I was fourteen. Sheep rancher. He couldn't do that anymore. We sold all of the sheep over the next year and moved to town. When he got where he could walk pretty good, my parents bought a café. I think a friend loaned them money for it. They've never said. Anyway, I had a younger brother and sister still in school when the draft came and I was still helping to support my folks so, they didn't draft me either.

"Big difference is, they're still both alive. I went to church with them this morning. I'm sorry you…"

"It's all right," Simms replied. "Been a long time now."

"Yeah." He looked back at the application. "You were a brand inspector for a little over a year. How did that go?"

"The beginning of the end, I'd say."

"It says you quit. Why?"

"There was a ring of rustlers. Eight guys it turned out. I went to school with four of 'em. One was a small-time rancher and his son. I'd worked with the other two a couple of times before. I knew all of them. It took me six months to figure it all out and gather enough evidence to arrest the first three. That gave me more evidence, and eventually led to convicting all of them. All of these guys were well-liked. I don't think anybody had a clue what they'd been doing, but I did my job and did it well. They all went to the Oregon State Pen. The rancher had two other kids still in school. They spent every cent they had and sold all their stock trying to beat it in court but lost it all in the end. The ranch. Everything. Wives of two of the others left town in shame.

"Pretty soon hardly nobody in the county would talk to me. I thought they were maybe afraid that I was trying to get more of their friends arrested. I don't know. My two oldest kids were in grade school. Other kids stole their lunches. Beat them up. You name it. Anyway, I quit. I figured if they hated the brand inspector, I wouldn't be the brand inspector no more.

"I went back to cowboyin' for the biggest ranch in the valley. A ranch that these rustlers had been stealing from for who knows how long. I thought I'd live out my days working for them. Live in one of their houses. Just do my job. It was a lot less money, but that would be okay. My family would be fine and that's what mattered…and it was good for about four months, just long enough to get settled in real good and folks started nodding an acknowledgment when you met them at the post office door instead of looking the other way.

"Then he fired me. Out of the blue. Cold turkey. I thought, 'what the hell?' you know? He had the foreman do the dirty work and when I asked why? He just said to talk to the boss. So, I did. You know what the boss said? He said that he just wanted to show me how it felt. That the wife of the rancher who had been rustling cattle was his wife's best friend and it was my fault they lost everything and this was his payback for what I done. It was right before Christmas and he gave me a week to get moved outta his house. He came to the house to give me my final pay. And right in front of my kids he says, 'how are they gonna feel when Santy Claus don't show up this year?' What can I say to them after they've heard that?"

"That was almost a year ago," Conor commented. "What have you been doing since?"

"Living in a grain shed. Working for a few days at a time here and there."

Conor turned to watch the children playing in the street. "All yours?"

"The four youngest. The two older boys are my nephews."

"What brought you here instead of somewhere else?"

"My brother-in-law. He used to work for the U.P. up at Winnemucca. His wife and mine are sisters. That's where we all met. Ten years ago, now. I was wranglin' for a horse-ranch at Denio at the time. Brought a hundred head of mustangs down to ship out on the railroad. By the time I made it back to the ranch, I was married and out of a job. Like they say, the rest is history.

"Bob and Sue Johnson was already married and settled in at the time. Sarah and me headed up to the Warner Valley looking for a home. Bob transferred down here a couple of years ago. He said they was buildin' a town out where the new dam is gonna be and there might be a chance to find work here. We got here two weeks ago. Looks like lots of other fellas had the same idea."

Conor nodded in understanding. "They don't ask this on the application, but they should. Why do you think you'll make a good deputy?"

"Well, I ain't never broke a law in my life that I know of." Carter Simms grinned then shook his head looking down at his feet. When he looked back up it was straight into Conor's eyes. "Contrary to what some folks might think, I was a damned good brand inspector. I can cut through a herd of five hundred cattle, read every brand, and not stir 'em up. I doubt that skill will ever need doin', but it takes an understanding of nature and a knack to do it right. I can track about anything with hair on it and do it better than most. I think I'm a pretty good investigator when the need arises and a good shot with pistol or rifle, but I hope I never need to be."

"You understand that this job can be dangerous."

"Can't be much worse than what I just came out of."

"We've had five murders this year and that's not counting two moonshiners that were killed in a shootout and a suicide."

"I understand. I can hold my own. I won't let you down, Sheriff."

"Be at my office at seven o'clock tomorrow morning shaved, bathed, and ready to work."

"Yessir, Sheriff. I'll be there."

* * *

## MONDAY NOVEMBER 3, 1930

Sheriff Conor Armenta hung his Stetson on one of the pegs by the door of the sheriff's office at six-fifteen. All four of the new recruits jumped to their feet when he walked in. He glanced at the clock on the wall. The smell of fresh-baked doughnuts filled the room as he sat two white paper sacks on the table beside the coffeepot. Each of the men held a coffee cup in their hand, appearing almost paralyzed for fear of making a false move.

"Better to be a half hour early than five minutes late," he commented as he glanced again at the clock while filling a cup for himself. "I expect you gents to be as clean and well-groomed as feasible under whatever conditions might dictate. I don't expect you to be tin soldiers. Manners and respect. That's what's important in here and out there." He pointed toward the window. "Help yourselves to a doughnut and clean up after yourselves when you're through. If the coffee pot is empty, make fresh. The ladies that work here aren't maids.

"I take it that you gents have met Hazel Corbyn. She knows more about how to run this place than all of the rest of us combined. She's a lady, as is Dottie Dickenson our night dispatcher. Treat them appropriately.

"Introduce yourselves around, if you haven't already and get to know each other some. I'll be ready for you shortly."

When he closed the door behind him, Conor sat down behind his desk. He hired both Ben and Whit shortly after being appointed interim sheriff following his predecessor suffering a stroke. One was to fill the vacancy created by his own advancement the other to replace a deputy that quit when Conor had been promoted ahead of him. The department had consisted of the sheriff and three deputies since he had joined it. A new era was now approaching Clark County, Nevada.

He stood and crossed the room to the safe that sat in the corner and spun the dial. Inside were three holstered Smith & Wesson .38 Special service revolvers. They were nearly new, purchased sometime before his term for an emergency posse, should the need ever arrive. He would deal with the pistols later.

In the rear of the safe, he found a small wooden case with a hinged lid. He opened it and removed four blue velvet pouches. He pulled the gold braided cord on one and dumped the contents into his palm. A gold-and-silver-plated bronze star, shined to perfection. 'Deputy Sheriff, Clark County, Nevada,' was embossed across the center of it. He returned it to the pouch, then placed all four on his desk.

Conor walked over to the supply cabinet and rummaged his way to a stack of booklets in the back. *Clark County Sheriff's Department—Code of Conduct.* Someone had compiled it some two decades ago, probably Hazel, Conor surmised, and had it professionally printed. There must have been a minimum quantity at the printing company because a stack of more than two dozen still remained in inventory. He took four of them and returned to his desk.

Taking the first book, he opened it to the first page, *Your Oath of Office.* He read it carefully as he had several times since taking the oath himself. Taking the four books and the four applications, he returned to the outer office and handed them to Hazel.

"Would you enter the applicants' names on page one and bring them to me when they dry?"

"Yes sir, Sheriff."

He turned to the candidates. "Come on in, gentlemen," he told them. "Bring your chairs. You can come back and refill your coffee and get another doughnut if you like. This will start out pretty casual."

Within a couple of minutes, the four were seated in Con's office with coffee and fresh doughnuts. Francois had his .38 strapped around his waist and McCoy and Simms each wore single-action Colts around theirs.

"Over a hundred men applied to become deputies of the Clark County Sheriff's Department," Conor began as he perched on the front of his desk. "Three professionals narrowed the choices down to the ten they felt were most qualified. Of them, I interviewed the four of you. You were each chosen because of your specific qualifications. I am authorized and it is my intention to hire all four of you. This is not a competition. In your interviews, I asked each of you if you understood the responsibilities and possible dangers of becoming a lawman. You all expressed a desire to accept the conditions of the job. You've had time to think about it since then. If there are any doubts, I appreciate the time you've taken to come this far and you are free to leave now without any prejudices."

Romeo Benelli shuffled in his seat but stayed there. "Is everything okay, Romeo?" Carter Simms controlled the urge to grin at the unique name but continued to give Sheriff Armenta his full attention.

Benelli blushed. "I don't have a gun."

"One will be issued to you," Conor reassured him as he glanced at Simms and McCoy. "And anyone else who might need one."

"Come in," Con responded to a soft knock at the door.

Hazel entered and laid the books and applications on his desk. "You'll need these for their files too," she told him as she placed duplicate copies of the oath beside them.

"Have Jesse come in when he gets here too," Conor told her.

"He's filling out a report from yesterday right now," she replied.

"When he's finished then."

He took the books and handed them out to the appropriate men. "You'll see on page one, *Your Oath of Office*. When you take that oath, you'll sign on the line at the bottom where it says, sworn officer. I'll sign where it says officiated by, and Deputy Jesse Slater will sign where it says witness. This will be your copy of the contract you are accepting when you become an officer of the Clark County Sheriff's Department."

He held up the file copies Hazel had brought in. "These are my copies and you will be bound to uphold them. This is serious business, gentlemen. No less serious than a contract at the bank or a marriage license."

"Or induction papers," Boudreaux added.

"Exactly," Conor agreed as a firm rap sounded at the door. "Come in, Jesse."

As Jesse entered, he announced, "Gentlemen, this is Deputy Jesse Slater. We have worked together since I first became a deputy. He saved my life, earlier this year when I was shot twice while assisting the Bureau of Prohibition southeast of here." The statement widened the eyes of every recruit. Conor continued as he turned to him. "Jesse, this is Romeo Benelli, Francois Boudreaux, you know Mark, and Carter Simms."

The last statement embarrassed Mark McCoy and drew expressions of a second revelation among his new peers. Con and Jesse, both noticed it.

"Let me reiterate," Conor began in a tone making it perfectly clear. "This is not a competition. You are all being sworn in on the same day, all with the same seniority, the same pay, and the same responsibilities. After you're sworn in, each of you will be on two weeks probation. At the end of that two weeks, I expect every one of you to become permanent members of the department. There will be no favoritism beforehand or afterward. Understood?"

"Now read and understand the oath of office, then take a few minutes to glance through the rest of the book. I want you to read it all by this time tomorrow. These are the rules that your signature says you'll follow."

Con strolled across the outer office to the coffeepot and refilled his cup, then took a doughnut and returned to his office. Jesse slouched beside Con's desk in the one office chair that usually sat in front of it. He sat up in his seat when the sheriff returned.

"Grab yourself some coffee and a doughnut, Jess. We've got a couple minutes."

Jesse left the room as Conor sat behind his desk then picked up the telephone and dialed.

"Good morning, Amy. Is Newt in?...Conor Armenta...sure."

"Hey Newt, Con Armenta. I've got four new deputies. We want to see how they shoot. Is your gravel pit available...yeah, maybe all week and then some...you bet. Thanks, Pard."

After hearing half of the telephone call, all four recruits' eyes and ears were glued on the sheriff when Jesse returned.

"Ben and Whit are here," he told Con.

"Tell them to grab some coffee. They can join us in a few minutes...and close the door too please."

"For lack of a better system, we'll do this alphabetically. Romeo? Come forward please."

Conor retrieved a Bible from his lefthand desk drawer and held it up about mid-torso high in his right hand.

"Raise your right hand and put your left on the Bible." After he had done so, Conor continued. "Repeat after me. I, Romeo Benelli."

"I, Romeo Benelli."

"As an officer of the Clark County Sheriff's Department."

"As an officer of the Clark County Sheriff's Department."

"Do solemnly swear."

"Do solemnly swear."

"To enforce and uphold the laws of Clark County."

"To enforce and uphold the laws of Clark County."

"The State of Nevada."

"The State of Nevada."

"And the United States of America."

"And the United States of America."

"To the best of my ability."

"To the best of my ability."

"So, help me God."

"So, help me God."

"You may lower your hands," Conor told him and picked up one of the velvet bags from his desk. He deftly removed the badge from it and pinned it on Romeo's left shirt pocket.

"As sheriff of Clark County, Nevada, I hereby name you Deputy Romeo Benelli."

"Thank you, Sheriff," Romeo said, choking back the lump in his throat as they shook hands. Romeo, Conor, and Jesse then signed his *Oath of Office*.

The ceremony was repeated three more times. Each one as emotional as the others, but perhaps for three entirely different reasons.

When all the oaths were concluded, Conor went to the safe and brought out one of the nearly new Smith & Wesson .38 Specials holstered and rolled inside a black leather police belt. He recorded the serial number on a receipt and had Romeo sign it.

"Mark." He beckoned. "Let me see that pistol."

Mark McCoy took the gun from his holster and handed to the sheriff butt first. "Single action. It's the same as the ones we used at the studio. Basically, just a newer version of the old Colt Peacemaker."

"And it's almost brand new."

"I just bought it a few months ago. To practice my quickdraw more than anything."

"You shouldn't be needing that quickdraw around here," he commented as he returned the revolver. "We'll buy your cartridges."

"Carter?"

He had his old Colt out of its holster and handed it to him as he walked up. "This one's about as old as McCoy's is new." He chuckled.

Simms was right. There was hardly a blemish of bluing remaining on the old revolver. The gun was probably a survivor of the previous century. Even though the exterior of the barrel had minor remnants of rust-pitting, the inside was spotless and the action and cylinder felt tight. Conor looked closely at the writing embossed on the barrel but failed to make it out.

"Smokeless," Carter translated his thoughts. "It was my father's. It looks a little rough, but it's not."

"Same goes," Con told him when he handed it back to him. "We'll buy your cartridges."

"Jesse, you can bring the other two in."

As Whit Ellis and Ben Neilly entered, the four recruits remained seated.

"You fellas can play Tiddledy-Winks or Pattycake or whatever you choose to decide, but two of you will relinquish your seats to your superiors."

Benelli and McCoy stood immediately and took a place against the wall. Conor made a mental note of it.

"This meeting was arranged before I ever knew we were going to be hiring four new deputies. I called for this meeting to recognize two of my deputies for performing their duties in an outstanding manner a week ago this past Saturday. We don't have little stars on a calendar or any other method to show praise for our peers. They didn't know it at the time, when they were called to investigate a kidnapping of sorts, that the suspect was in fact a multiple murderer and wanted by the FBI." Conor continued with a detailed account of their exploits that morning. "In a very, very touchy situation that could easily have cost the lives of three innocent civilians, Deputy Slater and Deputy Ellis kept cool heads thus averting a catastrophe. When the victims were out of danger, they pursued the suspect on foot for more than a couple of miles. He only escaped when an accomplice picked him up in a truck on a road south of town."

"What happened to the suspect?" Boudreaux asked.

"He died last Tuesday in Arizona."

"So, after our guys risked their lives here, some clown in Arizona gets all the glory for killing him?" Boudreaux questioned in disgust.

"That's not what happened, and it's not about 'the glory,' as you put it. It's about doing your job and doing it right. Read your *Code of Conduct*. Memorize it.

"Deputy Neilly is just as good an officer as Ellis and Slater. He was working nights by himself last weekend. Just as dangerous

or more so. He just wasn't the one who got that particular call."
He looked each new deputy in the eye as he perused the room.
"If each one of you don't get that, you're the wrong men for this
job. And I'm not nearly as good a judge of character as I thought I
was."

"If the boys over in Arizona didn't kill him, what happened to
the murderer?" Simms questioned.

"He fell down a five hundred foot deep mineshaft with four
hundred feet of water in it. Sheriff Armenta had been tracking
him since his last murder," Mark McCoy answered.

"How do you know that?" Boudreaux persisted.

"It's been all over the newspaper for the past three days.
Sheriff Armenta wounded him up north sometime last week—"
McCoy began.

"The bullet hole in your hat," Benelli interrupted in shock.

"And Sheriff Armenta chased him into an abandoned mine in
Arizona where he fell to his death nine days later," McCoy
finished.

"Holy cow," Carter Simms exhaled the words.

"Regardless of what the newspaper said, I'm not the hero
here. Jesse and Whit are the two men that deserve 'the glory'
today for the innocent lives they saved a week ago. Including my
father's."

"That brings us to the other reason this meeting was originally
called. As can be seen here in this room this department is under-
going a rapid growth spurt. The Clark County Commissioners
authorized creating a new position in the department. Undersheriff. Following the recommendations of Judge William Tucker and
District Attorney Donald D. Davis, Deputy Jesse Slater has been
selected to fill that position. I discussed it with him on Friday and
he accepted the promotion. For the most part, he's been
performing that duty for some time. Now it's official. Whenever
I'm out of reach, Jesse is in charge."

"Hear, hear!" Ben hollered, followed by loud applause joined
by everyone in the room.

"Benelli and Boudreaux, you'll be riding with Jesse today. McCoy and Simms, you're riding with Ben. Tomorrow night one of you will ride with Whit. The schedule will rotate. Everyone will work with each senior deputy. Everyone will work at least three nights in the next two weeks. Jesse and Hazel will work out the schedule by this evening. It will be on the board and someone will show you how to read it."

# 19

C onor Armenta entered the sheriff's office at six-thirty.
The past three days had been troubling as his four new
recruits kept trying to compete against each other when
no competition existed. He just couldn't seem to get through to
them that there were four openings and four of them to fill those
openings. Hazel was on the telephone when he walked in.

"Hold on a second, he just walked in." She held her hand over
the mouthpiece. "Duncan Blackwood."

"He losing more cattle?"

She shrugged her shoulders. He pointed toward his office and
headed that way.

"What's going on, Dunc?" he asked when he picked up the
telephone.

"Harris just called me. One of his riders saw a truck with
stock racks driving up the old Wagon Road with no lights on this
morning."

"When?"

"Just before dawn. About two hours ago, or so."

"You still got cattle up in the high-country?"

"Just those steers up on the mesa. I planned to bring them in on Saturday. We brought the heifers down from Kiel Spring last week."

"I'll head right up there. Don't send anybody out that way. I don't want anything to tip them off."

"I'll be waiting to hear from you, Con."

"Be patient, Dunc. It might take a couple of days."

"Okay."

Duncan Blackwood had been missing cattle, one or two or three at a time every month or so for several months. It had taken Sheriff Armenta a while, but he had figured out part of how the rustlers had been working and hoped to catch them in the act. He had found evidence previously of their operation at both the mesa and Kiel Spring and planned a route to sneak up on the mesa from the spring.

"I'm going out near the end of the old Wagon Road. My pickup will be at Paddy's," Conor told Hazel as he nearly ran out the door. He drove to his house and changed into a khaki work shirt. He placed his badge in the pocket and slipped on his old leather vest. He filled his canteen with fresh water and carried it with his rifle and scabbard to his pickup. Back in the house he checked the inventory of his saddlebags and added a generous stock of lamb jerky. Running Dog watched the entire process and stood to join him in anticipation as Conor slung the saddlebags over his shoulder.

Con grabbed his new Stetson from the back of the kitchen chair where he placed it when he arrived. He paused just short of putting it on and exchanged it for its bullet-ridden predecessor. In doing so, his bedroll appeared in the corner. Noting the elevation he was heading to, he picked it up, also.

"Just in case," he commented to himself as he walked out the door.

At a quarter 'til eight, he stepped into the saddle. His beloved bay gelding, Bob was anxious to be on the move and progressed from a fast trot into his smooth ground-eating lope without encouragement. He rode northwest past Blackwood's house in the distance and into the cut leading to what Blackwood called his deer pasture and school section pasture, then on to the old Wagon Road.

Just past nine o'clock, Conor closed the wire gate exiting the school section pasture. He was a half mile from the old Wagon Road and more than a dozen miles from the Kiel Spring pasture. Turning left onto the old Wagon Road when he reached it, the familiar sight of Charleston Peak loomed straight ahead on the western horizon. He would be less than five miles from it when he left the road and continue toward Kiel Spring. At the first mile, the road forked. The branch to the left turned due south for a half mile before wandering in a generally westerly direction for three or four miles to the Harris place, the man who called Duncan Blackwood this morning. Conor continued straight ahead on the less traveled main road. A fresh set of tracks from truck tires with good tread on them continued up the main road. Bob followed them at his comfortable lope.

Running Dog took the point position for the past mile and followed the road more traveled. In biblical fashion, he soon discovered the error in his ways and repented by cutting cross country to intersect his master's path and fall in behind him. At Bob's ground-eating pace, they reached a section of severely eroded road that marked the end of travel for less than enthusiastic motorists. Conor slowed him to a walk as they negotiated the mile-long obstacle course. At the far end, the tire tracks from the truck were all that remained on the road.

Bob returned to a lope for a half mile before Con turned him into a side canyon that ran to the northwest. A mile of gradual incline brought them to the fence of Blackwood's Kiel Spring pasture. The rancher had installed a new wire gate since his last visit. As they continued on, the canyon began to narrow. The slope to the northeast provided good grazing and still offered edible tufts of grass even after carrying Blackwood's heifers through the summer. The slope on the southwest side gradually grew steeper until it became a vertical cliff at the spring and a mile from the gate.

Running Dog eagerly lapped water at the spring. Grass was sparse there, trampled by the heavy traffic of the heifers coming to drink, but he led Bob to partake of the fresh water there anyway. The air was cold in the shadows of the cliff at seven thousand feet in elevation and Conor was glad he thought to tie his denim jacket to his bedroll on Bob's saddle. He retrieved it now and put it on.

Looking ahead, the canyon narrowed to just a few feet wide and made a sharp turn to the right just a few yards from the spring. Taking a handful of jerky from his saddlebag, he stuffed it into the pocket of his jacket. He kept back one piece to eat along the way as he swung his leg over the saddle. Running Dog dashed ahead as he rode into the narrow slot of the canyon and around its abrupt turn to the north.

In less than a quarter mile they emerged into a small valley. Conor calculated the mesa should be directly above them to the west, but the terrain that direction remained far too steep for Bob to negotiate. The eastern side was much more maneuverable. They immediately began the climb up the sidehill. In just over a half mile, they circled the head of the canyon and turned back west to arrive on the slope just above the mesa.

The diversion took more than an hour, but the rustlers would never suspect his arrival from this direction. The top of the mesa averaged about a quarter mile wide by a little more than a half mile long. It fell off quickly in every direction except the longer ends north and south. Near the center was a small rise topped by a jumble of boulders. Conor knew from his previous investigation that they would access the mesa from the southwest. He kept the rise between him and where he expected the rustlers to be as he made his approach.

A scrubby juniper tree stood twenty yards from the pile of boulders. He dismounted and tied Bob to the tree. He took his field glasses from the saddlebags and slid the strap around his neck, then loosed the thong from the hammer of his 1911 Colt. Running Dog followed as he made his way to the rocks. He suspected if anyone spotted Running Dog from any distance, they would mistake him for a coyote. Sprawling out on a large flat rock he began sweeping the mesa to the south with the glasses.

He soon spotted a man walking about seventy-five yards away. He was taking long, odd, and jaunty strides as he followed two fat steers southward. The man turned and looked right toward them for a moment, then turned and continued a few yards behind the steers. His face had looked familiar, but Conor couldn't place it.

He lowered his field glasses and caught Running Dog in his peripheral vision. He was chasing a ground squirrel or some similar prey among the rocks. Conor returned his attention to the rustler. The first steer dropped below his line of sight into some unknown indention in the terrain. Then the second steer did the same...and finally the rustler followed. Conor scanned the surrounding area with field glasses to no avail.

The two steers finally emerged some distance beyond where he'd last seen them. They stopped, standing broadside to him and looking his way, or more likely at the rustler. At that moment, Running Dog released his low almost imperceptible growl.

"Stay where ya' are and call off yer hound," Roscoe Taylor commanded.

"*Nukwi Sari-chi,*" Conor silenced Running Dog.

"You stand up nice'n slow and keep yer nose pointed south an' yer hands where I can see 'em. Ain't no point in ya seein' my face an' we both live ta regret it."

Conor rose to his knees and Running Dog moved to stand beside him, his eyes on the man behind him. Then Con, holding his hands in the air, rose awkwardly to his feet.

"Right neighborly of ya ta leave yer Winchester on yer pony," he said as he pulled back the hammer.

At that instant Running Dog half barked, half growled, and lunged at the threatening man. The report from the rifle was deafening. Running Dog yelped and Conor heard his body hit the ground simultaneously with the sound of Taylor levering another round into the chamber of his Winchester. In a reflex reaction, Conor had begun to turn to his companion.

"Don't be stupid as that mutt o' yourn!" Roscoe yelled, bringing Conor to an abrupt halt.

"Now, mister lawman...real careful...slip the thong back onto the hammer of that otto-matic pistol in yer holster. We sure don't want it to go off accidental."

Conor obliged. He didn't know who the rustler was, but he knew he was armed and dangerous...and at this point seemed to have nothing to lose. *What was it he had just told his deputies two days ago?* He thought to himself. *Keep a cool head...or wind-up dead*, Sheriff Baker had added when he was hired four years ago.

"Ya see that brindle steer ta yer left?"

"Yes," Conor answered. The first word he spoke since this confrontation began.

"Put yer eyes on it an' nothin' else."

Conor could hear the rustler's feet shuffling on stone toward his right. He was very close.

When the shuffling ended, he spoke again. "Now turn yer head an' body to face him."

Conor again followed the instruction.

"See the Hereford now?"

"Yes."

"Eyes only. Same thing."

He submitted. Roscoe again sidestepped his way to Conor's right.

"Last time," Roscoe commented. "Look at yer horse."

He did. He avoided glancing down at Running Dog. He didn't want to see him lying there dead. He could hear Roscoe moving to a new position behind him.

"Now start walkin'. Right past yer dog an' yer horse an' jus' keep a goin' 'til I say stop."

He looked down at Running Dog when he passed. He couldn't help it. It might be the last time. He glanced at Bob when he was near to him. The best horse he'd ever ridden...and kept walking. *Keep a cool head,* he thought to himself. As he approached the edge of the mesa he began slowing down. It seemed there was a steep shoulder before the vertical drop off the cliff.

"Stop," Roscoe ordered. "See that ravine to the left?"

"Yes."

"Walk to it."

Conor angled to the left and resumed walking.

"Stop," Roscoe ordered when he reached the top of the ravine. "Where's the keys ta them cuffs in yer hip pocket?"

"My vest pocket."

"Take 'em out with yer left hand an' show me."

Conor got them and held his hand up with the key dangling from his index finger.

"Slide 'em inta yer left hip pocket. Ya can climb down the first twenty feet, but you'll need both hands. Ya gotta do it face first. Don't go lookin' back up here at me. I'll tell ya when ta stop."

Conor began working down the steep incline. He definitely needed both hands on rocks and little ledges often sliding on his hind end.

As he reached a small somewhat flat area about twenty feet from the top, Roscoe yelled, "Stop."

He obeyed.

"Take them cuffs outta yer right hip pocket with yer right hand and show 'em to me."

Again, Conor obeyed.

"Put 'em on in front of ya."

He did and stood with his hands hanging in front of him.

"Hold 'em up wheres I can see 'em."

He held his handcuffed hands above his head.

"It's a couple o' miles ta' Kiel Spring. There's places ya might hafta turn around an' go down backerds, but ya can make it. That's a damn fine horse ya left back up yonder. Don'cha worry none. I'll take good care of him."

Conor waited a count of ten then turned around and looked up. No one was there. He began walking down the ravine. At first, the descent was relatively steep, but manageable to walk down remaining upright. In the first quarter mile it became a narrow canyon. It seemed he could touch both walls if his hands were free. It was there he confronted the first obstacle, a near vertical drop of fifteen or twenty feet covered in a jumble of rubble and boulders. He stopped and looked up the west wall toward the mesa. The top was not visible.

Considering himself quite agile and consequently flexible, he contorted his body in every manageable way trying to reach the precious keys in his hip pocket. The rustler seemed to fully understand the limitations of movement in the human body when choosing his method of restraint. It was not humanly possible, at least not for this particular human.

Following the rustler's advice, he turned around and began working his way down. Near the bottom of the incline was a stick wedged among the rocks that caught his attention. It was a branch from a juniper tree an inch in diameter on the small end and about two feet long. It was fairly fresh and strong and the small end was broken off at a sharp angle. It gave him an idea. Wrangling it free, he tossed it to the bottom.

Conor knew that juniper wood was quite stout. When he recovered it, he examined it more closely and determined it suitable for his purpose. Holding the large end between his hands, he torqued around, resolute on inserting the sharp end into his left hip pocket. Finding his mark, he pushed down as hard as he could. If he could poke a hole in the bottom of the pocket, he hoped to work the keys out of the hole and unlock himself. Try as he might, he could not force the point of the stick through the pocket.

"Old Levi Strauss was right," he spoke aloud in disgust as he tossed the stick away. "They are tough as iron."

He continued down the narrow canyon another half mile before encountering another steep drop. Looking down, it appeared at least twice as high as the first one and there had been no place from the beginning to escape the canyon and detour around it. When he reached the bottom his hands and knees were scraped and bruised from negotiating marginal foot and hand-holds with limited mobility.

Fortunately, the floor of the canyon improved to a moderate downgrade as he continued. It also began widening out intermittently into small grassy patches twenty or more feet in width and twice that in length. It encouraged Conor, seeing he might soon reach the larger canyon above Kiel Spring that he and Bob had scaled earlier in the day. It was getting late and he hoped to reach the spring before dark.

He was soon disheartened by a large obstruction at the far end of one of these little meadows. A very large bull facing away from him, swished his tail lazily as he munched on the patch of grass. Conor had never seen this particular bull, but he quickly identified him by appearance and reputation. The cowboys in these mountains called him Old Hickory, in honor of the late Andy Jackson, for his strength and stubbornness. His reputation was legendary. He was a Hereford-longhorn cross and well over ten years old by now. His left horn was twisted and broken off a foot from his eye and he had lived all but a few days of his long life in these mountains.

Legally he belonged to Duncan Blackwood, but he was slave to no one. He was born up here to a longhorn cow and Hereford bull at a period when Dunc was trying to put more meat on the hardy longhorn calves he was producing. He somehow got missed in the fall roundup that first year and amazingly survived a hard winter in the peaks. They brought him down as a yearling with the rest of the herd the next fall.

The men had him in a corral with others to be branded and

because of his age had him stretched out between two mounted horsemen. They had burned him and prepared to castrate him. When he felt cold steel in an area he was particularly fond of, he kicked loose from the lariat around his hind feet and nearly killed the man holding the knife in the process. The horseman who had his horns lost his dally when he bolted past and lost two fingers when he hit the end of the rope. Old Hick crashed through the corral fence and never slowed down until he was back home up here.

Now Conor afoot and with wrists cuffed together had to face him. He reached around his right hip and managed to slip the thong from the hammer of his pistol. There was an abundance of small rocks scattered across the canyon floor, and he gathered a half-dozen of them. On his first attempt of throwing with his hands bound together it made less than halfway to the target. The second was no better. He split the distance and tried again. When the stone landed near the bull's ankle, he turned his head just far enough to eye Conor without pausing in eating his supper. The next bounced off the bull's right hip and he swatted at it with his tail like a fly.

His final attempt struck the bull in that very personal area that had drawn so much attention in the corral all those years ago. Old Hickory jumped straight up and two thousand pounds of beef made a hundred and eighty degree turn in midair. The snort he blew through his nostrils expelled a rocket of snot that nearly reached Con as he scrambled to get his Colt from its holster. He had it out and leveled between the eyes of the red-eyed bull just as Old Hickory pawed a mountain of dirt into the air with his front feet for the third time.

Sweat dripped from Conor's forehead and down his cheeks in the cool mountain air. The smell of the dust drifting in the scant breeze from the bull's recent display of force reached him. Conor had faced down men shooting to kill him in the past. None scared him like the monster now less than twenty feet in front of him.

"Now, Hick." He spoke as calmly as he could knowing full

well that the bull could smell the fear in him. "I really don't want to kill you, but I just saw how quick you can move. If you so much as flinch, I swear I'll pull the trigger and pray it kills you before you can get to me."

They stood there in a Mexican stand-off for what seemed like eons of time. It felt to Conor like Old Hickory must have understood the challenge he made or read his mind. Maybe he remembered the day one fall all those many years ago. Regardless, he pivoted effortlessly on his hind feet and with a final snort trotted off down the canyon.

Conor exhaled and fumbled to remove his hat and wipe the sweat from his brow on his sleeve. He reached Kiel Spring in the last moments before dusk and fitfully managed a much-needed drink of water without drowning himself. He hurriedly sought a comfortable looking spot to rest away from the water so not to interrupt wildlife seeking the same refreshment in the night.

Remembering the jerky in his pocket he stretched out in a likely spot. With his crumpled hat for a pillow, he stared at the stars as he chewed on lamb jerky. Light from the full moon had no more success reaching to the depths of the canyon than that from the sun had at midday. His neck and shoulders ached from the restriction of movement caused by the handcuffs. He made a mental note to remember that in the future when dealing with prisoners.

* * *

*FRIDAY, NOVEMBER 7, 1930*

The direction of the canyon at Kiel Spring and the channel cut through the mountains to the east offered the perfect combination for the sunrise to strike Conor's face in the morning. When he moved to shadow his eyes from its glare he was reminded of the manacles around his wrists. He sat up to improve his angle of view and began chewing in a fresh piece of jerky. The movement also retold the degree of pain in his aching neck and shoulders. He puzzled once again over how to access his keys to the handcuffs.

As a variety of scenarios drifted through his mind, he considered that if his range of motion would allow it, he could stand on his head and the keys might fall from his pocket. As this thought meandered past, he laughed at how stupid he would look trying to perform such acrobatics. That introduced the realization that no one would see him out here anyway. And that understanding somehow suddenly provoked a whole new train of thought.

He scrambled to his feet and began unbuckling his gun belt. Just as he was about to drop one end of the belt, it struck him that if this scheme failed, he would be unable get the belt back on. It only took a moment to ignore the possibility and let go. After laying the belt in the grass, he quickly unfastened his jeans and dropped them to his knees. He bent over and scooped the keys from the pocket. After half a day and all night, he was free in seconds. In less than an hour, he reached the old Wagon Road.

The inbound set of tracks left by the rustler's truck were beneath a fresher set going the other direction. He had slowed to a crawl maneuvering over the washed-out section of road with his heavy load. He sped up after crossing it but often drifted nearly off the road.

"Driving without lights," Conor surmised aloud and picked up his own pace.

An hour later he heard a vehicle approaching and a game warden's pickup soon appeared around the bend. He slowed to a stop when they met.

"You're Sheriff Armenta, aren't you?" he asked when he recognized him.

"Yes I am." Conor pulled the badge from his vest pocket.

"What're you doin' out here afoot at this hour?"

"Chasing a cattle rustler who also became a horse thief yesterday. It's a long story."

"Well, I got one call from yesterday morning and two from

last night of someone driving on this road with no lights in the dark. They figure it's a poacher," the warden told him. "Three calls. I gotta check it out."

"I can assure that it was a rustler. He came out before dawn yesterday and left sometime in the middle of last night. He was driving a truck with stock racks." Con told him. "He had two fat steers belonging to Duncan Blackwood and a horse belonging to me when he left."

"Well, I'll be damned. The folks who saw him were down closer to the highway, but I just figured a poacher would be headed out here somewhere. That fills the bill for me. You need a ride somewhere?"

"You know where my brother's place is?"

"Can't say I do."

"How about Dunc Blackwood?"

"Yeah, sure."

"It's right down the road from there. I'll show you where to turn."

An hour later, they rolled in at Paddy's yard. The game warden had saved him at least two hours by driving the road and twelve miles hiking across Blackwood's ranch.

* * *

While Conor was riding with the game warden to his brother's ranch. Hazel received a telephone call at the sheriff's office.

"This is John Meriwether, is Sheriff Armenta in?"

"I'm sorry, he's out on an investigation."

"Have him call me at the Moapa Trading Post as soon as he can."

"Can someone else help you?"

"Nope. Only him."

"Can I tell him what this is about?"

"I've got a message from Rayno Pete. It's important."

* * *

At eleven o'clock, Conor walked in and hung his crumpled Stetson by the door. He caught the shocked look on Hazel's face.

"You look like..." she began, as Con held up his hand to stop her.

"Don't ask. It'll be in my report."

"John Meriwether from the Moapa Trading Post called about an hour ago," she read from her note. "He said to tell you, and only you, to call him right away. He has a message from Rayno Pete and it's very important."

Conor poured himself a cup of coffee and sat down behind his desk. He picked up the telephone and dialed the operator.

"Sheriff Armenta," he told her. "Get me the Moapa Trading Post."

After a few clicks it began to ring.

"Meriwether," he answered on the third ring.

"Conor Armenta. You need to talk to me?"

"Rayno caught a ride in here this morning. He said your horse showed up at his house before daylight."

"Rayno's never seen my horse."

"He said it's a good-looking bay gelding, and you know as well as me that he don't like horses. It has your canteen, your saddlebags and bedroll, and your rifle tied to the saddle."

"That's my horse. What do you mean, 'he showed up?'"

"That's what he said. He went out the front door before daylight this morning and there he was, tied to the rail on his front porch."

"No tracks?"

"No tracks. He said he back-tracked him a mile up the road and the tracks disappeared among all the tire tracks and whatnot. No tracks at the house. He said it was like he just walked up and tied himself to the rail."

"A ghost horse."

"I never said that, but he did."

"Tell Rayno I'll be there as soon as I can."

"I doubt I'll see him."

"If you do, tell him."

"Sure thing, Sheriff."

"Hazel," he beckoned. "Where's Carter Simms?"

"He and Benelli are riding with Jesse."

"Can you find them?"

"I think so. What's going on?" she asked as Conor donned his hat.

"I need a brand inspector. I'll be back in an hour to pick him up." He stopped at the door. "Call the Mesquite Café and order two roast beef sandwiches and two bottles of Coca-Cola. We'll pick them up on our way out of town."

"To where?"

"Acton."

Jesse dropped Carter off at the office a half hour later and Maggie delivered the lunches ten minutes afterward. "What's going on?" she asked Hazel.

"I don't know, but it's big," she told her.

Maggie suddenly noticed Carter sitting anxiously waiting for her son. "You're one of the new deputies?"

"Yes, ma'am. Carter Simms," he introduced himself as he scrambled to his feet.

"Maggie Armenta," she replied, holding out her hand which he accepted. "You're going with him?"

"Yes, ma'am."

"I'm his mother. Try to keep him from getting killed," she added as she released his hand.

"Yes, ma'am," he replied to her back as she hurried out the door. He turned to face Hazel. The questioning expression on his face needed no oration.

"I don't know. It doesn't normally get like this, but I think that might be changing."

"You ready to go?" Conor asked Simms when he entered the door a few minutes later.

"Yessir, Sheriff."

"We need to swing by the café and pick up lunches on our way," Conor added.

"Your mother dropped them off a few minutes ago," Hazel interrupted as she handed them to Simms on his way out the door.

The blue roan in the back of the Model-T stock-truck sitting in front of the office caught Simms by surprise.

"His name is Smokey and for now, he's property of the county. The saddle belongs to my little brother. I thought you'd like it better than the McClellan that came with him."

"Yessir," Simms replied as they climbed into the truck and hurried north out of Las Vegas on the Arrowhead Trail.

"This truck belongs to my brother. It's a little slow, but steady. We've got two more horses to bring back when we come. It'll be a full load."

"Two more?"

"Yeah, mine and another confiscated horse, like Smokey here."

Conor had Simms dole out their lunches and Coca-Colas as he drove.

"These sandwiches are on me," he told Simms. "I don't want a growling stomach to tip the rustler off. He killed my dog when he growled at him yesterday."

Carter didn't know if the sheriff was joking or serious. He chose to accept serious and eat crow later if need be.

"It's two hours to Moapa, maybe a little more," he told him. "Acton's not far beyond that. We'll ride from there."

As they ate their sandwiches and motored up the graveled highway, Conor began telling the story of his previous investigation of the rustler and his debacle yesterday. He then explained his association with Rayno Pete and chasing Altaha in the Mormon Mountains. He finished by adding how his horse had mysteriously appeared at Rayno's house early this morning. Conor was making a bold move on a hunch, but it all made sense to him. He was made a fool of yesterday and was pretty sure the rustler would think him to still be stumbling down the mountain west of Las Vegas.

They rolled into Rayno's yard at a quarter past two. Bob's saddle was on the porch rail. The horse was in the corral with Rayno's three mules and the Mexican pony. Rayno came from the barn when he heard them pull in.

"Rayno, this is deputy Carter Simms," Conor told him. "Carter, Rayno Pete." Rayno accepted his hand but looked skeptically at the new recruit.

"Carter was a brand inspector up in Oregon for a period of time," Conor explained. "I figured he'd be the right man to have along when arresting a cattle rustler."

Rayno nodded solemnly without comment.

"Where's this Howling Moon guy live, Rayno?"

"Northeast of Guelph, why?"

"I'm pretty sure he's the rustler I've been after, the one who stole Bob over there." That comment brought a little more interest in his Paiute friend's expression. "And killed *Nukwi Sari-chi*, yesterday."

"*Nukwi Sari-chi* is dead?" he asked in anger and disbelief.

"Yes. I'm sorry, my friend."

"I will show you where he lives."

"That won't be necessary, Rayno. I have Deputy Simms with me."

"Friends?" he questioned Conor's authority.

"Yes. Friends."

Rayno Pete went in the front door of his house and returned immediately with his well-worn Colt revolver tucked in his pants.

"Deputy?" Conor questioned.

Rayno tapped his chest and grinned. "Inside."

Rayno had Toohoo saddled and ready to go almost before Conor had Bob to the front of the house. He saddled Bob and checked his rifle. He dug two additional cartridges from his saddlebags and slid them into the magazine, then returned the rifle to its scabbard.

Carter Simms sat tall in the saddle atop Smokey.

"Comfortable?" Conor asked.

"Perfect fit." He grinned. "Even the stirrups. Your brother must be about my height."

"Actually, my fiancé was the last one to use that saddle. And yes."

Rayno led out at a fast trot. They were at Guelph in a half hour. He rode on through the scattered houses and turned right past the last house and stopped in the middle of a sandy track leading toward a weatherbeaten shack five hundred yards ahead.

"That's it," Rayno told them.

"No truck," Conor commented.

"There's a wash behind with a road down into it," Rayno explained. "I've seen him driving the truck up out of it."

"How wide and how deep is the wash?" Conor asked.

"Fifteen or twenty feet wide. Ten feet deep. That little rise you see behind the house is on the other side of the wash."

"A wash?" Carter questioned, unfamiliar with the term.

"A gulley," Con clarified. "Dry creek bed."

Carter nodded.

"Know any good places to cross it?" Conor asked.

"The road behind the house." Rayno grinned.

"Besides that?"

"About three hundred yards below the house, there's a sheep trail that crosses it. The wash makes a bend between it and the house. You can't see the trail from there."

"Okay, if Howling Moon is my rustler, he knows both me and my horse. I'll take the back. I'll ride down and cross the wash. When you see me on the other side, start for the house. Put your badge in your pocket," he told Carter. "He won't know you or your horse and hopefully won't suspect you, Rayno. When you get to the house, I'll be covering the back with my rifle. If no one's there, move to the wash and I'll come in from above on the other side."

"Rayno, don't do anything if you don't have to. You're our backup, okay?"

"Okay, Conor."

"Carter?"

"I'm good. I'll stand my ground, Sheriff."

Conor rode south and found the sheep trail Rayno had described. He followed it across the upper ground on the west side of the wash and down the bank to its bottom. The dimensions of the wash were about as Rayno described and Bob had no problem scrambling up the far side. He waved to Carter and Rayno and waited for them to begin their advance. When they started, so did he, but a little slower since they had more distance to cover.

As Conor rode around the bend, he caught a quick glimpse of the wash behind the house. He could see the truck at the bottom and a brush corral like the ones that were built near the pastures in the mountains. Someone was moving near what looked like some sort of hoisting frame and then it all passed from his view. His quick view reassured him that Howling Moon was his rustler. It also boosted his confidence that no one would be in the house. He took his rifle from the scabbard and watched the rear of the house as Carter and Rayno disappeared from view at the front.

A moment later they both were mounted again and coming down the trace of road to the wash. Howling Moon heard them and went to the passenger side of the truck and got something from it. He wore a long apron covered in blood as were his hands. It was then Conor realized what was hanging from the hoist was a partially skinned steer.

Howling Moon moved around the front of the truck and greeted them. "What can I do fer you gents?" he asked.

Carter was in front and stopped his horse, then casually leaned forward. With the reins in his left hand, he lazily rested his left elbow on top of the saddle horn. The horse stood at a slight angle to Howling Moon and Carter's right hand was completely hidden from his view.

"I was just passin' by," Carter began, "and noticed you were butcherin' a steer. I'm a State Brand Inspector and I's just wondrin' if you'd mind if I had a look at the backside of that hide?"

Howling Moon was pretty calm himself as he casually pulled a Colt 1911 from inside his apron. Conor could see from behind him that the gun wasn't cocked. "I ain't never kilt no lawman, mister inspector. So why don't you jus' turn that pony 'round an' take yer Injun back up the hill with ya?"

"Well now," Carter began. "I'm not sure just how you kill a lawman with what's left of your face pokin' out the back of your head?" he said as he raised his Colt enough to be seen over the pommel of his saddle.

"Or with the back of your head blown out through your nose," Conor added from close behind the rustler.

Howling Moon dropped his pistol and slowly raised his hands.

"Now that's the smartest thing I've seen you do in two days, Mr. Howling Moon," Conor told him. "Deputy Simms, why don't you holster your pistol and put your handcuffs on Mr. Howling Moon?"

"I'd be honored, Sheriff Armenta."

Howling Moon's long curly locks were pulled back tight into a ponytail to keep them from dragging in the bloody chore he was in the midst of.

"Behind his back, Deputy," Conor instructed as he approached.

"Yessir, Sheriff."

"When you've got him secure, cut that filthy apron off him and turn him around so he can look me in the eye."

When he did so, Conor was shocked. "Well isn't that a surprise. When I saw you yesterday with my field glasses up on the mesa, I thought I recognized you through all that curly hair, but I just couldn't place you. With that out of the way, now I know who you are. You're the miner from the train. The man with the wrong ticket.

"As soon as you knew where Dutch Wagner was cuffed to the seat and where I was sitting, you could call George Altaha and tell him. He sat right here in your house, the only telephone out here, and waited for the call. That gave him plenty of time to ride up the canyon and get set up before the train came. The freight train would be moving slow up that grade. George already checked his range. It wasn't that hard to account for the speed of the train. He had his mark.

"After the train stopped, he shot my hat off to make me think I was the target and not Dutch.

"After I shot him in the arm over on Toquop Wash two days later, he went to the doctor at St. Thomas, who couldn't get the bullet out. He left his horse there and got on the train, but not before calling you to meet him in Las Vegas. The doctor there got the bullet out and Altaha made a run for his money. After getting chased around by my deputies south of town you picked him up and took him to Searchlight.

"In Searchlight you bought that blue roan right there"—he pointed at Smokey—"from Bert Haygood. Loaded the horse and hauled him away. Sent him and Altaha across the ferry into Arizona and said adios.

"You're Roscoe Taylor. Army Sniper and George Altaha's one and only true friend."

Awed by what the sheriff knew, Roscoe had to find out what happened to George. "How'd you get the horse?"

"He was standing outside an abandoned mine in Arizona."

"But what happened to George?"

"Inside the mine was a five hundred foot deep vertical shaft with four hundred feet of water in it. George Altaha fell into it."

Conor waited for that to sink in before he continued, "Roscoe Taylor, you are under arrest for aiding and abetting George Altaha in the murder of Gary D. Wagner, for the rustling of cattle

from Duncan Blackwood, kidnapping an officer of the Clark
County Sheriff's Department, and assaulting two officers of the
Clark County Sheriff's Department. Furthermore, you are wanted
for questioning by the FBI."

While searching Roscoe's truck afterward, Sheriff Conor
Armenta stumbled on the "cow-shoes" Roscoe had made to
successfully disguise his tracks for several years while rustling
cattle.

# 20

*Three Weeks to the Wedding*

For the second morning in a row, Conor was awakened by the brilliant sun shining in his face. This time it was midmorning. The sun had already risen above his neighbor's house to reach into his bedroom window. It had been well past midnight when he and Paddy unloaded three horses into his corral, but Conor could not remember the last time he had slept so late into the day. He looked into the mirror above the bathroom sink at a man with three days' growth of beard and weary eyes. As he ran hot tap water into his shaving mug, the telephone rang.

"Con," he answered.

"Good morning, sweetheart. You made it home," June greeted him. "I spoke to your mother last night; did you catch the rustlers?"

"Yeah. We caught him. He's in jail right now."

"That's wonderful. Are you busy today? There are wedding plans we need to decide about."

"I'm not too busy to see you."

"Lunch?"

"Sure."

"Noon then?"

"Perfect. That gives me time to get cleaned up."

"I love you, Conor Armenta."

"You too, June Sommers," he responded before she hung up.

Two hours later, shaved, bathed, and dressed in clean clothes, Conor's brown Chevrolet coupe pulled up in front of June's house. She met him on the porch with a warm embrace and a modest kiss. She felt the need to keep her hormones in check today...at least for a few hours anyway.

"Where's Running Dog?" she asked when she realized he had not bound from the rumble seat upon his arrival.

Conor's face lost its smile and suddenly sobered. "He's gone, June. Running Dog is dead."

"What happened?"

"The rustler shot him," he replied then proceeded to recap all of the events of the past two days as they sat on the porch swing.

She picked up Running Dog's empty dish from the front porch when they went in to eat their lunch. "I will talk to April," she told him. "She really liked him, you know. I'm not sure how she will take the news."

"We should tell her together," Con reasoned.

"Tomorrow, after church?" she asked.

"I suppose. Where is she now?"

"She and Donna are at Campfire Girls. Olivia is picking them up afterward and she's spending the night with them again."

As they ate their lunch, Conor broached the subject. "So, what did you want to discuss about our wedding?"

"Leonora Campbell and Mrs. Westcott came to the office

yesterday morning. They quite often drop in to discuss things with Mr. Westcott, but this time they came to see me."

"Oh? What was that about?"

"Since both of my parents are deceased, the Campbells and Westcotts want to adopt the role of 'father of the bride' regarding our wedding."

"Well, what will that entail?"

"In its simplest form, Mr. Westcott walking me down the aisle and giving his permission for me to marry you. In the most extreme? Everything."

"What do you mean by, everything?"

"Everything from the ceremony to the reception, right down to the wedding dress."

"You mean they pick all of that stuff out?"

"Yes, they would be heavily involved with all of it...and they pay for it...everything...except for the person officiating...that is the groom's responsibility."

Conor was dumbfounded. "You mean, they want to pay for our wedding?"

"Yes." She nodded. "And they even want to have Velora Huckabee make my dress."

"Who's she?"

"Only the best dressmaker in Las Vegas and probably the state. She even makes gowns for the governor's wife."

"Sounds pretty fancy to me."

"They want to hold the wedding and reception at the Campbell estate," she said it quickly to keep from stuttering. "Leanora is estimating fifty or more guests and holding the ceremony and a catered reception in the rear courtyard if the weather cooperates or the foyer and dining room if not."

"Matt McCoy was murdered in that foyer just a few weeks ago," Conor noted superstitiously. "Besides, we've already talked to my parents about a small ceremony, maybe even at their house, a dozen people or so. My mother might be upset if we do something different."

"And I discussed it with your mother on the telephone last night. She's elated."

"So, I'm the missing link in the chain. Everybody else has decided. You're all just waiting for me to go along with it?"

"Yes, we have all agreed."

"Okay, I guess, but somebody needs to tell me what I'm supposed to do through all of this."

"Kiss the bride," she said while leaning across the corner of the table and kissed the groom.

\* \* \*

*SATURDAY, NOVEMBER 15, 1930*

*Two Weeks to the Wedding*

Conor arrived at June's house for breakfast at seven thirty. April danced with excitement of the upcoming wedding. She was heartbroken over the loss of Running Dog, but the sadness of the loss soon was overshadowed by the prospect that she and Donna would be flower girls in the ceremony. Both of these experiences were outdone by implications of the wedding itself. The anticipation of Conor becoming her father outshined all of the previous events in her life. She could hardly contain her eagerness to call him Daddy.

She leapt into his arms and kissed his cheek as he mounted the front steps.

"Only two more weeks, Con," she whispered into his ear.

"Until what?" he asked while forcing a quizzical facial expression.

"'Til I can call you Daddy!" the whisper strained in its desire to become a scream.

"I forgot all about that," he replied in mock amazement.

"Did you forget that I love you too?"

"I could never forget that, sweet pea. And you know what? I love you too," he responded before giving her a peck on her forehead and setting her on her feet.

He stepped back to look her over. "What's all this about? New blue jeans? And cowgirl boots?"

"Mama bought them for me." She tugged on his shirtsleeve, beckoning him to bend over, and again whispered in his ear, "They're boy's. We couldn't find any girl's ones, but Aunt Olivia said it's okay."

"Aunt Olivia?"

"She said it was okay for me to call her that now too."

"Hmmm. So, why are you wearing boots and jeans?"

"We're going out to Uncle Paddy's house."

"Oh, we are?"

"That's what Mama said."

June's white straw hat hung beside the hook he hung his own on. In the kitchen, she wore her riding skirt and boots beneath her apron.

"Breakfast is ready except for the eggs," she said without mentioning her attire...or any other greeting for that matter Conor noticed.

"Thank you," he said as April hurried to the coffeepot on the stove to fill his cup. "Good morning."

"Good morning, dear. Did you see April's new clothes?" she asked as she busied herself at the stove.

"Yes, I did," he replied cheerfully, but short of further comment, still wondering what she might be going to say.

June laid her spatula beside the skillet and brought a platter of bacon and biscuits from the warm oven. "I'd like to go visit Smokey today," she finally said as she sat the platter on the table.

"Did Bert Haygood plant a seed?" Conor asked before taking a sip of his coffee.

June turned back to the stove and flipped the eggs. "I suppose he did," she replied without facing him. "Can I ride him?"

"Yes, you can ride him. He seems like a good horse."

"Too good for dog food?"

"Yeah, probably too good for dog food."

"Do they really make horses into dog food, Con?" April asked, joining the conversation.

"Yes. Sometimes they do," he told her hoping to avoid expanding on the subject.

The conversation lightened over the breakfast table and Conor mentioned that Carter Simms had ridden Smokey up at Acton the previous week. "We only rode about ten miles, but Carter really liked riding him and he seems to know horses."

"Does he want to buy him?" June asked.

"Possibly, but he has a family to feed. I doubt he will, even if he has the money to."

"How much will he cost?"

"There's no way of knowing. Bert sold him to Altaha for forty dollars, but slaughterhouses rarely pay over two or three."

"You can buy a horse for two dollars?" April chimed in in amazement. "I have that much saved up in my piggy bank."

Conor could see the wheels turning in April's eyes.

"Not a very good one usually, but money is tight right now. You never know."

An hour later, the soon-to-be family arrived at Patrick Armenta's sheep ranch. Bob was in his paddock behind the house. Paddy's two horses and the two impounded horses were all in the corral by the barn. The young cowgirl rode in the rumble seat with the sun on her shoulders and wind in her face. She shrieked when she saw the horses and hurried from the seat to the fender, rear bumper, and the ground, almost headfirst. The process was certainly unladylike, but she didn't care while reveling in her freedom from wearing a dress.

"Where did the little brown one come from, Con?" April squealed. "She's just my size."

"Well, she's a he and he's in the same boat as Smokey," Conor answered while holding June's door.

"Are you sure she's not your daughter?" June asked as April climbed to hang from the top rail of the corral.

"Not for another two weeks," he grinned.

"He sure is pretty," June mooned over Smokey as she dug a carrot out of her pocket.

"You know what to do," Con told her. "Go ahead."

June crawled between the rails of the corral. She slowly walked toward the roan with her hands lowered, palms up and held away from her body. "Smokey, boy." She spoke softly to him. "I have a present for you." He stood stock-still watching her, ears perked searching for the slightest sound.

It had become apparent to Conor earlier that June had contracted the equine flu. Now both of the women in his life seemed to have been infected by the disease.

"You stay here for now, April. I need to take a closer look at this little brown horse that you like."

Patrick walked up as his brother climbed through the fence. "What do you know about him after a week," Conor asked.

"He's a little shy, but really smart and well-trained, I think. I left him ground-tied the other day. He was standing in bare dirt for a half hour over by the house and never made a move to eat the grass in the yard. I rode him three or four times. Just around close here. He likes that old Mexican saddle the best...and he reins pretty good."

"He was owned by an Apache. Maybe for a long time. I don't pretend to know their methods, but some of it might not have been too kind."

"That could explain the shyness and the obedience both."

"How old do you think he is?"

"I looked at his teeth. Five or six, I think. He has really good feet. Unshod right now and he might never have been. I trimmed his feet up a little, no splits or big chips. Hooves are hard as iron. I really had to work with the nippers to cut through them."

"Anything else I should know?"

"He has a Mexican brand on his right hip. I've never seen it before, but they all have a look of their own. There's another brand on his left shoulder that I thought was Mexican too, but after what you said? Maybe Apache?"

April had been hanging on every word even though she probably failed to understand most of what was said beyond shy and well-trained.

He looked up at her. "Do you think sweet pea here could ride him?"

"Some horses treat inexperienced riders gentle as a basket of eggs, others dump them off as quick as they can and head for open country. It's hard to say. I'd start with carrots."

Conor chuckled. "They've both seen that trick." He looked to June who was gently petting Smokey's cheek.

"What have you been calling him?" Con asked while patting his neck.

"Bashful."

"We'll try that for a start and hope it doesn't change to Thunderbolt." Conor chuckled.

A half hour later, April had coaxed Bashful into submission and Con had him saddled and the stirrups adjusted. June saddled Smokey by herself and Paddy was helping her make final checks and adjustments before climbing aboard, while Conor began saddling Bob. He had given April basic instructions on reining, how to tell the horse what she wanted him to do and leaning to help make his job easier. He left a halter on Bashful beneath his headstall and attached a lead rope. She could practice simple maneuvers while being led by Conor and Bob. June pretended not to watch as he slipped his belted pistol into his saddlebags. They were ready to go within a few minutes.

"Go ahead and lead off," he told June. "We'll mosey along behind you."

"Where should I go?"

"Wherever you want to take us. Feel free to put Smokey through any kind of test you choose. I don't think we'll get lost."

"What about me?"

"You can't go more than two or three miles in any direction without coming to a fence. Follow the fence either direction and sooner or later you'll end up back here. You'll recognize most of anything you see when you come to it. You just might not remember where it was when you saw it."

"Thanks for the reassurance." She chuckled.

"I doubt you'll be very far ahead of us at any point. If you're not sure and you can't see us, just take a break, we'll be along shortly."

She galloped up the road behind the house and stopped as it crossed a low saddle between two hills, turning Smokey broadside in the road, she waved her hat in the air like the silver-screen cowboys do before riding off into the sunset. She smiled so broadly both Conor and April could see it plainly as they waved back to her. Then she turned her back and disappeared over the hill.

"Will Mama get lost?" April asked.

"I doubt it, and not for very long if she does."

Perhaps a half mile up the trail they followed; April giggled from behind him.

Conor turned in his saddle as they continued walking. The lead rope was slack and April was basically riding by herself. "What's so funny?"

"If I put my knee right here"—she showed him as she did,—"he goes that way. If I put my other knee on the same spot on the other side, he goes the other way." She repeated the move and giggled again.

"He's been trained to do that, sweet pea. Do you remember what I told you about rubbing the reins across his neck to tell him when to turn?"

"Yes."

"If you remember to do both at the same time, it reassures him that he's doing what you want him to. Then if sometimes you can't do both, he'll still know what you're asking."

As they approached two miles from the house, they found June about two hundred yards ahead of them. She was waiting, still astride Smokey at a fence and wire gate, still grinning from ear to ear.

"How are you two doing?" Conor asked as they rode up to her.

Perspiration followed loose strands of blonde hair down her temples, and she could not stop smiling. "Oh my," she gasped, "is he ever fun to ride." She leaned forward and patted his glistening neck.

"Do you remember how to get to the top of the hill above the house?"

"I will never forget that spot." Her grin almost becoming a smirk being reminded of its significance.

"Take it easy as you go so you and him both cool down slowly. You can trot from time to time so his muscles don't tighten up but hold off on the speed. Too much of a good thing can lead to trouble, you know." He winked, and she blushed.

"The hill," she acknowledged as she pointed Smokey back down the road.

"We'll meet you there," Conor confirmed as she rode away.

After the invigorating way they made getting there, Smokey was anxious to return in the same manor. It took some effort to hold him to a walk for the first quarter mile where she let him trot for a similar distance.

Conor and April were only a few yards behind when June let Smokey pick up the pace. He had April ride up along him.

"Do you remember how I told you to tell him to speed up?"

"Lift up my reins and lean forward a little bit. If he doesn't get it, nudge him just a little bit with my heels."

"Yes, but there is more. We want him to trot, but not run. If he starts to run, you need to lean back and pull back a little bit on the reins. You just keep pulling back a little harder and a little harder until he slows to a trot. If at any time it feels like you might fall off, pull back until he stops. It's very important that you pull back with even pressure on the reins and not jerk on them. If you jerk on the reins, he might get confused or excited and start to buck. Do you understand all of that?"

"Yes. I understand."

"Good girl. I'm gonna be right here beside you, so don't be scared. Do you remember why?"

"Yes, because he can smell me if I get scared."

"Yes, you're really smart to remember all of that. Go ahead and try it out."

Conor urged Bob ahead and he tried to go into his lope, which was usually what he wanted, but not this time, Con eased back on the reins and Bob slowed his pace. Bashful paced himself with the larger horse and had to work a little bit to keep to a trot alongside the longer stride of his peer. All worked well until April's foot slipped from a stirrup and she panicked. Conor saw what happened and brought Bob to an immediate halt.

Anticipating the lead rope to come taut, Bashful turned a bit sideways awaiting the jolt and April began to slip from the saddle. Feeling the shift of his lightweight passenger, Bashful sidestepped to center himself beneath her. April crashed into Bob and nearly fell as Conor grabbed the saddle horn in his left hand in order to reach around her waist on the shorter horse. With his help, she regained her balance as both horses and riders stopped in the middle of the road, catching their breath.

"Are you all right, sweet pea?" he asked shakily. Had she fallen between the colliding horses, Conor understood how seriously she might have been hurt. He struggled to control the surge of adrenaline.

"I'm okay," she said confidently. "I was scared for a minute, but I'm fine now."

"You did real good, sweet pea," he encouraged while regaining control of his breathing. He had just survived his first real-life experience of being a father.

A half hour later, he and April rode up the hill overlooking his brother's ranch yard. June awaited them enjoying the view in full light of day for the first time.

"Do you know where we are, April?" June asked.

She shook her head no and looked around. Noticing the distant speck of green identifying Las Vegas, she commented. "That's home." Then recognizing the barn and Paddy's house below them she added, "and that's Uncle Paddy's."

"You're right," June agreed, "and you know what else?" A euphoric glow overcame her with the reminder of what had happened here. "This is where Conor asked me to marry him,"

* * *

*THURSDAY, NOVEMBER 20, 1930*

*Nine Days to the Wedding*

At five minutes before ten, Conor and the county clerk stepped out the door and onto the courthouse steps. Three men he identified as representatives from meat processors stood to the side idly chatting. Though competitors, he suspected they were scheming to control the bidding. June rounded the corner in her usual business attire and walked hurriedly up the sidewalk, forcing herself not to run in her excitement. No one else attended.

"Good morning, gentlemen. I am Sheriff Conor Armenta, and as advertised, we are here this morning to auction two horses to the highest bidder. The successful bidder will pay cash for the amount of the bid immediately following and receive a signed bill of sale from the Clerk of Clark County, Nevada. The animals must be retrieved before noon tomorrow or you will be charged an additional two bits a day when you pick them up. I presume that you three are those who accompanied my deputy yesterday to look over these two animals. They both appear to be healthy and little else is known about them." While he spoke, June scaled the steps and stood a short distance from the three men. Conor tried to keep from focusing his attention on her. He had coached her last evening on what to expect.

"Are there any questions?" he asked without response. "Okay. We will begin with the bay gelding. I would estimate him to weigh less than seven hundred pounds. Can I get an opening bid of ten dollars?"

All three of the men scoffed. June fidgeted.

"Can we start at five dollars?" Conor asked.

The tallest man of the trio extracted the cigar from his mouth and pointed to the sheriff with it. "I'll give you a buck," he snorted sarcastically.

"Two dollars," June spoke solemnly with a straight face.

Her bid brought a moan from the trio.

"Three!" Cigar-man yelled, stabbing the air with his smoke.

"Four dollars," June replied almost before Cigar-man got the words out of his mouth.

Cigar-man waved his hand back and forth at his throat indicating he was finished.

"Are there any other bids?" Conor asked.

All three men shook their heads. June approached the clerk and shakily handed him four silver dollars. The clerk filled in the blanks on the bill of sale and signed it before handing it over for Conor to do the same. He signed it and passed it to June's shaking hand with a wink.

"Next," he began. "We will sell the roan gelding. I estimate him to weigh under nine hundred pounds. Will someone open the bid at ten dollars?"

"Ten dollars," June replied.

Cigar-man threw his hands in the air and stomped down the steps. The other two men followed less flamboyantly as they

mumbled back and forth between them. June fumbled nervously
in her purse to bring out a ten-dollar bill.

\* \* \*

## THURSDAY, NOVEMBER 27, 1930

*Two Days to the Wedding*

David McLeod joined his sister Donna and April in a game of
hide and seek around his grandparents' yard. Mom, Grandma,
and Uncle Con's fiancé were busy in the kitchen baking a turkey
with a host of traditional side dishes thus giving his grandfather
a holiday. Grandpa normally spent ten-hour days, six days a
week cooking at the Mesquite Café. Uncle Con helped Dad adjust
the carburetor on their family car while Grandpa snored on the
couch through the special Thanksgiving Day edition of his
favorite radio program.

An hour later, Dad and Uncle Con scrubbed automotive grime
from their hands and examined their Sunday best clothing for
accidental grease stains. By the time the trio of youngsters filled
their plates and scooted on the living room floor up to the coffee
table to eat, the adults had filled their plates and Grandpa was
asking the blessing for the meal they were about to share at the
dinner table.

While the adults in the adjoining room were engrossed in
conversation over the upcoming wedding, Donna and April
giggled over their best-friend-secrets. David, barely a teenager
tormented them for being childish.

\* \* \*

*FRIDAY, NOVEMBER 28, 1930*

*One Day Before the Wedding*

Conor was a bundle of nerves throughout the evening wedding rehearsal. Judge Tucker, Newt Campbell, and Robert Westcott did their best to help calm him. Juan and Patrick Armenta, being nearly as nervous as Con, were of little help. Stuart McLeod was busy trying to blend in to the empty courtyard with little success. June had asked if Juan could give her away and Robert Westcott was more than pleased to comply. June's sister, Julie Moore arrived on the train that afternoon to be her maid of honor and Patrick was Conor's best man. David McLeod was the ring-bearer, his sister and April the flower girls. Judge Tucker was offi-ciating. He insisted on waiving his customary two-dollar fee for performing the service.

When they moved into Leanora Campbell's dining room afterward for the rehearsal dinner, eighteen were seated, six more than Conor had originally expected for the total number of guests. Leanora had placed Conor and June side by side at the head of the massive table. Newt Campbell and his girlfriend, Amy Slater sat immediately next to Con. June's sister was seated beside her followed by April. No less than four men in white shirts and jackets with black bow-ties served the meal. Conor lost count after the fourth course was served. His nervous stomach soon settled when food was added. He had no idea what most of the dishes were, but they were all delicious. When dessert arrived, April was thrilled to have vanilla ice cream.

Leanora Campbell seated herself at the far end of the table. Soon after dessert, she tapped her spoon against her crystal water glass. Its bright ring gained everyone's attention.

"As all of you know, the Campbell family has endured some

troubling times this past year. Due to the exemplary detective work of Sheriff Conor Armenta, justice has been served and we can now all sleep restfully at night. I am certain Sheriff Armenta will tell you that he was only doing his job, but as our expression of gratitude for doing it so well, we asked that we might host he and his bride, our lovely June's wedding. They graciously accepted.

"Through planning and preparing for this beautiful union to take place here tomorrow afternoon, we discovered that they were both too dedicated to take time off from work for a honeymoon." She handed an envelope to one of the servers who carried it to June. "They have planned to spend their wedding night at June's lovely home on Third Street. I thought they deserved at least one night of a more private and romantic setting after the reception tomorrow. Would you open the envelope please, June?"

June's hands shook nearly uncontrollably as she opened it and read the paper inside. She handed the paper to Conor.

"What does it say, Conor?" Leanora asked.

He held it up momentarily to show everyone present then began. "It's on Hotel Nevada stationery. To Mr. and Mrs. Conor Armenta upon showing a validly signed marriage license on November 29, 1930; one night's stay in the executive suite, including unlimited room service until noon November 30, 1930. It's signed Leanora Campbell, Newton Campbell, Amelia Westcott, and Robert Westcott." He looked around the table at each and every one of them. "Thank you all. We thank every one of you very much."

# 21

SATURDAY, NOVEMBER 29, 1930

*The Wedding Day*

The wedding ceremony scheduled at one o'clock went off without a hitch, but not without the extensive planning directed primarily by Leanora Campbell and her daughter Amelia Westcott. June, Olivia, and Maggie were also major contributors, but were unable to devote as much time to executing the tight schedule due to their employment responsibilities. They were overjoyed to have Leanora and Amelia take care of so many details of the elaborate affair.

Leanora had it all worked out in her head, if not on paper. The bride and her maid of honor were to be at the Campbell estate precisely at ten o'clock for hairstyling, dressing, and makeup. She avoided telling them about the makeup since June hardly ever wore any, but felt a very modest application by a professional would only further enhance the ladies' beauty.

The groom, best man, ring-bearer, and acting father of the bride, would arrive at eleven o'clock to be poured into their tuxedos, complete with bow-ties and cummerbunds, custom made from the same pale-blue cloth as the bridal gown. Their boutonnières were white roses to match the bridal bouquet.

The flower girls were also to arrive simultaneously with the men for their own turns with the hairstylists before the ceremony.

Leanora had every detail covered right down to the transportation of the wedding party and who should ride with whom. Since Julie was staying with June and they were the first to arrive, she insisted they drive her late husband's LaSalle home from the rehearsal dinner and return with it in the morning. When they arrived, Leanora met them in the driveway and asked June how she liked the car.

"It is beautiful. I've told Conor we may have need for a sedan soon. We want to have more children. He would say, the car matches my beautiful blue eyes." She laughed as she handed Leanora the keys. "He seems mesmerized by them, but I am fairly certain he loves the rest of me too."

Patrick rode with Conor since he spent Friday night on his brother's sofa. Juan picked up the children at Stuart and Olivia's so they in turn could pick up Maggie before for the ceremony.

By the time the reception began, Conor's euphoric daze had been growing continuously for over twenty-four hours. He could not have described the magnitude of his bliss, but knew he wanted it never to end and June was right beside him throughout, equally enamored with every moment of it. He picked up April at one point during the reception and carrying her in his arms with hers wrapped around his neck, he danced around the courtyard to whatever tune the live quartet played at the moment. April shrilled with joy, Daddy, Daddy, Daddy, Daddy nonstop into his ear until the music ended.

At six o'clock, Conor sat two small suitcases down in front of the desk at the Hotel Nevada and handed the clerk their marriage license.

"Very good, sir. Would you like to use the lift?"

"Sure," Con answered as he assessed the safety of the iron cage across the hotel lobby. When he reached for the suitcases, the clerk was already carrying them into the open door of the contraption. He turned and beckoned them to follow.

Conor turned to June. She wore the yellow dress she had worn on her birthday. The one with the lower than usual neckline that accentuated her bustline. Her blue pearl pendant hung invitingly at the top of the valley between her breasts. *She is the sexiest woman in the world,* Con thought to himself as he laid her hand over the arm of the white dress shirt he'd worn with his tuxedo in their wedding. He strutted proudly as he escorted his bride in boots and jeans to the awaiting elevator.

On the second floor, the clerk rushed across the hallway to unlock their room and stand aside. "Perhaps you would like to carry your bride across the threshold, sir?"

He swept June from her feet and into his arms almost before she realized what had happened. June knew that she was no longer the thin waif she had been before April's arrival, and Conor's strength astounded her. In the lounge area of the suite, he gently returned her to her feet and kissed her fervently for a long time. "Pleased to meet you, Mrs. Armenta," he told her when their lips barely parted.

"A gentleman called me that at the reception," she told him. "He was unknown to me and I caught myself glancing around the courtyard for your mother when I realized he was talking to me...the pleasure is mine, Mr. Armenta."

The clerk cleared his throat. "When you are ready for supper, just call the desk. There's a menu on the bureau. Anything at all you need at any hour, someone will answer." He held out the key for the room to Conor. "Your key, sir."

He accepted it and the clerk disappeared out the door, closing it behind him.

They looked around the room at a large bouquet of flowers and a basket of fruit adorning the table in the center of the room. Between them was an envelope not unlike the one presented by Leanora last evening. June picked it up. *Mister and Missus Conor Armenta* was scrawled across the front. She handed it to Conor who opened it and removed two sheets of paper. The letterhead read *Wagner Trucking Company.*

*My Dearest Conor and June Armenta,*

*By the time word reached me of your wedding, Leanora and Amelia were already well underway with the planning...to Leanora's wishes I am sure...and not necessarily yours. I understand. Now I am guilty of the same interference for your honeymoon. Please don't hold it against me. I've arranged it with your employers and you aren't expected back on your jobs until Wednesday, December 10. April also has known of this plan of mine for a week. And don't worry about her. I know that Julie told you she was leaving Sunday on the train. She is, but actually not until next Sunday, after she spends the week with April.*

*Both of your suitcases are packed and ready to go in the bedroom of your suite. This service was performed by Olivia McLeod and Julie Moore for Mrs. Armenta; and Maggie Armenta and Newt Campbell for Mr. Armenta. Be assured, your privacy remains intact.*

*My mother and father never had a honeymoon*

when they were married and it wasn't until just a few weeks before my father's death they ever took a vacation. Mother told me repeatedly over the years that it was the most romantic time of her life. I have duplicated the portion of their trip that was most memorable to her. I didn't want the two of you to wait thirty years like they did to share that kind of experience.

You may not realize it, but the two of you have had a profound effect on me since I met you both. I'm sorry I couldn't attend your wedding. This is my gift to you. You will find your itinerary on the next page. Your meals are included with your suites. Should the mule trip to Phantom Ranch at the bottom of the Grand Canyon be canceled due to weather, you will enjoy three nights at El Tovar.

May this week be the beginning of a lifetime of wonderful memories.

Katherine "Katie" Brumbaugh

June looked into the adjoining bedroom and bathroom. "Our suitcases are in here," she confirmed. "And this place is fancy. The sink in the bathroom is the shape of a giant seashell." She returned across the room and wrapped her arms around his neck. "But that is not what is important right now." And she kissed him amorously.

When they broke the embrace, she indicated with her raised index finger and added, "Give me one minute." June grabbed her small suitcase and dashed into the bathroom.

A moment later, she emerged from the bathroom. She wore

the sheerest of negligées. Every feature of her nude body within was visible. Conor stood in awe staring, wanting to look away in modesty, but he could not. She came to him and began by removing his cufflinks. From there she unbuttoned his shirt beginning at his open collar and pulled the tails loose from his jeans when she reached the bottom.

"Let me make you more comfortable she whispered," she said as she slid the shirt off his shoulders and let it drop to the floor.

* * *

*SUNDAY, NOVEMBER 30, 1930*

*The Honeymoon, Day One*

June awakened to bright sunlight filtering through the draperies. Conor's bare chest was exposed as he lay sleeping beside her. She found her negligée and slipped into the bathroom to freshen up and comb her hair. She returned wearing the negligée with its less revealing matching robe and ordered coffee. When it arrived, she put it on the table then returned to bed and kissed Conor awake.

"What time is it?" he asked when he opened his eyes.

"After sunup is all that I can tell you." She kissed him again.

Conor lifted the sheet and blushed when he confirmed that he was still completely naked.

"Would you like for me to pour coffee while you use the bathroom?" she asked.

"Uh. Yeah. Uh. Sure," he stammered as she left the bedroom. Collecting his underwear and jeans from the floor, he made a dash for the bathroom.

June sat at the table reading the menu and drinking her coffee when he returned.

"Have you ever had eggs benedict?" she asked as he sat down across the small table from her and filled the cup in front of him

"I don't think so."

"You should try them. That is what I am having. I think you might like them. If not, you can always order something else."

He agreed and she called in their order, including a second pot of coffee. After Conor checked his pocket watch, they were already too late for church.

"So, where are we bound for today?" June asked as they finished their late breakfast.

"The Hotel Brunswick in Kingman."

"How long will it take to get there?"

"Four or five hours, I think."

"I am sure that Julie will take April to the Episcopal Church this morning. They should be home by eleven and I would really like to say goodbye to April before we leave. Will that be okay?"

"Of course."

June came around the table and seated herself on Conor's lap.

"What shall we do until then?" she asked, mocking her innocence as she pressed her breasts into his bare chest as she kissed him.

At a few minutes after eleven o'clock, Conor carried the two large suitcases and June the two smaller ones out the front door of the Hotel Nevada. They had left Conor's Chevrolet coupe only a few spaces from the entrance. Now Brice Campbell's light blue LaSalle sedan occupied the space. A note on the windshield was held in place by the wiper blade.

*None of us have felt comfortable driving Brice's LaSalle since we lost him. Newt, Amelia, and I all felt it was the perfect wedding gift for a growing family. I'm sure Brice would agree.*

*You will find your Chevrolet at June's home.*

*Leanora.*

"I...I just...there are no words," Conor uttered. As he handed June the note, a tear rolled down his cheek. As June lowered her hand, still clinging the note after reading it, he took her in his arms and kissed her passionately. A passing motorist knowingly honked the horn as he drove by. They were in love and they didn't care about the spectacle they were displaying. At the moment, they were the two happiest people in the world.

When they arrived at June's home, she rushed in wanting to chastise her sister and daughter for keeping secrets, but instead found herself thanking Julie for staying with April then began kissing and hugging both of them goodbye for the week. While she was inside, Conor transferred both his rifle and pistol from beneath the seat of his car to the LaSalle. June saw him and considered reprimanding him for bringing guns on their honeymoon. She decided instead that she would rather he bring them along than leave them unattended in front of her house, *their* house she corrected herself mid-thought.

*** 

MONDAY, DECEMBER 1, 1930

*The Honeymoon, Day Two*

Neither Conor nor June had ever enjoyed a lifestyle allowing them to laze around until midmorning. Because of her previous marriage, June was less inhibited than Conor, but he was becoming more relaxed and enjoying the new experience of exploring June's body. They had eaten a hearty breakfast soon after sunrise, then returned to bed for a fun and an intimate frolic lasting late into the morning.

Shortly before noon, the LaSalle rolled out onto the newly

oiled highway sixty-six. The first twenty miles were nearly straight and flat where Conor opened up the throttle to sixty-six miles per hour for a short distance just to see what it felt like. He had no desire to travel any faster. They were in no hurry to cover the short distance to reach the Hotel Escalante at Ash Fork. After slowing considerably when the oiled road turned to gravel, they made a sweeping righthand turn and began the climb up Truxton Wash.

Just past the community of Hackberry the road made a similar turn to the left and continued its climb up Truxton Canyon. Conor continued on up the graveled highway at a leisurely pace of twenty to thirty miles per hour. As they passed the Truxton Canyon Indian School at Valentine, it brought reminders of what Jimmy Garza had experienced in a similar school at Fort Mojave. Where the railroad line proceeded up the Truxton Wash, a couple of miles past Valentine, highway sixty-six branched to the left, up Crozier Canyon. At the top of it, the terrain began leveling off and the highway continued at a much milder grade.

A couple of miles west of Peach Springs they rejoined the railroad for a short distance before again meandering through the hills north of the tracks. Ten miles farther was a sign advertising the Yampai Caverns, twenty-five cents. They turned off and followed a dirt road a short distance to a less than attractive facility. The business offered sandwiches and drinks for excessive prices before partaking of the guided tour. Since it was midafternoon and several hours since breakfast, they chose to pay the price for the meager snack then joined the purported professional guide for the hour-long tour.

They were the only clients at the time and coaxed the guide to take their picture near the entrance with June's brownie camera. Neither having ever been inside a cave admittedly found the rock formations colorful and interesting. Conor was skeptical, however, of the display of two mummified bodies claimed to be those of ancient cavemen, especially when remnants of what appeared to be fabric clothing could be seen in the dim light.

Upon returning to the surface, they assessed the value of the excursion and concluded it had been fun but were anxious to enjoy a more palatable meal later at their hotel.

The bathroom in their suite at the Hotel Escalante had a very large cast-iron bathtub. June was anxious to wash her hair and get into the tub to soak away any creepy-crawly things that may have hitch-hiked out of the cavern with her. She also made Conor promise that he would do the same as soon as she was finished. Further impressing her, the hotel offered overnight laundry service. She promptly made arrangements for them to pick up every stitch of clothing they wore in the cavern.

June drained the tub as she finished her bath and instantly began refilling it for Conor. She added an ample supply of bubble bath before calling him in. Wearing a fluffy robe provided by the hotel, she collected all of her clothing and stacked it outside the door, as instructed by the desk clerk. When returning to the bathroom unannounced, she embarrassed her modest groom while he soaked beneath a sea of bubbles. She gathered all of his clothing to join hers in the hallway, then rang the front desk to have them picked up.

Moments later, she went back to the bathroom. While standing in front of him, she dropped her robe to the floor. As he sat there staring with mouth wide open, she climbed into the massive bathtub with him.

*  *  *

*TUESDAY, DECEMBER 2, 1930*

*The Honeymoon, Day Three*

Conor woke early in comparison to the two previous mornings. He drew back the draperies of their second-floor suite just far enough to peer outside. The sun was just beginning to peek over the horizon casting long shadows from anything daring to obstruct its light. At nearly a mile in elevation, the cool night had left a heavy coating of sparkling frost blanketing everything in view.

He slipped on his jeans and quietly closed the door to the bedroom. With a glance, the menu offered eggs benedict, a treat he knew June loved from Sunday morning at the Hotel Nevada. He called the front desk for a pot of coffee, and two orders each of cheese Danish pastry, eggs benedict, bowls of fresh fruit and orange juice. When he answered the door a short time later, the Harvey Girl blushed at seeing his bare chest, then wheeled their breakfast in on the cart and placed it all on the table.

When she left, there were two bundles outside the door wrapped in brown paper and tied with string. Bringing them in, he noted "Mr." penciled on one and "Mrs." on the other. Opening the one marked Mr., he found his clothing from yesterday; clean, starched, and pressed; right down to creases in the legs of his jeans.

Opening the door to the bedroom, a beam of sunshine broke through the gap in the drapes. June lay on her back in bed, the sheet spread across her just low enough to reveal her left breast. He bent down beside her and gently kissed it, causing a brief stir. He moved to her lips and finished kissing her awake.

She smiled back at him as her eyes opened and sat up in the bed, totally uninhibited that the sheet had fallen to her waist.

"Good morning, sweetheart," he told her as he moved to sit facing her on the edge of the bed. He slipped his arm around her waist and pulled her to him as he kissed her more ardently. She was smiling when their lips parted then suddenly the expression turned to shock as she realized he was seeing her for the first time with unkempt hair.

"Oh, my God, Conor. I must look a fright," she exclaimed. "I've not even combed my hair."

"You are beautiful," he replied and kissed her again.

The flathead V-8 of the LaSalle rumbled along smoothly as they made the gradual sixteen-hundred-foot climb spread over twenty miles to Williams. The well-maintained gravel highway was smooth and Conor eased the speed up to forty miles per hour as June pored over the roadmap he had purchased in Kingman.

"It says it is sixty-four miles from Williams to the Grand Canyon and the road is 'improved dirt.' What does that mean?"

"It means they run a road-grader over it once a year when it dries out in the spring," Conor replied sarcastically. "Bring your own elephant to pull you out of the mudholes if it rains for the rest of the year."

"Poo." June snickered. "It cannot be that bad."

"There's a reason most tourists leave their cars in Williams and ride the train to the park," he replied in defense of his sarcasm.

They enjoyed the change of scenery to ponderosa pines dotting the area surrounding Williams and turned north on the "improved dirt" road just east of the town. To Conor's surprise, the road was in good condition allowing them to maintain around twenty miles per hour most of the way to El Tovar.

At nearly seven thousand feet elevation, the temperature at the hotel hovered around forty degrees at two o'clock in the afternoon. June dashed for the lobby pending unpacking more suitable clothing while the bellman hurried to get their luggage before Conor could unload it from the car.

"Good afternoon," the mid-fiftyish manager welcomed June as he crossed the lobby to introduce himself. "My name is Palmer,"

"June Sommers," she responded and started to offer her hand, but Palmer's were clasped together at his back. This oddity was perhaps what joggled her senses. "Oh!" She blushed. "June

Armenta," she corrected. "In all of the excitement for the past few days, I guess it has not quite sunk in yet."

"Ahh, the newlyweds." Palmer beamed. "We've been expecting you and are so happy you've arrived safely."

At that moment, Conor and the bellman came in the front doors.

"And you must be Mr. Armenta. My name is Palmer and I am at your service, sir."

"Please take the Armenta's luggage to the honeymoon suite," Palmer told the bellman.

Their suite was at the end of the hotel and offered one-hundred-eighty-degree views of the canyon and river three-quarters of a mile below. Photographs and paintings both had seen over the years failed to capture the immenseness of the chasm. John Wesley Powell had chosen the name well. It would be difficult to find another single word that could better describe it than 'Grand.'

June and Con found warmer attire and changed into it before returning downstairs to have a late lunch in the dining room. Seated next to a wall of windows, the view was spectacular accompaniment to a nice meal.

"Better than lunch yesterday?" June asked with a chuckle.

"Definitely." Conor grinned.

When finished, they chose to walk the canyon rim trail east of El Tovar Hotel for about three miles to Mather Point. June brought along her brownie camera. Seeing no one else around, Conor and June took turns taking snapshots of each other along the way. It was nearly dark when they returned to the hotel and opted for hot bathes and supper in their room in lieu of eating in the dining room.

The bathtub was less inviting than that of the Hotel Escalante the evening before, but they found plenty of time to romp in the comfortable bed afterward.

\* \* \*

WEDNESDAY, DECEMBER 3, 1930

*The Honeymoon, Day Four*

At six o'clock Conor and June were cheerfully enjoying breakfast in the dining room anticipating the arrival of dawn. Their pack mule trip to Phantom Ranch at the bottom of the canyon was scheduled to depart before sunup, at seven o'clock. It was recommended to dress in layers since it was common for temperatures to get warmer the deeper they descend into the canyon. Presently, it was fifteen degrees outside the hotel.

After a hearty breakfast of ham and eggs accompanied by fried potatoes, biscuits and coffee, June and Conor joined the packtrain. They presented their maximum one small suitcase per couple, packed with necessary belongings for a one-night-stay in a cabin at the bottom. Because of the season, there were no other guests on the trip, but eight pack mules carried supplies for the caretakers of the facility below. They moved out to the Bright Angel Trailhead.

They took their first break at the at the one-and-a-half mile resthouse directly below the El Tovar Hotel. They were only a quarter mile from the hotel, but it was nearly a half mile from there to the trailhead, then a mile and a half, fourteen switchbacks and nearly two hours to reach it by the trail. The sun had been up for most of that time but had yet to reach their depth in Garden Creek Canyon.

The scenery was forever beautiful as they rode. They made another quick pause at the three-mile resthouse, fifteen switchbacks later. June stopped to take occasional snapshots as they went. They paused for a lunch of beef stew cooked over an open fire at Indian Gardens where regional natives had grown corn and squash in past generations.

From that point the trail became more gradual and in a little more than three miles, they were a stone's throw from the river. The trail however followed its south bank for three more miles. It was midafternoon and sixty-three degrees when reaching the tunnel that led to the south abutment of the black bridge, built two years earlier. The previous bridge could not be crossed by mules, making it necessary to hike the last mile to Phantom Ranch in years past.

After a day of riding and breathtaking views they enjoyed relaxing under the sun in rustically crafted Adirondack style chairs. Both of them dozed while holding hands and listening to the music of Bright Angel Creek tumbling its way down to the Colorado River.

\* \* \*

*THURSDAY DECEMBER 4, 1930*

*The Honeymoon, Day Five*

Neither June nor Con could ever remember sleeping so soundly as they did in the little cabin on the hand-stuffed cotton mattress. It was the most peaceful place to rest June had ever experienced. Though Conor had experienced many peace-filled nights on a bedroll under starry skies, the bed was more comfortable and he shared it with the woman he loved.

Wishing they could stay longer; they enjoyed a good breakfast in the canteen just a few steps from their cabin and climbed aboard the mules for the return to El Tovar. As was expected, they reached the hotel late in the afternoon. As they approached, Conor noticed a yellowed piece of paper beneath the wiper blade on the windshield of the LaSalle.

When they dismounted, June watched as he walked over and took the paper from the windshield. He leaned against the fender and read it. Lowering the paper, she watched as he seemed to stare off into nothingness, then lift it and read it again and repeat the process. As he began reading it for the third time she walked over to him, arriving just as he again lowered it.

"What does it say?"

"It's written in not very good Spanish...it says, 'You've taken my guns, you've taken my horses, you've crippled my arm, and put my friend in jail. Leave me alone. Altaha.'"

# EPILOGUE

An eight-year-old Chiricahua Apache boy sat across the fire in the dark of night listening to stories. He was a White man but told stories in Apache. Joseph Wren's mind was nearly gone. Too many bouts of week-long drinking. Too many days in the sun looking for gold and too many days, deep in a hole without enough air digging for it. His mind was gone and so, soon would be his life.

The old men, the warriors who were young when they fought alongside Geronimo, were tired of listening to the crazy White man who had been raised by their fathers. He rambled on and on about some mystical place under the ground, the *Heart of the Dragon*. He would always begin with how to find it. Starting at the north end of a mountain range in Hualapai country. All of the landmarks. The washes and hills and valleys. Then turn up the hill here and turn down the hill there. He talks Apache, but he was not Apache. He was a crazy White man. It was always the same.

The young boy was the only one left. All of the others had left the fire.

"Never trust the White man," Joseph Wren told the boy. "There will come a time when a White man will be chasing you. I saw it in a dream. You are running away from him. Sometimes he's close and sometimes he's far away, but he never gives up chasing you. Run to the *Heart of the Dragon*. You can get away from him there," Wren told him.

"You are a warrior. The son of warriors. The son of sons of warriors. And their fathers before them. Your very name means powerful men of the mountains. You can beat them. The White men.

"When you get to the hole in the side of the mountain, take your knife and leave everything else. Run into it as fast as you can. It will be dark. When you get to the end, there is a hole in the ground. It's the dragon's throat. You must jump down the throat of the dragon. There's water down there. A long way down. You must hold your breath and swim back to the surface when you fall into the water. Just below the surface of the water, there is another hole. It's smaller and in the side of the dragon's throat. Swim into it. Just a little way and the hole goes up and there is air.

"This hole is smaller than the others. Too small to stand up in, but you can crawl on your knees. All the way out the other side of the mountain. You will have your knife and you will be free. They will think you are dead, but you will be free, George Altaha."

# YOU MIGHT ALSO LIKE
## DARK PRAIRIE BY JOHN D. NESBITT

**In a town where indifference and disbelief cloud the pursuit of justice, one cowboy vows to right their wrongs.**

Taking up work at the Little Six Ranch in Winsome, Dunbar finds himself immersed in the dealings of Tut Whipple, a prominent water project developer. What begins as a simple inquiry into stolen beef soon spirals into something far darker with the disappearance of Annie Mora.

As Dunbar delves deeper into the young girl's disappearance, he becomes embroiled in the intricacies of Whipple's schemes and the mystery surrounding a recently constructed dam and reservoir. With each step closer to the truth, he faces off against increasing dangers.

But in a land where ruthless men hold sway, Dunbar welcomes a showdown on the dark prairie.

*AVAILABLE NOW*

# ABOUT THE AUTHOR

Jefferson Glass grew up near the Klamath Indian Reservation in the ranch country of southeastern Oregon. Influenced by the stories found in his grandfather's collection of Zane Grey novels, his young imagination went wild in these rural surroundings. At an early age, he often hiked with his dog over countless miles of public land that bordered his family's property. The only rule was to be home by suppertime. As a teenager, his wanderlust gave way to working the hayfields of a nearby ranch.

In 1981, Jefferson moved to central Wyoming where he began his writing career. He has written numerous articles on Western history for *Annals of Wyoming, True West Magazine* and WyoHistory.org. His non-fiction books, *RESHAW: The Life and Times of John Baptiste Richard* and *Empire: The Pioneer Legacy of an American Ranch Family*, won a Western Writers of America Spur Award and a Will Rogers Medallion Award respectively.

Jefferson began research in 2020 on his Conor Armenta Mystery series, set in 1930s Las Vegas. While exploring Clark County, Nevada, and surrounding areas, he and his wife stumbled across Kanab, Utah, where they purchased a home and relocated. The magnificent view of The Grand Staircase-Escalante out their back door is certain to inspire years of future writing.